The Heart of a Lynx

Trisha St. Andrews

Dedicated to my husband Rich whose belief in me fortified and encouraged me to follow my dream.

Acknowledgements

Thank to the San Diego Writers' Conference, –specifically to Drusilla Campbell and Judy Reeves, who inspired and taught me about the art and craft of writing.

Thank you to my two book clubs, THE CLASSICS and FRIENDS OF DIANE, who read the manuscript and lit a fire under me after my sitting on it for years.

Thank you to Lisa Hogue for your valued evaluation and to friends Joan Weatherhead, Heidi Wiessner, Liz Weatherhead, Terese Walton, Heather Haith, Cheryl Takeda, Karin Lange, Carmen Heston and Donna Moore for your encouragement and support.

Readers, please go to Amazon.com. Your comments will be inspiring or elucidating. I welcome them all.

Chapter 1

"If only I hadn't opened the letter."

Tess exhaled an anxious breath as she spoke out loud and finished her walk through the park. On any other day, she felt alive when she walked. She felt momentum, direction, purpose, when she walked. But on this April morning, she only felt her heart pounding. Puddles of early morning rain splattered the hem of her coat and myriad trails of shoe prints, puppy paws and bicycle tires stretched out before her, leading to destinations unknown. What would happen, she thought, if she followed another set of prints, another path? Another set of problems? It wouldn't solve anything. She knew that. All people drag around their own complications, perhaps even their own "letter." She needed to go home and reread it.

In a matter of weeks, the world would look so different. Blankets of snow would melt, exposing tiny baby blades of grass. Poppies, hyacinth and daffodils, promising to bloom. Winter air would heat to a simmer and other people's children would decorate sidewalks with pink and blue chalk. Honking Canada geese would disappear and yellow warblers would migrate from the south on a still breezy night. Oh, that life for a human be so effortless and predictable.

She rang her doorbell to hear the chimes; a ritual reminding her of a Parisian chapel she'd once visited which appealed to her sense of reverence. The aroma of bran muffins and raspberry jam

1

lingered in the kitchen. Swathed in Southwestern pastels and inhabited by porcelain coyotes, her home had recently had a face lift. Costuming rooms was like changing clothes to Tess. She felt as comfortable with Corinthian columns as Mexican pavers. She felt sorry for people who lived with the same décor year after year. Change equaled interesting.

The telephone rang. She dodged past the clay cacti and plucked the phone before the answer machine activated.

"Hello."

"Hi there, you sound out of breath." It was Troy, her younger, but self-proclaimed "wiser" brother. "I'll be passing through town on Thursday night. Can I entice you and hubby with an invitation to dinner? You choose the restaurant. My treat."

"You're on. I'll make reservations at Emilio's. But just for two. Rennie's out of town until Friday. Call me when you get in."

"Fabuloso, mia sorella. Arrivederci."

Since his trip to Italy, Troy practiced his "Beginning Italian" with anyone who'd listen. If his audience was indulgent, he'd accent his English with Italian inflections which was either amusing or ridiculous. Tess was pleased that he was coming to town. She'd hint at the contents of the letter and read his reaction.

She approached her antique desk and withdrew the silk-brocaded oval box Ren had bought for her at the festival in Andorra the previous September. Since then it had assumed its post as The Guardian of Correspondence. She ceremoniously opened Pandora's Box, took out the letter and placed it on the square glass coffee table. She stalled, staring at it long and hard as if she were about to tempt Fate. She needed Mozart. She needed the Mozart Clarinet Quintet in A. She'd read somewhere that Pablo Casals listened to it every day because it mystically relieved the pain of his arthritis. Perhaps it would anesthetize her edge. She turned on the power button and poured a glass of chilled Pinot Grigio. Mozart and Dionysus, harmonious companions.

She picked up the letter, her hand shaking. The envelope was addressed to:

T. Monson

1320 Brookside Circle

Swannsong, Mississippi

She still used her maiden name Monson, but only professionally. The letter written in blue ink and perfect penmanship had been forwarded from her former address.

Dear Ms. Monson,

If this reaches you, please read it when you're alone. My name is Cristin Shanihan. I'm twenty years old. My parents recently died in an auto accident. I was their only child. Our home will have to be sold so I've been sorting, storing, throwing and giving away its contents. It's been an enormous, painful and tedious job. Until last week.

I came across a locked drawer in my father's desk. After an exhaustive and futile search to find the key, I broke into the drawer with an axe. Inside were legal documents, insurance papers, a marriage certificate and some love letters from my father to my mother. But then I found a document of adoption, my adoption. My parents never told me that I was adopted so you can imagine my surprise. I wouldn't have loved them less if they had. I would have loved them more for choosing me.

Tess laid the letter on the sofa and tasted, savored, her wine. She closed her eyes, firmly ran her tongue over her lower lip and gnawed on the inside of her cheek, in rhythm to the pulse of Mozart. *I could tear it up*, she thought. *Pretend it never existed.* But just as she continued reading it the first time, she proceeded once again.

Needless to say, my life went into overdrive. I ripped through every drawer, every diary entry, and every personal paper I could find. When I was no longer expecting to find any clues, I found the letter you wrote to my parents shortly after I was born. It was a beautiful letter and I understand you must've had valid reasons for giving me away. I forgive you. The only thing that matters now is that we meet. I'm your daughter and I want to know you. I won't cause you any trouble and I don't expect you to take me in. If you have other children and a husband, I'd love to meet them. Or if I shouldn't, that's okay. But please contact me. You're not listed in the telephone directory in Swannsong.

If there was ever a time in my life that I needed you, Mother, it's now. I miss my parents so much. I don't want to go through life unconnected. Please write to me at P. O. Box 625. Nevada City, Ca.

Your daughter, Cristin

Tess slumped into the folds of the sofa. First of all, the child wasn't hers. Not having a baby had been the most profound sadness of her life. She knew she would've been a wonderful mother but her maternal feelings had been lavished on nieces and nephews, other people's children. She'd been cheated. Her chest tightened, her throat closed. She wasn't obsessed with her misfortune. Preoccupied was a kinder word.

What to do. Her first inclination was to write the girl and tell her she was mistaken. But the return address in Mississippi was specific and disturbing, leading her to question if anything at all unusual had occurred twenty years ago. She pulled out a photo album marked "1977" from the bookcase. Standard shots, mostly nature photos, her trip to Montana, pictures of Katie. Pictures of Katie. Her older sister Katie had briefly visited after separating from her husband Stefan. She'd left her family for five months while she "found herself." Was it possible that Katie had delivered a baby girl between her stopover in Mississippi and her return to Boston months later? Would Stefan or the children have known about it? Probably not. But why wouldn't Katie have confided in her? Aware that she was jumping to conclusions, she searched for other possibilities, but came up short. If Katie had given birth to a child during that time, chances were that Troy and their younger sister Tia didn't know anything about it. Katie was close to Mum so Mum would have known. But Mum had died a year ago.

And now Katie was in an alcohol rehab center and far too fragile to handle Tess's questions. Whom could she ask? Who would possibly have the answer? Katie's best friend, Sondra... decent, kind, trustworthy Sondra. Tess remembered sitting for hours with Katie and Sondra, playing a game called "On My Honor." Sondra always lost because she didn't know how to bluff. Sondra was the key.

But first she needed to think it through before involving Sondra. Why had the letter had been mailed to her former address, to T. Monson? Katie's legal name was Katrina but her family had called her Trina in her childhood so perhaps she'd assumed her childhood name for the purpose of anonymity. It was a long shot. If she contacted the girl, she couldn't involve anyone else. And she didn't dare acknowledge a blood relationship, even if there was one. Perhaps she'd explain that the correspondence had mistakenly reached her, that she couldn't possibly be her mother but would like to help her. That, at least, would safely open the door.

And what would Ren say? She hadn't mustered the courage to discuss the letter with him because it didn't seem like an appropriate topic for a long distance conversation. More to the point, her intuition told her he wouldn't understand. Until she at least knew all of the facts, she wouldn't mention it.

Fact: if Cristin came to Minneapolis, Tess would have a "daughter" in her life, blood or no blood. Fact: if Cristin turned out to be her niece, even if she did meet Katie, it was unlikely that identities would ever be discovered in casual conversation. Fact: she needed to verify the truth through Sondra. Fact: she'd come up with a plan and would write to Cristin before Ren returned on Friday.

She opened the doors to the balcony. The piney, robust evening air flooded the living room as if a dam of cool wind had broken and spilled. She walked outside to discover that hours had passed. The sun had set and Orion the Hunter guarded the horizon with masculine dominance. For half of the year, Orion was her secret love; huge, strong and watching over her.

~ ~ ~

Morning was Tess's toughest time. If she lay in bed, immobilizing demons descended. They lined up to take their turns. Her first intruder was Disappointment: why hadn't she the discipline to lose the ten pounds she'd recently gained? She'd fast. No moderation. Deprivation was the solution. Then the ugly head of Frustration: her novel in process didn't have that magic quality that transfixed publishers and transformed readers and she knew it. The most recent newcomer to the morning, Anguish: how could she benevolently manipulate a situation without anyone's knowledge? No one would approve. No one would support her decision even though it was harmless. She jumped out of bed to plunge into the day, leaving the restless shores of early morning behind.

The aroma of brewed Colombian coffee beans soon filled the house. She poured herself a cup and headed for the verandah overlooking their backyard. Birds flew among the conifers and deciduous giants. Soft furry creatures scurried across the flower bordered pathway that led to the swing Rennie had built for her birthday. The garden was magic, a labor of love. The perennials in shades of purples, blues and pinks. She and Ren had designed their yard as if planning the layout of The Tuileries. But Nature had gifted the colors, textures, shapes and sweet, sweet smells. A perfect co-creation.

Sitting in the sycamore tree, no more than forty feet away, sat a rough-winged hawk. It stared at Tess as if it knew her thoughts and she stared back at its piercing, yellow-eyed scrutiny. What was this magnificent bird doing in her backyard? Only a few hawks were indigenous to the area and she knew the rough-winged hawk wasn't one of them. In her childhood, for hours upon end, Katie, Mum and Tess had played with Native American medicine cards which taught the meanings of animals appearing in one's life. The hawk symbolized vision and observance, circling from above to gain perspective. For moments, Tess and Mr. Perspective glared at each other. Until the phone rang.

"Tess, it's Tia. I hope it isn't too early. It's night time here and I'm at Cafe Etienne with Yves and Yvette. I miss you, Tess. I wish you were here."

Her little sister Tia, attending the University of Grenoble as a graduate student in International Business, was inebriated.

"It's 11 a.m. and I'm communing with a hawk in the back yard."

"Oh, Tess, you live the life I long to live. Do you miss me?"

"Of course, little one. When are you coming home?"

"Not 'til January. I want to fly directly to Minneapolis to see you and Ren. I want to take long walks in crunchy snow and make angels in your backyard and spy on the snowy owl in your oak tree and gaze at Sagittarius and Orion and the guys. Remember those times, Tess?"

"Honey, they were great times. We'll share them again. Did you say your friends were named Yves and Yvette? Are they twins?"

"No, pretty weird though, huh?"

"Listen, sweetheart, you just stay well and come home safely to us, okay?'

"Okay, sis. Je t'aime. Au-revoir. Bye."

First the hawk, then Tia. Tess felt doubly blessed. Triply blessed, for she'd had a reprieve from fixating on the letter. She reheated her coffee and returned to the verandah to find that the hawk had flown away.

Chapter 2

Sondra Rampling hated Aurora. It was a crummy little town. She'd been transferred by her company but it hadn't been worth the extra money or the prestige, as there was nothing to do and no one to meet. She was a city girl, stuck in a prairie town where polished nails, dinner rings and an accomplished vocabulary were frowned upon by the grocer, the mail carrier and the preacher's wife. The fact that she was unmarried and drove a German sports car only compounded her unfortunate image. Life became increasingly intolerable as she assumed the role of victim and boredom poisoned her discretionary hours.

She surveyed the flat, monotonous fields of golden wheat and blue flax that seemed to touch the sky on the horizon, a zillion miles away. Perhaps, she thought, if she moved to the interior of town, rather than living on the edge of it, she wouldn't have to stare at the tedious, infinite landscape. The phone rang, startling her, shooting adrenaline through her veins of self-pity.

"Sondra, this is Katie's little sister Tess."

"Oh my God! What a surprise! Is everything all right? Where's Katie?"

"She's fine. I mean she's relatively fine, in alcohol rehab. Safe."

"Yes, I know about that. How are you, Tess? How did you find me?"

"By association, believe me. Katie mentioned the town you were transferred to, Aurora, and it stuck. You remember? I love the stars, so Aurora was easy to remember. Actually, I'm lucky I didn't try directory assistance for Borealis."

Sondra chuckled and paused to hear the reason for the call.

"I wish we didn't live so far away, Sondra, because I need to ask you something and it's a bit sensitive. I hate doing this over the phone but I don't know anyone else I can turn to. It concerns Katie but considering what she's going through right now, I don't want to stress her out." Tess audibly inhaled.

"I'll help you if I can." Sondra held her breath.

"Thank, you. I recently received a letter from a twenty year old girl who thought that I might be her biological mother. As you may know, I've never been able to have children, so this is impossible. However, twenty years ago, Katie did leave Stefan and the kids for five months. Remember? It was about four years before Heidi was born. She popped in on us in Mississippi but didn't she stay with you for a while?"

"Yes."

"Well, I have a theory. I think that she might have been pregnant and gave the baby up for adoption".

"Tess, that's preposterous."

"I don't want to go to her and Stefan about the matter. Who knows what the problem was then. But she might want to know about the girl now. I'd hoped that you could shed some light on the matter."

Silence.

"Sondra, I've no intention of telling the girl. She can't trace Katie except through me and I'd never hurt Katie. You know that. I just need to know the truth. Anything you say is safe with me. On my honor."

"That's so far-fetched. I'm really sorry, Tess, but it couldn't possibly be true. I would have known about it. Listen, I was just walking out the door. Sorry I can't help you. But it's good to hear your voice again. Bye."

Suddenly Aurora was exactly where Sondra wanted to be. A simple, quiet place, far away from problems of the past and complications of the future.

~ ~ ~

Tess, the journalist, had a deadline to meet. She'd been hired to research the migration of gray whales off the coast of British Columbia. But concentration didn't show up as a willing participant in the creative process that day, so she quarantined herself in the office and forced herself to fall in love with the subject. Pressure was her pal. Hours later, she emerged, knowing more about gray whales than she had previously thought possible. She was now on target to meet her brother at Emilio's in forty-five minutes. Ren called her ability to go from frumpy to fabulous low-maintenance. She called it skill.

The shower refreshed her. Her new hairdresser, Alonzo, from New York City, vowed that her new short 'do made her eyes look enormous. Ren agreed, and the best part was that she could comb it out in two minutes. Fastidious about her wardrobe choices, she most often dressed for Ren. But that night, she dressed only for comfort. Before leaving the house, she slipped the letter into her purse. The prospect of touching it during the evening made Cristin feel real.

Emilio's smelled like the Italian region of heaven, the blends of garlic, oregano and basil steeping the air like an invisible herbal tea bag. Troy sat at a table in the corner with a bottle of Sangria and a basket of hot homemade focaccia.

"Buona Sera, Bella," bellowed her one and only brother as he stood, gallantly standing and watching her approach.

Tess's face flushed to match her lipstick, "Embarrassed Red," as Troy's thunderous voice craned every neck in the room to see the object of his salutations. Lasered with scores of eyes following her path and smiling politely, she self-consciously made her way through the maze of small red and white checkerboard tables.

"SShhhh. Keep it down," she whispered in his ear as she hugged him. "The whole room is watching."

"Who cares? I'm never going to see any of these people again." In spite of his cavalier manner, his voice dropped to a muted roar.

"Well, big sister, how's life treating you?"

"You know me. Taking on too many assignments to do them justice and still not having time to work on my novel. It's frustrating, I feel like I'm swimming in molasses most of the time. Let's talk about something else like Suzanne and the kids."

"Buona Sera, senor y senora." Wearing an apron with a map of Italy on the front and an irresistible Adriatic smile, a handsome blue-eyed waiter with short curly hair stood before them like Michelangelo's David with clothes on. As he spoke, his voice caressed each "special" like an invitation to make love and Tess secretly wished he would go on forever.

"Where in Italy are you from?" she asked.

Troy couldn't help himself. "Let me guess. Northern Italy to be sure. Florence."

"Close, senor. Milano, home of La Scala, Leonardo Da Vinci's Last Supper, Brera Palace and the finest sauces in the world. You must try the cioppino. Delicioso."

So cioppino it was.

"Where were we? Oh yes, the kids."

While Troy fumbled in his wallet for a recent picture, she noticed that he'd lost the childhood freckles that had given him his mischievous Dennis the Menace appearance. His eyes were hazel and bordered with enviably long lashes, the kind that never bless the girls of the family. She wondered if Cristin had long lashes.

"Ah ha," he exclaimed, as he proudly exhibited a recent family photo of nine year old Lindsey, five year old Max and the picture-perfect Suzanne. How had a high school screw-up like Troy ended up with a Kodak family? Of course she was happy for him because he was genuinely one of the good guys but wondered how he'd ever fallen for a mindless Barbie doll like Suzanne.

Through the ecstasy of the cioppino, Troy gave her a rundown on the family routine, sports schedules and upcoming vacations. Hearing that little Lindsey loved to read pleased Tess no end. Then came the opening that she had been waiting for all evening.

"Tell me about your novel, Tess."

She laid down her spoon as the pulse in her ears began to throb and the aberrant sounds of the restaurant faded.

"Well, I've actually put it aside. It was weighing me down. I'm writing a short story about adoption. I'm intrigued with the complications that can arise from adoption." She looked away from him and said, "consumingly intrigued." With piercing intensity, Tess shot a stare at Troy and said nothing.

His eyes widened. "You're not thinking of..."

"No, heavens no," she said. "Not at our age. But bear with me. Sometimes children come forward to find their birth parents or a biological parent tries to find his or her child. And of course, there is a legal system in place that protects the anonymity of all parties, to a certain extent, but there have been recent changes in privacy laws. If both parties consent to finding each other, it can be a beautiful thing. Or a disaster. There are so many variables. I think the subject has rich story potential. After all, don't you know anyone who has given up a baby? Someone who prays that the child was placed in a loving family but wants to find the child?"

Troy looked puzzled. "I guess I can't say that I do." He bit down on a huge succulent tiger prawn, dripping with sauce. He didn't have a clue.

Tess heard him talking, but the nagging chatter of her own internal frustration drowned the body of his faraway words. Had her imagination run amuck? Was she needy? And if so, was her neediness consuming her good judgment? She reached into her purse and touched the letter.

"Tess, where would you go?"

"What? I'm sorry, what did you say?"

"Where would you go, Portugal or Argentina?" He paused, accusingly miffed. "You haven't heard a word I've said."

"Of, of course I have," she stammered. "Argentina. You know how I love waterfalls and I especially want to see the one on the Brazilian-Argentine border. I don't remember the name. It starts with an 'I' and is in desperate need of a consonant as I recall. But it's magnificent. And the birds! The scarlet macaw and the resplendent something-or-other."

"Well I think we've decided on Portugal but I'll let you know."

Troy did have an aggravating way of discounting people, unintentional as it was. He had no interest in what she'd just said. Then again, she'd ignored his last few minutes of monologue and apparently hadn't camouflaged her lack of concentration. One thing was certain: Troy knew nothing about this chapter of family history if there even was one. Beneath the tablecloth, she touched the letter again, then closed her purse.

She returned from Emilio's, full of questions and hungry for answers. The phone rang but she let the answer-machine pick up. It was Sondra.

She bulldozed over her writing table and papers went flying. "Hello, Sondra, I'm here, I'm here!!"

"Are you alone? Can you talk?"

"Yes, I'm all alone"

"Is the recorder turned off?"

"Yes."

"Tess, I need to tell you something in strictest confidence, because if I don't, you will hurt Katie and her family and I know you wouldn't want to do that. You haven't called them, have you?"

"No, of course not."

"Tess, you can't go to Katie and Stefan with your suspicion because Stefan doesn't know anything. It wasn't his baby. There, I've said it." She paused and inhaled all her available air. "I've been terrified you might attempt to reconcile their family by saying something to them. But you can never tell anyone, not even Katie. No one can know this. Tess, I feel like I've betrayed my best friend by telling you so you have to promise me that you'll not say a word. Please, Tess. On your honor."

"Why didn't Katie tell me? Oh, my God. So Cristin is my niece."

"Tess, you have to forget about Cristin. Think of your sister."

"Of course I'm thinking of my sister. What a dreadful time it must have been for her. But Sondra, how could she have been so careless, so stupid?"

"Stop."

"I'm sorry. I don't mean to be judgmental but I'm in shock. You must have been so stunned when I called. It involved another man? Did she love him? Who was he?"

"Tess, I can't discuss this. I feel awful as it is. Promise me that this information stops here. Please, Tess, Katie is my best friend."

"She's my sister, Sondra. I'd never hurt her. Thank you for the truth."

As abruptly as the conversation began, it ended. The worlds of Sondra Rampling in Aurora and Tess Parker in Minnetonka had collided.

~ ~ ~

The following day, Ren was due home from his business trip. The day dragged. Tess resolved to respond to the letter prior to his return. But first she needed to take a shower, prepare the dinner, set the table, make some phone calls, edit her whale tale. She was a master procrastinator. Her dad had said a million times that whether one does something now or later, it takes the same amount of time. The burden of relegating its time frame to "later" only increased its emotional burden, it's mass. Tess hadn't mastered the "Just Do It" concept.

When finally she'd run out of excuses, she picked up the pen, shamelessly invoked God, Buddha, the "saints" of all religions, leveled her stare at the empty stationary and wrote:

Dear Cristin,

My name is Tess. I'm not your mother. I have never given birth. However your letter did arrive a week ago and I opened it because it was addressed to T. Monson. It had been delivered to my former address in Mississippi; so naturally, I believed that it was intended for me.

First, let me say how sorry I am to hear that you have recently lost your parents. It's a painful loss to bear and my heart goes out to you. I wish I could shed some light on your search for your mother but I'm clueless. Whoever wrote that letter must have lifted my name from a telephone book to protect her anonymity.

Tess stopped and took a deep breath. It was a necessary lie but still went clunk in the face of the universe. She continued.

I'm so sorry that I haven't better news but I am concerned about you. I live in a suburb west of Minneapolis, so if you'd like to come to the Twin Cities, please feel free to contact me and I'll be happy to meet you and help you in any way I can. My best to you, Cristin. I look forward to your response.

Sincerely,
Tess Monson Parker

There. It was done. Succinct and to the point. Tess deposited the letter in an ecru envelope and walked to the mail box down the street. The sensation of the envelope slipping through her fingers into the mouth of the big blue box was titillating. She had stepped over the border of safety into a land of uncertainty. Of course, there was no real risk. No one could be hurt. Perhaps the girl wouldn't even look her up. But whatever happened, Tess had hidden the truth without jeopardizing their chance to meet.

As she turned the corner, Ren pulled into the driveway in his conservative Chrysler 300M. She picked up her pace, running the last few steps into his arms. He smelled like fresh air; his arms and chest felt strong and the light in his eyes showed her he was glad to be home.

"Where were you?"

"Oh, just mailing a letter," she said. "I'm so glad you're home. I really missed you this time, Rennie."

"Do you mean that sometimes you don't miss me?" He hugged her tighter.

"I have a special dinner planned tonight. I even bought a bottle of your favorite Cabernet Franc."

Except for the black bean relish which was a bit too spicy, dinner was perfect. A cucumber and mango salad, tortilla soup with side dishes of avocado slices and limes, pork enchiladas on a bed of cilantro and corn tamales with salsa and cheese. They'd discovered Mexican food three years before on a deep sea fishing vacation in Cabo San Lucas. On that trip, they formulated a lifestyle, either to eat simply and healthily or to dine. Most of the time, due to their schedules, they ate simply: protein, fruits and vegies. But when they created an event, they dined. Ren spent as much time in the kitchen as she did. Walking in from an appointment and smelling garlic or cilantro or freshly baked bread, courtesy of her capable husband, ranked right up there as one of life's richest pleasures.

The night brought cool breezes that blew the chiffon bedroom curtains into the room like ghosts at a dance. Tess always slept better when her husband was home. His low volume snore comforted her as she lay motionless and barely breathing. It was warm for a spring night, a harbinger of the hot, sticky summer nights ahead when sheets would feel heavy and darkness would feel endless.

In the middle of the night, Tess awakened when Ren rolled over and his big bear like arm swallowed her into his chest. Her eyes widened in the dark as her heart hammered and her thoughts began to fistfight. It became increasingly clear that she had no intention of telling him the truth about Cristin. She had never kept a secret of this magnitude from him and it felt lousy. But he wouldn't understand. He wouldn't approve.

Chapter 3

Inside the entry of Woodrose Rehabilitation Center, a bulletin board with crayoned pictures of dinosaurs and suns wearing sunglasses welcomed patients and guests; to the right, a chapel. The stark white corridors smelled of uncertainty and fear; a theater of endings and beginnings, some happy, some not.

Holding a lavish bouquet of lilacs, Stefan Shepard winked at the receptionist and headed for room 172. He opened the door to an empty room. A schedule of activities, posted on the wall, indicated that his wife was in her private therapy session. A heavy-set nurse with graying hair tightly fastened in a bun resembling a moldy doughnut, poked her head into the room and with the vocal delivery of a train conductor, announced, "Mr. Shepard, your wife will be here shortly."

Stefan stared at the pink peony bushes outside the first story window. Katie could open the window and pick a bouquet every morning if she wanted to, but she wouldn't. She was far too conventional to break the rules and face the consequences.

He didn't like being there. Rehab establishments induced a memory of the nauseous smell of ether from his childhood appendectomy and that alone was enough to keep him clean and sober. His mind wandered into threatening territory. He knew he was the reason Katie had started drinking so heavily. His philandering had taken a toll on her. Admitting her to Woodrose was a humiliation and just another example of how he'd let her down. In her square, bare room away from home, he privately vowed to make it up to her. Somehow. The scary part was that she could relapse and with one drink, end up back at Woodrose. He wondered if for the rest of his life, he'd feel like he was walking on eggshells. Would he have to guard his every word to avoid upsetting her? What kind of a life would that be?

Katie appeared at the door with blood shot eyes and a swollen face. She looked so different without makeup that he tried to find the resemblance of the girlish features and confident demeanor he had fallen in love with twenty-five years before. Her mouth was contorted in a grimace and her head hung in defeat, as she avoided looking at him.

"Katie, what happened? What did they say to you?" He jumped up to hold her.

She pressed her forehead against his chest. "I can't do this. It's too hard. I don't think I'm strong enough to fight back, Stefan. And you're going to hate me for this...I really want a drink."

She began to sob.

He'd been warned by her sponsor and the staff psychiatrist that his wife's recovery was intimately tied to his support and patience. But he didn't know what to say.

"Let's talk about the kids...or the house."

Katie didn't even hear him. Her grief poured into the room as if a dam of shame and frustration had finally burst.

"I'll never be happy again. I want to scream but I'm afraid I won't stop! Oh Stefan, my head is so heavy. I'm so sorry. I'm so sorry."

She shook her head from side to side as she spoke. The room felt oppressive and mournful.

Stefan rocked her as a father would rock his child and she clung to him for what seemed like hours. Eventually, a shapely young nurse with green eyes and curly auburn hair asked him to leave. She had pouty lips and a flirtatious smile. At least that was the image Stefan seemed to conjure to divert his pain to pleasure.

~ ~ ~

The Shepard home stood on the southeast side of Boston in the college town of Wellesley. A more charming setting in all of New England could not be found. When Katie and Stefan had fallen in love, living in Wellesley had almost been a prenuptial agreement. Fortunately, Stefan graduated in architecture and jobs were aplenty in the region, so Katie's dream came true. Their ivy covered colonial governed an impressive acreage, populated by oaks and towering elms. Two hundred year old rock walls bordered the lot like an artist's mat and winding dirt roads framed the picture.

By the time Stefan approached the driveway, the sky had clouded over, and the yard, shaded in a dismal foreboding gray, fit his mood precisely. Ingrid's car was parked out front. *Thank God someone was home.* He hated walking into an empty house. The rain began to fall in large heavy drops when he remembered that the garage door needed repair and was temporarily inoperable. As he ran to the house, pummeled by the sudden downpour, he stomped a bed of newly planted pansies.

"Damn it!" he yelled as he fumbled with his key, opening the front door. "Ingrid, I'm home! Ingrid? Is anyone here?" No response. His luck, an empty house.

He thought of Katie and how afraid of thunderstorms she was. Had she been at home (and sober), the lights would have been on, with the aroma of beef stew and the sound of Schubert lieders filling the air. Instead, the house was cold, dark and bleak. He walked to the bar, poured a scotch and water, sat down in the study and stared out the window into the frowning, wet woods on the southern perimeter of the property. Life was tough but he was a very lucky man. He had three terrific kids.

Years ago, to please his mother, he asked Katie to christen their children with Austrian names. His son was born Franz Joseph

Shepard. When Franz entered the eighth grade, he announced to his family and friends that his name was Shep. Thirteen years later, Stefan remained the only person who refused to call him Shep. Franz was his given name.

Ingrid was twenty-two and had graduated from Sarah Lawrence a year earlier with a degree in political science and a minor in drama. She had procrastinated finding "a real job" and had elected to wait on tables and audition for dramatic parts at the local supper clubs and starving artists' theaters. Stefan was disappointed but the subject wasn't open for discussion. Not having to work in order to survive was an attitude of growing up in a well-to-do family in the nineties. Young women tended to be headstrong and rebellious, and felt entitled to do what they wanted, when they wanted. Survival was never an issue; it was a given.

After six years of a four person household, Heidi Joy was born. A little princess she was, with golden hair and her father's brown eyes, a virtual Heidi of the Alps. She was now a sixteen year old social butterfly and co-captain of the dance squad, with endless activities and revolving-door boyfriends.

A deafening bolt of lightning struck close in the neighborhood and jolted Stefan from his thoughts. It had been years since he'd heard a crack loud enough to hammer hearts for miles around. *Katie must be terrified. And where in the world was Heidi? And why was Ingrid's car in the driveway?* Stefan turned on the hall light and opened the heavy oak entry door. The spring rain soaked the thirsty tree bark and nourished the newborn carpet of grass. The blended scent of wet leaves and flowers perfumed the air, creating that special, singular smell that only rain can bring. He'd forgotten to clean out the eaves, the consequence being a solid sheet of water from the roof to the front steps. He could see nothing but its backside and hear nothing but its splattering on the bricks below.

Headlights approached the house and shone through the watery cascade. He heard two doors slam and squeals of young females bolting toward the house. The next thing he knew, his girls blasted through the wall of water, shrieking, giggling and drenched.

"You're soaked! Don't come near me," he said. But they threw down their shopping bags and hugged him, front and back, as he playfully fought them off.

"Oh Dad, you should have seen us in The Mall parking lot. There was a sale, so we had to park miles away and the rain was pouring cats and dogs. You should have seen Ingrid's face when we started making a run for it. It was awesome! I have to change my clothes. I'll be down in a few minutes." Heidi vanished as quickly as she'd materialized.

"Me, too. I think I'll take a shower though. I'm freezing," said Ingrid. Then she too was gone.

Seconds later, from the top of the staircase came the small, apologetic voice of his older daughter. "Dad, I'm so sorry I didn't ask. How was Mom today?"

~ ~ ~

Katie trembled in the dark, as she huddled in the perfectly square corner of her perfectly square room. With her knees pulled to her chest, her hands clenched and her eyes closed tightly in anticipation of the next clap of thunder, she braced herself. She didn't recall the last time she'd been by herself during a storm. Her loneliness was agonizing enough but loneliness coupled with her most harrowing phobia was hell. She wrapped herself in her mother's quilt and unraveled one of the worn corners. Her room filled with supernatural light, courtesy of Zeus, Hurler of Lightning Bolts, as she anchored her feet against the floor. Within an interminable few seconds the dreaded strike and rumble had passed.

She needed something to take her mind off the storm, any memory to occupy her thoughts. She focused on the time she met her grandmother's train when Troy was born. Her father had awakened her at five in the morning to drive to South Station to greet Grandmum. The icy car windows outlined gifts of lacy stencils from Jack Frost's visit and she studied the designs all the way downtown. The train station boasted of vaulted ceilings, ornate frescoes and granite floors. The stuffy waiting rooms filled with tired people, waiting for departures, draped themselves over wooden benches. The stale smell of cigarette smoke made her queasy but the draft from the doors leading to the trains laid a path of fresh air that would lead them to Grandmum. Katie held her father's hand tightly as they walked next to the train pulling into the depot. The brakes screeched as the iron giant traced the filthy black track. People appeared and disappeared in and out of the steam that hissed and spouted from the guts of a locomotive which sounded like an angry dragon. They walked for blocks as Negro porters, dressed in stiff white jackets, placed stepping stools on the ground to help the passengers disembark. Katie scrutinized each window in search of her Grandmum's face, until she discovered her, waving and smiling through the glass, smudged with decades of fingerprints, tear stains, lipstick kisses and hot breath. The anticipation of Grandmum's first hug made her heart pound. The fur stole she wore around her shoulders felt softer than velvet, its fuzzy creatures' heads still intact. Grandmum's neck smelled like gardenias and Grandmum loved her"Trina."

Thunder interrupted Katie's memory but soon thereafter, she sank deep asleep into her corner of the world and slept.

~ ~ ~

Woodrose awakened early. Shifts changed at 7 a.m., the maintenance crew arrived by 7:30 and the staff, by 8 o'clock sharp. Katie jerked awake. She stood up to straighten out, discovering aches from her neck to her buttocks, which had pressed against the cold tile floor all night long.

Her first responsibility was a 9 a.m. group therapy session. She craved a drink but knew she couldn't have one that day. That's what they'd told her. One day at a time. She didn't have to face the rest of her life, just one day, one hour, one minute, one decision, one at a time. She could do that.

Although reluctant to share her life with a room full of strangers, Katie conceded that group sessions were certainly the most interesting part of the day. The group facilitator sat by the only door and faced a circle of chairs. Katie guessed that this was to discourage anyone from leaving in the middle of the session. The patients filed into the room like ants with antennae high in the air, shooting self-conscious but curious glances at one another. No one wanted to be there.

The analyst introduced herself as Dr. Chambers and politely welcomed everyone. She looked too young to be a doctor and too pretty to be single, as the bare finger on her left hand suggested. Katie couldn't help wondering how Stefan would look at her.

"Who would like to begin this morning?"

With no eye contact and no volunteers, Dr. Chambers selected Mr. Dhansa, a young eastern Indian, perhaps in his early twenties. He'd become involved with the wrong crowd and messed with cocaine. His parents discovered the problem when they realized he'd drained thousands of dollars from their bank account to support his habit. Rehabilitation or disinheritance was his choice. It was his first time in rehab.

"My name is Harish and I am a drug user. Call me Harish, not Mr. Dhansa, please."

Dr. Chambers nodded in compliance.

"This is humiliating. I've brought dishonor to my family name. I really thought that I could control my desire for the stuff. I never meant for it to get out of hand. And my parents? Well, I intend to pay back every cent plus interest. That's all I want to say now."

No one there was supposed to judge one another but Katie couldn't help formulating opinions. In Harish's case, on an odds-of-success scale of ten points (ten being high), she gave him a nine. He was young, he'd made a mistake; he understood his intolerance of chemicals and his breach of ethics. He had the support of his family to boot. He'd be out in two weeks.

Day by day, the patients had peeled away their masks, relaxed and some had begun to heal. Patients had come and left. This morning a new and young uninhibited woman appeared.

"My name is Lonni and I'm an alcoholic and drug user. I'm thirty-two and as you can see, I'm gonna have another kid. I'm here because there're three more at home, no husband and my life's a disaster. I figured that if I drink and do drugs, maybe my baby 'll be deformed. I can't handle that."

"Lonni," asked the doctor, "if you were not pregnant, would you have come to Woodrose?"

"No, probably not, cuz you see, I don't do shit in front of the kids so it don't affect them. They don't even know I'm here. My mom gave me the money and she told them I went to visit my sister Candi in Cincinnati. I was just worried about the baby because I've heard things can go wrong."

"Does anyone have any questions for Lonni?" asked the doctor.

Katie found herself jumping into the ring.

"Lonni, my name is Katie. I' m an alcoholic. Have you thought about what you 'll do if your baby isn't healthy?"

"Yes, I'll give it away. And if nobody wants it, the state hospital'll take it. They have to. My friend told me it's a law."

Stunned by the answer, Katie didn't respond. This woman wasn't fit to be a mother. And Katie's own sister couldn't conceive a child. An injustice of magnitude. Had Katie known twenty years ago that Tess could not have children, she would have…. She hadn't examined that brutal chapter in her personal history for years. She blocked it out. What right had Katie to condemn another woman when she herself had borne the child of another man and never even told her husband? Disconnect.

To Katie's left, a heavy-set Irish woman in her fifties began to speak. "My name is Maureen and I'm an alcoholic. I've been drinking for twenty some years cuz my husband cats around."

"Maureen, remember that your husband's alleged affairs…"

"They aren't alleged! They're real. Every one of them!" She yelled, defending her anger.

Dr. Chambers continued, "Maureen, look at me. Remember, your husband is the only one who can take the blame for his decision to have affairs. That is a separate issue. You're responsible for your drinking and that's what we're working on together, to help you control yourself so that you can, with dignity, deal with any crisis that comes your way."

"You don't understand. I wouldn't be an alcoholic if he'd been faithful to me."

"Maureen, you know that's not true. Has your husband ever opened your mouth and poured booze down your throat?" No response. "Maureen, you drink because you decide to drink, not because someone coerces you."

Maureen began to cry. Katie put one arm around her chubby round shoulders and the stranger's greasy head slumped to Katie's chest. The session continued with a few others sharing their stories. Maureen calmed and sat up. No words were spoken between them but Katie acknowledged Maureen's gratitude by the faint, warm squint of her eyes.

Harish spoke up. "Lonni, it bothers me that you're willing to keep your baby only if it's perfect. In my culture, responsibility is a counterpart of freedom. If we're free to make choices, we take responsibility for them. To respond to whatever life gives us, to respond with dignity and honor, not selfish convenience."

"Are you calling me selfish for not wanting to care for a crippled baby? I have three other kids at home."

"I'm not calling you anything. I'm merely suggesting that you examine your code of honor, that's all."

"Code of honor? What are you, a knight of the Round Table?"

Dr. Chambers intervened. "Let's go on. Is there anyone else who hasn't spoken who would like to share?"

"I would," said Katie. "Harish, I like your code of honor idea. I hate feeling like a victim of my circumstances. Maybe if I figured out what my code of honor is, I wouldn't keep reacting like I do, crisis after crisis. I'm exhausted. I don't want to question who I am when the going gets tough anymore. I just want to decide who I am and act it out until I become that person. I want to learn from everything and everyone...and be happy. That's all I have to say."

The group applauded. Katie looked around at the approving faces and suddenly, they didn't look like strangers anymore. They were friendly, supportive people who shared her struggle and she'd made progress.

Hours later, lying in bed, safe beneath Grandmum's quilt, Katie reviewed her day. The night before, she'd cowered in hopelessness. Now as she succumbed to sleep, she thanked Harish for his vision of life with dignity. She thanked Lonni for holding up a mirror so that she could see herself more honestly. She thanked Maureen for showing her the fallacy of blaming Stefan for her present predicament. She thanked God for clarity. The web of life was intricately spun, one seemingly unrelated strand at a time, with no definitive pattern, until woven through time. She fell asleep with a contentment that she hadn't felt since childhood.

That night she dreamed she stood in a shroud of dense, heavy fog on the balcony of her master bedroom. Suddenly a narrow hole opened in the sky above her and she peered through the natural periscope to behold enormous, brilliant icicles like stalagmites in space; miles high and reflecting the blue sky and sunlight from above. She hollered for Stefan to come out and see it but he couldn't hear her. No one could. It was as if it were meant for her eyes only. She couldn't take her eyes from the spectacle. When the hole closed, she was left alone in the fog, but with a vision of the beauty that existed beyond.

Chapter 4

On the last day in May, a large "Welcome Home" banner hung on the garage of the Shepard home. Standing at attention and wearing fresh new green uniforms, the poplars lined the east and west boundaries of the property. The front lawn, manicured with precision, appeared much larger than Katie remembered. Fiery red poppies bordered the driveway. Over two months had passed since she'd been at 127 Arlington Road. She felt like a guest about to reenter her own home.

Stefan grabbed her suitcases from the car.

"Kate, we're home. Just like old times."

"Old times" hadn't been so great, she thought to herself, but acknowledged his good intention with a smile.

The front door opened and Charley, the family German Shepherd bolted toward the car, jumped on Stefan and barked at Katie.

"Hey boy, it's me, Katie." Charley, recognizing her voice, jumped up to lick her cheek, practically knocking her down. She laughed and it felt so good.

"Who's making all the racket out there?"

Startled by the deep male voice, Katie swung around to be swept off her feet by her muscular, playful only son.

"Shep! Oh my God! I didn't know you were going to be here! Stefan, did you know about this?"

"Of course. You said you just wanted the immediate family and we took you at your word."

"But I didn't mean...I hope it wasn't..."

"Mom, chill. I couldn't miss your homecoming. Let's go see the girls. They have a surprise for you."

Inside the entryway stood two little French maids, with net stockings, black skirts, white aprons and caps perched high on their heads like tiny white tents. Adorable.

"It was Ingrid's idea," said Heidi, bursting with teenage zeal.

"Welcome home, Mom," said Ingrid, as they simultaneously hugged her. "Tonight you will not lift a finger. Heidi and I have done the cooking. We'll do the serving and the menfolk will bat cleanup."

"What? No one asked for my two cents worth." Shep asked.

"What would you have said, bro?"

"I would have refused."

"Precisely, that's why we didn't ask you." Heidi smiled after sticking out her tongue.

At this point Stefan intervened and announced, "I'm going to help your mother take her things to the bedroom".

"Don't be long, you two. We've got a great dinner planned. Hors d'oeuvres in fifteen minutes," said Ingrid as she dashed off to the kitchen.

Apprehensive, Katie entered their bedroom. She'd grown accustomed to sleeping by herself, rather enjoying her privacy. Weeks ago she had adjusted to strange surroundings, never dreaming that she would face an adjustment upon returning home. Stefan followed her into the room, dropped the suitcases and pushed the door closed with the side of his foot. He turned her so she faced him and embraced her.

Her body stiffened and she whispered in his ear, "I just need a little time, Stefan. Please."

He released her and without disguising his disappointment, he nodded and abruptly stated, "I'll be downstairs with the kids when you're ready. Take your time."

Katie knew she'd hurt his feelings but couldn't help her response. She walked to the bookshelf and examined the titles as if she were in someone else's home. *Magic Mountain, Atlas Shrugged, Portrait of a Lady, Madame Bovary*...all familiar. These were her books, her friends. The large watercolor that hung over their bed depicted The Champs Elysees on the Seine. She and Stefan had bought it from an art vendor on a sunny Parisian boulevard on their tenth wedding anniversary. She walked into the bathroom to wash her face and looked into the mirror, discovering deeper lines than she'd remembered, lines furrowing her cheeks and across her forehead. She hadn't really looked at herself at Woodrose. Changing the lighting in the bathroom would be number one on the to-do list. She washed her hands and noticed the blue veins beginning to protrude from skin marked with small dark blotches. Why had she thought that she'd be immune to aging? No one believes they'll age, she thought, until they do.

Barber's "Adagio for Strings," one of her favorites, filled the downstairs "auditorium." She'd heard it first at her grandfather's funeral when she was six years old. It was strange how the mind selected memories to be relived in Technicolor and stereophonic sound, when most of life faded into oblivion. Her past was a skeletal sequence of events on a horizontal timeline but most of the details were as blurred as the watercolor that hung over their heads at night. "Adagio for Strings" was very real.

"Mom, the canapés are ready."

"Canapés? Since when do we serve canapés in this house?" she shouted from the top of the staircase.

When she reached the kitchen, her eyes welled with tears.

"It's really so good to be home," she announced with a broad smile. Looking at her family's faces, she momentarily felt beautiful.

The telephone broke the mood. "Which line is it?" Heidi pealed.

"It doesn't matter," Ingrid yelled. "Dinner is served in five minutes. Nobody answer it!"

Too late. Shep would have to endure the wrath of his little sister as he'd already picked up the receiver.

"Dad, it's Aunt Mattie."

"Tell her I'm not here."

"Daddy, she can hear you. Sshhh!" Heidi said it in a vain attempt to silence her father.

"Hey Dad, she knows you're here. She heard you," said Shep.

"Good God! I forbid anyone else to answer the phone tonight," he ordered as he wrestled the phone from his son.

By the time Stefan joined them at the dinner table, Katie had offered the standard family grace.

"Dad, why don't you like Aunt Mattie?" Ingrid asked.

Stefan pensively chewed his corn relish for what seemed to be an eternity, then responded.

"Because she's weird. Do you know what that was all about? Your Uncle Les had a heart attack six months ago, remember? Well, he's afraid that if he gets too excited, his heart might stop again. Can't blame him for that. Anyway, your Aunt Mattie is hysterical because she's afraid she'll never get laid again. And she's calling me to tell her tale of woe. What the hell can I do about it? I told her to write her chaplain."

"I've got a suggestion, Dad," Heidi said.

"About Uncle Les's impotence?"

"No." She snickered. "But I think Aunt Mattie might feel bad when you yell that you don't want to talk to her. Maybe you could be a little nicer to her."

"She doesn't know when I'm being rude. Believe me, I know my sister. It makes me nervous that we were in the womb together." Obviously amused by the thought, Stefan peered over the rim of his glasses like an old schoolmaster, while his family laughed.

By the time the smells of roast beef and Yorkshire pudding reached the table, Charley could no longer contain himself. He inched his way off the hardwood floor and onto the forbidden carpet under the dining room table. Katie was the first to feel his pleading paw, followed by a large, moist tongue. It was comical how quickly his memory had revived. He had no trouble at all remembering that she was the sucker of the family. A tender piece of meat inconspicuously slipped under the table but Charley's chomping blew his cover.

"Charlemagne Shepard, are you under the table?" Stefan barked.

Charley's tail began to pummel the floor making him an easy target to locate. A gentle boot from his master sent him scurrying down the hallway.

"Dad, I have tickets to the Bruins playoff game on Sunday night. Would you like to go?" Shep asked.

"You guys are such brutes. I think hockey is so violent, they should ban it from sports," Ingrid said. "I mean, there was a guy at my school who actually wore a T-shirt with a red cross on it, and you know what it said? 'Give Blood. Play Hockey.' That's gross."

"Do you realize, Ingrid, that the same injury that keeps a second baseman out for the season keeps a hockey player off the ice until the next line shift?" A fierce hockey fan, Shep defended his sport to the death.

"Mom, you don't like hockey, do you?" Heidi asked.

Katie had finally been addressed ."Actually, honey, hockey is my favorite sport. The strength, the finesse, the speed. I love it. But remember, your grandparents were Canadians. I grew up listening to my father defend his Montreal Canadians and curse his neighbor Roget Lambert, who cheered for the Toronto Maple Leafs. Hockey was a topic of conversation at every evening meal. So Shep comes by it naturally. It's in our blood."

Ingrid protested. "Well it's not in my blood."

"Have you ever thought you might be adopted, Ingrid?" said Stefan.

"Nice try, Dad. But I look just like you." It was true. All of the children looked strikingly like their father, almost as if Katie hadn't participated in their conceptions. Stefan had strong Austrian features so it really was no wonder that his were the dominant genes. Even Heidi's blond hair had darkened and she'd lost her Irish fairness.

Katie didn't remember when she'd last had an uninterrupted island of time with her whole family. Perhaps eight years ago, on some uneventful evening when Shep was still in high school. So much life had lapsed. They had been together for holidays but holidays were artificial days, staged with predictable activities, overeating, overdrinking, exaggerated expectations and stressful deadlines. Had she realized the preciousness of a simple night together, she would have been more grateful. She would have paid more attention.

After dinner, Shep seated himself on the ottoman in front of his mother and took her small hands in his.

"Mother, how are you?" His dark eyes probed for a sincere answer. Stefan cleared his throat as if a reminder that he too was in the room and shared his son's concern.

" I'm much better, honey. Thank you for asking. It was hard being away for so long. That first week was tough. I've never felt so alone. I'd wake up in the middle of the night, crying my heart inside out. And no one showed up to rescue me. So I rescued myself."

Katie paused, then added with a hint of levity, "But honey, I'm exhausted. Let's table it for tonight."

Her special child, the child who most closely connected with her, looked at her adoringly. The moment was a gift and this time she paid attention.

~ ~ ~

The bedroom was cold. In the late afternoon, she'd opened the windows and fresh air flushed through the room. The kind of air that stimulates wild, imaginative dreaming. Katie closed all but one of the windows, and turned to face Stefan, who sat with slumped shoulders on the edge of the bed.

"What's wrong?" she asked.

He shook his head, appearing to deny that anything was on his mind but begging to be asked again.

"Stefan, talk to me, please."

"Did you think about me when you were there?"

"What do you mean?"

"Have you forgiven me, Katie?" His voice faltered.

She could hear him trying to swallow the lump in his throat. Katie sat down beside her husband and pressed her forehead against his cheek.

"You weren't responsible for my drinking. I was. Your decisions in the future will never drive me to drink again."

Stefan pressed harder, persisting.

"But do you forgive me for the hell I've put you through, Katie? Do you forgive me?"

"If forgiveness means that your affairs were all right with me, then no. But if forgiveness means that I'm willing to make a fresh start with you, if it means that I won't dwell on the past, if it means that there won't be secrets between us, then yes, Stefan, I forgive you."

As so many times before, he collapsed in her arms, and she knew that her husband probably felt absolved of his sins, perhaps hoping that he could be true to his Katie. But this time they made love as if there had never been anyone else. Katie found it curious that he fancied himself a Casanova, pleaser of women. He really was a selfish lover, self-conscious of his manhood as the center ring attraction. The possibility of "training" him as a lover had long passed, and suggesting he alter his sexual routine would only emasculate him. It wasn't worth the effort. She probably couldn't forgive him but she accepted him. She accepted her marriage. End of subject.

That night when the rest of her world slept, Katie designed flower beds, salivated over the sweet tomatoes and the lip puckering rhubarb she would plant the following spring. Tomorrow would be "Prokofiev Day." She would play his Fifth Symphony, then "Romeo and Juliet," then maybe his Second Violin Concerto. She shared her mother's love of "those Russians," as Stefan called them.

Her aberrant thoughts drifted to her childhood family. Tess liked the German composers better. But Katie and Tess had different tastes, and style. Katie had always felt unfairly judged by her sister, only two years her junior. Fortunately, distance and time had eased their feelings of incompatibility. Troy was nine years younger and Tia had been a complete surprise to the family twenty two years ago, and practically the same age as Ingrid. It had been strange to be pregnant at the same time as Mum.

On this homecoming night, Katie's family slept under one roof and she felt content. At Woodrose, she'd lived with the humming of an air conditioner outside her window and the cold, stale, recirculated byproduct of the noisy monster. On her first night home, she stayed awake for a long while to inhale the fresh air, to smell the night-blooming jasmine sweetly scenting the breeze, and to hear the wind chime made of tiny shells sing outside her window. In the distance she heard the hooting of an owl, or was it the cooing of a dove? She'd never learned to distinguish the sounds of birds very well. That was Tess's expertise. Did Tess know about her release from Woodrose? She would call her tomorrow.

~ ~ ~

The household awakened to Charley barking at the rabbits in the backyard.

"Shut up, Charley!" yelled Stefan. "Shut up! That damn dog can't catch those rabbits! He's so stupid!"

"You named him. I think he's trying to live up to it. Charlemagne, Mighty Warrior, Conqueror, Killer of Rabbits." Katie grinned.

"Very funny. Since when are you a comedian?"

"Since now. It's about time, don't you think?"

He playfully wrestled her to the bed and with a dastardly pirate-like wail, pinned her down. She laughed and realized she liked the idea of being taken. His weight was heavy and his shoulders broad above her. But then the tickling began. She squealed for mercy and fought him with all her might, finally screaming, "I'm going to wet my pants. Stop! Please stop!"

"What's going on in there?" Heidi heckled from the hallway, delighted that her parents were having fun. The atmosphere of their home had been strained for years: her dad would often come home late at night and her mother would wait out his return with Captain Morgan.

"None of your business!" roared Stefan, who sat up just long enough for Katie to wriggle herself free.

"Hey Shep, Ingrid! Dad's molesting Mom!" Heidi yelled.

"Go for it, dude!" he yelled.

Katie pleaded. "Stefan, stop it. This is embarrassing. Those are our children out there."

He smiled and tenderly kissed her. And all was well in their world.

~ ~ ~

The gray morning welded into midday. Katie had forgotten how the afternoon sun shone into her kitchen with beams of light, so distinct, so visible, they almost appeared solid. She'd always been fascinated by light and shadow. That's why she loved early morning and evening photography. Slanted light minimized glare and allowed the depth of color to come out and play. It danced across her fruit bowl and illumined the red of the ceramic strawberry pie on the counter. As she sliced cucumbers, her mind drifted to the people she'd met at Woodrose. She'd been right about Harish. His release had been quick, just as she'd predicted. The young girl who was pregnant lasted only four days, and Maureen, whom Katie had befriended, was still there. Maureen had a good heart but was a struggling soul with limited ability to see through a window of truth without the heavy shade of confusion crashing down. "God bless Maureen," Katie prayed under her breath.

Ingrid climbed onto a stool at the counter.

"Spence and I are going to a foreign flick down at The Harbor View, Mom. So I think I'll be staying at his place tonight and then going home to my humble little hovel on Sunday night."

"Honey, do you love Spence?" Katie eased into the conversation. "I mean, are you planning a future together?"

"Mom, it's not a big deal." Ingrid already sounding irritated. "We just really like each other."

Katie felt Ingrid's indignant Irish temper flair, as well as her own. They were headed for disaster. "So let me get this straight. You sleep with men you just like. That's all it takes?"

"I know how you feel but times have changed. You are so in the Dark Ages, Mom."

Katie interrupted. "What happens if you get pregnant, Ingrid?"

"I'm out of here." Ingrid jumped off her seat and headed for the front entry. But before she slammed the door, she muttered, "Since when are you so interested in my life? You haven't talked to me in years. You were drinking, remember?"

Katie suppressed her tears as her heart raced. She'd been home for less than twenty-four hours and within minutes of being alone with her daughter, they'd come to blows. Par for the course. Ingrid had opened a wound that now seeped with injury. Katie hadn't been there for her children but she didn't have the option of turning back the clock. Ingrid's verbal attack had been accurate. Disrespectful, but accurate.

"Mom, Aunt Tess is on the phone!" Heidi yelled from her upstairs bedroom.

Katie gulped her ice water and ran to the telephone in Stefan's office for privacy.

"Tess? I'm so glad you called. I intended to call you today. Honestly. But you beat me to the punch."

"I called Woodrose and they told me that you were released yesterday. This is great! How are you feeling?"

"Truthfully, better than I've felt in years. Of course, I just put my new found courage to test and ended up alienating your darling niece, Miss Ingrid, and she plunged a dagger in my heart. Your phone call is great timing. Let's change the subject. How's life?"

"Fine. Keeping busy."

"How's your novel coming?" Katie didn't have a writing bone in her body and would rather walk over hot coals than have to write even so much as a resume or press release. She couldn't imagine wanting to write a whole book.

"I was blocked the last time I checked. I'm writing some short stories though and magazine articles, here and there. But I'm ready to really sink my teeth into a story that moves me."

"About what?"

"Oh I don't know. I'll know when it hits me. Maybe a story about adoption gone awry. " Tess gulped. "Enough of that. Tell me about your stay at Woodrose. How are you?"

"I'm okay. A little shaky...you know, reentering family life. I met some interesting people at Woodrose. One in particular, a patient named Maureen. Here's a story line for you. She has an Uncle Jimmy, homeless, who hangs out on the banks of the Charles River. Anyway, he's been on skid row since he returned from WWII, fifty-some years ago. Apparently he was a tail gunner over Germany, survived the war and returned as a fragmented soul. My God, he has to be seventy-five, maybe eighty years old, and totally alone in the world, except for Maureen. Before she went to Woodrose, every Saturday she brought him food and sat underneath the bridge and they talked. He always wears the same dirty blue hat and a green flannel shirt and picks wild flowers along the river bed for the centerpiece on the rock they use for a table. Can't you picture it? I guess he's a smart old codger though."

"Why doesn't your friend bring him home?" asked Tess.

"He won't leave his territory. And he doesn't know that she's in rehab. Poor guy. I envision him picking flowers for her arrival every Saturday and sitting alone, wondering where she is." Katie exhaled an audible sigh. "Why am I rambling on about this? There's nothing I can do about it. But what about you, little sister? Any adventures in your future?"

"Not really. We may have company sometime this month though. I have an opportunity to help a young girl who has recently lost her parents."

"Where did you meet her?"

"Well I haven't actually met her yet. And who knows, perhaps there's very little I can do for her. I'll let you know what happens."

"Now wait a minute. How do you know about her? Is she a friend of a friend?"

"Not exactly. She's just someone who needs a helping hand."

"What are you going to do for her?"

"I don't know. Help get her a job. Be nice to her, be a friend."

"I'm confused. How do you know this girl?"

"I don't know. She's at right place at the right time, I guess."

"What does Rennie think of your playing The Good Samaritan?"

Tess paused. "Well I haven't really told him yet."

"You haven't told him? Why are you so cryptic about this?"

"Listen. It's no big deal. I promise to keep you posted. Katie, I have to go but I'm so glad you're home. Heidi sounds so grown up on the phone. Say hi to everyone for me and stay strong."

"Okay. Thanks for the call. Bye."

Katie hung up the phone. *What was that about?*

Chapter 5

"Now boarding for the Twin Cities, Minneapolis and St. Paul. Now boarding, Twin Cities, Gate Two."

"*Finally*," thought Cristin Shanihan as she stood from the wrought iron bench which had numbed her lower extremities. She stretched, identified the gate and headed through the Dubuque bus station toward the big blue "2." This would be the final day of her travel. Her duffel bag, heavy with belongings, banged against the side of her leg, leaving the promise of a bruise. At the head of the bus line, a young boy cried as his mother showed a photograph to the bus driver and asked that her son be safely delivered to the man in the picture. A huge, fat woman in front of Cristin smelled as if she hadn't taken a bath in weeks. Cristin winced as she contemplated the long journey in an enclosed space.

But maybe things would work out well for her in Minneapolis, she thought, as she climbed the steps onto the bus. Maybe this would be her last bus trip ever. She took a seat and pressed the side of her face against the cool window as she scanned each stranger who entered the bus. A parade of faces she would never see again. An old man with a carved wooden cane sat next to her and asked if she minded if he laid it on the floor at their feet. She shook her head, then closed her eyes to discourage conversation, and relaxed.

Inside her eyelids, she saw her father, not his face, but his slow gait, walking away in his gray cardigan sweater and baggy trousers. She watched her mother compulsively fold laundry in orderly piles on the kitchen table. And she felt the heat of fire. The drone of the bus engine lulled her to sleep.

She awakened as the bus made its first stop. Staring out the window, she watched young boys playing Kick the Can and a store owner sweeping the sidewalk in front of his hardware establishment named "Nails and Pails." An Asian woman, carrying a flowered parasol to shade herself from the noontime sun, stood on a corner and observed a pair of street people digging for treasures in a trash bin. Across the street she saw a young man and woman kissing on a park bench and Cristin wondered if she would ever marry. Past the park she saw headstones in a cemetery and wondered when she'd die.

"You can read it upside down, you know." The old man next to her pointed to the carved numbers on his cane."1961...you can turn it upside down and it still reads 1961, the only year in my lifetime that it happened. It won't happen in yours. John F. Kennedy was inaugurated 35th President of these United States that year and those pinko Commies built The Berlin Wall. And Dag Hammarskjold died and Yuri Gargarin orbited the earth and Chubby Checkers sang "The Twist." What year were you born?"

"1975." Cristin mumbled, discouraging a litany of historical events linked to that year as well.

"Tough year. Watergate, South Vietnam's surrender, Patti Hearst." His voice wavered. "The year my son died. Tough year, 1975."

Cristin took out her Guide Book to the Twin Cities and feigned interest. Her eyes followed the print, but two pages later she realized she hadn't read a word. She thought about the man losing his son. Maybe he'd really loved his son, been a good father, never beaten or abused him. She wondered if his son had suffered or if he'd died suddenly, and if his final thoughts included his father. It didn't matter. She wasn't really interested in other people's lives.

~ ~ ~

Minneapolis was an extraordinary city in June. "The Land of Sky Blue Waters," canopied with perpetually moving incandescent clouds, and boulevards appliquéd with emerald oak archways that bowed to each other like dancers at a ball. Tess forgave the brutal winters. Her relatives thought she was crazy because they had no tolerance for its harshness but she liked to come home to a roaring fire, feeling rescued from the bite of an arctic blast. Summer however ripened the land, setting the stage for mallards and their babies to waddle in single file across lawns between the latticing of nearby lakes. Squirrels and chipmunks scurried and rabbits left their warrens to nibble whatever bill of fare the neighborhood gardens had to offer.

Tess and Ren planned to attend an outdoor symphony concert that evening, so Tess packed a picnic dinner and a bottle of Chardonnay. The last time they'd visited the amphitheater, she'd forgotten the corkscrew and in an attempt to open the wine, spilled Merlot on her husband's light pants. "Once forgiven, twice, a fool," as Mum used to say. This time Ren wore dark pants, and she'd packed white wine and a cork screw.

Before they left for the evening, she took a few moments to sit on the verandah and survey the back yard. To the south, she could see everyone's property all the way down the street. To the north, a thick border of evergreens. Behind this living fence lived an eccentric old lady whose only visitor seemed to be the young man who delivered her groceries. For years, Tess and Ren had listened to the sound of water from her yard which they presumed to be a fountain. The serene sound of running water often put them to sleep at night so they'd nicknamed their mysterious neighbor Madame Serena. Every Tuesday from Madame Serena's windows, the aroma of paprika, perhaps Hungarian goulash, drifted from yard to yard on a breeze that slipped under doors and strained though window screens. Every Tuesday. It was as predictable as the sunrise.

When they arrived at the concert, people on the hillside behind them sat on blankets and peered through binoculars into the lives of the attendees in the box seats, perhaps presuming better seats signified lives with more fortune and fewer worries. Tess and Ren had a box seat with a table for two, twenty rows back and slightly to the left of center stage so they could see the keyboard if a pianist was featured. She dressed their table with a small lace tablecloth, a candle and a diminutive bouquet of pansies. As they ate, the orchestra practiced particularly difficult passages, warming up their fingers and tuning their instruments.

Finally the lights on the stage brightened, the concertmaster and conductor appeared and Bernstein's "Overture to Candide" exploded. It was over as quickly as it had begun. Rachmaninoff's Second Piano Concerto, as always, was like a beautiful dream that ended in tears. At intermission, they stood and stretched but Tess declined Ren's suggestion that they take a walk. She needed time to mention the letter and although it was possibly safer to discuss the potentially volatile subject publicly, she needed his undistracted attention. Her heart jumped when the bell rang warning the audience to resume their seats.

"Rennie? I keep forgetting to tell you something." She spoke in her most nonchalant tone. "I received a letter a while ago from a young girl whose parents recently died in an auto accident and she was searching for a relative. Somehow, by mistake, the letter was delivered to me. I responded, telling her that it had been misdelivered but that maybe I could help her anyway."

Ren interrupted. "You what?"

"Rennie, just listen. It's such a sad story. This poor girl has no one. I just offered to meet her."

"Why?"

"It seemed like the right thing to do."

"But you have no idea who she is, Maybe she's a psycho."

"Rennie, she's just a young girl who needs help. I think it was fate that I received the letter by mistake. Besides which, I don't believe in coincidence."

"I do."

"Rennie, be fair."

"I am being fair. So how was it left?"

"She dropped me a postcard that said she was coming to Minneapolis for a visit I'm going to meet with her once, take her to lunch, just see if I can help her, okay?"

"What's her name?"

"Cristin Shanihan. Cristin with a 'C'. It's Gaelic for Christine."

"When is this all going to happen?"

"I don't know yet. She'll call me when she arrives, maybe this week."

Strutting like a peacock, the conductor returned to the stage. The audience applauded and Ren took his wife's hand, placing it between his warm, massive palms. She'd told him and he had nothing further to say about it. And why would he be upset? She was just meeting a young girl for lunch. She muffled a sigh of relief. The second movement of the Beethoven 7th symphony was exquisite and on this particular night, she and the music were one, melodious and uncomplicated.

~ ~ ~

Tess arrived at Pang's, a Chinese restaurant downtown and sat so that she could see the front door. The restaurant was decorated with brightly costumed Chinese dolls encased in glass, landscapes on ecru silk and framed in black lacquer, and exquisite porcelain vases, delicately hand painted with birds, boughs and blossoms. An ornamental lantern adorned each table and bamboo railings separated the booths. The air smelled of ginger, soy and lemon. Rennie always said that a Chinese restaurant filled with Chinese customers indicated the food was good, and assessing the clientele, Tess looked forward to a delicious meal. She glanced anxiously at her watch. What if she and Cristin had come this close to meeting and didn't actually connect? What if she didn't recognize the girl?

Suddenly her eye caught a beautiful young lady in a coral dress, standing in the entrance, scoping the customers' faces. Tess smiled and raised her eyebrows ever so slightly. The girl smiled and approached the table.

"Hello, Mrs. Parker?"

"Yes. Cristin?"

"Oh yes, it's me. And it's you. I can't believe it."

"Please have a seat. I'm so pleased to meet you." She didn't resemble Katie at all, but none of Katie's children did. "How was your trip?"

"It was all right. I'm not crazy about bus travel but it was the cheapest way to get here. Minneapolis is a beautiful city. I hear there are 10,000 lakes."

"Not in Minneapolis proper but throughout the state there are more than that. I think there are closer to 14,000. And that doesn't include all the little ponds and puddles. Thanks to Paul Bunyan." Tess smiled.

The waiter came to take their order and suggested they try an assortment of tastes by ordering "The Beijing Platter." Cristin agreed.

"Please, tell me about yourself, Cristin. What was it like living in California?"

"Well, I didn't live near San Francisco or in the Redwood Forest or anything. I just lived in the hills. It used to be a center of the gold mining industry. So there's lots of history. People come from all over to visit. I lived outside Nevada City though. It sounds like it should be in Nevada, doesn't it?"

Tess nodded in amusement.

"Well, anyway, it's a pretty cool little town. Lots of antique shops, old Victorian houses with flower gardens and white picket fences. Main Street looks like a postcard. There's even a red fire station and a church with a white steeple."

As Cristin spoke, Tess studied her face. She was beautiful in a classic sense. A gold barrette at the back of her crown swept her thick dark hair away from her face, accentuating her chiseled bone structure. So young and unmarked.

Cristin continued. "There isn't much to see there. But in Grass Valley, there's a house where Lola Montez, the exotic dancer, lived with her pet bear."

Cristin chattered and Tess smiled.

The waiter arrived with a platter of egg rolls, bacon-wrapped water chestnuts, Cantonese pork, sweet and sour spare ribs and sesame shrimp.

"Help yourself. Doesn't it look delicious?"

"I'll say."

"Where are you staying, Cristin?"

"At the YWCA."

"How long can you stay?"

"I haven't decided, Mrs. Parker."

"Please call me Tess. Mrs. Parker is my mother-in-law's name."

"Okay, Tess." Cristin collected her thoughts. "I haven't decided because I really don't have anywhere to go. I have no family and since I couldn't find my mother, I can really start over anywhere."

"Why don't you try Minneapolis?" Tess jumped in. "I mean, perhaps you'd like it here. I could help you find a job".

"That would be wonderful. I do like it here. My parents left me some money but I will have to find a job. I'd appreciate any help you can give me."

The afternoon was friendly and promising. Tess felt pangs of maternal protectiveness and took a private vow of custody over this person who had been mysteriously handed to her. A divine and serendipitous hand had reached down to favor her with a child, Katie's child. But no one would ever know that. No one would be hurt.

~ ~ ~

On her way home Tess stopped at an Armenian delicatessen near the University to buy some dill lavoshe, Ren's favorite. The bakery section smelled of yeast and caramel, sweet and warm. The male clerk behind the counter, perhaps in his mid-sixties, wrapped her bread as if he were wrapping a baby in swaddling clothes.

When she arrived home, Ren's new BMW was in the garage and his ex-wife's Pontiac was in the driveway. Lissa, Ren's fifteen year old daughter, was staying with them for the weekend.

"Hi, honey, I'm home," Tess announced as she entered.

"We're out on the verandah. Lissa and Mel are here."

"Hi, Lissa. Hello, Mel," Tess said, nodding in deference to the witch-mother and feeling a twinge of her own duplicity. Merely a nicety for the child's sake.

"How long will you be able to stay, Lissa?" Tess asked.

The child shrugged her shoulders. "Till Sunday."

Mel squawked. "I'll talk with my attorney next week, so consider yourself warned."

Ren shook his head. It was a broken record coming from a woman who sat home all day, every day, watching soap operas and game shows, gaining fifteen pounds a year and virtually destroying any possibility of building a life or meeting a new partner. It had been ten years since their divorce and every night, Tess counted among her blessings, that she had not been "the other woman." It hadn't been a "messy kill," in that respect. Ren had just become unwilling to devote his life to Miss Piggy any longer.

"We've been through this before, Mel." He entreated Tess with his eyes.

"Lissa, I need your help in the kitchen, honey."

The child snapped, "Don't call me honey."

"All right. Well, I'm making giant popovers tonight so we need to get a head start. Besides which, I'd love to hear what new videos are on MTV this week. You're my lifeline to the world of rock, you know."

Within hours, Mel had returned to her cave, Ren had been fed and Lissa experienced an unargumentative family dinner. As predictable as the coming of winter, the first couple of hours with Lissa were always exhausting but once her mother was out of sight, the household resumed a sense of normalcy and equanimity.

~ ~ ~

The following evening Tess walked by the guest room which Lissa never used as she preferred to fall asleep in front of the television and not claim any room as her own. The girl's analyst explained to Ren that this was because she didn't want anything or anyone too permanent in her life, for fear it would be taken away, "a normal adolescent reaction from a child of divorce." Ren didn't buy it and attributed it to the bull-headed stubbornness from her mother's side of the family.

The guest room was substantial, the most prominent feature being a bay window and window seat, piled with cushy pillows, overlooking the backyard. Where the walls met the ceiling, a pastel floral border edged the perimeter of the room, in a print that perfectly complemented the curtains. The bed was covered with a star quilt Tess's Grandmum had sewn. The quilt was so special that when company stayed overnight, Tess folded and tucked it safely away in the linen closet.

But here sat an empty guest room and Cristin was staying at the YWCA. Surely she could use it while she was getting herself on her feet again.

Tess found Ren downstairs reading the day's normal array of newspapers, *The New York Times, The Wall Street Journal* and *The Christian Science Monitor.* In the family room, Lissa buried her attention in a romance novel, with a cover of a muscular brute dragging a voluptuous woman in a torn, tightly fitted skirt, with enormous breasts gaping out of an untied bodice. Tess couldn't imagine why anyone would want to read such a book, but reserved comment for the sake of family harmony.

"Rennie, could I talk to you about something?"

Ren took off his reading glasses and gave her his attention. Lissa left the room. Suddenly Tess felt that she should have rehearsed what she was about to say.

"Honey, I haven't had a chance to talk with you. Yesterday I met the girl I told you about. Cristin. We went to Pang's for lunch."

"How was it?"

"It was delicious. She's bright, quick-witted and charming. As I mentioned before, her parents died and to her knowledge, she has no living relatives. She lived in California but has come to the

Midwest because it's more affordable. She has some money for school but needs to find a job."

"I hear the intonation of "rescuer" in your voice and it's making me nervous, Tessa," he said. "What do you have in mind?"

"I just want to help her get on her feet, Rennie. Make a couple of calls for her, perhaps vouch for her if she needs a reference, and maybe offer her the guest room...temporarily."

"In our house? Our guest room? Tess, you don't even know this girl. She's a stranger. We don't invite strangers to live with us. What are you thinking?"

"For God's sake, Rennie, she's living at the YWCA!"

"I don't care if she's living in a cardboard box, she's a stranger. Case closed."

Tess pursed her lips, clenched her jaw and stormed out of the room into the backyard, praying that Ren would not follow her. He didn't. She grabbed a hoe and started aerating soil in the west corner of the yard where the blue spruce provided too much shade for anything to thrive. She hated this job. She hoed with fury, sweating out her anger. In time, glimpses of solutions began to surface and a plan developed. Initially, Cristin would come to dinner. She would gradually be integrated into their lives. But their future house guest would first have to earn Ren's trust.

An hour later Tess glanced at the verandah and saw him standing beneath the Casablanca fan. *How long had he been there? How long had he been watching her?* She laid down the hoe and headed for the house. As she neared the verandah, she saw a look of love on his face that she treasured, a look that made sense in her life. It didn't indicate he had changed his mind. Quite to the contrary, he wore an expression that he was sorry he couldn't change his mind.

~ ~ ~

The following morning Ren agreed that an invitation to dinner was not out of line. The compromise was a partial victory. During her agitated night, Tess remembered that only a week ago, their neighbor Jodi Taylor had mentioned that she was going back to work at an architectural firm where she'd been employed before her children were born. Her husband was not in favor of the decision but had finally acquiesced. The two Taylor children were in need of full-time day care. Enter Cristin, a bright young girl, "between engagements," as Ren referred to the unemployed. It was a potential match.

By 9 a.m., the phone call was made. Jodi was delighted at the suggestion.

"When can I meet her?" she asked.

"Hopefully, she's coming to our house tomorrow evening so we could stop by before dinner, let's say 5:30?"

"Terrific. We're going to the zoo tomorrow. That will give me time to clean up the kids. Tess, if this works out, I wouldn't have to go through the hassle of advertising. And the interviews! If you could spare me that aggravation, I'd owe you one."

"I haven't mentioned it to Cristin because I thought I'd talk with you first but I'll be speaking with her today. I'll call you tonight."

Tess hung up and smiled. If this worked out, Cristin would be living in a guest house down the street, keeping her close and accessible.

~ ~ ~

Tess knew that it was Tuesday because the bouquet of Hungarian paprika and cayenne hung in the air like colorful aromatic balloons. Madame Serena had once again established a culinary eminent domain of the airways. Tess closed the windows so their home didn't set the scene for "A Night in Budapest" but did set the stage for her own personal drama. She set the dining room table with Mum's sterling silver flatware and Ren's favorite china, collector dishes with hand-painted Audubon birds on the margins. She chose the American goldfinch, the scarlet tanager and the indigo bunting plates, and then picked tiger lilies from the yard for the centerpiece. It was already 4:30. As usual, she always packed too much activity into too little time. She could hear her dad saying, "Be a respecter of time, Tessa; other people's as well as your own."

Traffic on Interstate 394 was backed up for miles between General Mills and the Farmers Market. Despite the fact that the air conditioning in the car blew full blast, her hands stuck to the leather steering wheel. Her eyes volleyed between the clock and the road as she complained out loud. "Where did they all come from?"

Then for some mysterious reason, the cars began to move. She stepped on the gas and began weaving in and out of traffic. She was finally making good time when she noticed the red flashing light in her rear view mirror.

"Damn!" She slapped the steering wheel.

Abrupt and unfriendly, the officer never once looked her in the eye. He informed her that she not only exceeded the speed limit but verged on driving recklessly. Because it was her first offense, he wrote her up for speeding only and she drove away, feeling thankful.

Cristin dismissed Tess's delay with poise, assuring her that the world was far too entertaining to ever be bored. The traffic home, bumper to bumper, offered them time to talk. Cristin agreed that the job at the Taylors would solve an immediate problem and appeared to be delighted at the prospect.

The farther they drove, the more picturesque the landscape, the more plentiful the lakes. The color of the month was green, with trees and grasses of so many shades and variations that through an artist's eye, green displayed a chromatic scale of colors. Lakes bordered with pussy willows, cat-tails and blowing reeds were intersected by roads, serving as bridges across the bodies of water and circumscribing their perimeters. A summer wonderland.

"Cristin, I need to talk to you about one detail of our meeting that would be best kept in confidence."

"Of course, Tess, whatever you say."

"First of all, I've told my husband that I inadvertently opened and read your letter. True. That it had been misdelivered to me.

True. I told him that you were searching for your biological mother and your adoptive parents had recently died and I wanted to help you. True. What I haven't mentioned is that the letter was addressed to my pen name, that you actually thought I was your mother. I don't want to bring this up because my not being able to conceive a child has been a sensitive and sad issue for us, so I would prefer that you not mention it. As a matter of fact, I would prefer that we don't talk about the letter again. The most important thing is that you're here."

"No problem, Tess. I understand."

Tess sighed. "We're almost home." She tried to imagine what Cristin was thinking. If the adage "normal is the neighborhood you grew up in," then there was no question in her mind that Cristin was retuning her comfort level.

"Do you live in one of these big homes?" she asked.

"It's a good sized home. It's an English Tudor and it does have a pretty garden. We've lived here for a few years now and have no desire to move."

She pulled up to the curb and stopped.

"Is this your house?"

"No, this is the Taylor's home. I told Jodi that we'd be here by 5:30 and it's past that time now, so let's run in and meet the family. Remember, two little girls, Lexi is four and Tori is two."

The sidewalk leading to the house snaked through a manicured lawn, bordered with pliant stalks of white narcissus and mixed wood hyacinths that stood at least a foot high. The two-story stone building, bearded with ivy, hung awnings the color of malachite. Jodi answered the door with a cheerful smile and two curious toddlers by her side. The children were indisputably sisters, both with big brown eyes and long black lashes, chubby cheeks, and frocked in identical red sun dresses.

An hour later, Cristin had a job, a home and a family. It was arranged that Tess would bring her back that weekend. She would live in the guest house at the back of the property, work five days a week with two days and all of her evenings to herself. She would have a car at her disposal for family errands and necessary chauffeuring and was expected to pay only for the gas that she used during her off-hours. Cristin looked stunned and grateful and glowed during the ride to Tess's home.

The front of Tess's home was dramatic, with lofty maples and birches and showcasing one enormous weeping willow tree whose branches swept the grass with its feathery tresses. The yard was scored with bird song and Cristin looked as if she had just landed in Oz.

"Listen to the doorbell," said Tess. "It's a ritual to ring it even if no one is at home. I'll tell you why later."

Ren wasn't home from work so they took a quick tour of the house. Paintings of Minnesota scenery hung in the upstairs hallway: Minnehaha Falls frozen in the grace of winter; the Split Rock Lighthouse seen through a veil of morning mist; and an autumn view of the Mississippi River with banks of brilliantly blazing trees that looked like watermelon and cantaloupe piled in parfait glasses. At the end of the hall was a lighted picture of Tess and a distinguished looking man.

"Is this Rennie?"

"Yes, that's my Rennie." She added, "but I think you should call him Ren. His name is Warren which no one calls him. But I'm the only one who calls him Rennie. It's a term of endearment, if you know what I mean."

Cristin smiled and turned the corner into the sunny guest room. On top of the mahogany dresser, Tess displayed pictures of their extended family and loved ones. Cristin pointed to one woman, asking who she was.

"That's my sister's family when her children were very young."

"What's your sister's name?"

"Katie. Her name is Katie Shepard." Not eager to discuss Katie with Cristin, Tess folded the topic into another. "I have a brother, Troy, who lives with his wife and two children in California and a younger sister, Tia, who is twenty-three and studying in France."

"Wow, your sister is only twenty-three? That's practically my age."

Tess smiled.

~ ~ ~

At dinner Cristin shared that she was an art lover and that she and her mother had spent hours together looking through art books, noting where each painting was displayed. She'd only been in Minneapolis for a couple of days and had already been to the Walker Art Center to see Franz Marc's "Blue Horses." As she spoke, she sparkled. And Ren smiled.

Later that night, after Cristin returned to the YWCA, Tess glossed over the consequence of the successful evening to minimize her own delight and expectations.

"Rennie, you'll never guess what happened to me today. A traffic cop stopped me for speeding. He almost cited me for reckless driving, but I flashed my baby blues."

"Were you going too fast?"

"I guess so."

"Were you reckless?"

"Come on...I just wanted to get there."

"Baby, reckless is a serious offense. Promise me you'll slow down. Promise me you'll be careful."

"Oh, I know what I'm doing. I'm not reckless."

Chapter 6

In September, Stefan and Katie vacationed in New England. They slept in four post beds beneath downy eiderdowns and family quilts. They dined and conversed with travelers from Belgium, Australia and Canada. They canoed around thickly-wooded islands, paddling through water that was still, deep and clear to the bottom, revealing "The Dance of Waving Reeds." As they regarded the scenery, they disregarded time, walking through forests of yellow aspen, copper oaks and blazing sumac. They watched the sunrises and sunsets paint backdrops for silhouettes of shorelines, tree lines and vees of geese. They awakened each morning to whispering breezes and fell asleep to the haunting call of loons. They talked; they accepted. They began to heal and reinvent themselves.

The camera was magic in Katie's hands, capturing the beauty of water lilies with white and yellow blossoms floating like aquatic jewels; a white egret's posture just before impaling his dinner; the reflection of fiery maples in blue waters; and an enormous blue heron taking flight with the slender extension and grace that inspires ballerinas. She changed her lenses frequently, zooming in on the veins of a single leaf as it floated on its back down the river and widening the angle to capture the mercurial palette of autumn colors on a distant bluff. In her personal life, there were times she'd concentrate on a general view, to avoid a painful specific; or focus on a detail to ignore a threatening bigger picture. Photography empowered her. She framed the world, to magnify or delete, to augment or diminish; her perception was her choice, and with it came the joy of authenticity or the risk of delusion.

****

Closing the door on a vacation was always sad. A few miles from home, Katie felt anxious and impatient to arrive. She'd taken one day at a time, every day, so surely her re-entry wouldn't be brutal.

After a two week absence, they opened the front door to the stuffiness born of stale air and humidity, accosting them like an escaping intruder.

"I'll get the windows downstairs. You open them upstairs," Katie yelled.

"Aye aye, captain."

She opened the kitchen window and filled her lungs. It was good to be home.

Later they met in the kitchen. The house felt alive with the smell of fresh air, pine trees and wood burning in neighboring fireplaces. Katie had returned from the market where the cantaloupes were the size of small soccer balls and the zucchini obscene. Stefan had retrieved Charley at the vet and picked up the mail.

"Hey, Kate, here's something from Woodrose."

"It's probably just an invitation to come back to talk with the patients. They mentioned that I might be hearing from them. I'd really like to." She ripped open the letter.

"Oh, ..no, oh no."

"What? What does it say?"

Katie read aloud,

Dear Mrs. Shepard,

We have repeatedly tried to reach you this past week. We regret to inform you that Maureen Shea took her life on the tenth of this month. Before she died, she wrote a letter, addressed to you. We made a copy of it for our records but felt that since it was intended for you, you should receive it in a timely fashion.

We apologize for this method of notifying you but we had no other recourse. We join with you in your sorrow. Please contact us when you return.

Sincerely,
Pamela Stockton
Executive Director

Katie opened the enclosed envelope. Stefan laid his hands on her shoulder, as he silently read with her.

Dear Katie,

By now I'm gone. I'm sorry, I truly am. But there was no way out. I knew that if I talked to you, you would have talked me out of it and that's not what I wanted.

I've lived a long life by anyone's standards. I'm unhappy in my marriage, I'm too old and tired to start over again, and I'm afraid of being alone. I want to go to sleep and not wake up. I know this will be hard for you to understand because you have a family and so much to live for.

Katie, no one ever treated me kinder than you did. I want you to know that. I do have one favor to ask of you. Remember my Uncle Jimmy who lives down by the Charles River? I'm sure by this time he's given up on me. But I worry about him. Would you go down there some Saturday in the early afternoon and try to find him? On the Cambridge side, across from the park. Tell him that I love him. I'll rest in peace knowing that you'll do this for me.

Remember me fondly and please don't be angry.

God bless you,

Maureen

Katie clutched the letter until her hands lost their grip and it dropped to the floor. *Maybe if she'd not gone on their vacation, Maureen would have called her. Maybe if she'd kept in closer touch, Maureen would have found a reason to live.* Attempting to shield her from the pain, Stefan threw roadblocks in front of each guilt-doused speculation. But Katie went through every "would, should and could have," exhausting herself with remorse.

Gradually her grief steamrolled into anger. Anger stemming from hurt and hurt rooted in loss. Loss of a friend and loss of someone who became so disoriented in the world that she couldn't find her way back. Katie's head ached with an unmerciful, pounding pain. It took hours to find the eye of the storm. But it was there that she thanked God for her own spiritual renaissance, and made a promise to the heavens and to one of its newest residents that she would find Uncle Jimmy and deliver the message.

The following morning, unrested and emotionally bruised, Katie awakened to the sound of the morning news. Stefan often turned on the television while dressing for work but this morning the stock market, the traffic and the weather reports were particularly inconsequential and annoyed her. Maureen was dead. Katie turned off the television and walked to the mirror to wash her face. She was an ugly crier. When other women cried, their eyes welled with a liquid sky that deepened the color and made them vulnerable and irresistible. But the aftermath of her tears left her eyes dry and caked shut; her face swollen like a blowfish. It was one of Mother Nature's practical jokes. Unappreciated.

As a child, she'd believed that if you went to school and followed the rules, you would graduate; get married; bear well-behaved, adorable children; and voila, you were an adult. Life became simpler because being a grownup implied a completed process of having grown up. *What a colossally foolish notion.* Life had turned out to be a constant barrage of challenges and complications as her inner circle expanded. The more people she loved, the more often she would be affected by their circumstances. It was an exponential nightmare, as well as a blessing. The ultimate paradox.

She sat in her kitchen with a cup of peppermint tea and opened the mail she'd not touched the night before. Trudging through piles of bills and junk mail, she eased into the incoming personal correspondence. There was a postcard from Tia in Grenoble, telling her that her next side trip would be to Munich for Oktoberfest. Katie's younger sister was more like a daughter in age. Tia had no idea of how fortunate she was to be traipsing throughout Western Europe, without a care in the world. Her weightiest responsibility was to show up for classes and pull grades.

The only other letter was from Tess. The girl Tess had referred to in their telephone conversation had arrived and worked as a full-time nanny at a neighbor's home. Reading between the lines, Katie could tell that Tess was extremely fond of the girl. That was no surprise as maternal feelings came naturally to her younger sister. Katie smiled.

Later in the day she visited Woodrose and was given an account of Maureen's memorial service. It had been poorly attended, only by a few members from The Center, Maureen's husband, and a nephew. The chaplain from Woodrose delivered the eulogy and a singer had been hired to sing "Danny Boy" in memory of her only son who had died at the age of six. There were no flowers. It was abysmal that someone could live a whole life and be so despairingly alone.

~ ~ ~

Saturday morning danced with autumn sunlight. The Wellesley area now had a sneak preview of the changes in color which Katie and Stefan had witnessed in New Hampshire the week before. Autumn was Katie's favorite season. The leaves would fall and be raked into piles, making yards ala mode. The gardens would bear chrysanthemums and asters, and the slanted light of a low sun would disappear into sunsets that gave birth to harvest moons. Autumn in Massachusetts made one acutely thankful for one's sight.

Her trip to the Charles River was dramatically out of character as she had never been a risk taker. She parked her car near the bridge that Maureen had described and began her descent to the riverbed. Wedging her heels into the dirt, she maneuvered sideways to maintain balance and navigate the bank's steepness. She slipped once and cut her hand on a jagged rock but erected herself and 'remanaged' her momentum. As she approached the bottom of the bank, she tripped over something in the weeds and let out a yell, flying through the air with the grace of a tumbling wildebeest.

"What the hell are you doing, bitch?" screeched the woman over whose body Katie had tripped.

"I'm sorry," Katie said in her best Wellesley manner. "I didn't see you." Her heart raced as she questioned her sanity for ending up in a place like this. She bent over to examine the throbbing pain below her knee. There was no question about it; she needed stitches. A man approached her and offered his dirty handkerchief to wrap her leg. She thanked him but declined his offer. She wrapped her scarf around the gash, applying pressure to stop the bleeding.

The old woman hollered again, "Get outta here. Go back where you belong, bitch!"

Wanting to get as far away from Sleeping Beauty as possible, she stumbled to an isolated grassy area below the bridge. She felt safer staying away from the groups. Determined to complete her mission, she yelled, "I'm looking for Jimmy, Maureen Shea's Uncle Jimmy. Can anyone help me? Please?"

A man beneath the overpass stood and started toward her. He wore a dirty blue cap and a green flannel shirt, just as Maureen had described her Uncle Jimmy. He hobbled as if crippled with arthritis, hunched over, fused in one position. His face was weathered and his eyes barely decipherable, the folds of wrinkled skin of his eyelids resembling an old lizard.

"Where's Maureen?"

"Uncle Jimmy?"

"Yes, I'm Maureen's Uncle Jimmy. Who are you?"

"My name is Katie Shepard. I was her friend."

"What? What's that supposed to mean?" He fidgeted with his fingers and stepped back and forth from one foot to the other.

"Jimmy, can we sit down? I hurt my leg."

He nodded and pointed to a log. When they both safely landed, she said, "Maureen and I met in a hospital a few months ago. We were both patients. Jimmy, Maureen passed away last week."

At that moment, she realized that she hadn't the heart to tell the old man that it had been a suicide. In this case, an incomplete truth had merit. God would forgive her.

Jimmy stared straight ahead for minutes as if transfixed by one of the office buildings across the river. He said nothing. Katie sat with him and stared at the water swirling randomly without pattern or design. After a time, Jimmy reached for her hand and cupped it in both of his worn, dirty paws. Never had anything so rough felt so tender.

"You're a good friend to come and tell me this. What did you say your name was?"

"Katie."

"Katie. Pretty name. Does it stand for Katherine?"

"No, Katrina."

"Hmmm."

"Jimmy, Maureen told me about her visits to you on Saturdays."

"We had some great talks, her and me did. But she walked down those steps to get here." He pointed to a stairway a block north of the bridge. "You came down the hard way...caused quite a ruckus. Who'd you step on anyway?"

"I have no idea but I'm going to have to doctor this cut as soon as I leave."

"You don't have to leave yet, do you?"

"No, I need to tell you something else. It was very important to Maureen that you know how much she cared for you. Her exact words were 'Tell Uncle Jimmy I love him'."

He pursed his lip and paused. "Were you there when she died? What she die of?"

61

"I wasn't there." She took a deep breath to gather her thoughts. "She died of heart failure."

"Hmmm."

He didn't press her any further. Her answer was convoluted but true. Everyone ultimately died of heart failure.

Her leg ached and the steps to the right became her stairway to heaven. "Jimmy, I'm so sorry to have had to tell you this but it was important that you not think that Maureen had forgotten you. I'm relieved that I found you."

"People meet for reasons, you know." He made a long drawn out guttural sound that guaranteed that he would not be interrupted as he conjured his next thought. "Would you come back some time to talk with me? I think Maureen would like that. If you can't, I understand. I'd just have to pass your kindness on to someone else. That's the way it works, you know."

He never once made eye contact with her but his request was clear. She was stunned that her assignment wasn't finished.

"Yes, I'll come back to talk with you. Maybe, next Saturday. How does that sound? Around one o'clock?"

"That would be dandy. I don't have a watch 'cause I don't need one but I'll watch the sun and expect you, Miss Katie."

It had been years since anyone had called her "Miss." She shook his hand and said goodbye. He told her that "Farewell" was a better parting phrase, and suggested she use it instead.

When she finished her ascent to the street, she looked downward. Jimmy hadn't moved a muscle, had probably watched every step she'd taken. And finally from a distance, he waved.

~ ~ ~

The ride home was uncomfortable. The bandage that the emergency care center had wrapped around her stitched leg made it difficult to bend her right knee while operating the pedals. The gash in her hand had been treated with a butterfly bandage but was stiffening by the minute. She longed for a vodka tonic with a twist of lime but muzzled that dream and replaced it with a tall glass of sun tea. When she arrived home, she would crawl into her recliner, take two pain pills and elevate her right leg and hand.

As she rounded the corner of Arlington Road, she saw Ingrid's car in the driveway. It had been months since they'd last spoken. Lousy timing. She wasn't physically fortified for confrontation. Katie's communication with her daughter had degenerated since Ingrid's high school years. She believed that they may have created a gap that couldn't be fused, that she and Ingrid would just travel through life on parallel planes, destined never to meet at one point. One thing was certain; after the shocking news of Maureen's demise and injuring herself that afternoon, she wanted to be alone.

She limped into the house and called Ingrid's name. Her daughter appeared, bearing an enormous hug, a few exclamatory remarks about the bandages, and demanding what, where, why, when and how. Katie tried to slough off the questions but Ingrid pressed to hear every detail. She found her way to her recliner, and when Ingrid brought her a glass of iced tea, recounted the story.

"That's dreadful, Mom. I'm so sorry about your friend. You're not going back to see the old man though, are you?"

"Why yes, I think I will. He may be dirty but he was decent and kind... and alone."

"But Mom, what could you possibly have in common with him? What could he ever do for you?"

"Maybe my meeting him isn't about me."

"But aren't you afraid it might be dangerous hanging out with bums? Does Dad know?"

Katie sensed an argument brewing and vowed she'd not participate. "Honey, don't worry about me. I'll be fine. Tell me what you've been doing? How are you feeling?"

"That's actually why I stopped by. I have some news for you and Dad but I want to tell both of you together." She grinned.

"Sounds exciting." She was ready for some uplifting news. Katie secretly hoped that her daughter had either applied to graduate school or she'd accepted a job related to her undergraduate degree.

"By the way, do you know where your father is?"

"He said he had to do some paperwork at his office. He should be home in an hour or so."

"Good." Katie sighed. "Honey, I need to take a snooze. Would you call Dad and ask him to bring home some food from that Peruvian restaurant down the block from his office? I think it's called "Inca Express." Maybe some curried chicken and their seafood/noodle combination? I don't want to cook tonight." She felt herself slipping away as Ingrid mentioned something about going up to the attic. Going, going, gone.

Upon awakening, her injuries pounded like pistons. She heard voices in the kitchen so she called out for pain medication which was followed by the sound of running water. Stefan knew that she had trouble swallowing pills. Not he. He could swallow a handful that would gag a horse.

He appeared in the doorway with glass and medicine in hand. "You don't need to say a word. Ingrid filled me in." As he fed her the pills and balanced the water to her lips, he added, "I should have gone with you. What were you thinking?"

Katie faintly smiled but didn't have the energy to defend herself. "I'm okay. The house smells great."

"I stopped at the Peruvian place. We'll bring dinner to you. Heidi won't be home until ten."

The dinner had all of the elements of a perfect meal; delicious, exotic, spicy, steamy and prepared by someone else. But as hungry as Katie was, she ate with small deliberate bites, as if her whole body had been injured and she needed to be exceptionally cautious.

"Well, Ingrid. You said you have some news for your mother and me. We're all ears."

"I certainly do. I'm glad you're both sitting down. First, I must tell you that I'm very excited about it." Ingrid's beamed. The room charged with anticipation.

"Katie urged her. "Spit it out, honey."

"I'm going to have a baby."

The room chilled. No one said a word. Ingrid looked into the stunned face of her father and the horrified face of her mother.

"Come on, you guys. I'm happy about it. It'll be great to have a baby around."

"Is it Spence's child?"

"Of course, mother. What do you think I am?"

"Are you and Spence getting married?" Katie asked.

"He isn't ready for a baby yet, but I want it so I've decided to keep it."

Katie shot an incensed look at her husband and when he said nothing, she turned to her daughter.

"Ingrid, listen to what you're saying. You're calling the baby 'it.' My God, this is a human being who deserves a mother and a father. If you and Spence are not going to be a family and make a home together for this child, for God's sake, let another couple adopt the baby."

"Your mother's right, kitten."

Ingrid gritted her teeth and began to shout. "I don't know why I thought for a goddamn minute that you two would be happy for me. This is the most exciting thing that's ever happened. For once, why can't you understand?"

"I understand that you're thinking of yourself. You're excited for yourself. But what's the best thing for the baby? Honey, there will be other babies for you. This child deserves a loving home with two parents." Katie's hands shook involuntarily.

"How could you ask me to give up my baby? You couldn't do it, I know you couldn't!"

Katie winced and struggled to find the right words. "Ingrid, I'm not saying it would be easy. I would hope I'd have the courage and the decency to put the child's needs above my neediness."

"You wouldn't, mother. I know you wouldn't! And since when did you nominate yourself Mother of the Year, Guardian of Children?"

Ingrid used sarcastic, demeaning words as weapons, stabbing Katie until both women were in tears. Stefan called for a truce, suggesting they talk again after having time to recover.

"Recover?" screamed Ingrid. "This is wonderful news that you are just choosing to view as a big mistake. Well, it wasn't a mistake. I wanted a baby."

"So let me get this straight." Katie tearfully persevered. "You made a baby on purpose, in an uncommitted relationship, because you wanted one?"

"That's it, Mom. You've got it." Ingrid's flippancy was intolerable.

"You didn't consider the sacrifice, the caring, the time, the resources involved in raising a child? To say nothing of the love!" Katie paused to breathe.. "My head feels like it's going to burst."

"You're not giving me much credit, Mother. I'll be there for this baby, even if you're not. I can give it all the attention and love it needs. I'll get a good job. There are support groups for single mothers. I know other single moms who have kids and they're doing it."

Katie continued. "Did you ever stop to think that men and women bring different valuable gifts to a child?"

"My male side is very well developed. I've got a grip on my masculine/feminine balance."

Trying to instill some sense into her inexperienced, psycho-babbling daughter was so bitterly exasperating that Katie could no longer control her anger.

"Balance? Since when are immaturity and selfishness balance?"

"That's enough!" Stefan yelled.

Ingrid took the cue and grabbed her backpack. The next sounds they heard were the slamming of the front door and the engine of her car.

Katie looked at her husband accusingly and yelled, "Why didn't you say anything?"

"You didn't give me a chance! You fired up so quickly there wasn't room to get a word in edgewise! My God, Katie, you could have held back a little. Now you've totally put her off. God knows when we'll see her again."

"Why can't you stop trying to be a buddy and act like a parent? I don't believe you're defending her!"

"I'm not defending her. You just made it impossible to discuss the matter," he retorted.

"There's nothing to discuss. She's wrong. As usual your daughter, Little Miss Rebel, is making poor decisions and taking no one else into consideration. But this time it involves an innocent child, Stefan. I don't think I can take much more. I want a drink so badly."

There. She'd said it.

"But of course, I'm not going to have one."

Stefan wore the shocked expression of a little boy having just been told that there was no Santa Claus.

"Stefan, my head, my hand, my leg are throbbing. My best friend from Woodrose has committed suicide, and our daughter has just informed us that she has planned a pregnancy with no intention of marrying the child's father. This is a nightmare! Tell me I'll wake up and these torturous problems will have disappeared." Katie paused to breathe. " I want to walk without pain, laugh with my friend, and give a baby shower for my happily married daughter. Is that too much to ask?"

Her voice was injected with sobs. Stefan cautiously helped her from her chair and up the stairs to their room. Walking past Ingrid's childhood bedroom, they noticed an assortment of baby clothes, Ingrid's baby clothes, laid out on her bed. She had brought them down from the attic for her own baby, but left in such a hurry, she'd forgotten them.

Tess asked her husband to open a window. Even though the night air was cool she needed to smell the gardenias. She needed to hear the serenade of crickets and the cicadas in the nearby fields. She needed a glimpse of beauty. She needed to sleep. She needed.

Chapter 7

Within the next few weeks, the winds of Wellesley smelled of burning leaves and the imminent coming of winter. Katie's physical wounds had healed, she'd made two trips to visit Uncle Jimmy, and no one had heard from Ingrid. Heidi, a high school senior, was so involved with school activities that Katie and she rarely shared a mutually satisfying conversation. Only brief, intermittent question and answer sessions. "When will you be home?" "At ten." "Where are you going tonight?" "A basketball game." "Don't you think that top is a little too revealing?" "No." Katie braced herself for the so-called "empty nest syndrome." In the past she couldn't imagine not having someone at home who really needed her. But her daughters' behaviors in recent months eased the transition. She shelved her dread of loneliness and closed the library. After all, she'd also dreamed of a time when she could pursue her interest in photography, taking side trips for hours at a time and not having to rush home to fix a pot roast.

The good news of the week was that Shep was bringing his sweetheart home to meet the family. Katie had not told him about Ingrid's foray into motherhood in hopes that Ingrid would tell him herself. He would surely align with his mother's strong values and talk some sense into his sister.

On a family conference call, Shep explained that his paramour Peri was the last child of seven in the Blue family and a daughter of hippies from the sixties who were creative in lifestyle as well as the naming of their children. Peri's name was actually Periwinkle.

"It's a bit unusual but wait 'til you meet her. You're going to love her."

"What are the other kids' names?" Stefan asked.

"Stefan, it's none of your business. I don't believe you asked that!" Katie laughed. "So what are the names of the other kids, Shep?"

"There's a brother named Slate and two sisters named Azure and Skye. I'll let your imagination come up with the others. Listen I've got to go. We'll see you tomorrow around 5. Bye."

"Bye," they chimed. They met at the bottom of the stairs and giggled like two children who'd seen someone's pants fall down. "Cobalt." "Sapphire." "Indigo." "Midnight." It was apparent to both of them that they needed to get it out of their systems by the following evening.

~ ~ ~

Charley's barking warned the household when anyone arrived. Charley leapt and jumped on Shep for his attention. So much so that he couldn't make it to the other side of the car to open Peri's door.

Katie watched a tall, lean woman exit the car. She wore a blue sheath and a copper scarf that hung to the hem of her dress, and dangling copper earrings that peeked through her long, straight golden hair. The length of her hair, the earrings, the dress and scarf accentuated her height and she floated like an apparition as she walked up the steps.

"How do you do? I'm Peri." She extended a long fingered hand at the end of a bare and graceful arm.

"We're so pleased to meet you, Peri. Please come in."

Katie turned to Shep who had managed to calm Charley and he hugged her tightly. "Hi, Mom. The house smells great. What's for dinner?"

"Your favorite. Beef stroganoff. Dad will be down in a minute. Come into the living room."

Just as they sat down, Stefan appeared in the doorway and Katie watched her husband's eyes widen as Peri stood to be introduced. Stefan poorly disguised his attraction to a beautiful woman, even when it was his son's girlfriend.

"I'm pleased to meet you, Mr. Shepard."

"Likewise. But please call me Stefan. Franz, is that a friend's car in the driveway or did you rob a bank?"

Shep addressed Peri with a quiet aside. "Did I remember to tell you that Dad insists on calling me Franz?"

Then turning to his father, he announced, "Dad, the car is mine. Business is good and I've always dreamed of owning a Ferrari."

"You mean to tell me dreams come true? It's a beauty. A mean, lean dream machine."

"You're giving your age away, Pops."

Heidi crashed through the front door and screamed, "Whose car's in the driveway?" She took one look at the dinner guests and squealed, "Oh my God, Shep, is it yours?"

He nodded and offered to take her for a ride sometime soon.

"Now! I have to ride in it now! Please, please."

"First show some manners. Come in and meet Peri."

Heidi breezed into the room and shook Peri's hand.

"Cool name...and I love your scarf."

Stefan and Katie held their breath in anticipation of Heidi's inquiry about Peri's name but she was far too excited about the car to be curious about anything else.

Shep hugged Peri and excused himself while he indulged his little sister.

Peri broke the silence by asking to see the home. Stefan poured a glass of Chardonnay for himself and two glasses of ginger ale for the girls and they began the tour. In each room, the curtains were tied back allowing natural light to fill and filter, with skylights strategically placed. Stefan explained that they had built the home and designed the window placement so the trees and flower beds could be seen from every angle. Katie loved freshly cut autumn flowers, so each living area had a colorful floral arrangement. Even the bathrooms had gardenias floating in crystal bowls.

When Peri spoke, she talked in a low voice, slowly, but not without enthusiasm. She had an appealing sense of sophistication and spontaneity and focused her attention on whoever spoke to her, as if what they had to say could change the world. She deliberately engaged her listener and digested his or her response before formulating her own. That was part of her exquisite charm. Katie began to understand why Shep was enthralled with her.

By the time they entered the family room, Peri asked if she could sit down because she was tired. Katie made a mental note of it. A sound as distinctive as the rumble of a Harley-Davidson approached the driveway. Katie imagined neighbors curiously peering, to catch a glimpse of the machine. Moments later, Heidi ran into the house with an artillery of superlatives that would make a Ferrari dealer blush.

Shep apologized to Peri for their lengthy disappearance and explained that they had driven to two of Heidi's friends' homes to show them the car. Peri smiled sweetly and assured him with a wink that she'd had a wonderful time and hadn't missed him at all.

"Well, Peri, Franz has told us that you come from a large family and your siblings have unusually interesting...jobs."

"When you come to think of it, I guess that's true. My oldest sister teaches sky diving by day and glass blowing by night. My next sister is a naturalist on a cruise line and just came back from her first trip to Antarctica. My middle brother is a painter in Marseilles. Let's see, Slate is a jazz saxophone player in Miami. Skye and her husband run a dude ranch in Wyoming. And whom have I forgotten? Oh yes, my oldest brother is the black sheep of the family. He's a computer consultant with a wife and five kids in Scarsdale, New York."

Katie almost laughed out loud. Stefan's transparent attempt to ascertain the names of the remaining Blue siblings had been in vain, learning absolutely nothing more than he already knew. She flashed him an amused "I know what you're doing" smile and segued into the next topic.

"But with all of you so spread out and in such different businesses, do you ever see each other?"

"Oh yes. You know how people have family reunions every ten or twenty years? We have one every year. The only one who was really at the mercy of a schedule last year was Ceri, the one who works on the cruise ship. But usually everyone comes. It's wonderful."

Stefan jumped in as soon as her voice faded. "Sari? That's an unusual name, is it a nickname for Sara?" he asked, thinking he'd discovered an incongruity.

"No, it's spelled CERI, it's actually short for Cerulean."

"Mom, did you notice these gorgeous earrings Peri is wearing?" Shep interrupted to camouflage his father's amused reaction.

"Yes, Shep tells us that you are in the jewelry business. Did you make your earrings?" she asked.

"As a matter of fact, they were a gift from my friend Marla. I'll tell her you like them. She'll be pleased. She works with copper and bronze. I prefer working with gold and precious gems. Shep, did I mention that I'm going to take a gem cutting course this winter?"

"I thought you were going to continue your French lessons?" he replied.

"I am." Peri shyly smiled at Katie and Stefan. "I'm a perennial student. What can I say?" She gracefully opened her expressive arms into the air until they settled gently in her lap. Katie could not remember so enjoying just watching someone move.

Everyone migrated to the dining room while Heidi and Katie worked the "last-ten-minutes-before-dinner-magic" that only a cook, serving guests in her own home, can understand. Every time Katie sat down with her guests at her dining room table, it felt like a small miracle.

As she pulled the rolls from the oven, the front door opened and in walked Ingrid.

"Hi, everyone! I made it, Shep." She greeted Stefan and Katie, hugged her brother and sister and extended her hand to Peri. "Hi, I'm Ingrid. Pleased to meet you."

Katie's stress level ignited. Shep hadn't mentioned calling Ingrid. But of course, why wouldn't she be invited? She was a member of the family too. In typical Ingridian fashion she acted as if nothing ugly or confrontational had ever taken place.

At dinner Heidi rattled on about the Ferrari, Ingrid was on her best non-disputatious behavior and Shep just let Peri shine, asking her questions that gave her center stage to glisten and glow. No more hints were dropped to ascertain the Blue family's missing names and no reference of the baby was made.

After dinner, Shep took Peri home early. Heidi hooked her ear to a telephone upstairs and Ingrid lingered. After the dishes were done, Ingrid appeared in the family room and straddled the ottoman.

"Mom and Dad, I have something to tell you. I've done a lot of thinking these past few weeks, since we talked and you were right."

Katie felt herself inhale as if she'd never stop, then bit her tongue and held her breath so that Ingrid could continue. But Ingrid said nothing more. She waited.

Stefan broke the silence. "Kitten, what's going on?"

"Daddy, I've thought about what was said that night when I told you both about the baby. I've realized that I really was thinking only of myself. A baby sounded so exciting. It gave my life meaning. There was a void in my life and I felt rather worthless, if you must know the truth. I wasn't passionate about my job, about the man in my life. A baby filled the void. It was a foolish plan, a selfish maneuver on my part. And I'm sorry."

Katie leaned over and embraced her daughter. She looked into Ingrid's eyes and said, "I love you. You have renewed my faith in humanity tonight!"

Ingrid beamed.

"Ingrid, you're giving this baby a chance to be raised by people who can't have a child of their own. It's completely unselfish and good. Honey, it won't be easy but your father and I will be with you every step of the way."

Ingrid's mouth opened but no words came out. Katie was so relieved that she didn't even notice Ingrid's shock. But Stefan did.

"Kitten, what's wrong? You look sick."

"I guess I haven't been clear," she said. "You're not listening. I mean, I realized you were right. I was in no position to have a baby and raise it on my own". Ingrid started to cry. "But Mom, I couldn't have a baby and give it up."

"What are you saying?"

Ingrid buried her head in her mother's shoulder and wept.

"Ingrid, what's happened?'

"I've had an abortion, Mother. I've had an abortion."

The words echoed in Katie's ears like a gong, and her own pain from twenty years before began to blister like an infected wound. Ingrid had had an abortion. That had been her logical remedy. She'd done what she believed was right. And why should she do otherwise? Katie had never spoken to her daughters about abortion.

That night as Katie lay in bed, she mourned how it had become common and acceptable to wipe out "a mistake" without conscience. And she knew that her own generation had failed their children by creating a society that was a playground without values.

Chapter 8

Since the day she'd received Cristin's letter, Tess had written only what she'd been paid to write. Preoccupied with having a child in her life, despite the fact that the child was grown, she manipulated time, people, and circumstances to satisfactorily align Cristin's life with her own. With that accomplished, she felt happy and prolific, free to write again.

Tess wrote because there was nothing she'd rather do than create characters who, in turn, created stories. She loved the wizardry and beauty of words and didn't strive to resolve profound conclusions but rather, to raise worthy questions. Writing was an honorable responsibility.

Her ideas were born in solitude. Even bird song or the sound of wind tended to disrupt her focus. Playing background music while she wrote was out of the question. The Russian composers were far too passionate, stirring her soul and fragmenting her concentration. The Germans left her no space to think because the beauty of their melodies lured her to other worlds. The only exception was the music of Mozart, the calming perfection of Mozart.

She did find that the sound of running water enhanced her creative mood....a gentle rainfall, a pounding storm, crashing surf; whatever the form, water was her link to the Cosmos, where imagination flourished. Madame Serena hadn't a clue how many characters and plots had been spawned by her backyard fountain.

There were, however, certain sensory experiences that induced the Muse. The metronomic ticking of a clock, windshield wipers, her breathing; or anything hypnotic, watching a fire in a fireplace or fish swimming in an aquarium. Stroking a piece of velvet. The aroma of vanilla in a slow-baking oven. A sip of Kahlua. All bridges to Beauty.

When writing, her world became myopic. Every person, conversation, sight and sound was scanned for applicability to her story. She became finely tuned and discriminating as to how she used each hour. Such a treacherous temperament to be so immersed. Thank goodness for Ren, her lifeline to the world. Convincing her that her raw material came from living her life, he had insisted that she participate in life outside the boundaries of her stories. In a spirit of cooperation and good will, they shared an active life, and in time, she realized the wisdom of his insistence.

~ ~ ~

The night of the hail storm was the first threat of winter. The sugar maples and oaks costumed the boulevard as umbrellas of bronze and yellow. The squirrels and chipmunks had gathered food in preparation for their season of repose. The nights cooled, the days shortened and the winds ferociously pursed their lips.

One evening Cristin came by to take her customary Tuesday evening walk with Tess. After two months of making up stories about households along their route, the girls had developed a portfolio of fantasies that were far from true but outrageously fun. The neighbors would have cringed at the conjured tales but the yarns were only discussed on the walks and unraveled before returning home.

They turned back onto their block just as it started to rain. They lingered like two giggling school girls, tilting their heads to the heavens and collecting as many rain drops as their open mouths could manage. Tess later contemplated trying to describe the smell of rain and discovered that it was somewhat like describing the color red. It wasn't a combination of anything else. One had to experience it to understand it.

Squealing, Tess and Cristin ran into the kitchen which was steeping with the aroma of hot peppermint tea, courtesy of Ren. Cristin shed her doggie-damp sweater while Tess hugged her husband. It was then that they heard the first hit. It wasn't identifiable until a few seconds later when the sound repeated itself. The periodic knocks accelerated to a pummeling, at which time, the three of them ran to the verandah to watch the show. Hail stones bounced off the earth like ping pong balls, a freak of nature that made children squeal and farmers cry.

The assailing of the hail lasted only a few minutes but the storm grew in intensity and the winds blew viciously from the Northwest. Within minutes, everyone in town knew that they had seen their last radiant autumn day. The leaves would lose their grip that night and the branches would wake up bare and shivering.

The neighborhood lost electrical power. Cristin wanted to stay but she conscientiously called the Taylors to see if they needed her help. They assured her that the children were having a great time with their flashlights and there was no need to come home. So there sat Tess with her husband and her niece, the two most important people in her life. Their faces, lit with candlelight, and the room, charged with magic.

"Tell me about your short stories, Tess," said Cristin.

"Well, I'm almost finished with my first collection, but I don't let anyone read them before my editor has had her way with them. But if you twisted my arm..." No one ever read her stories before her editor, not even Ren.

"Well, Cristin, you rate pretty high on her list. You just heard an unprecedented offer," Ren remarked.

"It probably isn't a good idea," Tess replied, trying to retract her offer.

"I think it's a wonderful idea. Please, I would be so honored, Tess, please." Cristin pleaded with puppy dog eyes.

"All right. I'll finish my last story by the weekend. You can be my first critic."

Tess was reluctant. Cristin was delighted. Ren was surprised.

Cristin continued. "I've had some wonderful talks with your neighbor, by the way. I was surprised to hear that you haven't met her."

"Which neighbor is that?" Ren asked.

"Betty, the older lady who lives next door."

"Tess, I think she's referring to you-know-who. The house to the north? Betty? Are you sure it's Betty?" He grinned.

"I'm positive. Two weeks ago, one of her bills was delivered at the Taylors by mistake, so I brought it to her. Her name is Elizabeth Morgan but she goes by Betty."

Tess started to laugh. Ren fell back into his lounge chair.

"I don't get it. What's so funny?" asked Cristin.

"I'm ashamed to tell you, honey. Especially, if she's a nice woman. You know how you and I fabricate stories about some of the neighbors when we take our walks? Well, let's just say we haven't been very good neighbors. We haven't taken the time to meet her. She seems rather..."

Tess looked at Ren for moral support but was met with nothing but sheer amusement. "Anyway, considering her reclusive behavior, her unusual style of cooking...Rennie, help me out," she deferred.

"Yes, her taste in music, her appearance, aahh..." he faltered.

"Considering the little we know about her, we have jokingly named our mysterious neighbor, Madame Serena." Tess's confession was out.

"Betty? I'm disappointed, Tess. Betty?" Ren started laughing.

Cristin appeared less amused. She liked Betty and didn't feel comfortable hearing disparaging remarks, however playful and harmless.

"Actually I call her Mrs. Morgan because even though she appears eccentric, she commands respect," said Cristin. "I've only visited her twice but we've had some intriguing conversations."

"Tell us more. Maybe we had the old gal pegged wrong." Ren smiled.

"I think you should both meet her. At first I couldn't put my finger on what was so special about her. But after listening to her talk I realized that it was her voice. She has a majesty about her. She's not rushed and she talks only about big stuff. I don't mean politics and religion...but beauty and appreciation, of the smallest kinds. The last time I left her, I was convinced that the dew on the spider web in her yard and the sparkling of the crystal pitcher in her kitchen were two of the most beautiful sights I had ever seen."

"Intriguing. Who is the man who brings her groceries? Her nephew, her grandson?" asked Tess.

"No, she has a service she can call when she needs anything. She hasn't spoken about a family. But Tess, would you like to come with me the next time I visit her?"

"Yes, I'd love to!"

"I'll leave it to you two to fill me in." Ren smirked. "Would you lovely ladies like anything from the bar before it closes?"

But it was getting late. Cristin hugged them goodnight and a curtain fell on the last act of the day.

Chapter 9

Nature had no manners. The first order of the day was to survey the damage of the storm. Silhouettes of leafless branches sprayed an eerie design against an austere backdrop of gray low-lying clouds. Tess wondered where birds hid during the storm and what a shock it must be when they returned to their favorite tree to find it stripped. Ren said she gave the birds too much credit. The front yards and streets were carpeted with large wet leaves that squished with each step and begged for a rake. The only leaves that survived the night were the copper oaks, always the last to let go.

Midmorning Tess lit a fire in the fireplace and resolved to finish her last short story. It was a tale of a woman who frequented cemeteries and became friendly with those who visited the resting places of their loved ones. In a lonely and forlorn attempt to connect and belong somewhere, she empathetically and pathetically made the visiting families her extended family.

In a matter of hours, the sun came out and inflated the air with the kind of humidity that malignantly grows mushrooms into giant mushy parasols. Tess heard the postman drop the mail and walked expectantly to the door to retrieve the usual assortment of bills and advertisements. There was a letter from Katie, written in green ink, Katie's signature color. They hadn't spoken for a while and she wondered why Katie hadn't just called, but she was delighted to receive a letter. The forgotten art of letter writing. It was more efficient to pick up the telephone or send an email. But there was something personal about the hand-written word. It took more time to create, so it made the recipient feel special. If something of a delicate nature needed to be communicated, a letter was less confrontational, because it didn't demand an immediate answer. One could read it over and over again and keep it forever. She opened the letter and began reading.

Dear Tess,

So much has happened and some of it isn't easy to talk about so I thought this time I would write you a letter. Remember how much fun we had rereading Mum's correspondence from her Aunt Hattie and Aunt Etta? Well, maybe someday, one of our grand-nieces will read this and appreciate the fact that it was written. I've often envied your talent for writing as I know I have none.

It has been a sobering season (pardon the pun). I lost my friend Maureen who took her own life a couple of months ago. I met her at Woodrose and we shared a great deal of living in a short amount of time. Her death was a shock and you can only imagine the guilt I feel, even though everyone assures me I could not have deterred her. Anyway, I think I mentioned her to you months ago.

Also, you will recall that I told you that Ingrid was pregnant and intending to keep the baby? Well she finally realized how selfish her choices were. However, instead of putting the baby up for adoption, she chose abortion. I'm just sick about it but I'm not angry. Just terribly, terribly sad.

Our last bit of news regards Shep. He recently introduced the family to his friend Peri. Do you recall that poem we had to memorize in high school? The one that started "She was a phantom of delight." This beautiful young woman brought that poem to mind within minutes of meeting her. She has a sense of style, a gracious elegance that you would love, little sister. She's an artist. She creates exquisite pieces of fine jewelry. She's a few years older than Shep and he has fallen head over heels in love with her. However this story is not a happy one. Shep has informed us that she has leukemia and does not have long to live.

Tess, this is as disturbing to me as any news I've ever received. This girl is so full of life. She's known about her condition for years and takes French lessons and art courses as if she's going to have the time to use what she learns. Except for fatigue, she appears to be healthy. She is a rare, lovely person and a living inspiration to me. I want to spend time with her but I don't want to coddle her. I want to help her but I don't want to pity her. I want to thank her for loving my son but I want to spare him the pain.

Tess, how would you face a tragedy like this? I need your help. You would know the right words to use. You would say the right things.

Waiting for your response.

Lovingly,

Katrina

Tess was stunned. How could she know the right words? She didn't even know the girl. She grabbed her jacket, ran out the front door and smacked into a wall of sticky air. The ground was still damp, the leaves had lost their crunch and Tess Parker ran three blocks before she questioned what she was doing. She wasn't a jogger but she wanted to run. No thinking, no plotting, no feeling, just the sound of her feet on the pavement, her heart pumping and her breath laboring. For a short while, she was ageless, agile and invincible.

The slanted rays of late afternoon sun highlighted the best in nature. White birch bark and amber leaves shimmered in the reflection of the blue pond to her right, and on her left, the creek had risen from the night's rain and now gushed in powerful torrents en route to the Mississippi River. The grass was accented with bursts of butterfly weed and wild asters; and now, this late in the season, only spruces and conifers dominated the tree line. Tess momentarily reflected on Katie's letter, but in an effort not to spoil her temporary hiatus, she tabled the topic and just kept running.

The following morning Tess's ageless, agile, invincible body had decomposed to a decrepit, aching old woman. Ren showed no mercy, thinking it rather foolish that she'd run for an hour without any conditioning. She wasn't twenty years old, after all, so what did she expect? It was difficult to accept the physical betrayal of aging, but every time she ignored it, she paid the price. Young people truly believed that they would never be vulnerable to afflictions or infirmities but there was justice and someday, they too, would suffer the consequences of a simple run.

She soaked in a hot tub, her body relaxing, her mind racing. Cristin was due to come by to pick up the short story collection sometime that morning and Katie's letter needed a response. Just as she surrendered herself to the task of Katie's challenge, the doorbell rang. Aggravated by the interruption and willing to ignore it, she didn't move a single aching muscle, hoping that whoever it was would go away.

A couple of minutes passed when she heard a voice from her back yard. "Tess? Tess? Are you home?"

Like an old woman, Tess gingerly exited the tub and wrapped herself in a towel. Peering from her bedroom window she saw Cristin below, dressed in a fuchsia vinyl raincoat that would brighten any dreary autumn day. "Hi sweetheart, I'm not quite ready. Did we set a time for this morning?"

"No, I'm just eager. Can I wait in the living room for you?" Cristin chirped.

"Certainly. I'll be right down." Tess watched her niece tiptoe around the corner, being careful to land on the stepping stones that twined through the season's surviving chrysanthemums. There were less than a handful of people for whom Tess would accelerate her morning, but Cristin was at the top of the list. Unable to disguise her soreness, she limped down the stairs.

"What happened to you?" asked Cristin with a sympathetic grin.

"Let's just say I got a little carried away yesterday. You'll understand in about twenty years."

"You know, we should go for a slow easy walk to loosen you up."

"I can't imagine wanting to do anything less."

"Come on, I'll get a jacket from the closet." Cristin opened the front door, helped her on with a bulky sweater and ushered her aching playmate out of the house.

The day was still and gray. The only detectable movement was the swirling of smoke from the neighboring chimneys, one of Tess's favorite autumn smells and visions. Cristin shared amusing episodes of the Taylor household and talked more of her desire to go to art school. Without admitting it, step by step, Tess became thankful for the "jump start." Toward the end of the block, they passed a window in the "castle house" through which she heard a familiar melody, one from a Gilbert and Sullivan operetta that Mum had played on an old record player in her grandparents' parlor. Tess stopped, grabbed Cristin's shoulder and whispered, "Shh...listen...I haven't heard this for years...I remember every word.

'Things are seldom what they seem/Skim milk masquerades as cream/Highlows pass as patent leathers/Jackdaws strut in peacock feathers'."

Smiling, she lost herself in a reverie of remembrances. "H.M.S. Pinafore, I believe. Mum loved 'Pinafore.' But this song always bothered me."

"Why?" asked Cristin.

"Oh, don't get me wrong. I love the music. But not the words. I mean what do you think? Are things seldom what they seem?"

"Please, don't shatter my world. Are you implying that all that glitters is not gold?" She laughed with a nastiness, a cynicism that Tess had never before detected.

"No, I'm serious. Do you think there's a big old reality out there or is reality only what we perceive? Are things what they seem to be? Or are they seldom what they seem? What do you think?"

"I don't know."

"But there has to be something real that we can count on, something substantial and constant, doesn't there?"

"Tess, this is too philosophic for me. But I have a great idea. I want you to meet Mrs. Morgan. You know, your Madame Serena? She said I could drop by anytime and you just reminded me of something she said that I can show you right now. Stop for a minute. Now, squint your eyes, and look straight ahead. Do it with me. When you squint, you can reduce your field of vision to nothing but shapes. Now, look at the roundness of the maples...the cone shapes of the evergreens...the rectangular roofs...the vertical telephone poles. When everything is reduced to shapes, you develop a natural appreciation for the modern artists who reduce 'reality' to geometric shapes. Okay, you win. Things are seldom what they seem. It's all perception. Pretty weird, huh?"

Instantly Tess thought about the constancy of her love for Ren. Her love was as it seemed. Her values, her personal ethics were as they seemed.

Cristin rang Elizabeth Morgan's doorbell and an old lady wearing a necklace of what looked like pasty black-eyed peas answered the door. Her face lit up when she saw the young girl.

"Come in, come in. What a lovely surprise."

"Mrs. Morgan, this is your neighbor, Tess Parker. Tess, Elizabeth Morgan."

They politely shook hands. The smell of raspberry coffee filled the air and the guests followed Mrs. Morgan's cane-assisted steps down a narrow hallway that was decorated with cuckoo clocks and china knickknacks. Even though the house was as cluttered as she and Ren had imagined, it felt cozy and comfortable. She wished that he'd been there because her attempt to describe the home would never do it justice which wasn't easy for a writer to admit. They took seats at the kitchen table.

"Tell me, dear." Mrs. Morgan addressed Tess. "Why has it taken us so long to meet? I'm not particularly mobile these days but I'm so pleased to make your acquaintance. Cristin speaks so highly of you, that I feel we've lost precious time. Tell me about yourself, dear."

Tess complied with the request. "There's not much to tell. I live with my husband Ren and I'm a writer."

"Are you happy? Do you enjoy your writing?"

"Well, yes. I'm very happy and writing is my passion." As she spoke, she wondered why she was sharing her feelings with a virtual stranger.

"It sounds like there is much to tell. Life may not be long, but as the Spanish say...'it's wide.' So we must be careful to say what we mean. We must think deliberately, speak deliberately, act deliberately."

Tess was stunned by the directness of the old woman. Mrs. Morgan had an aura of clarity about her, to be sure, and her instructive style was surprisingly neither arrogant nor offensive. Perhaps her age gave her license to say what she meant and not be judged harshly.

"Mrs. Morgan," said Cristin. "This morning I shared with Tess the story of squinting your eyes to experience shapes."

"Oh yes, that was helpful to me. I was never much of a modern art appreciator. I'm still not. I prefer art that identifies the specifics of my world. I feel more comfortable with it because I like to share a common experience with the artist and other people. But when I learned to squint at the world from time to time, I acquired a different perspective. It's important to accept change even if you don't subscribe to it, don't you agree?"

"Yes, I do, Mrs. Morgan."

"Please call me Elizabeth." As she poured the coffee, she strung a necklace of thoughts so lovely and unbroken, that Tess understood Cristin's appreciation for their "new" neighbor. She smiled and continued. "People have a difficult time adjusting to change because of our conditioning, don't you think? Mind you, very habitual conditioning. As a species, we were given the gift of the mind to see past our needs and securities. Once our needs are met, we actively seek change. If we want only that which is familiar, our lives become stagnant, having only memories repeated over and over. The willingness to walk into change gives us the promise of growth, the gift of adventure, the unveiling of the mysterious, the birth of new ideas. Change is our birthright and the gateway to our evolution."

Cristin peered at Tess over the top of her dainty china coffee cup with a look of "I told you so."

At that moment the sound of flowing water started up in the back yard and the faces in the kitchen nodded in appreciation.

"My husband and I love the sound of your water fountain, especially as we go to sleep. It is a water fountain, isn't it?" asked Tess

"Would you like to see it?" Elizabeth stood. "Come with me to see my Pan."

They followed her. There in the middle of the yard was a splendid water fountain, with a statue of Pan playing his pipe, spraying water high into the air. It was much larger and more dramatic than Tess had visualized. And of course, there was a story attached to it. It had been a gift from Elizabeth's son many years ago.

Inside the home every item had a story which was written down and either tucked inside or taped to the bottom of the object. Tess discovered this when she asked about the origin of a purple vase. Elizabeth suggested that she read the paper stuffed inside the vase. It read "This is a gift from my dear friend Silvia whose father smuggled it out of Ashkhabad in 1917." Inquiring about a sculpture of a "pas de deux," she was told to turn it upside down to read about it. "This gift is from Marie Ortelle, my dancer friend from Budapest, 1956." Every displayed item, painting, ceramic, photograph, etc., was identified by origin, date and meaning. Elizabeth's reason for doing this was to immortalize her friends.

She continued, "When you get to be my age, you naturally become a philosopher. Everything, even the smallest of things, has meaning because you come to understand that there are no small things. Everything matters. Every word, every thought, every action, every memory, every gift, every dream. They all weave together into a tapestry that tells your story. Every thread is accountable and used. The universe is economical, you know." She smiled.

Enchanted, Cristin asked her, "When you look back, what was the most difficult part of your life?"

"I'll tell you what hurt me more than anything else. Betrayal. The sting of betrayal is like none other. More than loss, more than death. The most treacherous feeling is 'That concealing pang [that] seizes the trusting bosom, when betrayed'." Elizabeth stared at nothing. Her eyes watered with past hurt. It was such an intimate moment that it was only appropriate that she break her own silence. "Please don't mind me. I'm a nostalgic old woman who shouldn't bore her guests."

At that moment Tess realized that "Madame Serena" had been a serendipitous and fitting choice of names and someday Tess would share the affectionate nickname with her neighbor. Tess and Cristin walked home that afternoon, arm in arm. They now knew that their mysterious neighbor had a son, many fascinating and generous friends; and had survived a painful betrayal.

Handing the collection of short stories to Cristin forced Tess to feel how much she wanted Cristin's approval and admiration. The tales were diverse. One was a twisted tale of a very intelligent psychiatrist who exercised his position of station and power to exploit a weak and dependent patient; another, a story inferred from a correspondence of letters between two people who never met each other but had discovered an impelling common bond. Would Cristin like the story of the imaginary friend? Or the account of the old woman making friends in the cemetery? Or perhaps the narrative about the doomed couple who didn't belong together but spent their lives "working" on their despairing relationship. Tess loved writing about the human condition. Words were her children and she didn't want Cristin to call her babies ugly.

After Cristin left, Tess snagged the portable phone off the kitchen counter and headed for the swing in the back yard. Her short stories were completed and she felt like celebrating with a telephone call to the East Coast. Mum had taught her children how to celebrate. "Celebrate the big things, the little things and everything in between," she had said. Tess had been known to celebrate the loss of five pounds, the vernal equinox, and the color of chocolate mint ice cream.

"Katie, it's Tess."

"I figured I'd hear from you after you received my letter. I was really having a tough night when I wrote to you. I'm sorry."

"Don't be silly. How are you? How is Peri?"

"I'm okay. She's remarkable. Now that I've gotten to know her, I have a hard time believing that she'll only be in our lives for a short time."

"That's not true, Katie. She'll be there forever. Just because she physically goes away doesn't mean that you can't think of her and talk to her every day for the rest of your life."

A long distance silence gave new meaning to the experience of silence. Katie swallowed, then clenched her jaw to fight the huge sob that was lodged in her throat. But she couldn't hold it back. "I'm having a hard time, Tess. This shouldn't be happening to such a beautiful young woman. And Shep is so in love with her. I just can't bear to think about what's ahead for him."

"I'm so sorry, honey." Tess paused as an empathetic reverence to Katie's hurt. "Do you remember that quote that Mum reinforced in our heads a million times...*A man is what he thinks about all day long*? Remember? Maybe this is a chance to understand it. Rather than living in the future pain, live in the present gift. Keep telling yourself how fortunate you are to know her and tell her how much she uplifts your spirit. Let her know that she makes a difference in all of your lives and none of you will ever forget her. I can only imagine how important those sincere and honest words would mean to me if I were dying. And furthermore, tell her that you intend to keep her memory alive. She'll live as long as her name is spoken."

Tess listened to her own words; the words that she had doubted and mistrusted would come. When she realized that Katie was listening with no intention of interrupting her, she continued. "And Shep? He will be a better, stronger man having known her and survived her. And big sister, if you are by his side, your link with your son will be like a steel coil, constructed fiber by fiber, and unbreakable." Once again there was silence. But Tess said nothing more and waited.

Finally, Katie spoke. "I would do anything to be able to say things the way you do. I understand what you say. I recognize what you say. But my words are not as clear. I wish I could carry you inside me and bring you out when I needed you."

"Now there's a picture. You know I'm far too visual to hear things like that. But I'm glad it helps to talk. How is Ingrid?"

"Since the trauma of her abortion, we've grown closer. I'll never understand why it is that so often it takes such difficult times to bring people together. That's certainly been the case for us. So once again, I must count my blessings despite the pain, right?"

"You've got it."

"I've been rambling on about my heartaches. Tell me, what's new in your life?"

"I finished my short story collection. As a matter of fact, that's what prompted this call. I felt like celebrating and no one was home so you received the honors."

"Congratulations! That's wonderful. When do I get to read the mighty words?"

In hearing the heartfelt support of her sister, Tess realized that they had more in common as adults than they'd ever had as children.

"Well nobody reads the 'mighty words' until the editor and I have hashed them out. Although this time, I did allow Cristin to look at them. Remember Cristin, the young girl I've told you about who is the nanny for our neighbor's children?"

"Oh yes, tell me about Cristin. It sounds like she's become important to you."

"She has. She came into our lives out of nowhere but I feel very close to her. So does Ren."

"That's wonderful, Tess. I'm happy for you. I hope to meet her someday."

Uncomfortable with the thought, Tess terminated the discussion and Katie was left hanging, wondering why they had so abruptly said goodbye. Tess sat outside for a while on the backyard swing, then began swinging high and vigorously. She pumped with her legs like she was a little girl. How high could she go? She felt the swing reach that thrilling point where it might wrap itself over the tree branch, three hundred sixty plus degrees. But of course, it never did. The wind whistled against her face and her hair matted over her eyes, until slowly she came back to earth and stopped, dead still.

It was time to play the "psychiatrist game." She imagined herself with a psychiatrist asking the Why? question that forced one to get to the root of the matter. She hadn't wanted to talk to Katie about Cristin. Why? Because she realized that she had no intention of ever telling Katie that Cristin was her daughter. Why? Because too many people would be hurt. Who? Katie, who had tried to do the right thing by having the child and keeping her affair a secret from her husband and family; Stefan, who had been deceived and then screened from the truth; Ingrid, Shep and Heidi, who might unfairly judge their mother; Sondra, who had betrayed a confidence in an effort to protect her dearest friend; Ren, whom Tess hadn't trusted enough to tell the truth, fearing his disapproval; Cristin, whom she now loved as a daughter but who might never trust her again if she realized that information identifying her biological mother had been withheld; and herself, Katessa Monson Parker, who had selfishly and deviously, although not maliciously, brought the girl into their lives. What had she done?

The swing didn't move. Neither did her body. Her head hung heavily like a steel ball on a tetherball pole as she stared at the ground, staring at nothingness. Her heart pounded, her breathing, undetectable. For the first time, Tess dared to comprehend the scope of her deception, her well-intending but deliberate omission of truth. After an undetermined time, she elected to go to inside, go to sleep and escape her new-born guilt.

That night the local wildlife provided melody and meter to Madame Serena's water fountain score. Ren didn't arrive home until Tess was sleeping. He slipped under the sheets and held his beautiful wife, his partner. He knew she slept because her patterns of breathing had become decipherable through the years. He gently felt the contours of her soft shapely body, as if he were stealing a forbidden pleasure. He pressed himself against the small of her back and wrapped her legs with his, as he reached to feel her sleeping nipples harden to his touch. He tenderly kissed her neck and felt the tiny hairs stand at attention. More than anything, he wanted to gently roll her over and feel her body trapped and submissive, beneath his manhood. But he didn't. He let her sleep.

Chapter 10

Days shortened, weeks passed and the air frosted with ice. Since Cristin's arrival that summer, Tess's spare time had been devoted to her niece. Only once had Ren questioned her amputation of civic activities, to which she responded with an "it's my life and I know what I'm doing" tone of voice. Fortunately he liked Cristin. He sometimes even referred to her as their daughter and openly called Tess her mother, just to see them both smile. Cristin had not only brought joy into his wife's life but had a positive effect on Lissa, who now visited more often, always asking when Cristin would be there.

An evening storm had knocked out electric and telephone lines in the middle of the night so Tess spent the morning doing housework that didn't require modern conveniences... reorganizing the upstairs closets and framing a print that Troy and Suzanne had sent from Portugal. She hadn't anticipated visitors and was startled when the doorbell chimed. She bolted downstairs and opened the door. There stood Sondra Rampling.

"Sondra?"

"I'm sorry I couldn't reach you, but my trip was sudden and the telephone lines are still out in this section of the city. I hope this isn't an inconvenience."

"No, please come in. I'm just so surprised. Let me take your coat."

Sondra entered the Parker home and felt a wave of envy as she surveyed the rich interior.

"Please have a seat."

"I'm in Minneapolis on a quick business trip but I'm here because I need to talk to you about the telephone conversation we had a few months ago. I feel so guilty about having told you what I did."

"You did the right thing, Sondra."

"Just tell me that you didn't contact that girl, Tess. That's all."

"Don't worry. Everything is fine. I haven't told a soul."

"Thank God for that. I have agonized for months about this. And you didn't contact the girl, right?" Sondra persisted, fidgeting with the clasp on her purse.

The secret she had so diligently guarded had obviously become a burden of the heart. At that moment, Tess realized the terrible onus inferred by a secret.

"Sondra, I do need to tell you something."

"Oh my God, you did write to her, didn't you? I thought you said you didn't tell anyone." She began wringing her hands in her lap.

"I haven't told anyone. Not even my husband. I did write to the girl and told her that her lead was false and she was mistaken. However, you and I both know that she is Katie's daughter and my niece. Knowing that, I couldn't turn my back on her. She had just lost both of her parents in an accident. I did what anyone would do. I offered to help her."

Sondra's gaunt face turned ashen as she listened to Tess's confession.

"How did you help her, Tess?" Sondra insisted.

"She came to Minneapolis and I helped her find a job. She works down the block as a nanny for a neighbor."

"Oh dear God. Do you have contact with her now?"

"We see her."

"How often?"

"A few times a week. But Sondra, she knows nothing. Please don't worry."

"What are you telling Katie about her?"

"I've just told her that Cristin needed help and Rennie and I decided to do what we could for her." Tess continued to defend her weakening position.

"Her name is Cristin?"

The front door opened and Ren called out, "Honey, I'm home for lunch. I thought I'd surprise you." He then saw the strange woman sitting on the sofa. "I'm sorry. I didn't know we had company."

"Rennie, this is an old friend of mine from school, Sondra Rampling. Sondra, my husband, Ren."

"I'm pleased to meet you."

"Thank you. It's a pleasure meeting you as well. I apologize for barging in like this but the phone lines were down so I couldn't give Tess any warning. I really do have to go."

"Don't run off on my account. I just ran home for a sandwich." The doorbell rang again. Ren smiled. "When it rains it pours."

Sondra stood and uncomfortably reiterated that she had to go when she heard Ren affectionately say, "Hi Cristin. Come on in. Your Mom is in the living room."

Tess froze. The timing was deplorable. Cristin bounced into the room and gave Tess a big hug. "Hi, I'm here to return your manuscript. I loved it! And yes, I can come to dinner tonight." It was only then that she noticed Sondra standing in the corner.

Tess broke the silence. "Cristin this is my childhood friend, Sondra. Sondra, meet Cristin."

They exchanged greetings and Sondra made a cursory exit from the room. Tess excused herself and followed her guest outside.

Sondra angrily lashed out. "I should never have come. I can't believe you brought this child into your lives. She called you Mom, for God's sake! Tessa, what are you thinking? I trusted you and you've betrayed me! I'll never forgive you for this."

"No one will ever know. Please trust me. I know what I'm doing."

"No, you don't. You just think you do. Meanwhile you're lying to everyone you love." Sondra got in her car, started the ignition and rolled down her window. "I don't know how you sleep at night."

As Tess watched her Jiminy Cricket drive away, her legs weakened and her mind whirred. Ren and Cristin were inside the house and she, without appearing upset, needed to face them. *Rally now, think later.* She would face Sondra's intimidating words later. She would assess her own conscience later. She would scream later.

Seemingly confident and unruffled, Tess entered her home like a queen enters her castle, with shoulders back and head high. She found Ren and Cristin making sandwiches in the kitchen and discussing how strange Tess's friend had seemed.

"What was that all about?" asked Ren. "She's a weird duck. You said you knew her from school?"

"She was actually my sister's best friend, but I knew her too."

"What was her problem? She was as tightly strung as a new piano wire. And the way she stormed out of here, you'd think we had the plague. What was going on, Katessa?"

Addressing a person with formality seemed to imply a degree of culpability in a conversation and it made her angry.

"Nothing." She could feel herself close. "Sondra was tired. She's had a difficult life lately, but she's really a very nice person. Seeing you home at this time of day is sure a surprise, honey. How long can you stay?" she moved on.

"Only a few more minutes. But Cristin, if you're coming for dinner, perhaps I'll call Lissa and see if she could join us. Is that all right with you?"

Relieved to be off of the subject of their noontime visitor, Tess agreed. Within minutes, her home was her own again and she was free to think. Sondra had been right. Tess knew what she was doing and deep inside could no longer play hide-and-seek from her own conscience. Her curiosity and neediness had compromised her integrity. She had taken a risk, justified every move with good intentions and now she prayed that the potential wreckage of her dishonesty wouldn't be discovered. The most judicious decision would have been to have never answered the letter. But she had answered the letter. The door to her world slammed in her face. She was now alone.

Chapter 11

Winter in Minnesota wasn't usually grueling until January. The first snowfall enchanted child and adult alike and for some strange reason, most often came at night, throwing a surprise party for early risers. One morning Tess discovered the season's first blanket of snow upon opening her bedroom shutters, which overlooked their front yard. Overnight, Mother Nature and Father Time had conspired to gift the world a wonderland. A striking male cardinal, calling to his mate, sat on a naked branch against a backdrop of pure white brilliance and the morning sun created long shadows of trees trunks and low-lying branches against the snow, providing magic paths for bunny prints and puppy paws. The garden would sleep until spring, the perennials would hibernate and the bulbs would lie dry and dormant in a dark corner of the basement. Even though winter was predictable, it was a change and a reminder of the precious and pernicious passing of time.

Cristin's responsibilities at the Taylor household had increased to include more duties and greater involvement with the children, so Tess saw less of her, making their time together even more coveted. Rumor had it that not only was Jodi Taylor's job demanding, but she also missed her children, so there was a distinct possibility that Cristin could be without a job by the first of the year.

Awaiting word from her editor, Tess took a hiatus from her personal writing and accepted a job researching the history of the iron ore mining industry in northern Minnesota. She spent most of her time gathering facts, but needed anecdotes and stories from former employees of the mines, so the job would require a trip up north. It wasn't glamorous but it paid well. Besides which, she needed time alone to think. She was sleeping poorly, as if Sondra's parting words had cursed her. She prayed that Sondra wouldn't reinvent her visit in the form of a phone call, a letter or a dream. She was reasonably certain that there'd not be another visit to the house. The dose of guilt administered on that intimidating afternoon didn't need a refill.

The good news was that Troy, Suzanne and the children were coming for Christmas. The basement had a back bedroom that was decorated like a fort and the kids would have the time of their lives. Tess had arranged for the children to go sledding and caroling with Jodi's family and Max had already sent a drawing of the snowman he was going to build in the front yard. Even Ren was looking forward to hearing the voices of children in their home at Christmas time.

One afternoon, Tess slipped over to Madame Serena's. A wonderful line of communication had unzipped between them and Tess had actually revealed "the nickname" to Elizabeth who found it so charming that she insisted Tess call her Serena. They were accustomed to perching in the kitchen in Serena's home, but on this particular afternoon, the pentagonal porch, paneled in wormy cedar and stacked with ceiling high windows, was the venue of choice. Serena wasn't about to forego looking at the fresh snow draping her bushes and quilting her trees. Pan stood frozen in time, his panpipe soon to be drizzled with the icicles of Janus.

"How fortunate we are to live in a land of climate changes," said Tess. "Where my sister lives in Boston, the seasons are much more subtle. In California, they're almost nonexistent. Did I tell you my brother's family is coming for Christmas?"

"No, dear, that's wonderful. Family is a blessing."

"Serena, you never talk about your family."

"Well, I'm afraid there isn't much to tell."

"I'm not going to let you get away with that. Do you remember what you said to me the very first time we talked and I said 'there's not much to tell'. You told me to think deliberately and speak deliberately and life was too short to beat around the bush. Remember?"

"I dare say I do. Did I also mention that words come back to bite you on occasion?" She laughed. "I have one son, James Hammond Morgan. He lives in New Orleans with his girlfriend Danita."

"And your husband?"

"I was never married, Tessa. At a time when it was scandalous for a woman to bear a child without a husband, I was a pariah within my own family. It was the most dreadful time of my life." Serena paused and collected her thoughts. "To spare you the awkwardness of asking, yes, I did love Jamie's father. He was the only man I've ever loved. His name was Cory." She paused, then continued. "Do you remember the first day that Cristin brought you here for coffee? She asked about the hardest part of my life? Do you remember what I said?"

"Of course. You said a betrayal."

"That's right. My Cory fell in love with my best friend. I lost my best friend and the love of my life one summer. And I never told him about the child. Cory married Theresa and they had two children of their own, a girl who never married and lives in Australia and a boy who married and moved to Nebraska somewhere and adopted two children. Girls, I believe."

"How do you know all of this?"

"I have a shallow, meddlesome sister, my dear, who under the guise of keeping me informed, finds a fiendish delight in gossip and hearsay."

"Serena, I'm so sorry you've had to suffer such heartache."

"Never mind, dear. I've learned through the years that one must live in the present. In the vernacular of a writer, that is a closed chapter in my story. On to the next."

"Who do you have in your life now?"

"I have you...and Cristin. And my Jamie calls me from time to time. And dear, one must ask not only "who" but "what." What do I have? I've given it a great deal of thought. It's the ultimate paradox. I have only what I give away. I am only all that I give, for without giving I am nothing."

"Serena, you are beautiful."

She laughed. "Now there's a topic of betrayal. Time is the Great Betrayer. You've yet to experience the shock of youth being plucked from you. I wasn't a bad looking woman in my youth, you know. I rather enjoyed the vanity of my early years. Don't get me wrong, dear, I wasn't beautiful. As a matter of fact, I didn't ever want to be beautiful. My mother, God rest her soul, told me out of truth, pity or kindness, that a beautiful woman never really knew whether her lover loved her for her beauty or her soul. I deduced from that statement that beauty was a potential curse, and I was forever after content with my looks. But what's so remarkable is that there's no transitional period between youth and age. You just wake up one morning and look into the mirror to discover lines in your cheeks, sagging eyelids and creases in your neck, and you realize you've crossed the border into physical maturity, shall we say. What an adventure you have in store, my friend. Thank the good Lord for a sense of humor." Serena threw her head back and laughed.

"Look, Serena! Look at the snowflakes!" The large translucent flakes slowly floated from the heavens like tiny lace doilies and melted into the whiteness of the snow. "Isn't it extraordinary? I love this. There's no way to describe this scene to someone who has never seen it, is there?"

"No, dear. Pictures can only transport one so far into another world. The whole three dimensional experience, the cool smell of winter air, the wet weightlessness of crystalline creations when they reach your tongue, knowing that each fragile flake is as unique as a finger print."

"I love the tiny dry snowflakes swirled in patterns on my driveway and the loud crunch of stepping on sub-zero snow and walking home at night when the streetlights make the snow sparkle like diamonds."

"Oh, Tess, that reminds me of a story about my Jamie when he was just a little boy. He was about seven and late for dinner, so I went out looking for him and found him walking across a field towards home, waving both of his fists above his head, like a victor or a champion before an cheering crowd. When I came within shouting distance, I asked him what he was doing and he told me that he was pretending that he was a giant, walking through a land of tiny people, and all of the sparkles in the snow were the camera flashes of his adoring public. Only a child could imagine such a thing."

Tess watched Serena as she lost herself in thought and concluded that Serena must have been a wonderful mother. Regarding her child's welfare, she had come to a different decision than Katie had. Two good people. She was struck by the commonality of human problems and the diversity of their solutions.

Tess continued. "I love to wake up in the morning to find the crystal patterns on my window that leave as mysteriously as they arrive. The designs are exquisite. I wrote a poem about it when I was a little girl. It went like this:

> *Jack be nimble, Jack be fast*
> *Jack Frost, paint my window glass.*
> *Carve some perfect figure eights*
> *With your shiny silver skates.*
> *Trace a dainty, lacy stencil*
> *With your tiny pixy pencil.*
> *Then embroider Paradise*
> *With your needle made of ice.*
> *Please Jack Frost, come tonight,*
> *While I'm sleeping, tucked in tight.*
> *In the morning I will see*
> *Your snowy masterpiece for me.*

"That's delightful, Tess. Did you write much poetry when you were younger?"

"I suppose a couple hundred or so."

"Recite another one of your very favorites."

"Are you sure?" Tess asked, feeling a little self-conscious. Serena nodded with encouragement.

"Okay. This is one I wrote when I was very young:

> *From mountains come thunderstorms*
> *Heaven, no one sees.*
> *Splashes hide in waterfalls.*
> *And breezes live in trees.*
> *I know I'm just a little girl.*
> *But these things I've understood.*
> *Colors come from rainbows*
> *And happiness from good.*

Serena looked at her like they had just been introduced and after an almost awkward amount of time, the eighty year-old woman spoke. "Are these poems published?"

"Well, no. I just wrote them for fun."

"Don't you think that someone else might enjoy them too? What good are they going to do the world if they're stuffed away in a file somewhere? You know that age-old question, *If a tree falls in the forest when no one's around, is there a sound?* Well, think about it. If you write something that's worthy but don't share it, it's as if it had never been written, only worse."

Tess was caught off guard. Serena certainly had a direct manner of looking at things. They talked for an hour about talent and the responsibility of sharing talent once it found its expression in form. Tess imagined a child looking up into a parent's face and squealing, "Read it again." And suddenly all she wanted to do was go home, dig out her old poems and give them away.

~ ~ ~

On the day she was to leave for the Iron Range, a fat letter from Tia appeared in her mail. She ripped it open, almost tearing the letter itself. Yes, Tia was coming home for Christmas, just as Tess had hoped.

An hour before Tess departed, Cristin came by, sounding like a mother having just escaped her toddlers for the first time in months.

"Lexi is so inquisitive. I just want to strangle her sometimes. Today she asked me where oil came from and why water was wet. I'm going to have to go back to school! Tori asks Why? to everything that's said. *Why? Why? Why? Why* must be the word of the week in preschool."

It was amusing to see Cristin exasperated, although a little surprising to sense the almost hostile impatience in her voice. Tess shared the news of Troy's family and Tia coming for Christmas and reminded Cristin of her own trip to the Iron Range that day.

"Oh, I remember. How long will you be gone?"

"Only about a week, honey. But it will be a long one. The Iron Range isn't exactly Bryce Canyon, you know. I wish it were. I've heard that the canyons and mesas of Utah are spectacular. Those geological formations, those spires, the bridges of sandstone and limestone..."

"Earth to Tess. Earth to Tess. Remember, you're just going to northern Minnesota."

"Oh, I know. But I'll take a side trip to the north shore of Lake Superior. It's gorgeous this time of year. The lakes are frozen, the ground is frozen, and even the mosquitoes are frozen. I love northern Minnesota in early winter."

"You're such a romantic. I swear you could make a car accident sound like a birthday party. Is there anything you want me to do when you're gone?"

"You might just check in on Rennie. He won't be home for hours so I might as well get on the road, but I'll be back before you know it. You can help me pack the car."

Within the hour Tess was heading north on highway 94 driving toward the Minnesota tundra, in search of a story. When she passed the city limits, she cranked up the volume of "Carmina Burana", rolled back the sun roof and cruised. High on the telephone poles, hawks perched and searched for the rodent du jour. Just that morning, on the birding hotline, she had heard that a boreal owl was in town and she wished she'd had time to scout him. She always got a kick out of finding that a specific bird was "in town" as it reminded her of hearing that a famous gunslinger was passing through the wild, wild west. People came from miles around just to get a glimpse of him.

By the time Tess reached the central part of the state, a light snow had fallen. Every branch, haystack, and cornstalk had a thin film of frost. Picture perfect. Far in the distance were two black stallions running behind a brown wooden fence that followed the contour of the earth like a roller coaster track. On the other side of the highway was a large bull, snorting heavy warm air into the cold ether, creating clouds of heat. There were barns with gables, barns with cupolas, barns made of rock, barns of wood and sheet metal. There were square traditional barns, round barns, and twelve-sided barns. Some were weather-worn, some were handsomely painted, some had tools hanging from the sides, and others had the farmer's surname painted on the roof. The saddest sight was a deteriorating barn, condemned to never again be useful after having been functional at a happier time in someone's life. The prettiest barn of the day was large and red with white trim and two connecting silos. Early evening sun had peeked through the clouds and momentarily the building, the red tractor next to it, and the windbreak of elms were reflected in the still unfrozen pond in the farmer's front yard. At that precise moment, Tess wished she'd been a painter, for it was an inspiring feast, delicious to the eye.

Late that evening she arrived at her accommodations. Rather than a hotel room, she had reserved a log cabin with a fireplace in the main room, and a wood burning stove and gingham curtains in the kitchen. The gabled roof line created one large interior ceiling and the few rooms were separated by seven foot high log partitions. Rustic and charming; just what she wanted. After she settled, she walked to the stream only yards from her cabin where broken ice shards of an arctic blue hue, overlapped each other on top of the frozen stream. She'd always associated moving water with time and somehow seeing the stream frozen connoted a timelessness that felt eerie and mystical and provocative.

Her interviews and research went well and by mid-week she was ready to detour to the north shore of Lake Superior where she could think about more personal matters. She watched the silhouettes of red pines and white cedars against a brilliant topaz sunset. She hiked the paths above granite bouldered cliffs that overlooked the lake and protected the vulnerable land from ravaging water. And she thought of Katie.

She took walks on rocky beaches and stared at colorful pebbles. The rock scape revealed bronze and burnt red ores, veins of quartz and the promise of agate. She stepped over twisted pieces of snow-covered driftwood that had been eroded by wind and water and charred by fire. And she thought of Sondra.

On the bluffs, she touched the surviving lichen, velvety orange and yellow. She took off her glove, and stroked it as if stroking a cat's fur against its grain. She stepped over tree roots in an aspen grove that led to the lake where she watched squalls approach the shore only to be transformed to sheets WOA(white on arrival.) And she thought of Cristin.

She listened to the calls of cardinals and blue jays and watched them pluck the remaining red berries from the mountain ashes. She imagined the glory of a hoar frost and the gargantuan icicles that would hang from the snow encased cliffs in the depth of winter and the snow banks that would prohibit any exit from the inside of cabins to the outside world. She recalled the red fox and blue heron tracks in the sand of summer and portaging a canoe along the boundary waters between northern Minnesota and southern Ontario. And she thought of her Rennie.

Chapter 12

Ren was home early that afternoon to prepare a dinner for his wife's homecoming when the phone rang. It was Sondra Rampling asking for Tess.

"I'm sorry, Sondra. I'm not expecting her yet. Is there anything I can do for you? Can I give her a message?"

"No, thank you. I thought she might be out of town. I'm here on business again and have called for the past three days. No one has been home. What time do you think she'll be back?"

"I'm hoping she'll be home for dinner. If you need to speak to her, why don't you come for dinner? It would be a nice surprise for her. I know you weren't able to stay very long last time you were here."

"Oh no, I couldn't. That's too much of an imposition. But I really do need to talk with her."

"Please come by at seven. She's sure to be here by then. I'll even make myself scarce so you two can have time alone. What do you say?"

"Well, if you really don't mind. But don't include me in your dinner plans. It would feel intrusive on her first night back."

"Don't worry about that. See you at seven."

Ren hung up the phone and walked to the sound system and put on The Dave Brubeck Quartet which always threw him into the late sixties, ripe with nostalgia. The kitchen braced itself for a southwestern dinner. The ingredients lined up in order of preparation: a black bean soup, roasted salsa spareribs, zucchini with corn and peppers, cilantro slaw, and a caramel custard flan. Tess teased him about expressing his "feminine side" when he put on his chef's hat, but he always reminded her that most of the finest chefs in the world were men.

Chopping the cilantro, Ren picked up the phone to call Cristin, extending a dinner invitation which she happily accepted. She arrived within minutes and spent the next hour mincing, chopping and laughing. Tess called to say she had run into some bad weather and had pulled off the road, so she'd be delayed, urging him not to hold dinner for her.

"I'd rather not, honey. Give me your best guess. What time do you think you'll be home? "

"You know how this is, Rennie. Nine, if I'm lucky, ten, eleven, if I'm not. One of the hazards of living in the upper Midwest."

"Well, don't take any unnecessary risks. We made a special dinner for you that I guess we're going to have to serve without you, that's all. I'm disappointed."

"I'm so sorry, Rennie. But who's 'we'?" She paused.

"Cristin came over a couple of hours ago to help me and your friend Sondra needed to talk to you so I invited her too. She's due any moment."

Tess froze before she could utter her next words.

"Sondra is coming tonight? What does she want?"

"She wants to see you. You sound reticent. What's going on?"

"Nothing."

Ren persisted.

"Tessa, this woman has something specific on her mind. You must have some idea."

"We'll talk when I get home. Don't worry, honey. It doesn't involve us. Everything's fine."

She hung up the phone and stared at the swirling whitewashed world through a dirty cafe window. She was surrounded by the chatter and commotion of strangers. She felt helpless to control the circumstances within her own home that evening. What if Sondra told Ren and Cristin everything? How would they react? What if Cristin took off? What if Ren wasn't home when she arrived? The pressure in Tess's head built until a merciful release valve opened and she began to cry.

~ ~ ~

Sondra arrived a little after seven, not expecting to see Cristin, and conspicuously nervous that Tess hadn't appeared. Ren hadn't mentioned to anyone that Tess would not be home for dinner because he hoped that Sondra would stay and perhaps leave a clue as to what it was that seemed so pressing. After an hour of exchanging niceties, they sat down to dinner under protest from Cristin who thought they should wait.

Their table conversation was no more enlightening. Well into the meal, Ren excused himself to answer the ring of a phantom phone that no one else had heard, then announced that Tess would be much later due to the inclement weather. At that point, Sondra visibly relaxed, leaving Ren with the impression that Tess's impending appearance, even though critical to her, was the cause of their guest's anxiety. The knots of conversation loosened and Sondra became chatty. She focused on Cristin by inquiring about her upbringing and her parents, then unleashing an unexpected and abrupt interrogative concerning Cristin's adoption.

"How did you know I was adopted?"

"Oh, I think Tess mentioned it. I'm sorry. Perhaps that's too personal. I have a lot of adopted friends and I find it an interesting subject."

"Why?" asked Cristin, suddenly appearing apprehensive to share anything further about the previously verboten topic.

"I do apologize, Cristin. I've touched a nerve."

"You didn't touch a nerve. I just want to know why you're interested in my adoption."

Ren intervened as the dinner dialogue deteriorated. "Ladies, let's change the subject. Tess has been trying to talk me into buying some outdoor Christmas trees. You know, those plastic frames that you string with lights and set in your yard. She wants to set the stage for all the company we're going to have. What do you think?"

Cristin and Sondra stared at him with a vacant disbelief that he had attempted such an obvious tack in the conversational course. But he was the host and they tacitly agreed to honor his tactic.

"I think it sounds beautiful." Cristin laughingly added, "Ren, why would you even question Tess's decorating ideas? She'd never steer you wrong."

"Listen, I'll be the one freezing my butt while assembling and stringing those suckers. But I suppose you're right. Tess is the queen of the castle."

"Your marriage sounds so healthy, so respectful. I'm envious." Sondra timidly smiled.

"We're very lucky to have found each other. Tess is a wonderful woman. I've never met anyone with such a strong sense of integrity."

"Really?" There was a challenging timbre to Sondra's response. Ren felt a sudden dislike for his house guest that left him with the same aftertaste that Cristin had experienced only moments before.

"Yes, really." He punctuated his words as if to communicate that this was an undiscussable topic and suggested that they move to the living room. Sensing the mood change, Cristin cleared the table and offered to do the dishes. Sondra curtly announced that she must leave.

Ren prodded one final time. "I would be more than happy to convey a message to Tessa for you. It sounded vitally important when you called."

"No thank you. It's rather personal. Please ask her to call me at The Hyatt tomorrow morning. I'll be there until 9 a.m. Thanks for the delicious dinner. You're an amazing cook, Ren. Goodbye, Cristin." Sondra grabbed her purse and coat. She insisted on showing herself out and melted into the frigid night air.

Cristin and Ren stared at each other. Cristin broke the silence. "She gives me the creeps. Come on. Let's clean up before Tess comes home." They didn't say much after Sondra's exit. Cristin said goodnight and Ren went upstairs to read and wait.

Tess's ride home was miserable, the longest drive of her life. The highway had been hazardous but she knew that the danger lurking in her living room was more perilous than the danger on the roads that night. It was 1:30 a.m. when she turned the key in her front door, foregoing the traditional chiming of the doorbell. She was relieved that Ren was not pacing the floors. If she could just quietly slip into bed, she could avoid his questions. But there was no escaping a sleepless night. If he were sleeping, she would stew about what he did or did not know. If she did talk with him, she would either be confronted with any allegations that Sondra may have made or be held accountable to his suspicions that something wasn't right. The lonely walk upstairs was like a defendant's walk into a courtroom. She peered around the corner of the bedroom and saw her Rennie sleeping in a sitting position with glasses askew on the bridge of his nose and his head drooped to his shoulder. His *Portable Emerson* had fallen from his hands. He'd probably tried to stay awake because he'd been worried. She gingerly took the glasses from his nose and placed his book on the bed stand, turned off the light, and slipped into bed. Ren rolled over and hugged her, mumbling how glad he was that she was safely home. She breathed a sigh of relief and closed her exhausted eyes. Just when she felt herself drifting off to sleep, Ren whispered in her ear, "By the way, sweetheart, your sister Katie called late last night. She and Ingrid are joining us for Christmas."

~ ~ ~

Dawn exposed a picture-postcard of white Saharan snow dunes, undisturbed by automobiles, footprints, or animal tracks. Ren was up with the cardinals to snow blow his way out of the driveway. Just as he finished, the snowplows came by to drift him back in. People in Florida and the Southwest didn't have this aggravation every December through March. Minnesotans were cursed with a geographic affliction. Before he left home, he scribbled a note that his wife should call Sondra at The Hyatt by 9 a.m. and Katie at home in Boston.

When she heard his car drive away, she opened her eyes to the blindingly bright glare of the bedroom. Even though the temperature was ten degrees below zero, the sun ruled a cloudless sky that reflected off the fresh white carpet of snow and bounced off her blazingly white ceiling. The effect was luminous and Tess's first thought was that she was thankful she'd not been drinking wine the night before. Apprehensive about her forthcoming talk with Sondra and the reality that Katie would meet Cristin, she'd slept very little.

She discovered the note on the kitchen table and dialed the number of The Hyatt.

"I'd like the room of Sondra Rampling, please."

She was connected and Sondra answered.

"Hello, Sondra, this is Tess."

"Hello."

"I'm sorry I missed you last night. The storm delayed me. Why did you come back? What could we possibly have to say to each other after our last encounter?"

"I need to tell Katie about Cristin, Tess."

"What?" Tess gasped. "What purpose would that serve at this point? Leave us alone, Sondra. We're all doing just fine without your interference."

"Just listen for a minute. The last time I saw you and met Cristin, she suddenly became real. She's a beautiful young woman and she's Katie's daughter. Katie has the right to know. I'm not going to announce it to the world. There isn't a reason to tell anyone but Katie. Just Katie. I'm her best friend and I owe it to her."

"Well, I'm her sister and I've decided differently. What's the real reason?" Tess demanded, her voice amplifying. "It has to be more than Katie's right to know. Tell me."

"Tess, stop yelling! Try to understand my position. I feel so guilty about telling you that Katie had a baby twenty years ago. I was sworn to secrecy. I've betrayed a confidence."

"So the real reason for informing Katie about her child is to ease your conscience? You suddenly have to walk the path of righteousness no matter whom you mow down along the way? I've never heard of anything so selfish in my entire life. You! You are the only one who would sleep better at night, Sondra. Saint Sondra, in your own mind only, I promise you. You'd not only drive a stake of mistrust between my sister and me but compromise my relationship with Cristin, who is as close to a daughter as I will ever know, and my marriage might not survive it. You want me to be concerned with your conscience? You have no right to do this! Sondra I beg of you, do not say anything to my sister."

Tess was shaking so convulsively that by default she stopped talking. Although her message had been articulate, fear choked her like a boa constrictor. A couple of times, Sondra had attempted to speak, but in vain. Now that Tess was finished spilling her heart, Sondra was at a loss for words.

"Tess, I'm sorry. Perhaps you're right. I'm sorry. I won't bother you anymore. Goodbye."

The telephone clicked and Tess felt disconnected from the entire human race. Her rage and fear and guilt…she couldn't isolate which emotion was more powerful, or destructive. She couldn't talk to anyone. No one would understand. For the first time she understood how people, pushed to the edge of their fears, could become violent. She stood at her emotional border, looking into a wild frontier, alive with untamed monsters, threatening and out of control, with lashing tails and gnashing teeth, all closing in on her.

She gradually calmed herself with the reassurance that the episode was over. She placed the incident on the top shelf of a dark closet in the back of her mind. But one by one, her demons began to pinch her. What if Sondra was not telling the truth? What if she intended to talk to Katie anyway? Tess realized that in her effort to muzzle Sondra, she'd forgotten to ask her about the night before.

She picked up the telephone and redialed Sondra's hotel. The phone rang and rang, leaving Tess no alternative but to leave a message. "Did you tell Ren and Cristin anything? Call me."

She then dialed Katie's home in Boston. Ingrid was the only one at home and informed her Aunt Tess of the newly laid plans. Knowing that Troy and Tia were coming to Minnesota made it impossible for them to stay in Boston. However Shep couldn't make the trip because of Peri's condition and Heidi had so many social activities that she'd elected to stay in Boston with her dad. Ingrid added how much she and her mom were looking forward to meeting Cristin. Tess's heart tightened.

That afternoon paranoia lurked in the marshes of her mind like a large, hungry reptile. Tess robotically paced from room to room. If Ren knew the truth, would their lives ever be the same? Would he ever trust her again? Would he love her anymore? Her guilt and feeling of being trapped led to negative conclusions on all counts. One thing was certain, Christmas would not be what she had hoped. On the contrary, she would walk on razor blades and have to make herself a high profile presence in an attempt to orchestrate conversations and circumvent indiscretions. Only when Katie returned to Boston would the tension ease.

Ren arrived home in a foul mood. Mel was threatening to take him to court for higher child support payments which he knew went directly into his former wife's food fund. The Vikings were losing an critically important game on national television and his stock broker had informed him that afternoon of some hapless reversals of fortune. As far as Tess could tell, he wasn't focused on Sondra's visit, which was an auspicious sign. Remembering that there were still groceries from the market in the car, she headed for the garage. Upon her return, she heard the end of an incoming message on their answer machine. *"Of course not. I'm truly sorry. Goodbye."*

"What the hell was that about? Wasn't that Sondra's voice?"

"Yes, that was Sondra all right." Tess sighed with relief.

Ren persisted. "Well? What's going on? Did you talk to her today?"

"Yes, at length."

"Okay. You said that we'd talk when you came home. I've got to tell you, this Sondra chick is spooky. You should have heard some of the weird things she was saying last night."

"Like what?"

"She hit poor Cristin with questions about her adoption. I was completely caught off guard. I didn't even know she was adopted. But why did you tell her about Cristin's past anyway? I thought you said you didn't really have much in common with her."

"It's true. I don't."

"Well, Cristin sure didn't like it. I think you owe her an apology. And furthermore, her insinuating tone of voice really rubbed me the wrong way."

"What did she say?" Tess winced.

"It doesn't matter. It was her tone of voice. I can't explain it. What does that message mean, 'of course not, I'm sorry.'? What's she sorry about?"

"It's really not that important. She and I, as adults, don't see eye to eye. I'm surprised because I really liked her in high school but she said some things about Katie that were slanderous and I defended my sister. I told her that there was no point of fabricating a sham of a friendship. Life is too short to be false in relationships. Her feelings are hurt."

"There's got to more to it than that, Tessa. What did she say about Katie?"

"She implied that Katie had had affairs."

"Has she?"

"Of course not, Ren. I know my sister. Sondra's accusations are totally unfounded and that's all there is to it."

"So you're saying that Sondra came to you two times in a couple months after not having seen you for twenty years to tell you libelous stories?"

"She's a troublemaker."

"There's something more here than meets the eye, Tessa." Ren looked askance.

"Are you calling me a liar, Rennie?"

"Of course not. I know you wouldn't lie to me."

~ ~ ~

Sunday mornings were the loveliest mornings of the week, no matter the season. Church bells chimed from sunrise to early afternoon and uplifted any human spirit, receptive to holy harmonies. Ren and Tess were not regular churchgoers because each of them professed a spirituality that organized religion seemed to taint. However, earlier that week, Tess had walked past a number of churches and noticed the titles of upcoming sermons on their announcement boards. The brick exterior of St. Stephen's Episcopal Church was strangled with ivy that almost hid the quote, "Thou shalt not bear false witness against thy neighbor"...Ex 20:16. The Lutheran church was a modern edifice with glass towers, blatantly snubbing the more architecturally conservative, threatening the promise of "progress." The announcement placard was practically buried by the snow, concealing times of the services, but revealing the words, "Except a man be born again, he cannot..." On the highest hill in the community the Immaculate Conception Catholic Church offered no information whatsoever, but pompously sat in judgment over parishioners and heretics alike from its lofty roost. In the past, Tess had attended all three churches in an unavailing attempt to discover a church home that aligned with her beliefs. Raised a Presbyterian, she'd found the Lutheran church too "sin-oriented" and the Catholic church too mysterious; by default, the Episcopalians gained her attendance one winter morning.

She climbed the steps of St. Stephen's and followed strangers, hidden somewhere inside fur coats, woolen hats, and winter boots. The Chinook from Saskatchewan had blown strong winds that night; the steps were shoveled and banked with freshly piled snow.

The organist played a prelude based on "Bring a Torch, Jeanette Isabella" and a dapper older man with enormous bushy eyebrows and wearing an ascot, ushered her to a pew within the sanctuary. The interior was decorated with cedar boughs that infused the air with a woodsy scent and the altar was lined with poinsettias, their pots wrapped in gold foil. Ah, the ambiance of devotion. No talking, no socializing. She closed her eyes, bowed her head, and entered into a quiet state. Whether she was praying, meditating, thinking or relaxing, she succeeded to be alone among a cast of hundreds. Her solitude was interrupted by a choir, robed in forest green with burgundy and white tassels, and singing "Oh Come all Ye Faithful" with full voice and consonance. She hadn't known that the Episcopalians could sing so well.

Halfway through the service, she noticed a blonde child, perhaps three years old, resting against her mother's shoulder, and looking back into the attentive congregation. She connected with Tess and gazed without blinking, then smiled ever so slightly before her eyelids closed and she slept. Her innocence, her beauty, her unawareness of the world's duplicity refreshed Tess's spirit, even if only momentarily.

Tess didn't hear a word the minister said because she'd entered her own world of complications that bound her so tightly, she was neither free to find her answers nor hear his. She was startled by a nudge from her right, handing her the offering plate. She smelled the sour breath of the woman, whose face looked embittered and alone. What had gone wrong in this woman's life that her smile had disappeared and the folded skin of her frown had become so indelibly pronounced? Tess glanced at the cherubic child still sleeping on her mother's shoulder and pondered the path from innocence to cynicism and her own placement upon that path. As she left the church, she shook hands with strangers and it occurred to her how naturally social human beings were. After her hour of interaction and introspection, she had resolved nothing in her life, but was better off for having spent the hour exactly as she did.

~ ~ ~

Night after night, the Parkers stayed up late to deck the halls with boughs of holly and angels and pine and ribbon and lights. Tess always insisted on two trees: one in the window of the living room, which guarded the house and overlooked the neighborhood; and one in the family room, adorned only with strings of cranberries and popcorn, gingerbread men noosed with red satin ribbon, candy canes from the local confectionery, and holly berries from the back yard. It was a replica of her mother's childhood Christmas tree that was not only charming but poignantly nostalgic. Ren bordered the roof line with strings of lights and had assembled the three lighted Christmas trees in the front yard, sarcastically calling them "The Three Wise Guys." Unwrapping each decoration was an intimately personal time for Tess each year. She greeted each ornament like an old friend having been away on an eleven month sabbatical. She had collected Santa Clauses for years and each one knew its familiar resting place. The house transformed and each room rivaled the famously adorned department store windows on Madison Avenue, N.Y.C.

On the night they expected Troy's family to arrive, they turned out all but the Christmas lights and took a walk through their winter palace. The music box tinkled movements from Bach's French Suites, as they sipped Yuletide grog and strolled arm in arm, from room to room. The stage was set. At the end of their tour, Tess announced that something didn't feel right. The reign of the Santas had ended and the following year she intended to replace the amassed fortune of St. Nicks with angels as she felt a strong pull from a secular to the spiritual celebration. Ren joked that perhaps they were growing up after all.

"Noel Joyeux! Noel Joyeux!"

Tess bolted for the living room where she found her little sister shaking off the snow and stamping impatiently on the entryway mat with wide open arms.

"Tia! You weren't due until tomorrow night!" In her woolen socks, Tess slid across the newly waxed hardwood floor into her sister's arms. "This is wonderful! Rennie, come here! Look who's here! I can't believe it!"

Tia yanked off her hat and playfully struck a pose. Her long auburn locks grown for a decade had vanished, and in its place she sported a short cut that framed her face like a European model.

"Tia! Your hair!" Tess screamed. "It's so French, tres chic." She twittered in approval.

Ren entered the room and whistled. "Look who grew up." He affectionately embraced his youngest sister-in-law.

"Am I the first to arrive?"

"Yes, but only by minutes. When I heard the door open, I thought you were Troy. But his voice is much deeper and he can't speak French worth a damn." She laughed.

The doorbell rang and Tess opened the door, pealing, "Grand Central Station!" There stood Cristin, wearing a long red coat against which her dark hair rippled and curled. She looked stunning.

"Hi! Is anyone here yet?" She hugged Tess and bounded into the room like it was her home. Tia, who had securely snuggled into a corner of the sofa with her stocking feet tucked beneath her and ready for whatever the moment offered, glanced at Tess with a look of curiosity as to who the young girl could possibly be. Obviously someone eager to meet the family.

Tess made introductions and explanations while Cristin shed her coat, revealing a gorgeous winter white angora sweater adorned by a single piece of jewelry, a heart shaped locket.

"Since I came to town Ren and Tess have been like family to me, so meeting all of you is very special. And you live in Europe? I want to go to Europe and study art someday." Cristin made herself at home and sat on the sofa with her Aunt Tia.

"Really? We'll have lots to talk about. I'm pleased to meet you. That's a beautiful locket, Cristin."

"Thank you. My mother gave it to me."

"Tess, look at this locket. Doesn't it remind you of the one Mum used to wear?"

Tess felt shivers run down her spine, which up to that moment, she had only believed to be an expression. She walked across the room to scrutinize the necklace.

"It's similar but Mum's was larger."

Tia persevered. "I don't think so. It looks identical. Whatever happened to that locket anyway?"

"I have no idea. Rennie, honey, would you offer everyone a drink? I'd like a Merlot."

She breathed a tremulous sigh. It looked exactly like Mum's locket. Cristin had unwittingly set the stage for a nightmare.

Instead of the proverbial "saved by the bell" scenario, there came a tiny knock at the door, the knock of a small person, perhaps under ten years old. Ren opened the door to two shy young faces who prompted by their parents in the background, began singing "We Wish You A Merry Christmas," accompanied by a set of jingle bells and two sets of off-key adult vocal chords.

The subject of the locket was forgotten and the Parker home became a love fest. Within seconds the room electrified with activity while the decibels of conversation amplified each excited greeting. The lovely Suzanne had gained a few pounds which ironically enhanced her curvaceous figure from modelesque to voluptuous status. Whether intentional or not, Suzanne had an aura of aloofness, a quality of unapproachable perfection. Tess knew that her sister-in-law didn't conceptualize words like "disheveled," "ordinary," or "passionate." As she helped young Max off with his jacket, Suzanne self-consciously bent her legs together with her knees slanted to the side, giving everyone the impression that she believed that everyone's eyes were following her every move. Her Barbie-doll demeanor and detached, vacuous dialogue made it impossible for Tess to feel close to her. But she was Troy's wife and the children's mother.

The children were in the house only minutes when they requested to go outside and play in the snow but because it was dark, the answer was "no." Max had Suzanne's blonde hair and was dressed in a colorful wool sweater adorned with teddy bears. With his legs extended behind his knees in an amphibious position that only a child can manage, he squatted in front of the Christmas tree, searching for his name on the gift tags. Lindsey, almost ten years old, was introverted in manner, much unlike her rambunctious brother. She appeared to be fascinated by Cristin and followed her every move, at first with her huge brown eyes, and soon thereafter, with her shadow. Cristin engaged everyone in conversation and blended into the family scene. Ren took Troy outside to look through the telescope while the women stayed inside where it was warm, chatting about what had been and might have been. Tess withdrew to the kitchen and Cristin followed her.

"Tess, could I talk to you for minute?" she asked.

"Of course, sweetheart. What's up?"

"Mrs. Taylor told me tonight that she's not going back to work after the holidays, so I guess I'm going to be looking for a job and another place to live. I just wanted to thank you for including me in your life. This will be the best Christmas I've ever had. I've never been happier and I just wanted you to know that I love you." Her delicate angora arms reached up around Tess's neck. Her hug was long and strong.

Tess looked into the face of the beautiful young girl in whom she'd invested her trust and her dreams and she heard herself say, "I love you too."

~ ~ ~

That night as they lay in bed, Tess and Ren decided what they would give Cristin for Christmas. After Ren fell asleep, Tess felt her pulse calm and she asked her God for His blessings. With her head sunken deep into her cool pillow, she watched the snow falling lightly against the light of the street lamps. So soft, silent, weightless, just as it had fallen for centuries. As she drifted to sleep, her last thought was that, before Katie's arrival, she would ask Cristin not to wear the locket.

~ ~ ~

The following morning in the library, Tess found Lindsey wrapped in an Aztec print afghan and reading *The Happy Prince*. It was a sad story and the youngster's face was intense, her forehead wrinkled and her jaw clenched.

"Lindsey? Good morning."

"Hi Auntie Tess. I hope it's okay that I'm reading one of your books."

"Of course it is. By the way, it's one of my favorites. It always makes me cry."

"Me too."

"You've read it before?" Tess inquired in disbelief. "Most grown-ups have never heard of that story."

"I read it last year. It's very loving."

"I hear that you read a lot."

"I like reading."

"Someday when you're older, you must read another Oscar Wilde story, *The Picture of Dorian Gray*. It's about what goes on within a person, his or her thoughts and personal feelings, the ones that no one knows about."

"I don't want to read it then."

"Why is that, honey?"

"It's private, Auntie Tess."

Tess realized at that moment that this sweet girl was harboring something painful, a sorrow, a heaviness that was more somber than mere shyness. The innocence that was every child's rightful endowment had somehow been prematurely plucked from this child.

Chapter 13

The advent of the holiday season gave people permission to escape their burdens, to decorate, to celebrate, to sing. Holiday wreathes donned halls and malls and "Jingle Bells" was piped into every public building in town. Memories were born and lives reconnected.

Everyone was struck by how well Katie appeared and how close she and Ingrid had grown. Ingrid's new found respect for her mother was not only long in coming but touching. Tess had asked Cristin not to wear the locket because it would be a reminder of the loss of their mother, still raw in their hearts. It was a lame excuse, but Cristin consented.

That week, Tia, Ingrid and Cristin were "The Three Musketeers," doing everything together. One evening they went into the basement and rehearsed for hours, and when they emerged sang "Silent Night" and "Adeste Fidelis" in three-part harmony. Their audience was biased but delighted and the night evolved into an old-fashioned sing-song. On another morning they rented cross-country skis and maneuvered through a local park until dark. They'd left together laughing and joking, and returned home, exhausted bunnies that needed the recharge that only a good night's sleep could provide. Another afternoon they spent hours decorating Christmas cookies with frosting, jelly, and sprinkles with Max and Lindsey, an afternoon the young children would long remember. For years to come, when Tess smelled the aroma of ginger, she would be transported back to the kitchen of that very berry afternoon.

Tess was relatively relaxed when Cristin was preoccupied with her new found friends, but whenever Katie and Cristin spoke, Tess carried an insufferable weight of anxiety. She tiptoed through a field of emotional land mines, set to explode and potentially injure everyone she loved. When in their presence, Tess seldom spoke, afraid that some slip or blunder might betray her. And when she did speak, she steered conversation into safe waters, finessing her unsuspecting guest from any providential discoveries of their own.

Tess and Katie had time to reminisce despite the fact that there were always people around them. Although quiet and aloof, Suzanne was often present, so the sisters obligingly included her in their conversations, as a measure of common courtesy.

Ren and Troy were dissimilar. But being intelligent men, they found common ground while speaking about sports or the stock market. Ren had always treated her family with generous hospitality and for this she was truly grateful. Life had been more complicated and uncomfortable during her first marriage because her former husband hadn't tolerated her family.

For weeks leading up to Christmas, various members of the house would disappear from the house, reappearing later with shopping bags, only to disappear again within the privacy of their rooms. They would emerge with brightly wrapped presents to display beneath the tree. Day by day, the presents and whispers grew in volume and numbers. The house was a flurry of whispers, which magnified Tess's uneasiness.

On Christmas Eve, Serena joined the family. The dining room table had never been so long, using every table leaf that, until this time, had been stacked in the front hall closet. Tia set the table, using a spray of cedar boughs with pine cones and sprinkling the centerpiece with silver sparkles. Each napkin was shaped like a bell and a white candy angel watched over each place setting. The tall red candles in crystal candle holders smelled of bayberry and were commissioned to stand sentry over the feast. By noon, the kitchen filled with the sounds of the turkey spitting juices and the smell of the swelling dressing. All afternoon Tess and Katie whisked away hungry visitors from the kitchen, each willing to taste test and sample.

The highlight of the holiday for Tess was seeing her family around her Christmas dinner table. There was something maternal, almost sacramental, to a woman who gathered and fed her family under her own roof, a feeling that was relative to other blessings, but had a supreme distinction all its own.

After dinner the family moved to the living room to exchange gifts. The children were delirious with excitement. Serena was visibly overwhelmed by the heightened level of activity and the boisterous exclamations of juvenile joy. She had brought gifts for only two people; a volume of Emily Dickinson for Tess and a copy of "Les Miserables" for Cristin. They were not new books, but gifts from Serena's own personal library, printed in the early 1900's. Tess was moved to tears for she knew that every page she would turn had been touched by Serena's eyes and fingertips.

Cristin gave Tess a statue of an angel with enormous gold leafed wings and a Botticelli face. The angel held a small gold dove in her delicate porcelain hands. Inscribed in the card was a request that each angel Tess received as a gift be christened with specified names. This one was Angela and the rest to be in the following alphabetical order: Beatrix, Celeste, Dulcinea, Eva, Felicity, Glori, Harmony, Ivy, Joy, Kinsey, Lilia, Melody, Nastassia, Ophelia, Patience, Qrystal, Rainbow, Stella, Tara, Ursula, Violetta, Whisper, Xyla, Yvette, and Zephyr.

The last present of the evening was from Ren to Tess. He presented her with an envelope wrapped in a red satin bow, along with a bottle of Dom Perignon, designated to be saved for the time specified inside the envelope. The room silenced as she ripped it open, discovering two tickets for a twelve day cruise on the Mexican Riviera, with ports of call in Cabo San Lucas, Mazatlan, Puerto Vallarta and Itapúa. Exuberantly, she threw her arms around her husband and hugged him. The room exploded with spontaneous applause.

The trip was scheduled for early March, the month that Minnesota magic mutated into frigid tundra where creatures without natural fur were forced to hibernate indoors. There wasn't a soul living in Minnesota that time of year who wouldn't relish putting on his or her snowbird wings and flying to the sunbelt that wrapped the Equator like a solar drenched ribbon.

When the evening settled, Ren and Tess asked Cristin to follow them upstairs.

"What's going on?" She followed them down the hallway, making a turn into the guest room temporarily strewn with visiting suitcases.

Ren spoke first. "Cristin, Tess and I have talked it over and we would like you to live with us. It would hopefully enable you to enroll in school without having to take on a full time job to support yourself. If you wish, the guest room will be yours as soon as our house guests leave."

Cristin's lower lip quivered and tears streamed down her cheeks as if someone had just told her painfully bad news. She let out a muffled cry, elevated herself on her tiptoes, and hugged Ren. "I don't know what to say. I don't know what to say."

"Say yes". Tess urged her with the broadest, most enthusiastic smile she could muster. She grabbed her niece and felt Cristin's sighs of appreciation resonate, indistinguishable from her own.

Cristin's effusive thank yous cast a spell upon the memory of the moment. Ren deposited a key to the house in her soft hand, with the understanding that she would always ring the doorbell in honor of their Parisian chapel. After all, it was a Parker family tradition.

After the carols were sung, the dishes dried and the lights turned out, Ren and Tess climbed the stairs to their bedroom. Only two more nights and they would be alone. Almost alone. As soon as the door closed behind them, Tess swung around, grabbing her husband, and together they toppled onto the bed.

"Thank you for the wonderful gift, sweetheart. I won't sleep a wink tonight thinking about it." She held him tightly as they playfully rocked back and forth on the cushy, padded mattress. "You do realize that I'll have to go shopping."

Ren whispered how happy it made him to please her, then abruptly changed the subject.

"Tessa, have you spoken with your brother today?"

"What? I don't want to talk about Troy right now. I want you. Come on, let's have a little cooperation."

"No, Tess, seriously. You apparently haven't spoken to him."

"No, why?" Her tone, annoyed.

"He didn't want to put a damper on the holiday, but since they are leaving tomorrow, he was going to try to talk to you today. I guess he wasn't able to. There is something you need to know."

"What is it?

Tess sat up, ran the fingers of both hands through her tousled hair and clenched her jaw, convincing Ren that she had made the transition from playfulness to attentiveness.

"He and Suzanne are getting a divorce."

"What? My God, Rennie, why didn't he tell me?"

"He wanted to but you were so busy. Inaccessible. He hasn't had a chance to be inconspicuously alone with you."

"A divorce? I can't believe you're telling me this. What happened?"

"According to Troy, Suzanne has been having an affair for the past two years. He's known about it for about six months."

"Rennie, no! What about the kids? Do they know?"

"Apparently Max doesn't have a clue, but Lindsey knows there's something wrong."

"Well that certainly sheds light on the conversation I had with her in the library a few days ago. Poor dolly. And it explains why Suzanne has been more distant than she usually is. Troy must be devastated."

"He is. But I think the hardest part is that Suzanne wants to stay in the house with their children."

"What? What rights does she have at this point? She has a man on the side with no concern with how it will affect her children. I have to talk to Troy before he leaves tomorrow. If she wants to continue her affair, she's the one who should move out and relinquish her custodial rights, not him! He shouldn't be punished. He has to take charge. I can't believe we're having this conversation." Her allegiance to her brother was spontaneous and vehement.

"Well, there's nothing we can do about it tonight, Tessa. But somehow, sometime before they leave, I will find a way to occupy Suzanne and the children so that you have chance to talk with him."

Tess sat down on her side of their bed as her concentration burned a hole through the air. So focused, she almost overlooked the envelope that was sitting on the nightstand.

"Rennie, is this from you?" She asked as she opened it. Inside she discovered Cristin's locket and a note that she read aloud.

Dear Tess,

I could not think of a gift I could give to you to express how much you have come to mean to me. This locket was given to me by my birth mother, whom I shall never know. I want you to have it because I think of you as my mother now and I know it reminds you of yours.

Merry Christmas. Love, Cristin

Ren broke the silence of the moment. "That's very special, honey. It's unusual that she'd be willing to part with it. She must really love you."

While holding the locket in her hand, Tess stayed inside Ren's arms until he fell asleep. She then unfurled from his embrace and turned over the gift. Squinting through dimmed light, she carefully examined the sterling silver heart and discovered on the back, the inscribed initials, C.L.M: Constance Larissa Monson.

~ ~ ~

Down the block, Cristin Shanihan smiled to herself with an exhilarating satisfaction of the playwright having successfully set the stage.

~ ~ ~

The talk with Troy took place the following morning when Ren offered to take the family to see the frozen cascades of Minnehaha Falls. Troy, who had been prompted beforehand, bowed out at the last minute. Suzanne watched him exit the loaded car. Tess could feel her sister-in-law's heartbeat accelerate. There was nothing as agitating to an in-law who had transgressed a sacred code like the alignment of strong family troops. Because of her warm reception, Suzanne had probably thought that she'd fly back to the land of milk and honey and into the arms of her lover without a tarnished reputation. But the die had been cast. Troy was neither to leave his home nor give away rights to his children, the brutal but just consequences of Suzanne's willful betrayal and Tess's intensifying wrath.

Later that afternoon when the California contingency exited the house en route to the airport, Cristin came running down the icy sidewalk, slipping and sliding with the ease a Minnesotan learns in order to survive. She hugged the children and joined the others waving goodbye. Tess grabbed her around the waist and whispered through her woolen hat, "Thank you for my special gift last night."

Cristin smiled.

~ ~ ~

There is nothing as unforgiving as a cold Arctic blast. Overnight a howling wind had come to town like a ravenous wolf.

Ren stoked the fire, and for old time's sake the family toasted chestnuts, filling the house with a familiar woody scent and cheery crackling. Two card tables were set up in the living room, one for

Scrabble and the other with scrambled jigsaw puzzle that Katie had brought from Boston. The family setting was a picture that Norman Rockwell would have paid money to paint. Tess set a buffet table that she replenished, as needed, and everyone helped themselves to the leftovers. Katie had used scraps of turkey for curried rice, Mum's recipe, as was the Monson custom sometime during the week after Christmas. Tess had forgotten the tradition, but its reintroduction was comforting.

By mid-afternoon gin rummy had replaced Scrabble at one table. Meanwhile, Tia had detected that the puzzle was an old photograph of the Monson family that Katie had sent to a catalogue company to be cut into hundreds of pieces. Once the subject was uncovered, the whole family turned their skill and attention to solving the mystery of the photograph.

"You all realize that I'm at a definite disadvantage because you all look so different and I don't even know what your parents looked like," said Cristin.

"I've got Grandpa's head!" yelled Ingrid.

"If I had half of Dad's head, I wouldn't have to work so hard," said Tess with a grin.

"You're plenty smart, little sister." Katie mused. "I'm the one who was shortchanged in the brain department."

"That isn't true. And besides which I love you just the way you are."

"Look at Troy," Cristin giggled. "He looks just like Max."

The resemblance was uncanny. The family became almost frenzied to fit the last pieces together.

"Tia you were just a baby, but Katie, look how young we look!" said Tess, startled at their youth.

When the last pieces were connected, they all hunched over the table with the celebratory camaraderie of a triumphant team, harmoniously reminiscent. At that seemingly inconsequential moment, Tess noticed her mother in the photo. More specifically, the locket around her mother's neck.

"Cristin! I need your help."

Tess gently snagged Cristin's elbow and led her away from the divulging picture. Apologizing for her abruptness, she said that she didn't feel quite herself, that she was suddenly smacked with pre-post-holiday blues. That, coupled with the picture of their family, made her maudlin and sentimental. She needed a break. She buried Cristin in the kitchen and busied her preparing a cheese ball and an assortment of crackers.

"Don't you think everyone is pretty full, Tess?" asked Cristin. "I mean, we've been eating all day."

"No, I think the timing is perfect. Besides which, my family will all be leaving tomorrow. I can't eat all of this food myself. I'll be right back." Embarrassed by her unreasonable request to serve more food and preoccupied with a way to turn attention away from the puzzle, Tess left the kitchen and entered the living room.

Tia pulled her over to the puzzle.

"Tess, look. Mum is wearing that locket that looks so much like Cristin's."

Tess had no choice but to look. "Yes, I see. But Mum's was bigger. I'm sure of it."

Ren stared and interjected. "Boy, Tessa, that's really interesting. It does look like the locket that Cristin gave you last night, doesn't it, honey?"

Everyone looked at her with incredulity.

"Well, how about some of Rennie's grog? Rennie, let's heat up a pot. Would you, please?"

Ren acquiesced with his usual good humor, and as soon as he turned she clumsily fell against the table, dismantling the puzzle, sending it spilling, piece by piece, onto the floor.

"Tess, are you all right?" asked voices in unison.

"I'm so sorry. I suddenly felt faint." Ren and Ingrid helped her to her feet. "I'm so sorry about the puzzle. I wanted to take a picture of it."

"What was that crash?" yelled Cristin as she came running from the kitchen. "Oh my God, Tess, are you okay?"

Tess assured her. "More embarrassed than bruised, I'm sure," Tess assured her

"Boy, I leave the room and miss all the action. What was going on, anyway?"

"Nothing really. We were talking about the locket in the picture that looks so much like yours," said Tia.

"Cristin actually gave it to Tess last night. That was a beautiful gift, honey," said Ren.

"I wanted her to have it."

"I'll bring it down the next time I go upstairs," Tess agreed, knowing full well she wouldn't honor her words.

The evening dragged. They resorted to playing bridge, as it was a game everyone knew except Cristin and Tia. The younger girls didn't mind. They were busy looking through old photo albums and laughing at the fashions and hairstyles of the past.

At one point Cristin shouted. "Look! Here's your spooky friend Sondra."

"Look at that page boy. A 'hum-dinger'." The girls pointed and snickered in playful ridicule. "Thank God we weren't born in the fifties."

"Did you say Sondra, Cristin? How do you know Sondra?" Katie asked.

Ren interceded to spare Cristin a long and perhaps uncomfortable explanation.

"Yes, we had the dubious honor of meeting your friend last summer. She was here on business and just paid Tess a social call. Very brief."

"Why do you say 'dubious'?"

"She was a little strange, Katie. The second time she was here, she had a bad attitude and asked some very personal questions," said Cristin.

"Definitely poor form," interjected Ren.

"I wasn't here that night." Tess glaringly addressed them in hopes of murdering the topic with visual daggers. "I talked to her the next day and she hadn't been feeling well. She apologized."

Katie persisted. "I can't imagine Sondra being anything other than a lady. What kind of questions did she ask you that were offensive, Cristin?"

Before Tess could interrupt, Cristin ingenuously blurted, "She wanted to know about my adoption."

"Your adoption?" asked Tia. "I didn't know you were adopted."

"Well no one ever asked me. But it isn't a deep dark secret, is it Tess? I figured that if you mentioned it to Sondra, it couldn't really be classified information. Truly, it's no big deal. I was adopted. Then my adoptive parents died. I moved to Minnesota and I've just spent the happiest months of my life with Tess and Ren. End of story."

"I hadn't realized that you and Sondra had corresponded these past twenty years." Katie spoke directly to Tess as she fought familiar feelings of sibling jealousy and searched her younger sister's face for any clue of collusion. "She visited you twice this year? I haven't seen her in years."

As there was no avoiding her inquiry, Tess explained. "I guess her work brought her to Minneapolis and she decided to look us up. She'd never met Rennie. And I was caught in a snow storm the second time and didn't even see her. Listen, I have a great idea. Knowing that you are leaving tomorrow, Serena sent over some lemon bars and rum balls. Cristin, will you help me again in the kitchen?"

They both withdrew to the kitchen like air sucked into a fan. The living room remained uncomfortable for a few moments until Ingrid asked Ren about his recent planet sightings. Katie sat quietly in the tufted leather easy chair. What had promised to be a lovely afternoon had been tainted by a ghost of the past. The mention of the locket, adoption, Sondra Rampling, reminded Katie of a time in her life that she thought she'd successfully buried in the basement of her memories. But with each drip of remembrance her heart flooded with sadness.

That night after Cristin had gone home and everyone had retired to bed, the smell of warm yeast in the bread machine lured both Katie and Tess to the kitchen. The clock ticked loudly on the wall to keep the nighttime visitors company. Tess made cups of hot chocolate, just like in the old days, and they talked.

Suddenly Katie interrupted her. "I'd like to see that locket before I go."

Shaking her head, Tess paused with reluctance. "Kate, it's not Mum's."

"I know that." She responded with surprise. "It couldn't possibly be Mum's. I'd just like to see it."

Knowing that Katie would never lay eyes on it, Tess finessed a lie once again. "In the morning. In the morning, okay?"

"Okay".

A few moments passed as they sipped their cocoas. Tess read her sister's confusion and for some inexplicable reason, she heard herself ask, "What ever happened to Mum's locket?"

Katie's hazel eyes stared into nowhere and she whispered her reply.

"She gave it to me."

Chapter 14

Twenty years ago he had come into Katie's life like a panther: strong, handsome and wild. He vanished with the slithering stealth of a snake. He had lured her, lusted after her and left her, to be sucked into a whirlpool of despair and loneliness. One day, she desired him as the love that should have been, and the next, she despised him as the man that buried her virtue. Now for the first time in years, she lamented her past indiscretion and prayed that she might receive God's grace of absolution or, at least, His protection from exposure. Excavated by suggestion and coincidence, her past shame no longer hid in the shadows of her conscience, but loomed in a spotlight of an excruciating self-recrimination.

The flight was half empty and the only sounds, other than the roaring of the jet engines, were the air conditioning blowing germs through the vents and a fussy baby at the rear of the plane. She watched Ingrid sleeping with her head pressed against the window. Katie closed her eyes and recalled the day that she went to work as a volunteer on Derek Northrop's political campaign. That ominous morning, when through the top of her Dutch door her rosy cheeked neighbor Marianne O'Connell, had appeared, balancing an apron full of apples gathered from her yard.

"Katie, how about some apples for a pie or cobbler? Or a brown betty?"

When she saw Katie's bloodshot eyes, she asked what was wrong.

"Nothing. I'm just tired," she'd replied tearfully. She attempted to camouflage her despair with a smile. Why would she share her personal agony with someone she barely knew? Because she was there? Marianne was not a good enough friend in whom to confide.

"Mind if I come in?" Marianne asked, as she presumptuously opened the lower door. Katie found it difficult to say no to people and a denial of entry would have been insufferably rude.

Although her advice was unsolicited, Marianne did mean well. "I've lived enough years to know the difference between tired and heartbroken. Whatever it is that's got your rope in a knot, it will pass. All things do, good and bad." She breathed one of those hissing nasal sighs that heavy older people make and she abruptly made a suggestion. "Come with me this afternoon to Derek Northrop's campaign headquarters. He could brighten anyone's day. He's so handsome."

"I really don't think so, Marianne, but thanks for the offer."

"Nonsense. You haven't left this house in days. I've been watching. I promise a change of scenery will lift your spirits. I'm not saying it will solve your problems, but it will help you make it through the day. I'll pick you up in an hour."

Katie didn't have the energy to decline. The children were at a friend's home until early evening. She suspected Stefan was having another affair. Staying with him was unthinkable, but leaving him was impossible. She didn't have any means of supporting herself and the children. But at that moment she also didn't have the energy to plan her future. So she didn't.

She changed her clothes and looked at herself in the long oval mirror on the back of her bathroom door. She looked tired and old. Her weeping had drowned the twinkle in her Irish hazel eyes. She breathed deeply and felt the tremor of her audible exhale. Mum had always said that her oldest daughter was a willow, pliant but strong. Katie braced herself against the bitter winds of fortune that had assaulted, but hopefully, not uprooted her.

Her next freeze frame of memory was walking into the campaign headquarters with Marianne. A virtual hive of activity, buzzing with volunteers, consultants, the media; telephones ringing, keyboards clicking, everyone focusing on the execution of an assigned job.

"Hi, Marianne," yelled a balding gentleman at the corner desk. "Did you recruit some extra help today?"

"I sure did. Everyone, this is Katie Shepard. She'll be helping me stuff envelopes."

Thankful to be busy, Katie steeped her mind in something other than her stale cup of tea. The day passed quickly.

That afternoon, just as Katie and Marianne were leaving, Derek Northrop arrived. He was tall with a strong square jaw and a confident, virile presence. As he strode into the room, he joked with the volunteers and yelled something about the ACLU which Katie didn't understand but which made the others uproarious. Then something unexpected happened. A sharp bolt of self-consciousness struck her and she neurotically avoided eye contact with him in hopes of disappearing before an introduction was made.

Marianne shouted across the droning activity, "Derek, I want you to meet a friend of mine."

Katie stiffened.

"Derek, the phone's for you. It's an advocate from the Labor Union. You'd better take it." His senior strategy consultant named Nick cuffed the phone and quietly briefed the young candidate as to what he should say. Katie informed Marianne that she needed to leave, but wanted to return and would meet the politician the following day.

She recalled every detail of the drive home that evening, as if it were yesterday. A chilly, waxen moon peaked out behind a bank of dark purple clouds. Dingy patches of snow lay in clumps on the front lawns of the turn-of-the-century residences that bordered the boulevards. The night was gray, but not a dismal gray, rather an impearling silver gray that gave the world iridescence. Marianne had been right: Change was good. The following day she would meet Derek Northrop and she would wear lipstick.

~ ~ ~

Their first meeting was informal and disappointing. His hands were warm and his eyes intent and flickering with other thoughts. He hadn't seemed to notice her as a woman, only as another volunteer. For the next few weeks Katie secured baby sitters for Shep and Ingrid as often as she could to work for the candidate. She took surveys, installed yard signs, worked in a phone bank, stuffed envelopes, and answered telephones. She studied his platform, helped to coordinate special events and clipped press releases on his private life, his issues, and his responses to his opponent. She listened to his budget meetings and memorized his constantly shifting schedule. Despite knowing that her fascination with him was inappropriate, she continued to fixate on the excitement and success of his charismatic maleness. Within days she mindfully campaigned for his attentions, at first subtly, then more flirtatiously. Her playful obsessions about him escalated to a dangerous game. The payoff was to feel alive again.

One night in early February, Northrop asked a few volunteers to stay late, so Katie made the necessary arrangements with her baby sitter. He brought in Chinese food and they worked until 8:30. One by one the others left, but she did not. As soon as they were alone, their conversation shifted from business to references of a more personal nature. As they spoke he moved closer to her, transferring from the sofa across the room to the chair next to her.

"Derek, I'm married," she nervously whispered.

"I know you're married, Katie. For that reason alone I have stayed away from you. You are a beautiful woman. You realize that, don't you?" He touched her leg above her knee.

"I don't feel beautiful. I'm very unhappy." She paused. "I shouldn't have told you that. Forgive me," she said apologetically as she pulled away and stood up.

Without saying a word, Derek Northrop stood and moved toward her with the strength of a pharaoh and the intensity of a beast. As if they were creatively choreographing a dance, she slowly positioned herself into a corner of the room as she watched him advance. When he reached her, his right hand turned off the light and his left hand took her arm and braced it against the wall. The next thing she remembered was the power of his body pressing against her, the sensuous warmth of his tongue deep inside her, and the thrill of an erotic seduction.

Weeks passed. They found places, times, and excuses for their clandestine trysts. Katie had never before known the joy of a man willing to explore the topography of her body. He was patient and heated, taking her back and forth between waves of pleasure and erotic spasms of passion, and always ending his love-making like a Beethoven symphony, powerfully punctuating and refusing to die. For a brief time, Katie lived two lives, one as a suburban mother of two, and another as a lover to a handsome, powerful man. At first she justified her affair as revenge. Stefan had earned the dishonor. What she hadn't foreseen was the plate of dishonor she was serving herself. Convinced that she was in love and discovering that she was pregnant, she hadn't anticipated his perfunctory response to the news, which insinuated that he'd given the speech before.

"I'll give you money for the abortion. The doctor's name is Schmidt, Mancel Schmidt. He's excellent. You'll be in very capable hands."

Katie's world crashed. Her heartbeat felt like it was bruising her insides; her vision blurred and the world looked like a photo negative, dark with outlines of indistinguishable forms. He wasn't going to stand beside her. He didn't want the baby. He didn't love her.

She protested in disbelief. "I can't have an abortion. This is a child, our child. I thought you loved me."

"Katie, Katie, Katie," he said in rapid succession. "I don't want to hurt you. I love being with you. I love making love to you. But a baby? What did you think I would say?" He reached out as if to embrace her and she forcefully, instinctively, pushed him away like her life was threatened.

"What were these weeks all about? Oh my God, I've been such a fool, such a silly little twit. What have I done?"

She shot a look of disdain, a dagger poised to pierce his arrogant male armor. Riveted with shame, she grabbed her coat and tore out the door into the deserted street. He didn't follow her.

Since that night, he'd won election after election, eventually becoming a state senator. There were mornings when Katie would pick up the newspaper on their front step and Derek Northrop's face would smile up at her. Her heart would ache for days. Sometimes while making dinner for her family, she would hear his voice on the television, or worse yet, see his face. Her shame of the past would flick on like a light switch. To complicate matters, Stefan liked Northrop's politics and became gruffly abrupt when Katie requested that he change the channel.

The only person she'd taken into her confidence had been her friend Sondra who orchestrated the adoption of the little girl-an agonizing time of Katie's life and one that she rarely relived. Citing "fragility of mental health," she'd left Stefan and the children for a few months. When the baby was born, Katie's only request of the new parents was that Mum's locket be given to the child on her sixteenth birthday. In Minneapolis, the mention of a locket and news of Sondra's visits rekindled Katie's past demons. She audibly moaned.

"Mom, Mom, wake up," said Ingrid. "We're landing in Boston."

~ ~ ~

Some things never changed. Katie, like her sister, always anticipated being met at the airport but rarely did her dream come true. Deplaning into the terminal, and heading for the baggage claim, she scanned the expectant faces of parents, friends and lovers, and searched the crowd for one of her own who might have rallied to pick them up. The escalators were lined with travelers, like armies of ants ascending and descending, all heading to separate, unnamed destinations. The directives shouted from the airport loudspeaker always made her feel like a prisoner in a concentration camp.

"I wonder what happened, Mom."

"If they don't show up in the next ten minutes, I'll call a cab, honey." Katie mumbled under her breath, angry at herself for her exaggerated expectations.

Stefan and Heidi came running across the concourse with a bouquet of flowers and remorse marking their faces.

"Traffic was terrible. We're so sorry we're late!" Heidi apologized.

Stefan gave his girls a heartfelt hug and they all bemoaned how empty Christmas was being apart. It was agreed that no one would leave during the holidays again.

Boston was a northern city, but had a much more temperate winter climate than Minneapolis. The forty-five degree temperature felt tropical by comparison. Charley welcomed them with effusive licks and tail wags. The first night home together was wonderful, a welcomed hiatus from the haunting memories exhumed during the past twenty-four hours. Stefan was as gallant as he had been when Katie first met him. She could hear her father saying, "Absence makes the heart grow fonder, Katrina." Perhaps he was right. Heidi actually took the night off from her social schedule to stay at home, putting her personal phone on vibrate, the ultimate sacrifice. The family spent most of the evening talking about Peri. She was now having blood transfusions every two weeks as she needed the fresh blood cells to carry oxygen to her body, without which she had virtually no energy. But her white count was rapidly declining and transfusions couldn't help because white blood cells only lived about forty-eight hours. Katie's inner world had shifted from depression to compassion as she resolved to help Peri as much as she could.

The following morning, she drove to Peri's home, which was located in a quaint part of town where the older custom homes wore charming roof lines and chimney top hats. The yards were defined by low stone walls and Alice-in-Wonderland gates that led to fairyed flower gardens. The streets were lined with pepper trees that gave them an impressionistic, willowy feeling, as if driving into a Pissarro painting. Katie parked her car on the street and walked up the brick sidewalk that was laid in a herring bone pattern. She was timid but resolutely put one foot in front of the other until she rang the doorbell.

A voice weakened by illness but struggling to be heard came from within. "Come in, Kate. Come on in." Peri had asked permission months ago to call her Kate because she thought it had such a youthful ring. So Kate it was.

Katie entered the living room and was greeted by two large china dogs that guarded each side of the bronze-tiled fireplace like twin Cerebri standing sentry to the fiery Inferno. The wood floors were accented with navy blue and burgundy oval rugs, gifts from Peri's spinster Aunt Marion who had taken great pride in dyeing, twisting, and braiding her own yarns. The green wooden shutters opened inwardly, showering the room with broad slants of sunlight that made the dancing dust visible. The house smelled of sandalwood, undoubtedly incense from Peri's childhood. Around the corner Peri lay on her sofa with her head propped against a plush pillow with tiny pink embroidered rosebuds on its casing.

"Good morning, Peri. I've missed you," said Katie as she hugged her young friend.

"I'm glad you're back. Please pull up a chair and sit down."

Peri's long straight hair was parted down the middle and hung close to her face on both sides like draperies, accentuating her gauntness. In her hand she clutched some old letters, dimmed by time and stained with the wear of fingertips.

"What are you reading?" asked Katie.

"Old letters I've saved. I figured if I didn't read them now it could soon be too late. So I'm taking a walk down Memory Lane this morning."

"Tell me how you're feeling."

"Well, they say it's the beginning of the end," she replied. "But I think it's really the end of the beginning."

Katie looked puzzled. "What do you mean?"

"I'm not afraid, Kate. I have a theory about how this whole life thing works. The best way to explain it is to think of how real a dream can feel. I know I dream in color because I've seen the violet in a rainbow and the yellow plumage of a bird. I hear people talk in my dreams. I mean, I actually hear their voices, their intonations, their accents. And you know the feeling of running from something or someone and you wake up and you're panting and your heart is pounding?"

Katie nodded.

"A dream feels as real as life when we're dreaming. We don't know it's a dream. We think it's real, right?"

"Right."

"Well, I think that when we die, we enter a state of consciousness that is as real as a dream, as real as our conscious state. It's just another level of awareness, but it's every bit as real."

"That's beautiful. I'd never thought about it that way." Katie's throat swelled with emotion.

"It's much more than beautiful; it makes sense. And somewhere in the depth of my soul, I not only believe it to be true, I know it, the same way I know that above a cloud cover there is blue sky." She paused for a moment, then smiled. "Time will tell."

"Please don't say that."

"I have to have a sense of humor, Kate. It lifts my spirits. I remember my first day in kindergarten. Having the colorful name that I do, I was teased mercilessly. We all were. I hated my name that day. But my mother told me I would have to learn to take a tease. She showed me that there was humor in my name. But she also showed me a picture of a periwinkle plant with tiny delicate blue and white flowers and told me that it was the flower that grew wherever angel dust was sprinkled."

Katie had never known anyone so vitally connected. She understood why Shep loved her so. But it was just so hard to believe that someday soon she would be in their lives in spirit only.

Katie attempted to dislodge the lump in her own throat by changing the subject. "I hear that some of your family is in town to see you."

"Oh, yes. I've actually had non-stop company since mid-December. I truly have a wonderful family, Kate. This is so difficult for them. They love Shep, you know."

"What's not to love?"

Peri yawned and stretched with the grace of a contented cat, then read Katie's face. "I'm sorry. I'm not bored, just rather tired. But I want you to stay, please. Stay at least until Shep arrives."

"Only if I'm not tiring you."

"No, I promise you're not. I would tell you so if it were true." Peri's delivery had become choppier, for it was increasingly difficult to get the oxygen she needed to speak in her usual mellifluous style.

"I'm curious. Why aren't you going back to your parents' home so that they can care for you?"

"Because I can't leave Shep, Kate. We have to be together. I love him."

These were words that every mother wanted to hear. Her son was truly loved. Katie's eyes welled with tears. She took Peri's cool long-fingered hand and pressed her love into Peri's palm.

"Please don't be sad."

"I'm so sorry. I have no right to come here and cry." Katie sniffled through a trembling voice. "You're stronger than I am. It should be reversed. I'm so ashamed."

Peri sat up and tightly hugged her knees as she posed herself only inches from Katie's face. Her large gray eyes were outlined by long eyelashes that accentuated the intimacy of every word. "Let me tell you something that you must believe is true, Kate. I love your son. And even though...we will not have a life together... we have both been so blessed. Most people never have in a lifetime... what Shep and I share. So don't feel sad. There is just one thing...

that I need to ask of you... Just a minute." She paused. "I need to rest."

Katie helped her lie down and waited.

"Shep is yet to give me his greatest gift. He doesn't know it yet. So you have to help him understand it." Peri paused again to catch her breath.

"Of course, sweetheart, anything you ask." Katie fought back tears.

"He will spare me the grief... that must be endured... after losing a loved one. I cannot imagine... if he had died before me. The only way I could survive... would be to find meaning... in his death. Sparing him the grief of being left behind would give meaning to my life. Don't you see, sparing me the grief I would face...if the tables had been turned...must give his life meaning. Kate, I want him to live a full and wonderful life. Promise me you'll help him."

Together they cried.

Peri requested a cup of green tea and asked for a face cloth to cool her eyes before Shep arrived. So they turned their attention to lighter subjects in anticipation of their privacy coming to an end. When Shep entered the room, he gave his mother a hug, but his eyes were on Peri. Katie was shocked at how tired he looked, how he'd aged.

She said goodbye to both of them and stepped outside into the big bad world. The day was bright. It seemed blasphemous that outside Peri's home there was so much life. Dogs barked, children played on the driveway next door, birds sang, and the winter primroses bordering her sidewalk were threatening to push through the earth and bloom. How dare they? She wished it were night; pitch black night. The sobriety of spirit should be sanctified at such serious times. Katie would always cherish her moments with Peri. Their souls had opened on such an intimate level that time could never injure their inspiration or their truth.

Chapter 15

On the first days of their cruise, Tess and Ren were at sea. As they leaned against the white side rails of the ship, the world offered an unobstructed view of sea and sky, interrupted only by intermittent island protuberances from the depths of the planet, which were paradisacally beautiful now. At one time they had been the result of erupting cataclysmic forces, too terrifying to comprehend. The sapphire waves were as mesmerizing as dancing flames of fire and as fascinating as a weeping willow touched by a fickle whimsy of the wind. The waves undulated with a constant yet random powerful motion, cresting between playful white caps, mirrored by fleecy white cloud caps above.

Tess stared at the horizon and inhaled the ocean air. From time to time a petrel or a shearwater flew into view, much too fast to keenly identify. She had often dreamed about being a bird, about flying. But never flying over land, always over vast horizonless expanses of water. There was freedom, a safety, a mystery implied by flight over water. Freedom to roam, safety from predators, mystery of destination.

The forward motion of the ship accelerated the movement of the clouds, providing a cinema of nature's pageantry. In early morning there was often a low fog that clung to the ship and disguised the sea in a cloak of invisibility. By afternoon the cumulus whip was usually so low that one could practically touch it and the animal clouds that hovered over islands left footprints of shadows on rugged terrain. By evening the few clouds that remained had blanketed the horizon in strata of pink, orange, and purple hues. How could something so visually real be so ephemeral? Tess hunted for the lines from a poem she had once written about clouds:

Nature has designed them so they mustn't wander past
The planet's atmospheric hold and poet's visual grasp.

Ren stood by the rail, three stories up from the main deck, and asked Tess to stand with him.

"I really don't like heights," he said. "Standing here this close to the edge spooks me. I feel like I'm going to be pulled over."

"Good God, Ren. What a morose thought."

"Or maybe, I'll be beguiled by some Siren or mermaid over whom I have no power."

"You're crazy."

"Whenever I get this close to an edge of anything, a ship's rail, a cliff's edge, diving board, church tower- anywhere I look over and down, there is a part of me I don't trust. All I'd have to do to end my life is jump like this." He jerked forward.

"Rennie!"

He threw his shoulders back and laughed with ferocity that only a man could muster. He grabbed her tightly. "Don't be silly. Why would I leave a beautiful creature like you behind? I would have to take you with me!" As he held her, he jerked toward the rail.

"Rennie! Stop it!" she yelled, as she squirmed out of his grasp. "What's gotten into you?"

"Sorry, babe. Just kidding. But it is a creepy feeling. I am aware of a pull, so seductive that it alarms me. Do you feel it at all? Do you understand what I mean?"

"No. No, I don't. Come on, sit down, sit next to me. Stay away from the rail. Now!" she implored, tugging at his shirt sleeve.

With an impish smirk of a little boy who had just scared a girl on the playground with his pet frog, Ren laid back on his chaise, folded his arms behind his head, crossed his bare ankles, and fell asleep to the sound of muted guitars above and surging wake beneath them. Likewise, Tess closed her eyes and thought about the tempting force that entices one to take risks.

The ambiance of the ship was appropriately Mexican. The Mariachi bands strolled the decks with the amplified sound of high piercing trumpets and frantically strumming guitars. Ladies in colorful twirling skirts, with stiff swishing petticoats, danced like whirling tops across the floor, a sight that excited the senses and dizzied equilibrium. By day, flowers floated in exotic drinks, and by night, in wreaths that encircled white candles adrift in the pools. Because the color of Mexico had been so expertly delivered to them via the ship's entertainment, atmosphere, and food, Ren and Tess agreed that they were perfectly content to stay on the ship without disembarking at the ports of call.

One didn't eat on a cruise. One dined. And viva la difference. The smells of cilantro escaped on wafts of ocean breezes while pelagic birds followed the wake, expecting better than normal bill of fare. The food preparation and presentation were superb, courtesy of a chef from Bridgetown, Barbados, and his serving staff from Indonesia, Mexico and the Philippines, a veritable floating United Nations. To top it off, the head waiter, the Secretary General so to speak, was from Iran, which led any thinking person to a paradox wrought with irony.

One evening after dinner, they adjourned to the library on the fifth deck. As the ship inched its way toward a vanishing horizon, the clouds in the east touched the water and reflected the rosy rays from the west, joined together in a concordance of natural beauty that is commonly present, but seldom witnessed. They sat together with large bulbous snifters of brandy and gazed through the picture window that framed the passing world. They talked about the world beneath the ship, the coexistent ecosystems so foreign in atmosphere and adaptability, yet independently sharing the same planet.

Ren pointed out that humans invade the territory of the ocean depths, never vice versa. Curiosity and the potential power to control surroundings were necessary human traits to advance the species but sometimes were precisely the qualities that spawned planetary discord. Tess loved talking with her husband. She loved the intelligence and humor he contributed to even casual conversation. She never tired of him. When they had first met, he'd stated, "Always expand the universe before you shrink it, Tessa" which had stimulated countless conversational journeys with general direction but no preordained destination. The eventual ports of arrival had dilated her perceptions and had indeed expanded her world.

Ren had exposed her to a love of sculpture and architecture. Prior to meeting him, she'd only thought of art as painting, strictly painting. She thought herself rather worldly, being able to recognize works of Michelangelo, Rembrandt, Van Gogh, and Picasso. But she learned to appreciate the beauty of sculptors: Rodin, de Vinci, Donatello, and Henry Moore. And in recent years she had actually driven through historic sections of cities for the sole purpose of looking at the buildings.

Being far from home, no one threatened to interfere with their lives. Tess infrequently even thought of anyone else. Cristin had moved into the guest room and was taking care of their home while they were gone. Tess did think about Lindsey and Max, with prayers that they would survive the storm of their parents' divorce. The damage of divorce was indisputably absolute. Only the degree of the damage was relative.

Having time away was therapeutic. The cruise had afforded her an opportunity to redefine relaxing as a necessity, not a luxury. She realized that she needed to start thinking of recreation as a time to re-create. She needed to trust that all would be well. She needed to live her life so that she could trust herself once more.

One of their favorite times together was late at night. Jupiter was high in the sky and the constellations were brilliant. One night they identified the haze of the galaxy Andromeda, a rare and personal victory. A black moonless sky, unobscured by city lights, was indeed uncommon to city folk. When the rest of the ship was losing cents in the casinos, losing sense in the bars, and gaining weight at the tables of midnight buffets, they chose to stroll the deck.

One morning in a port of call with a romantic Spanish name, they drove to a sleepy Mexican village and hired a local to take them to a secluded beach. The water taxi skimmed the surface which was a color intangible to describe. With the naked eye they could see tens of feet down and watch brightly colored tropical fish weave in and out of a web of sparkling sunlit paths.

Rounding the corner of an enormous jagged cliff, the taxi pilot pointed to a private beach between spires that rose from the sea as towers. He suggested in sign language and broken Spanglesh that they disembark and he would return in a matter of "dos horas, or so." Ren was leery of the "or so," but Tess urged him on. After all, the worst that could happen was that they would be stranded on a romantic and breathtakingly beautiful beach for more than a few hours. Ren reluctantly acquiesced with the condition that the pilot not be paid until he returned to reclaim them to the real world. It was a utopian retreat with golden sand and water as warm as a bath. They dived off the side of the boat to swim among the bright yellow and iridescent purple fishes. When they surfaced they laughed like children and waved goodbye to their deliverer.

Stepping onto the shore they could see that the beach was an isthmus. They walked only a hundred feet to the other side where the waves of the Pacific savagely slammed the shore and tossed foam high into the air. Majestic in sight, frightening in power. The tide left behind broken jewels of a mysterious deep, a peace offering from Poseidon. The sand was mounded hot and high, exposed to the sun and thirsty for drink. Like children on a scouting safari, Ren and Tess explored the caves, climbed the eroded rocks, and then returned to the tranquil side of the isthmus where the waves caressed the sand.

Knowing that the water taxi pilot would not return for hours and that no one knew where they were, they shed their bathing suits and together, hand in hand, ran into the diaphanous sea.

Ren ferociously dived and swam as if he were in contention for an Olympic gold medal. Tess loved his masculine, aggressive nature. In some primal sense it made her feel protected and safe. She floated on her back and watched the magnificence of the frigate birds and couldn't help but smile at the goofiness, the prehistoric awkwardness, of the brown pelicans, one of God's subtle reminders of a world, primeval and uncivilized.

She watched the waves swathing the shore in layers and angles that touched the artist in her soul and lightly kicked as she made her way toward her husband who was standing in water up to his chest. She grabbed him from behind and he clutched her, spinning her around until her legs clasped his waist and her arms encircled his neck. He then gently laid her torso into the water as he kissed her full buoyant breasts. With her hair freely floating, her dark lashes glistening in the sunlight, and the foam bubbling over her tanning body, she hoped that Ren was capturing the beauty of his lover in a glance that he would call to mind for the rest of his life.

The cruise ended much too soon but the reentry was cushioned by a night's stay at "The Hotel Del," as the natives referred to it, on the Coronado Peninsula off the coast of San Diego. The hotel was a perfect example of Victorian seaside architecture. Its style and extravagance was an architectural aficionada's dream. The exterior was an arrangement of turrets, cupolas, domes, and towers, constructed from wood, painted in luminous white, and crowned with a ruby red shingled roof.

As they approached the entrance, they were dwarfed by the colossal rotunda to their right. They entered the Grand Lobby, showcased by the immaculately polished woodwork, an exquisite chandelier, plush patterned carpets, cushy sofas and easy chairs. Enormous arrangements of flowers and the smell of affluence seduced them to erect their posture.

They checked in at the registration desk, then browsed in the sumptuous shops that flanked the long, narrow hallways of the palatial establishment. They poked their heads into a "private party room" that was filled with ladies playing bridge, each face framed in smoke and cawing like crows. They wandered into the garden patio, lush with tropical banana plants, orchids, and azaleas that had obviously been imported from faraway places. It was the perfect ending to a dream vacation. They sat on a bench and breathed the salty ocean air, trying to fill their lungs, so that when they returned to The Midwest Territories the following day, they would take with them its fresh bouquet.

"Rennie! Look over there. Isn't that Senator Northrop? We're not even in Hollywood and we're seeing famous people."

"Yes, I think you're right. Son of a gun, it's Derek Northrop. But Tess, the woman he's with. The woman he's kissing. Doesn't she look like Suzanne?"

"I guess." she said in disbelief. "But of course, it couldn't be." She paused. "Could it?"

They stared incredulously. As if cued by a stage director, they simultaneously stood up and walked toward their target. Ren, who was known to have an offbeat sense of humor, began whistling "It's a Small World" as they ambushed the rendezvous.

"Tessa! Ren! What are you doing here?" Suzanne exclaimed. "You're in California?"

"Hello, Suzanne," said Tess. "Aren't you going to introduce us to your friend?"

"Oh, of course," she said, flustered by the surprise. "Senator Derek Northrop. This is Ren and Tess Parker."

"How do you do? I'm very pleased to meet you. How do you all know each other?" he innocently asked.

"That's very simple. Suzanne is my sister-in-law, my brother's wife, our ten year old niece's mother, and our six year old nephew's mother. And how do you know each other?"

The verbal abyss that followed rendered even a politician speechless. In the War of Whoever Speaks First Loses, Tess held fast her position of silence and dominated. It had long been known that she had inherited her father's caustic tongue and although few had ever heard it unleashed, it was instinctively feared.

"Tess, please don't do this," implored Suzanne.

"Do what, Suzanne? Tell the truth? God forbid that I tell it like it is, you spoiled southern bitch!"

Ren didn't move a muscle to stop her. After all, Troy was her brother and this was her battleground. It was show time and there would never be a more appropriate time to confront her enemy.

"My brother loved you, cared for you, gave you children, and a beautiful life. And you, you self-righteous has-been beauty queen, you threw him and your children away like bags of garbage."

"How dare you talk to me like that! I love my children."

"That's why you're trying so hard to preserve your family, right?" Tess added sarcastically.

"You should talk. You've been divorced!"

"My ex-husband was a drug addict and a philanderer. Yours is a decent, loving man who never did anything to deserve your self-centered behavior. The sight of you makes me sick."

"That's enough!" interjected Senator Northrop. "I won't allow you to speak to Suzanne in this manner."

"Won't allow it? What are you going to do to stop me? Arrest me? File an injunction? This is a joke. You, the promoter of family values. Hell, you don't have a clue what family values are. You not only don't have a family, but you're wrecking one that isn't yours. You've got a major credibility problem, buddy. This will be great press for your upcoming campaign. And don't think I won't make a stink!"

"You can stop right now." Northrop yelled

"You're right. I can stop. But I'm not playing 'Captain, May I,' Senator. And unfortunately for you, I'm not finished. My husband and I have just returned from a cruise and this is the last night of our vacation. Thank God we stopped here. I wouldn't have missed this for the world. Listen to me, Suzanne. If you haven't the decency to gracefully relinquish complete custody of the children to Troy, I'll see you in court. Have a nice evening."

Tess grabbed Ren's hand and triumphantly marched across the patio like a victor of war. He had never watched his wife in action before, but secretly saluted her with a clench of his fist. Not a word was spoken until they reached their room. The moment the door of their suite slammed behind them, they frenziedly tore off each other's clothes. It was the most impassioned night either one of them could remember. Making love, talking, whispering, laughing, reenacting, whispering, making love for hours.

~ ~ ~

They arrived in Minneapolis at dusk the following evening. Cristin picked them up at the airport. She chattered about her classes at The College of Art and Design and squeezed every detail from the tube of their trip. Ren drove and Cristin requested to ride shotgun. Silhouetted with bare tree branches, the Minnesota landscape dimmed, creating a bas relief of gray and black, and bringing to mind an Ansel Adams photograph. They took a back route, following the serpentine course of Minnehaha Creek, which slithered its way through the shivering city like a vein of agate in a mountain of granite. Amorphous piles of dirty snow bordered the street curbs and darkness descended on cue like a heavy velvet curtain on a stage in the round.

Although it was always exciting to get away, it was equally as comforting to be home again. The house was filled with wondrous smells. Cristin had prepared what she termed "a dinner to die for- a Mediterranean Delight." It was decreed that Ren and Tess were to unpack while their live-in house guest "slaved" in the kitchen. The menu for the evening consisted of grilled Portobello mushrooms with a balsamic vinaigrette, which impregnated the house, accosted the senses, and induced a Pavlovian response; a mild soothing cream of broccoli soup; a Caesar salad with freshly grated Parmesan cheese and ample anchovy; a Penne Siciliana with zucchini and tomato cream sauce; and an almond custard filo pastry for dessert (which she'd picked up at a local Italian bakery.) Cristin admired Ren's proficiency in the kitchen and had obviously set out to impress him with her own. His generous praise not only complimented the chef but compensated her efforts.

After dinner, Tess retired to the office to sort and read the mail. Ren retired to the living room to watch the news and read the heap of newspapers that had accumulated during their absence. It was remarkable how out of touch they had been and how little it had mattered. After Cristin finished the dishes, she joined Ren, sitting next to him like a daughter might sit next to her father.

Tess noticed a letter from Katie, postmarked ten days prior, and opened it with timid curiosity.

Dear Tess,

This is one of the saddest days of my life. Peri has died. There is a gaping hole in the heart of my heart. Little sister, I need you. I wish you weren't so far away. I wish you were home from your cruise. My cup is spilling with sadness. I must write to you, but I apologize in advance and thank you in perpetuity.

Peri was the most remarkable person I've ever met. She had so much to give. She was wise at a tender age. She would have grown to be a wizardess, a priestess. She was given to us for such a brief time, plucked from us so prematurely. I'm repeating myself. I'm so full of questions, so empty of answers and it hurts like hell.

And Shep? He's distraught, lost without her. She forewarned me. She asked that I help him when she died, but now that the time is here, I feel powerless. What kind of mother am I? What can I possibly say to him? I can't even comfort my own son. I feel so lost, so inept.

Two nights before she died, she said something that I'll never forget. She said that beauty was man's bridge to God, that people had such a tough time trying to figure out the God/human connection, that He made it possible through beauty. Beauty was His way of uplifting our spirits to commune with Him. She asked (and I'll do my best to paraphrase), why do we look at the red of a poppy, smell the scent of a gardenia, hear a Mozart divertimento, follow a Monarch butterfly across a garden, and we feel uplifted? Because man's nature is inclined to be uplifted. We're constantly striving, consciously or not, to align with goodness and beauty because we feel reconciled with a higher knowing.

She said that she was about to join the universe and be integrated into all that we saw that was beautiful. She asked that we talk to her every day and she would hear us. She asked that we not be sad, because she would be able to help us more than she ever could on this planet. She asked that we keep her memory alive by living without fear. Oh Tess, I'm going to miss her beyond words.

At her memorial service, her brother said that if the secret of dying was unlocked by the mastery of living then Peri had held the key. It was a beautiful service, Tess. I wish you could have been there. The program stated 'Those of us present today must take this time to go within our collective soul, to express our gratitude to Peri for being the guiding star she is within our lives. It is you whom she loves, honors and touches, which binds us all together with a cord that can never be broken, by a chord that will never be unsung.'

I loved her so. Call me when you return.

As ever,

Katie

Tess laid down the letter, raw with sadness but uplifted by the words. As much as she wanted to procrastinate and place the call to Boston the following day, there was urgency implied that she couldn't ignore. After her bath she would call Katie upstairs from the master bedroom. As she passed the living room, she noticed Cristin sitting sideways on the sofa, eyes closed, back resting against Ren as he read his newspaper. And Tess smiled, thinking how cozy it was to feel like a family.

Upstairs, Tess drew her bath and watched ghosts of steam creep up the mirrors and mystically erase her image. The air thickened and cloaked the room with alchemy of moisture and warmth. She eased into the silky water, softened by beads of jasmine oil, and slipped under the blanket of bubbles. Her head rested on the back of the tub and she deeply breathed the floral aromas through flared nostrils, filling her cavities with the healing balm that centuries before had been discovered by mystic peoples in distant lands. She reflected on how fortunate she was to be exactly where she was, in history and in the world. The late twentieth century, a woman, in America, with a partner, a "daughter," living in a wealthy, beautiful community and lying in a steamy warm bubble bath. Life was good.

An hour later Tess propped herself up on their bed with telephone in hand. She was wrapped in a plush terry cloth robe that Ren had ordered for her from a Victoria's Secret catalogue. She had noticed that when he sorted the mail, the V.S. catalogue was always placed in his pile. When they had first married, his "periodic voyeurism" bothered her, but when gifts were delivered at the front door, courtesy of her husband and "Vicki's Place," as he playfully called it, she didn't complain.

"Hi, Katie? It's your sister."

"Thank God you're home. When did you get back?"

"Just tonight. I read your letter. I'm so sorry to hear about Peri. How is Shep?"

"It's so tough. He's lost weight. He looks like an atrocity victim. Thank God he has a buddy who is handling his accounts. It's truly awful, Tess. He won't talk about Peri, but she's all he thinks about. Lines of communication have completely shut down. I'm just sick about it. I swear, the older children get, the graver their problems become. It was much easier being a mother to toddlers. It took more time, but much less worry. What I would do to turn back the clock for one day and see my little boy happy again."

"Give him our love when you see him, Katie. I know that doesn't help but I don't know what we can do."

"I appreciate it, honey. There really is nothing you can do except lend a sympathetic ear to your pathetically helpless sister. I haven't even asked you how your trip was."

"It was wonderful. When Ren and I are alone, all is right with the world. But we're thrilled to have Cristin living with us now. She picked us up at the airport today, prepared an elaborate dinner (I'm sure, to impress Rennie), and she's sleeping downstairs, leaning against my husband as we speak, while he reads his arsenal of newspapers. We're a regular family and it feels terrific, Katie."

"That's good. I'm glad you're so happy. By the way, have you heard anything from Troy?"

"Oh my God, Katie. I forgot to tell you. You will never believe who we saw in San Diego?"

"San Diego? When were you there?"

"San Diego was the city of disembarkation. And we stayed in town for a night at The Hotel del Coronado. You know that gorgeous hundred year old hotel? Fabulous place. Anyway, Rennie and I were sitting on the patio in the huge inner atrium and there in the full light of day was Miss Suzanne and her lover."

"I can't believe you're saying this. The world is so small, it's frightening."

"You've got that right. She had no idea we were scheduled to be in California for a night, let alone in her back yard. I mean, Katie, what are the odds that we would end up within twenty yards of Troy's sorry excuse for a wife and her gigolo."

"Oh Tess, you confronted her, didn't you?"

"You're damn right I did. I've been waiting my whole life to lay into someone like Suzanne. And I didn't miss a beat."

"What did Ren say?"

"He just stood there and let me roar. God, it felt great. We not only caught her completely off guard but when Mr. Wonderful tried to defend her honor, I laid into him as well. Katie, you would have been proud."

"What was he like? The man?"

"I can do better than that. You know who he is. You've seen him on television and on the front page of *The Boston Globe*. The bastard is a public figure with a notorious reputation. She's such a little fool."

"Who is he?" asked Katie expectantly.

"Brace yourself, big sister. It's Senator Derek Northrop."

It was fortunate for Katie that she heard the story through a telephone line. Her face aghast would have exposed a reaction that could not have gone unexplained. Once again her memory was charred by pain of the past. The connectedness within the world was ruthless.

"Katie? Did you hear what I said? Derek Northrop."

Katie remained speechless as her throat filled with a fiery sensation of fury. What could she say?

"Wait a minute," Tess flashed. "Didn't you tell me that years ago you worked on one of his campaigns? Wasn't it Derek Northrop?"

"Yes. It was. He was a bastard then, too. That's why I quit working for him." Katie fumbled, trying to find a semblance of composure. After an uncomfortable pause, she said, "You know, Tess, it's been a long day. Thanks so much for calling, honey. We'll talk soon, okay?"

"Sure. Are you all right? Katie?"

"I'm, fine. Just tired, that's all. Goodnight, sis."

"Goodnight."

Tess hung up and laid back on the propped pillows. Within seconds she heard talking in the hallway.

"Goodnight, Tess. Welcome back," yelled Cristin.

Tess bounced off the bed and bounded around the corner of her room to see Cristin hugging her husband goodnight.

"Goodnight, sweetheart. Thank you for the great dinner and picking us up."

Tess's heart was full.

~ ~ ~

The door closed and they were alone to share the comfort and familiarity of their bed once again. When the lights went out, there was quiet talk, the intimate sharing between faceless souls when the sense of sight is missing and the sound of a voice, the scent of breath, the taste of lips and touch of skin heightens communication. In soft whispers they shared their feelings, but on this particular night Tess was not the only one guarding an apprehension. Ren felt an uneasiness regarding Cristin's open affection. But he was ashamed to share his wariness because his wife would not believe him. Besides which, his intuition was not strong and he was probably just not used to having another woman in the house. His mother had told him when he was only a little boy that he "tuited" better than he "intuited." He was a scientist, after all. Perhaps young girls expressed their caring to a father figure in just this way.

~ ~ ~

Meanwhile, Cristin lay awake in her dark room. She thought through the night, how it felt to be close to Ren, how she'd soaked in his warmth, and felt the movement of every muscle in his arm when he turned his pages. The man, who spent his hours looking through microscopes by day and telescopes by night, didn't see what was threatening within his own home.

Cristin stared at a painting that hung over a bureau of drawers. It was a fantasy entitled *On the Edge of a Dream* and pictured a swan floating under a filigreed bridge. Through her window, the light of the winter moon shone like a spotlight on the graceful creature in the painting and Cristin imagined herself straddling the swan that would bring her to Tess's husband. And he would seduce her and she would submit.

Chapter 16

Tia Shepard
8 Rue Montaigne
Grenoble, France

Dear Cristin,

You must come to France! It is the most romantic country in the world! The language alone makes me weak in the knees. I've learned the words and phrases that I need in order to survive but my accent is really atrocious. I can understand people pretty well when they speak slowly but I know I sound like those Vietnamese children who were immersed in English in grade school. And we all giggled at them. "Oh, woe is me," as my Aunt Thelma used to say. Living in a foreign country dulls a sharp tongue. Having now experienced the rank of foreigner, I am humbly grateful for a kind reception and a tolerant ear. Interesting- I don't even like the word "tolerant" anymore. It implies arrogance and a conceit that I despise, but you know what I mean. Maturity certainly has its rude awakenings, doesn't it?

I don't ordinarily write letters. I'm more of a postcard gal. But today is a rainy day in Grenoble with alternating bouts of downpour and drizzle and I have a sore throat. I mean, what's a girl to do? Expose myself to damp, wet wind, and cold? And since I know that a woman can justify anything to suit her purposes, I chose to play The Justify Game and cut my classes today.

Anyway, every once in a blue moon I feel like writing a letter. (Did you know that a blue moon is the second full moon within the same month? In second grade, Casey Cassidy's grandma told me that gem.) Cristin, I'm going to apologize right now for my writing style. People tell me that I write like I talk, kind of a stream of consciousness thing. Sometimes the flow takes a bend in the river and suddenly you're heading in a new direction. Oh well. It sure does explain why my English composition grade always brought down my GPA. This morning, I actually felt like writing a letter so you are the lucky beneficiary.

I understand from Tess that you are living at their house now and have enrolled in school. That's great! Are you working or just studying like a maniac? Being a full-time student is the ticket if you can afford it. The real world is going to have its way with me soon enough-bills, a house, a husband, children. I get spasms of terror just thinking about it. Perhaps I'll be a hermit and escape the trappings of society. But that's doubtful, despite Thoreau's warnings about the pitfalls of conformity. After all, some of the world's institutions, like marriage, have survived for good reason. I'm restudying the Transcendentalists this semester and can't believe what I didn't pick up the first time in high school. It makes me wonder what I'll learn a few years from now if I were to reread the same essays.

I suppose you've heard about Peri. I never did meet her, but Katie's family really loved her. So sad. I guess my nephew Shep is having a rough go of it. He's such a great guy. Handsome and smart. And rich. You've got to meet him, Cristin. He's a doll.

Seriously, think about coming to France, perhaps this spring or summer. You could stay with me in Grenoble. I live in an apartment across from Victor Hugo Park. I watch old men playing bocce ball, babies being pushed in old-fashioned carriages, and geese "following the leader" on their paths to the lake. The air smells like freshly baked baguettes from local boulangeries and is filled with a language so beautiful, it sounds like music. We could travel with my friends, Yvette, Desiree and her boyfriend Yves. It would be great fun. Loving art the way you do, you'd be in heaven. This country reeks of culture.

We could take the TGV to Aix en Provence and see the white cliffs immortalized by Cezanne. Then drive to the French Riviera, experience the nude beaches of St. Tropez, the nightclubs in Cannes, the cosmopolitan charm of Nice. Only miles above Nice is Saint Paul de Vince where there is an art museum consecrating Matisse and Chagall. Then on to Monte Carlo. You'd love Monte Carlo! The winding streets loop and curl like an unending piece of Christmas ribbon candy. The castle, the casino, the port. Then we could slip across the border into Italy and eat!

The food here is delicious, unsurpassed. Patisseries, outdoor cafes, restaurants on every corner. Paris! That will be our first trip. (You notice I'm writing as if I've assumptively convinced you to come?) We'll eat escargot and French onion soup covered with a thick toasty crouton and smothered with Gruyere; and watch the flower vendors sell bouquets to the Frenchmen who are homebound to their wives after rendezvousing with their mistresses. Can't you visualize it? It's another world.

And the men, Cristin, the men. They are gorgeous and so romantic. They'd love you. I guarantee that if you wore a long silk scarf and spiked heels down the Champs Elysees, you'd be approached no less than a dozen times. I'm serious. France, the land of romance.

But enough about France. Please write and tell me how you like your new life in Minneapolis. My sister and Ren are terrific people as you already know. They are so good together-my role models. You're lucky to be with them and I know how happy they are to have you there. Good luck with school this semester. Tell me what courses you're taking. Who are your favorite artists? Be good. Au revoir.

Love, Tia

Cristin found the unopened letter on her bed that afternoon which meant only one thing: someone had come into her room when she wasn't home. It had been agreed that her room was her private domain and no one would disturb it. She stared out the window and noticed some rippling of the glass, suggesting movement within the pane. She would have to ask Rennie about the phenomenon because he had explanations for everything. But on to the issue at hand, an invitation to France. How her life had changed. She had once been poor and unhappy, until the day she met the girl who had shared a secret. And that secret became Cristin's ticket to a new life. Now she lived in a beautiful home, in a gorgeous neighborhood. She had no money worries, a job, a chance to be near a man like Ren, and now an invitation to France! Her present was on cue, her future promising, and her past irrelevant.

She would speak to Ren and Tess at dinner. Perhaps she would convince her professors that an independent study would be in order. Traveling with Tia and her friends might be a hoot. Sure, she'd miss Ren. But there were other men in the world. It didn't have to be Tess's husband. And Tia was the perfect companion. There was something naturally vulnerable, naïve, and good about her. Tess's little sister was a perfect pawn, predictable and unsuspicious, easy to manipulate, just like Tess. Cristin had always been attracted to nice people, and fortunately for her, she had the chameleon ability to appear as virtuous as the Madonna herself. No one but her parents had really witnessed her dark side and her parents were dead. Cristin reread her letter and thought about what it must be like to have known an Aunt Thelma or Casey Cassidy's grandmother. Envy simmered inside her and for an instant she hated Tia.

"Tess? Ren? Is anyone home?" Cristin yelled from the hallway.

There was no answer. Cristin strode down the hallway into the master bedroom. She walked into their bathroom and with her fingernail she engraved her initials into Ren's soap, then walked to his side of the bed and laid down, burying her face in his pillowcase to smell his lingering scent. There on his bed stand was a picture of Tess, sitting on a swing, with bare feet and crossed legs, hair blowing in the breeze and a smile that probably melted his heart. She slammed the frame face down, breaking the glass.

Suddenly, the doorbell rang and chimes echoed throughout the house. Tess was home early. Cristin deftly, silently jumped from the bed and entered the hallway, faltering in neither stride nor heartbeat.

"I'm home," Cristin's cherubic voice pealed

Startled, Tess jumped. "Cristin! my God! You startled me! I didn't think anyone was here."

Smiling, Cristin intently peered over the banister. "Tess, why did you go in my room today?"

Tess stared at her with her mouth slightly open. Cristin's accusatory tone was unambiguous and alarming. "I only dropped a letter from Tia on your bed," said Tess almost apologetically.

"But I thought you said that when I moved in, my room was my room and no one else would be allowed in it without my permission. That is what we agreed, isn't it?"

"Well, yes. It is, Cristin," she stammered. "All I did was drop the letter on your bed. But if you prefer, I'll just leave your correspondence on the front hall table."

"That's perfect. Thank you." Cristin bounded down the stairs and gave Tess a hug, as if the confrontation had never occurred. "Let me take your coat and hang it in the hall closet." Her icy inflection had melted into a warm, embracing resonance.

"Thank you. Aren't you home from school early?' she guardedly asked.

"My last class canceled and I don't have to be at the museum until 4:30." She had a job at The Art Center as a docent, giving tours of the galleries five times a week. The curator had not only been willing to accommodate her schedule but she earned extra credit towards her art history class.

"So you won't be home for dinner?"

"No. As a matter of fact, I should be going. I'll get my things together and be home around nine."

She bolted up the stairs and left Tess in the hallway. She knew that Tess was psychoanalyzing the scene, questioning whether she had reason to be insulted or concerned about her guest's sudden unyielding demand for privacy. She would probably conclude that it was all a misunderstanding.... that Cristin may have been violated in the past and was paranoid about her belongings. *Whatever.*

Cristin left the house with a feeling of power and a sense of independence. She knew she was smarter than most people-she was on track.

The afternoon smelled of budding trees and thawing snow. Despite the cool air, the melting ice and softening breezes promised the coming of spring. The winter had been unsubtle and long, and all of its captives were looking forward to their release. The boulevards were stained with dirty thawing snow that gushed into the gutters and echoed in storm drains like the sound of micro-waterfalls. Although the temperature still hovered around thirty-five degrees, young machismic men wore short-sleeved shirts and unbridled children rode their bikes through the water in the streets.

With Berlioz' *Symphonie Fantastique* blaring through her car speakers, Cristin entered the parking lot of The Art Center. The lot was full, which meant she had a large flock to lead that night. Rather than entering through the employees' door at the rear, she elected to walk up the wide, steep front steps. The doors were solid oak, thick and carved with panels that depicted a story of the settling of the area, like Midwestern Baptistery Doors. She pushed them open and entered a compartmentalized different world.

Her first tour began with a bombshell. As she looked into the faceless sheep, she thought she saw Sondra Rampling, dressed in a hooded raincoat, common apparel for nocturnal Minneapolitans. Cristin hesitated and paused. Also in the crowd, her supervisor Ms. Stapleton, assessed her employee's effectiveness with a stern uplifted eyebrow. Cristin recovered her poise. By rote, she extolled the virtues of early twentieth century German painters and rerouted her eyes to ferret out Sondra who had vanished.

Between tours, Cristin took a brisk walk into the night which had fallen like an iron curtain. Her eyes batted quickly as her mind focused on the bizarre sighting in the gallery. *Perhaps it had only been someone who looked like Sondra. Probably not. Was it sheer coincidence that Sondra be visiting the place where Cristin worked? Probably not. Didn't Sondra live in another city? Be that what it may, why hadn't she stayed? Why had she disappeared without any acknowledgment?* There were no reassuring answers.

During her second tour, when she entered the third gallery, she smelled a familiar musk in the air. She quickly turned and saw him. Cloaked in a long tweed overcoat and smiling proudly, Ren stood like an illumined Greek statue at the back of the room. Suddenly the tour group evaporated and she was speaking only to him. He would have to sense her attention and would probably chalk it up to him being the only one she recognized. But his attendance was a good sign. A good sign indeed.

~ ~ ~

Ren's arrival home was delayed because the rain had embossed the side streets with a slick shiny rite of spring, necessitating his drive to be slow and deliberate. Tess greeted him at the door, dressed in concern, lips pursed, brow knitted.

"What's up?" he asked as she moved towards the sofas and motioned him to sit.

"I was worried about you driving on these slippery streets."

"That's all? You look anxious."

"Well, I need to run something by you, honey. Something did happen today that's really bothering me." She nervously adjusted her skirt and brushed the hair from her face. "This morning, before I left to do my research, the mail arrived and there was a letter to Cristin from Tia. I threw it in on her bed. When I came home this afternoon she was here. When I greeted her, she jumped all over me. Her exact words were, 'Why did you go into my room today?' She then proceeded to sternly remind me that we had told her that when she moved in with us, her room would be her own, with total privacy. Rennie, I wasn't prying. I merely dropped a letter on her bed. But she insinuated that she felt violated. The incident has bothered me all day."

"Are you sure you're not overreacting?"

"I've gone through it a dozen times. I don't think I am. Part of me feels guilty for even bringing this up. I love Cristin. You know I do. But I wish you could have heard her voice. It was so 'in my face'. "

"It's probably just an isolated episode. Hormones. I'm sure she'd feel terrible if she thought she'd offended you. She's a kind, sensitive woman."

"Woman? She's in her early twenties."

"What should I call her, a girl?"

"I suppose you're right. I think of her as being so young, it hadn't occurred to me that you look at her as a woman, that's all." Tess adjourned to the recesses of her insecurities and envisioned Cristin as a man might see her, then quickly changed the subject.

"I'm writing an article for *Rainbow Publications* on bird migrations, honey. I took a hike on the golf course this morning and the herons and egrets are back and I saw seven sand hill cranes tracking mud all over the seventh green. You would have loved it. Oh, and a blue heron spotted me and took off with his enormous wings spread and his skinny legs dangling, stretched out behind him. I swear he wasn't more than twenty feet from the weeds where I was standing."

"How did you know it was a he?"

"You just love to hear me admit how gorgeous male birds are, you rat."

"But I'll be the first to admit in the human species, it is the females that win the beauty contests." He deferred with an adoring grin.

"By the way, I had a call from Serena tonight. She wants me to stop by sometime this week to discuss something that she won't broach over the phone."

"That's a bit mysterious. Be sure to tell her that Lissa thought that she was, and I quote, 'the coolest old lady' she'd ever met."

Tess shook her head and rolled her eyes in amusement to think that her husband thought that a remark like that would be received as a compliment.

Shortly after dinner, Cristin came home. She wandered into the living room and gave each of them a hug.

"Tess, I want to apologize for snapping at you this afternoon. I'm a little sensitive about the privacy of my room. I always have been. But I had no right to question you the way I did. Will you accept my apology?"

Tess glanced at Ren with a look of shame that she'd been so shallow as to have wrongly judged the girl. "Think nothing of it, sweetheart."

"Oh, but I do. I'm truly sorry. You both have been so good to me. I would never mean to hurt or insult you in any way. I hope you know that. And Rennie, it was wonderful to see you at The Art Center tonight. A familiar face among strangers is a sight for sore eyes, believe me."

"Art Center? Tonight? " Tess asked, not concealing her bewilderment.

"I forgot to tell you. On my way home, I stopped by to see our little docent in action. I caught most of her second act...I mean, tour. And by the way, Mademoiselle, you were terrific. I was very impressed. Tessa. You need to see her in action."

"What do you mean?"

"Well, you never know when hot fresh talent will be discovered. The next thing you know, she could be anchoring the six o'clock news."

"You are far too flattering, Rennie. But thank you. I really do like my job. Tess, I'd love it if you'd come down some night too. I hadn't realized before tonight how much it means to me to have someone I know there. Oh, and before I forget, guess who I saw tonight! Your friend from high school, Sondra."

"Sondra? What was she doing there? Did you talk to her?" asked Tess without reserve, while mentally noting that Cristin had twice called her husband Rennie.

"No. She vanished as quickly as she appeared. Listen, I'm beat. I'll see you both in the morning. Goodnight." She was gone in one fluid movement.

Tess and Ren stared at each other with the look that either meant I don't know what to say or I don't know where to start.

"How about a drink?"

"Would it sound too melodramatic to say 'make mine a double?'" Tess attempted to jest.

"Sweetheart, I'd pour you one if you knew what you were talking about. Let's face it you're a classy lady who drinks nothing but fine wine." Ren intended his comment to be a compliment and punctuated it with a wink. Extolling the virtues of fine Napa Valley wines, he opened a bottle of chilled Chardonnay and asked, "What's Sondra doing in town this time? Did she call you?"

"No, she didn't. I haven't spoken to her since her visit when I was caught in that storm."

"Why do you suppose she went to see Cristin? After all, it's a bit of a coincidence that she just happened to be at The Art Center when Cristin was conducting a tour. She doesn't even live here. I remember having asked this before but I'll ask it again: What's going on?"

"I haven't the slightest notion. Let's chalk it up to coincidence. After all, she didn't even stay to talk to Cristin. Maybe she didn't recognize her. Maybe it wasn't Sondra. We're making too much of it. May I make a toast?"

"Of course."

"Here's to not worrying. Not about Sondra and not about Cristin."

They entwined their arms as was their personal custom and savored the smooth blend of fine California grapes.

"Excellent toast. And you must promise to honor your toast. As you witnessed tonight, Cristin is fine, never better. She's not angry with you. That was a sincere apology if I've ever heard one."

"You're right. How is it that I married such a wise man?"

"You just got lucky. Any other questions?"

"Only one," Tess paused dramatically, momentarily biting her lower lip. "Did you hear Cristin call you Rennie?"

"No. Any more questions?"

"Just one more. Why didn't you mention that you went to The Art Center tonight?"

Chapter 17

The following week. Cristin was sheer perfection. She returned phone calls for Tess, bought groceries, organized closets. She arose at dawn taking care of household chores before she left for the day. There were no incidents breeding doubt or bearing hints of ill will. None whatsoever.

Tess had buried the isolated incident until the afternoon she visited Serena. As she stood at her neighbor's front door, she inhaled the fragrance of the trees and noticed that she could no longer see her breath suspended in the air like small vaporized clouds. Spring had arrived and the promise of new beginnings was heir apparent to every one of nature's details. Serena greeted her with a locked embrace and a dancing smile that confirmed her genuine affection.

"Come in, my dear," she said with her raspy breathy inflection. Serena took Tess's hand and ushered her to kitchen, like a mother guiding her young child. The house smelled of cinnamon, apples, brown sugar and lemon. Hot apple pies lined the kitchen counters like pastries in a bakery window, each with golden crusts, fluted with expert symmetry, and appliquéd with patterns of tiny golden leaves.

"Oh Serena, they smell so good and they're beautiful. Tell me your secret."

"There's no secret. Like everything else, it takes practice. But perfect practice. Practicing something poorly will give you poor results. Practicing perfection leads to perfect results. The caliber of practice makes the difference. End of lecture. Please sit down and forgive an old lady for sermonizing. At my age, when time feels lamentably finite, shall we say, there is an urgency to say only what really matters. I regret I didn't understand this sooner."

"Another existential moment with Serena! You should have been a minister." Tess squeezed her friend's shoulder, conspicuously lacking in muscle. "You could have called that little sermonette *From Pies to Piety*."

Serena laughed. "You know, I think I'm making up for lost time. I so admire your generation's sense of freedom to say whatever is on your mind. Granted, it has its pitfalls, but all in all, it is a blessing. I was raised in a generation that was to be seen and not heard. As far as I can tell, it had many negative consequences and only one blessing. We learned how to listen. That one skill has served me well but I've decided to live in the best of both worlds and go out speaking my mind." She chuckled. "Enough! Enough! Tell me about your writing. What project are you working on?"

Tess smiled. But before she could utter a word, Serena almost nervously continued to prattle. "I hope it's a good one, because I'll now freely admit that I live vicariously through your stories, Tess. They season my life like salt and pepper. And paprika, of course."

Tess smiled. "Well I don't know how interesting they are, but I'm doing an article on bird migration and another on drug use in local high schools. Is that diverse enough for you?"

"Variety is my favorite spice. What else is going on?"

"Well, my agent hasn't called to tell me that my short story collection has been picked up by a major publishing house, if that's what you mean. And very frankly, my novel is dying from terminal writer's block."

"Dear, tell me, are you writing a novel or writing a story?"

Tess reflected on the question and smiled at Serena's perceptiveness.

"Perhaps if you concentrate on writing a story, it will revive. After all, there's no right or wrong. It's your story."

"Thank you. I needed to hear that. Serena, on the phone the other day, you said you needed to talk to me. You sounded rather serious."

Serena poured the tea that had been steeping, inflating the air with peppermint. The lines in her forehead deepened and pensively pursing her mouth, she spoke.

"I had a disturbing visit from Cristin the other day."

"Disturbing? What happened?"

"It isn't what happened. It's what was said. She asked me some questions that I found disquieting. She disguised them in lovely verbal gift wrapping, but they were troublesome, nevertheless. She's a very clever girl. She asked if I knew if and when you were leaving town this month. Not both of you, but specifically you. She then proceeded to make a passing reference to her profoundly unhappy childhood."

"What?"

"Tess, how much do you really know about this girl? Our young friend is obviously appareled in a sweet nature and proper manners but something is not ringing true. I thought you told me that she had a loving family and her parents had recently died."

"That's what she told me."

"How did you come to meet her?"

"It's a long story."

"I hope I'm not out of line, Tess. I don't mean to alarm you but I'm genuinely concerned. Forgive me, but does she have any reason to hurt you?"

"Hurt me? Of course not! I'm the one who helped her when she had no one. Why would she want to hurt me?"

"I don't know. Why would she want to know when you were going to be out of town?"

Each question took Tess farther and farther into a world where delusions roamed like behemoths. Her head whirred with uncharted suspicions that felt neither comfortable nor plausible.

"You were right to say something, Serena. Thank you. I'll talk to her tonight." She resolved to do so as her mouth clenched like a lobster cage.

Walking home, carrying a pair of pies wrapped in plastic, Tess noticed young children playing and prancing like puppies on the front lawn across the street. The air smelled of crocus and crackled with the electric joy of children shouting. The talk with Serena had left her anxious and edgy and the night promised to be long. Rennie wasn't home and Cristin wasn't due for hours, which gave Tess all the more time to conjecture and conjure. It wasn't productive time, for the demons of her imagination stomped destructively on the floor of her heart. Cristin, ungrateful and deceptive? It couldn't be. There had to be an explanation.

Hours later, the sound of the Jeep in the driveway warned her that Cristin was home. She heard the ceremonious ringing of the doorbell, then the door slam.

"Anyone home?"

"I'm in•the kitchen." Tess girded herself with courage and braced for the inevitable confrontation.

"Hi! How was your day?" Cristin entered the interrogation room with a canvas, draped in plastic, under her arm.

"Fine." Pointing at the object she asked, "Is that something you've painted?"

"Yes. I brought it home to show you and Rennie."

Tess bristled at the sound of her husband's pet name.

Cristin uncovered the canvas and revealed a macabre depiction of a young woman holding the limp body of younger girl. It was startling in composition, but grotesquely well-defined and demanded an emotional reaction.

"What do you call it?"

"I haven't decided. Either 'Victory' or 'Coming of Age.' They both work for me."

"But the younger girl looks dead."

"She is."

"But why?"

"I'll call it 'Coming of Age'. The more mature girl laying to rest the little girl of her past life. What do you think?"

"You're the painter. It's up to you. Cristin, please sit down. I need to talk to you."

"You sound serious. What's the matter?"

"I visited Elizabeth today."

"Is she sick?"

"No, she's fine. But in casual conversation, she mentioned a couple things you shared with her that concern me. I need you to explain."

"Of course, Tess. Ask me anything."

"Correct me if I'm wrong. You told me you had close to an idyllic childhood, did you not?"

"Yes, I had a wonderful life, why?"

"Because Elizabeth said you referred to your unhappy childhood. What was that all about?"

"Oh, there was a time in my early teens when I was very depressed, but it passed. It was one of those girl things. I felt unpopular and different."

"Why did Elizabeth think you had a miserable life?"

"I have no idea."

"Cristin, why did you ask Elizabeth if she knew when I was going to be out of town this month?"

The room became eerily quiet. Cristin, speechless, appeared crushed under the weight of Tess's glare. She broke the silence with a statement that Tess could not have anticipated.

"I don't want to tell you."

"What kind of answer is that? Be truthful with me. We invited you into our home to share our lives and you repay me with ambiguous mumble-jumble? Be straight with me, please. Why did you want to know if I was leaving this month?"

"You're spoiling everything."

"Tell me," Tess demanded.

"Your birthday's this month! I wanted to have a surprise party for you, and I thought it would be easier to surprise you if you weren't around a few days beforehand, so I could call people and plan the party. That's all."

Cristin's soft brown eyes welled with tears giving her the appearance of a wounded puppy.

"I'm so sorry," said Tess. "I'm so sorry."

Cristin left the room and climbed the stairs to her inner sanctum where she was safe from recriminations of any kind, leaving Tess, alone and stunned. Tess's fears had been unwarranted. She had single-handedly lodged a cleaver of distrust into the tender young heart of her niece. She couldn't tell Rennie. It was too humiliating.

~ ~ ~

Cristin closed her door and clasped her hands together in a spirit of demented victory. Her wits had saved her once again. *A birthday party? Where had that spark of brilliance come from?* One thing was for sure: after being so spurnfully interrogated, there would certainly not be a birthday party this year. This "retracted' gesture would be Tess's unspoken punishment. And as for Elizabeth Morgan, she was not to be trusted. Cristin had underestimated the old lady's acuity. But it wouldn't happen again. Lesson learned. She was still royalty in a game of pawns.

That night when the lights were extinguished, Tess whispered to her husband, "Rennie, has Cristin mentioned anything to you about a birthday party?"

The answer was no.

~ ~ ~

For weeks, every time Tess passed Cristin's bedroom door she felt pangs of guilt and remorse for her groundless suspicions. She suffered, stoically and silently. As with most families, both the sting and bruise of misunderstanding lingered for a while but faded with time. This was true for people with healthy consciences.

Tess's birthday arrived and departed like a tide, bearing celebratory phone calls and cards. There was no surprise party. The only tension within the house was within Tess's mind. Cristin seemed comfortable and uninjured. Her correspondence with Tia had escalated and she had decided that a trip to Europe was imminent. She had enough money to get there and back and informed the household that she planned to leave in June. It would be an open-ended arrangement. Meanwhile, she said she spent her free time studying the art museums of Europe in order to orchestrate itineraries once she was abroad.

A month before Cristin left on her sabbatical, Tess came home one day to a pungent smell permeating the house. She guessed the sickening odor to be paint and knocked on Cristin's bedroom door.

"Cristin, are you in there?"

There was a scurrying inside and Cristin opened the door. She was dressed in a white smock, splashed with evidence of red, orange and yellow paint.

"What are you doing? The house reeks of paint. We agreed that you would leave the paint at school. I thought that was clear."

"Sorry," responded Cristin. "I'll open the windows. I wasn't expecting you home this early. I'll air it out right away."

Cristin closed her door as soon as Tess walked away. Dazed by Cristin's second unwitnessed display of insolence, Tess descended the stairway. Passing the hallway table she noticed a polished linen envelope, addressed to Ms. Tessa Monson in formal typeset. It was postmarked New York City with a return address from a publisher to whom she had sent her short stories months earlier. She ripped into the letter and read,

Dear Ms. Monson,

Congratulations! We are pleased to inform you that we have read your manuscript entitled Tears in the Ocean and wish to speak to you about having the exclusive rights to publish it.

If you are still interested in its publication, please speak to your agent about arranging a meeting with our legal department to discuss the terms of the contract.

We look forward to hearing from you, and once again, congratulations on your fine work.

Sincerely, Patricia Shelby Brookstone

Tess felt a lump of joy lodge in her throat, past which no sound could escape. Then her scream resounded and echoed through the house.

Cristin ran out of her room and hung over the banister "What's going on? What happened?"

"My book! My book! It's been accepted!"

Cristin pounded down the stairway in her stocking feet and hugged her with unrepressed enthusiasm. Swept up in her moment of glory, Tess perceived Cristin's reaction to be authentic. They were friends, they were family, sharing good news.

"This is the moment I've waited for, the feeling I've dreamed about. I can't believe it. I feel so light. I feel like I could fly." Then grabbing Cristin's shoulders and lightly shaking her, Tess exclaimed, "Oh Cristin, Rennie will be so proud of me! I must call him! Thank you for being here, right now. I'll never forget that I told you first. I'm so thrilled, really thrilled!"

Like a little girl, Tess twirled and slid across the hardwood floor in her woolen socks on the path to the telephone. She momentarily recaptured a feeling from twenty-five years earlier when Jeff Chandler had invited her to their high school prom. She could even smell the chocolate chip cookies she was baking in the oven at the time. How strange it was that she could remember so little from those days but she could recapture the excitement of that instant and actually smell the cookies.

Cristin ascended the stairs and locked herself within her room, cloistered from the rest of the house. The locks which she had installed on her bedroom and closets doors earlier that week became her security, her protection from the outside world. She opened her closet door and continued to paint.

Tess couldn't reach Ren and decided not to call anyone else before she told him. She sat down and tasted the triumph of the delicious moment. The world was finally going to read her short stories. Millions of people were going to share her thoughts and feelings. Her mother had once told her that if she couldn't express her thoughts, she didn't truly understand them. That was her rule of thumb. Of course she made allowances for the ineffable. Tess loved to live different lives through her characters, experience the unknown, and explore those behaviors that she morally chose not to act out. Writing gave her boundaries to cross and a discipline that gave meaning to her hours.

She thought about her parents and how pleased they would have been. If only she had she started her stories earlier in life so together they could have shared moments such as these. But she could hear Mum saying, "No regrets, dear. If you live your life honestly, you must never look back with regret. Play out the cards life has dealt you." And her father with a mischievous lilt in his voice would have said, "I always knew you had it in you, girl." Tess missed her parents at times like this.

Mum, Constance Larissa MacIver, was born in 1922, the second daughter of Cameron and Christine MacIver of Sherbrooke, Quebec. She was the middle child, with an older sister, Patience, and a younger brother, Gilander. Although her parents, Scottish immigrants, were poor, they were self-educated and lovingly sacrificed their lives for the betterment of their children in a land of opportunity. For years, Mum spellbound her children with yarns of their Scottish heritage. And a wonderful storyteller she was. She spoke of the Scots as a fierce, proud people, hardworking and stubborn, who had passed on a legacy that was strong and principled. Coming to Canada, Tess's grandparents intended to travel farther west and settle in Ontario, but the beauty of Quebec had arrested their spirits as they settled in an eastern township of the picturesque province of the fleur-de-lis.

The stories Mum told of her childhood were idyllic in a storybook kind of way. The lifestyle was simple, unsophisticated, and demanding. But the memories were warm and charming, and contained an intimacy of shared experiences involving few people and fewer settings. She told of summers at her Uncle Roderick's farm where the kitchen always smelled of the next meal: nothing fancy, just delicious and plentiful. Every morning her Aunt Mattie would fix a huge breakfast of fried eggs broken from fresh brown shells, thick slabs of bacon and ham, or hand-stuffed sausage, fried potatoes, buttermilk pancakes with maple syrup from Vermont, and thick toasted bread with gobs of homemade strawberry jam. The table was laid with a white cotton tablecloth with a blue rooster print and a beautiful blue glass pitcher brimming with milk, so white you remembered it for the rest of your life. Her Uncle Roderick and Cousins Douglass and Russell would inhale the food with vigor, grab their jackets, and leave for the day. Aunt Mattie would then bake either berry pies or loaves of bread, alternating every other day, followed by the preparation of the largest meal of the day, "noontime supper," which was then packed and brought to the fields when the sun was high in the sky and furious with heat. Delivering supper was thrilling for a young city girl, as one could practically taste the sunshine infused with wheat and alfalfa. The sky was bigger than she'd ever see again, a cloudless dome that covered the world like a big blue cake cover. The children dangled their legs off the back of the rickety old wagon piled with hay and they watched the farmhouse disappear from view. The only sounds that could be heard were the buzz of insects, the creaking of wagon wheels and squeals of young voices over bumps on the narrow dirt road.

Mum's favorite time of day was when the menfolk came home at sundown. The boys would disappear upstairs and Uncle Rod would take off his shirt, revealing an enormous barrel chest and muscular arms, her introduction to the appeal of the male body. As an evening ritual, he would draw water from the kitchen pump into a large pewter pitcher and then pour it into a white tin bowl in the parlor. And she would watch him scrub, first his hands, then his face and head, his sunburned neck, under his arms and his mammoth chest. Then as certain as the day was long, he started the ritual all over again. But this time he sang, in a deep baritone voice, the kind that would make everyone in the house stop what they were doing and listen. Every evening Uncle Rod reverently, in full voice, sang "In the Garden." It was his way of thanking his Lord for the benediction of the day and the blessing of the evening to come.

Mum told charming stories that would fill her listeners' minds with images and tastes and smells that were as real as if they'd been there. But the most spellbinding story of all was how she had met their father. The story had bred complicated feelings within her family but was delightfully romantic nonetheless. On the afternoon of December 19, 1942, she had headed home on the train from McGill University where she'd just taken her exams and was dining in the dining car alone. The man at the next table was also dining alone. They smiled at each other with a look of acknowledgment, nothing more. After their entrees had been cleared, he asked if he could join her for dessert. His company was comfortable, unpretentious, and intelligent, and she found herself losing track of time as she smiled into his Irish eyes and wondered what it would feel like to be kissed by him.(Mum's story would become more detailed and sensual as her children grew older. She would blush, and they would urge her on.) She was sorely disappointed when the trip was over and they parted ways. His name was Thomas. He was visiting a family east of Montreal and that's all she knew. She gathered her things and took a bus for the last leg of her trip. She barely remembered anything about the ride. All she saw was his face. Perhaps this was the man she'd been waiting for and had lost him forever. Mum had been raised, reading *Anne of Green Gables* and its sequels, so she was hopelessly romantic, with a flair for the dramatic. As she always said, "To borrow a phrase from Anne, the thought of losing Thomas was 'beyond endurance'." She arrived home to a household of welcomes, hugs and kisses. Even the neighbors were there to greet her. She was the one in the family who had made the grades, so she was the one to attend the university. She was the star.

Shortly after arriving, she excused herself to freshen up after her journey. She entered her old bedroom and laid down on her childhood bed. She nestled into the plush eiderdown and smelled the familiar scent of down feathers, stared up at the four posts of the Maplewood bed that her father had built, closed her eyes for a moment to think of Thomas, and fell asleep.

She was awakened by the creak of the door opening and Patience tiptoeing to her side, and whispering. "There's someone I want you to meet, lassie. He's come all the way from Toronto. Get up. We'll be waiting for you in the living room."

Mum knew she was home because only within her family home did anyone call her lassie. Her father had chosen her middle name Larissa and called her his little Scottish lassie. It felt good to be home again. Sleepily disoriented for a minute or two, she remembered feeling a bit embarrassed that she'd fallen asleep. She ran a brush through her long chestnut hair and stumbled into the light of hallway, squinting to focus.

"I'd like you to meet my sister Constance," said Patience with pride, as she introduced a handsome young man.

"Constance?"

"Thomas? What are you doing here?" Mum asked in disbelief.

"You've met before?" asked Patience.

"Yes, on the train. Just hours ago," explained Mum.

As Mum told the story, she and Thomas knew that their meeting was fateful. Within few brief hours they recognized a chemistry of enthusiasm and a mutuality of values that one rarely comes across in a lifetime. The weeks to come were awkward for the family, especially for Patience, who was also in love with Thomas. But Mum and Thomas Carlyle Monson were married within the year and moved to Boston. Mum's children never really knew Aunt Patience. Tess suspected that Patience would tell the story quite differently.

Thomas Carlyle Monson was born in Dublin, Ireland in 1912, and died of heart disease in 1972 at the age of 60, only months after Tia was born. As a boy, he was a street fighter and an altar boy, defending his friends with his fists and honoring his family with his candles. His father taught him pugilism; His mother taught him manners. He was both a lady's man and a man's man; both a lover and a fighter. He was strong, rugged, opinionated, and stubborn and operated from a core of integrity. He was gentle and courteous, honoring both the outer and inner beauty of the fairer sex. He was a charming Irishman who knew who he was, and during the seventies had great difficulty understanding people who deserted their families "to find themselves." "Selfish delusion, nothing but selfish delusion," he would mumble with disgust. Mum was his "Wild Scottish Rose" and he openly subscribed to the adage that the greatest gift a father could give his children was to love their mother. Tess remembered very little about her father from her early childhood, but was mindful of a protection that he represented to her. He was her daddy who could slay the dragons and shield her from harm. During her high school years when he was in ill health, he was more approachable, mellow, willing to express his thoughts with an enviable eloquence. Tess had the sense to talk with him, ask him questions and listen to his insights. For those hours on earth, she was eternally grateful, not only for the gift of human intimacy but for an insight of mortality and a compassion for the infirm.

Frequently at the dinner table, Thomas the philosopher would insert a famous quotation within his blessing. Prayers such as "Dear Lord, we thank Thee for this bounty. May we be always be grateful and remember what Socrates taught us, 'An unexamined life is not worth living.' Amen.; or "Dear Heavenly Father, May we take this moment to express our gratitude for our many blessings and remember what Victor Frankl taught us-that there are only two races of mankind; the decent and the indecent. Amen." Thomas took his children through Philosophy 101 by the time they entered high school. She recalled him saying that when a man's lies dying, when he reassesses his life, he does not think about material things or accomplishments. He only thinks about the people he loves. Love was all that mattered.

Tess had been blessed by two extraordinary parents who'd been taken from her too soon. She could still hear her mother saying, "There are those who look, but do not see, those who listen, but do not hear." And her father saying, "When the student is ready, the master appears." *If only she could have one hour with them now. She would listen and she would hear.*

Tears broke her reminiscences. Her acceptance letter had sparked a confidence that dreams were not only necessary but also attainable. There was nothing more onerous than striving without reward. There was nothing sweeter than recognition of creative endeavor. Rocking from side to side, with a smile that ached, she wrapped her arms around herself and hugged her soul. Her world was frighteningly ephemeral. The disillusionment that had painfully stabbed her an hour beforehand had evaporated, and she felt invincible.

Chapter 18

"Pardonnez-moi, Monsieur."

A man whose face was buried in the morning edition of *Le Figaro* glanced, then gazed, at the coy beauty with the resonant voice, the woman who had now disarmingly interrupted his petit dejeuner. She proceeded to take her own table without acknowledgment of his watchfulness.

Cristin knew how to move. As a child she had studied the pros. The posture of Grace Kelly, the pout of Lauren Bacall. She'd practiced a balance of aloofness and attention and was always on stage.

The gentleman watched her coat drop from her shoulders, exposing a pearl pink cashmere sweater that dramatically revealed her curvaceous chest. He stared at a cameo that dropped from her slender neck and lodged in her cleavage; he appeared to have forgotten what he'd been reading, sipping his café au lait without calling attention to his attention.

As she ordered from the menu, she softened her voice to disguise her accent. She had the spark of an American, but the style of a French woman. She knew it was a luscious combination, the excitement of a foreigner iced with the elusive mystique that only French women had mastered. Crossing her legs slowly, titillating her participating voyeur and deliberately dangling her shoe from her delicately angled ankle, she raised her eyes to him with a blinkless, penetrating stare that demanded privacy. With a twitch of her eyebrow and a refined yet barely decipherable nod, she hinted a smile and looked away.

She'd only been in Paris for a few days and had adapted like a chameleon. Tia was right. It was truly a city of style. Learning one's way around a new city was normally an ordeal. But this wasn't Cleveland; this was Paris. The Latin Quarter, the Left Bank, the Seine, the Eiffel Tower, Notre Dame, the Louvre, the Sorbonne. With a few landmarks cemented in her mind map, she was ready to explore. In the morning she visited the Centre Pompidou and watched street performers; mimes, artists, and musicians in the open plaza. She fed bread crumbs to the pigeons and listened to the passers-by. She had an ear for languages and easily distinguished the French and Spanish dialects from the Dutch and German that were remarkably common. Her own accent was primitive, but she tried to speak French without butchering it, which was all the natives asked of her.

Tia was visiting a former teacher who had moved to Paris and Cristin opted to spend the day exploring on her own. She headed for the Musee d'Orsay, taking her time as she walked across one of the numerous bridges that spanned the Seine. Both ends of the bridge were capped with colossal gold sculptures, hovering over the river. She passed a group of eight elderly men, talking in rapid-fire French, and pointing to an object below. She peeked through the iron filigree in search of the curiosity, only to find a dead duck floating down the river. Nothing particularly unusual, she supposed. But wasn't it interesting that the men not only had the time, but took the time, to discuss such an inconsequential scene. It would never happen in America.

The air battled between sweet blossoms and rank river life. The familiar sounds of birdsong and barking dogs were practically muted by the unfamiliar sounds of barges and foreign taxi horns. Cristin wasn't thinking about Ren or Tess or Tia. Neither was she planning her next manipulation. Rather, she relaxed, basking in her new sense of reckless anonymity and freedom.

Paris was grand and rich and inspiring. Around each corner was a magnificent cathedral, boulevard, or park. Cristin closed her provincial closet door and walked through a looking glass into a wonderland that Alice would have been too young to appreciate. And for the second time in her life, she actually felt blessed.

She entered the Musee D'Orsay like a princess occupying a palace that was rightfully hers. The converted train station was gloriously enormous, bigger than life, much bigger than she had imagined. The hallways were wide and light streamed from the skylights in shafts. Renoir, Monet, Degas, everywhere she looked. She strolled through the galleries, pausing in front of works she had studied in her childhood. Her mother's art book had been one of her few childhood joys and had prepared her for the appreciation of this visual feast.

The light issuing from Millet's *Spring* looked authentic. *How did he do that?* she thought. She vowed to go to the cliffs at Entretat after a storm to experience what Delacroix was able to capture. She smiled as she walked past Whistler's *"Portrait of his Mother,"* as it looked out of place, commonplace. She stared at *Angelus* and wondered who had just been buried and what or who had been responsible for his death. Every piece of art had a story to tell; of people or places; in morning sun or evening mist; in lily ponds or dance salons. The world was an ever-expanding composite of stories, nothing more. Stories destined to be remembered or forgotten. Cristin would paint stories, devise them for her own amusement, and for the seduction of others.

Hours later, her aching feet wailed that it was time to go. One in front of the other, they steered her to the street alive with puddles, trickling waterways, and the dancing drops, all evidence of the unexpected rain. She glanced at her watch, discovering that six hours had passed. She had lost herself in a time warp. Pulling her coat over her head, she ran toward the café across the street, while thinking, "My kingdom for an umbrella."

As she passed the customers in the café, they smiled at her, as some of them had surely seen her dashing across the boulevard. She found a seat by the window, shook out her coat, and ordered a hot bowl of onion soup and a glass of wine from the Bordeaux region. She then checked the faces around her. The couple to her right were in love. She felt envy. The old man to her left smelled and looked lonely. She felt disgust and pity. The gentleman to her rear was engrossed in reading his menu and hadn't noticed her at all. She felt snubbed.

Through the water-beaded window, she gazed at the flower vendors. Ravel's *Jardins dans la Pluie* played in the background. A strange synchronicity. The world seemed connected, which prompted her to think that if there were a God, He had a complex sense of humor. After sipping her soup and slowly "chewing" the richness of her wine, she paid her bill and exited the café, but not before deliberately bumping into the unadoring stranger behind her and forcing him to notice her. The satisfaction was elusive but necessary.

Darkness fell on The City of Lights like a guillotine as Cristin approached her accommodations. The perimeter of the courtyard was bordered with pomegranate bushes and commanding center stage was a fountain of Poseidon, trident and all. She entered the parlor where citrus potpourri, jasmine candles, and eucalyptus firewood charged the air, reminding her of a soap and candle shop in Minneapolis. The clock chimed eight o'clock with a resonance that suggested an ineffable holiness as the innkeeper welcomed her home, in French of course, informing her that her friend had arrived minutes earlier. There was a delight in understanding a foreign tongue, a personal triumph of sorts. She passed two old men playing chess in front of a blazing stone fireplace which looked to be at least three hundred years old. As she climbed the narrow spiraling staircase, she heard one of the men bellow the French equivalent of "Checkmate!" as he exploded with a guttural, coughing fit of laughter which rather vilely declared his victory.

"Welcome back," Tia greeted her.

"Thanks. How long have you been here?"

"Only a little while. Did you have a good day?"

"Incredible. How about you? How was your teacher?"

"Madame Masimbert is a wonderful friend. But she's looking so old and frail. Her illness has taken a toll. I was shocked."

"What's wrong?"

"I'm not certain. But she's made arrangements to be cremated. And she gave me some of her books. Look, her copy of *Candide*. And she even inscribed it."

Cristin opened the inside cover and read, "To Tia, my dear student. Remember to always cultivate your own garden. Much love, Madame."

"Wow."

"I know. This has been an emotional day. I can't imagine Madame not being here. And when she's gone, who is even going to remember her? She doesn't have any children. She had students. But how long can I keep her memory alive? My children will hear of her but their children probably won't. And then she's lost as if she never was. I mean, that's a sobering thought. How much do you remember your grandparents?"

"I barely remember my parents."

"That's awful. You don't mean it, do you?"

"Yes, I do."

"Whatever happened to your parents?"

"They died in an auto accident. But I don't want to talk about it."

"I'm sorry. But doesn't it make you wonder what life is all about? If even the next generation will think about us? It's so melancholy, so depressing."

"Tia, you take everything far too seriously. No one is going to remember us. It's egocentric to think otherwise. I think of life as more of a game, an amusement."

"How can you really believe that? I hardly think the starving people of India or Africa see life as an amusement."

"Life is to enjoy. Make the most of it. Have fun. That's all."

"But that sounds so shallow. You know, hedonistic. There has to be meaning. I feel too deeply for this all to be for nothing. How do you explain beauty?"

"I don't. I just enjoy it."

"But what about our search for truth?"

"Your search for truth, Tia. I'm not searching. I'm enjoying."

"I can't believe you. How can you be so smart and not think about these things?"

"I just don't. At least I'm honest. What you see is what you get." Cristin stood up and walked to the iron bathtub with lion's paw feet. "I bought some plumeria bubble bath at the parfumerie at the Centre Pompidou this morning. You're welcome to use it."

Cristin saw Tia open her volume of poetry, probably to ponder her mortality, questioning her "egocentric" need to find meaning in beauty and the search for truth. She poured hot water into the "animal" tub that frankly looked more like an ornamental piece of furniture than a serviceable bathtub. The smell of plumeria permeated the air with each bucketful of added water.

Standing next to the tub, Cristin dropped her dress to her ankles. She immodestly stepped out of her panties and unsnapped her white lace bra with no sign of self-consciousness. She knew that Tia could peripherally see her step into the tub, like a woman watching another woman in an eighteenth century boudoir. Cristin slipped into the warm water, piled her heavy, silky hair on top of her head, and proceeded to follow the curves of her large, full breasts with a soapy sponge.

Tia watched from the corners of her eyes. Then to break what seemed like an awkward silence, she spoke. "The plumeria smells wonderful."

Cristin leaned into the suds, noticing the rainbow reflections of green and pink in the bubbles as they crackled. "Yes, it does smell good." She paused. "There's no meaning in it. It just smells good."

"Shut up." Tia smiled as she rolled over on her bed and cracked open her book of poetry. Her eyes landed on a famous passage, highlighted in yellow marker and she read it aloud.

> *"Beauty is truth, truth beauty-that is all*
> *Ye know on earth, and all ye need to know."*

"John Keats said it. So there."

Cristin smiled. She figured that with the assurance of John Keats, Tia felt sane and intelligent. She could tell by the satisfied smile on her romantic friend's face that the last thought that probably crossed her mind was that she liked that Cristin played the devil's advocate-because Cristin was open and honest.

~ ~ ~

Traveling alone had its advantages. For one thing, a sole traveler was infinitely more approachable. So the spectrum of new experiences and the likelihood of meeting interesting people and opportunities increased exponentially. Contrary to popular opinion, it was also less expensive for a young woman to travel alone; for almost without exception, Cristin was joined while dining and her check was picked up in exchange for the pleasure of her company or the prospect of seeing her that night. Of course, when alone, the joy of sharing a Mediterranean sunset or the aroma of freshly baked bread while walking past a boulangerie wasn't possible. But Cristin preferred the loneliness of privacy to the camaraderie of sharing. Tia had gone back to school for the semester, so Cristin had taken off through Provence, en route to The Riviera.

It was in St. Tropez that she met one of Tia's acquaintances, a tall woman with long straight raven black hair and grey eyes that could laser through steel. Cristin had been eyeing a piece of burgundy silk, a transparent wrap for evening wear, when Yvette interrupted her concentration.

"Pardon. Are you not Tia's friend from Des Estates Unis? We met at the Farmer's Market in Grenoble, no?"

"Oui. Je m'apelle Cristin?"

"Please, may I practice my English? I am Yvette."

"Of course. What a coincidence to see you here. I don't know another soul in Europe, so this is remarkable."

After a few minutes of polite interchange, Yvette asked, "Would you like to join me and my friends for dinner tonight? I'm here on holiday for a few days and I'd love it if you could."

"Done. Where? And when?"

"We're staying at the Hotel Solitaire. I'm in a hurry now but you can meet us in the lobby at 7:30. Dress is casual."

"7:30. I'll be there. Thanks for the invitation."

The lobby of the Hotel Solitaire was attired in "European Splendid" and crowned with sculpted artwork within each panel of a cavernous vaulted ceiling. The sofas of Louis XIV vintage, uncomfortable and upholstered with rich brocaded fabric screamed that they were pieces of art, not merely furniture. Rather than one enormous arrangement in the rotunda, as in luxurious American hotels, small bouquets of flowers crowned each sitting room table. Then again, America's lavish display of affluence would be gauche to the French. The lobby smelled of age. Old floors, old walls, and old money. Cristin arrived early and walked from the lobby to the balcony that ran the length of the hotel and overlooked the ocean boardwalk below. The Mediterranean smelled like a history of military and mercantile, from Africa to Byzantium, from Europa to the Straits of Gibraltar. She mused at the stories it could tell.

Yvette and her friends made a raucous entrance from the elevator into the lobby. Cristin spun around to catch her first glimpse of the group and was surprised at the number of them. There must have been close to a dozen.

"Cristin! Come here, mon ami. Meet everyone. Everyone, this is my American acquaintance, Cristin, not Christine-Cristin. Introductions later." Yvette quipped, as an aside, "You'll never remember their names anyway."

"Nor want to," remarked the man directly facing her. He looked like an art student from the Sorbonne: Bohemian dress and handsomely manicured. "Don't mind us. Hello, I'm Francois," said the handsome Frenchman as he extended his hand.

Cristin responded. "How do you do?"

A blast of cold evening air slapped the party as they stepped onto the boulevard. The sun was setting and a flock of flapping geese honked overhead en route from their afternoon feeding grounds to their nocturnal resting place.

"Do you have geese in America?" Francois asked in his delicious French accent.

"Of course," Cristin replied. "I don't know how similar they are to French geese. But a goose is a goose, right? The only goose I know is the Canada goose. It's beautiful with a white strap neck marking."

"I read once that geese mate for life. Really quite admirable, n'est pas?" coaxed Francois.

"If monogamy is a virtue, then yes."

"Do you, an American, not espouse true love?"

"Of course. But you were talking about fidelity, were you not?"

"Can you separate the two?"

"Hey, you two, nothing existential before we dine." Yvette interrupted as she nudged Francois from the rear.

They walked a couple of blocks during which time Cristin found herself caught in a web of high energy and intelligent banter. It occurred to her that perhaps she'd been flying solo too long. They turned into an Italian trattoria like a flock of geese following their leader in perfect formation and hit a wall of garlic and extraordinary sauces. She'd never eaten Italian food abroad before and the striking aromas seduced her appetite.

Sitting around a round table together accelerated the process of getting to know strangers. Cristin was physically in proximity to everyone present, within eye contact and hearing range. Even if not speaking directly to another, impressions would be made.

Francois manipulated to sit next to Cristin, which was amenable with her as she'd not spoken to anyone else. On her other side sat Hannah, an Austrian girl from Salzburg, who appeared rigid and smelled of nicotine. Cristin experienced her first "family style" dining in a French Italian restaurant. Everyone ordered what they wanted with the understanding that all of the entrees would be passed around the table for everyone else to sample, a mandatory buffet of sorts. The idea seemed barbaric, but Cristin later reevaluated her judgment and concluded that she quite enjoyed the variety, adopting the adage "When in Rome..."

The wine flowed like the river Seine, belts and tongues loosened, and eyelids began to droop.

"Did you know that Reno, Nevada, is west of Los Angeles, California?" exclaimed the young French woman with the tinted granny glasses, resting on her Caligulan nose.

"That's preposterous," responded Yvette. "Even I know that California is west of Nevada and I'm not particularly educated in American geography."

The trivia queen persisted. "Did you know that most of South America lies east of the United States? If you fly due south from Maine, you graze the west coast of Peru."

"Cristin! Jump in at any time. Ms. Magellan here needs to be put in her place!"

"Geography was never my forte," admitted Cristin, who saw the room whirling to a bacchanalian dance.

When the crowd became sufficiently satiated and the conversation lulled, Francois took up the gauntlet and announced to the table, "On our way to the restaurant tonight, Cristin and I were discussing fidelity and love, whether they were virtues or follies."

"And what did you conclude, oh great philosopher-king?" taunted the heavy set man who reminded Cristin of Orson Wells, his beard dribbled with alfredo sauce.

"We were cut short. But as I recall I was about to ask Cristin how one could embrace true love but not uphold faithfulness as an ideal."

Cristin retorted, "Faithfulness, an ideal? Yes. A reality? Difficult."

"But are we only to practice what is facile? Is not upholding an ideal that may prove difficult, what separates us from dogs?" suggested an anonymous female across the table. "I'm curious. What do you feel about bedding a married man?"

"If we're in love, I have no qualms about it," admitted Cristin.

"Do you not honor the commitment of marriage between him and his wife?"

"Why should I if he doesn't?"

"In vino veritas," interjected someone from the end of the table.

"Have you ever had an affair with a married man, Cristin?"

"No, but I wanted to and I would have had I'd the chance. You'd understand if you'd ever met Rennie." She heard her slip, but deduced from the foreign French faces that her faux pas hadn't been translated.

"I thought only French men had such lack of scruples," remarked Hannah facetiously. "I feel a case of indigestion coming on. Let's change the subject."

"I find your views amusing, Cristin," said Francois. "You must either be a maverick or a pariah among American women."

"Very frankly, I've never had this conversation before. It is nevertheless the truth."

"No, it's not the truth. It is what you truly believe. There is a distinction," remarked Francois.

"Perhaps you should learn to think through moral issues rather than feel your way," suggested the female stranger under her breath.

"Okay, new topic," exclaimed Francois in an effort to appease. "How long do you intend to travel, Cristin?"

She cleared her throat, subtly acknowledging his attempt to calm the turbulent waters of conversation. "Oh, perhaps a few more months. I've been traveling for over a month now. I love the freedom of total detachment."

"You haven't talked to Tia in over a month?" asked Yvette.

"No, should I have?"

"Well, let me put it this way. I talked to her yesterday and you might want to give her a call. Her handsome, filthy rich nephew is due in town this week. The French girls are already queuing up to meet him. You wouldn't want to miss the opportunity, would you?"

Cristin hadn't known that Shep was visiting abroad. Instantly she adjusted her plans to head back to Grenoble. The remainder of the evening was blurred by the effects of alcohol and her refocused concentration on Tia's nephew. The buzz of senseless conversation became almost exclusively French as the evening progressed, partially because tongues were relaxed, and partially because Cristin had obviously tuned out and there was no necessity to accommodate her.

Le Group emerged from the trattoria like a drunken flock, now following their leader with one-eyed peripheral vision. Then the unexpected happened. As they approached the corner of Chantreuse and St. Jerome, they witnessed a horrific accident. A young boy racing across the intersection was struck by an oncoming automobile and catapulted into the air like a scarecrow uprooted by a tornado. The merry, garrulous group collectively screamed and momentarily paralyzed. Francois ran to the boy where a crowd was gathering. The child's head was hanging to the side, neck broken, and his left leg bent behind his back and under his opposite shoulder. The innocent life had been snuffed out like a candle and all that remained was a facsimile of a rag doll, soaked in blood. There was no attempt to revive him, as his death was certain. Women wailed and men bellowed. Having entered his own living hell, the driver of the car, which had hit the child, cried in agony. These strangers knew of the boy's death before his family did. His mother was probably making dinner and his father rehearsing the lecture he'd deliver concerning his child's tardiness. And in one appalling moment, the child was dead and the driver would never again be the same.

"I feel physically ill." Yvette leaned her head into Cristin's shoulder.

Cristin didn't raise her arms to comfort her comrade but quietly said, "I think I'll wear my new scarf."

~ ~ ~

The following morning Cristin drove to Marseilles. The waves of the Mediterranean lapped the shores on her left, the sun following her like a persistent admirer. In the city, she called Tia to inform her of her arrival, and then caught a train that slithered through the valleys of Provence, like a speedy, silver snake. Tia met her at Le Gar and within minutes together, Tia burst with excitement about the arrival of her nephew. Like two French schoolgirls, arm in arm, they shopped for pastries, flowers, cheese and wine, in preparation for Shep's arrival.

Tia was happy that Cristin was back. They spent the evening swapping adventures and eventually focused on Shep. He was due the following day and had made plans to take a room a few blocks away in the home of a French family. His purpose in coming to France was to start anew; new country, new language, new people. And although not solicited, Tia intended to be instrumental in his healing process. After all, she knew dozens of lovely French women who would die to spend time with a devastatingly handsome American. Her nephew was a symbol of all that was good in men. He was kind, strong, and honest and was the standard against which all other men were measured.

"Tell me about Shep," asked Cristin as they lay on the rug in front of the hot flickering fire.

"He's wonderful. He's my sister Katie's son, my nephew, even though we're about the same age. To be perfectly frank, I've always been somewhat in love with him."

"Somewhat in love? Isn't that like being somewhat pregnant?"

"Cristin, you're outrageous. I've never met anyone like you." Tia rolled over and laughed.

Cristin remarked, "He would be the perfect man if he were rich."

"Oh, but he is. He is rich, young, handsome. Very handsome and very rich. Rumor has it that he's far richer than his very well-to-do family. You know, investments. Wise investments. Cristin, I'm so glad you're back. Shep is going to love you. It's great timing. Otherwise, you might have missed him."

Not a chance, thought Cristin.

~ ~ ~

On the morning of Shep's arrival, Tia was up with the birds and brimming with energy. As she filled croissants and arranged bouquets of irises and gladiolas, she chirped like a parakeet. She sporadically broke into song with a soft, soprano voice, resembling Snow White preparing the cottage for the arrival of her little men. Cristin maintained a more subdued demeanor as she sat at the kitchen table and sipped chamomile tea. She politely observed and marveled at the frenzy of activity created by only one woman.

"Six more hours and he'll be here, right in this very room!" Tia squealed. "We'll have to leave for the train station by three. What are you going to wear?" asked Tia.

"I've decided I'm not going to the station. I think it would be better if you met him alone. I'll meet him later tonight."

"Don't be ridiculous, Cristin. He called yesterday morning and I told him you'd be there. You can't disappoint him."

"Aren't you being a little melodramatic? I've never even met the man. It couldn't possibly be a disappointment. You go to the station alone. I'll see you both tonight." With that, Cristin rose from her chair like a Pharaoh's queen. With authority and finality, she knew that Tia had once again miscalculated and underestimated her.

~ ~ ~

Shep flew into Charles de Gaulle. He attracted the attentions of women wherever he went, and although, generally speaking, he didn't find French women beautiful, they were alluring. They were alluring and he was charming. And as Barrie once wrote regarding charm, "If you have it, you don't need to have anything else, and if you don't have it, it doesn't much matter what you have." On the plane to Paris, he'd met a lovely Swiss woman named Simone who was en route to Montreux. She had invited him to accompany her, but he'd promised Tia that he'd arrive in Grenoble that afternoon and was a man of his word. However, Paris was a living, breathing magnet. It took more than an iron will to escape its attraction and he vowed that he would soon return.

The train ride to Grenoble was like a slide show. While the ambient French conversations provided a muted nondescript soundtrack, images flashed inside his recent memory and outside the whirring windows. He was grateful for his blessings, but was no longer blessed with Peri. If only he had her, he wouldn't ask for anything else, but because he didn't have her anymore, nothing else mattered. Time passed slowly when he was inside his pain- a long, dark tunnel with no escape routes. He recalled how time had passed so quickly when he'd been happy. He stared out the window at a blur of thatched roofs, flower gardens and faceless figures. Perhaps a geographical change was only a futile effort to escape his pain. Time would tell.

An enormous porter with an accent a la Francais, a voice as deep as Porgy and as commanding as a James Earl Jones, walked through the car to announce the approach into Grenoble. Shep's heaviness lifted as he anticipated seeing his aunt, two years his junior. The engine slowed, the brakes screeched. He filled his heart with the love of family that would safeguard his survival.

He spotted Tia trying to act like a lady, but unable to contain her girlish glee. Her smile widened like a Cheshire cat and she bounced in her step as she shadowed his window. It felt good to feel the blood rushing from excitement, not anxiety. As he neared the exit, he smelled the grease from the tracks as steam spurted through the grated iron floor between passenger cars, momentarily shrouding his vision.

"Shep! Shep!" shrieked Tia. "Oh my God, you're here! You're really here!"

He dropped his valise as he stepped onto the platform and swung her around like a May pole ribbon. "Let me look at you," he said as he set her down. She had matured in face and body. Her eyes were Monson green and the freckles he had once teased her about had faded. She was in that wonderful stage between youth and maturity that she would grow to appreciate in the next decade.

Tia beamed; she exuberantly began to catalogue all the places they would go together and the scores of people she wanted him to meet. She then begged to hear first-hand information about the family. Hours later, as the wee small hours of the morning approached, Tia remarked that she was concerned about the conspicuous absence of her friend.

~ ~ ~

After the lights were extinguished, Cristin approached the house. The trellis at the end of the walkway was abundant with flowering jasmine, transforming the dewy night into a natural parfumerie. She breathed the bouquet with the intelligence of a chemist and the appreciation of a poet. She presumed that Shep had left earlier in the evening and she would make her entrance into his life the following day. Cristin would orchestrate their first encounter and he would surely find her captivating.

Quietly feeling the floor through the soles of her shoes, she entered the house with the stealth of a nocturnal feline. With her hands extended like a blind woman, but with the elegance of a dancer, she felt her way through the familiar rooms, lit only by slanted moonlight that seemed to accommodatingly bend corners. As she passed the sofa in the parlor, a deep male voice startled her.

"Who's there?" he asked.

"No! Oh, my God. You scared me half to death. What are you doing here?" she asked.

"Who are you?"

"I'm Tia's friend, Cristin. Who are you?"

"I'm Tia's nephew, Shep."

"My heart is pounding. You startled me! I thought you had a room at another home. I didn't know you were staying here!"

As her eyes adjusted to the dark, she could make out a large bare chested male physique sitting on the sofa. Bent over with his head in his hands, he said nothing, and made no move to turn on a light.

"I'm sorry I disturbed you. I'll see you in the morning." Cristin headed for her room.

"See you," he replied.

She groped her way to her room and flopped on her bed, staring at the ceiling in disbelief. Her first encounter with Shep could not have been more awkward. Her eyes dilated to "Blinkless and Shrewd" and she spent the next hour sculpting her second impression. Morning would come too soon.

~ ~ ~

Shep had already formed his first impression. He had watched the intruder as she gracefully felt her way through the room like an apparition floating through a dream. Her silhouette had impressed him as being lithe, yet sumptuous. Her voice was sweetly low and raspy. But what he couldn't shake was her scent. Still lingering in the air was a fragrance that he'd never forget. He'd not seen her face. And morning would not come soon enough.

Chapter 19

During her trip to southern France, Cristin had grown very fond of flowers, particularly sunflowers and water lilies. But in the land of Delacroix and Monet, that was not surprising. "When you're not near the one you love, you love the one you're near," so someone had said. And she supposed that this applied to flowers, as well. She arose early and visited Tia's gladiola garden. The stalks were bursting with new growth and it would only be a week or two before they'd be in full bloom.

Shep awakened, threw on his pants, walked through the lower level, and found the patio door open. As he stepped onto the cool pavement with his bare feet, he saw Cristin, dressed in a silk kimono with a sash cinched at her waist, swelling her breasts. She was bent over a gardenia bush and smelling the swollen blossoms of white.

"Good morning, fair night prowler."

Cristin stood and turned to face him. He was shirtless and stunningly male; more handsome than she had expected. Tia had forewarned her but her imagination had not proven accurate. He was broader, taller, and darker. His chest was massive and solid. His face was kind and his jaw line resembled the proverbial "lantern jaw" that she had heard of, but never really seen, except in Calvin Klein ads. Later she marveled how she could have had so many distinct impressions of him in the space of a second or two.

She slowly approached him and hoped that he was studying the details of her female figure that the sunshine revealed through her kimono.

"How do you do. I'm Cristin."

"How do you do. I'm Shep," he responded.

Cristin extended her hand and felt it swallowed up by a massive counterpart that was warm and strong.

"Well, I see you two have met." Tia chimed in from the patio door." I had hoped to make formal and proper introductions last night, but Cristin, you were nowhere to be found. Where were you anyway?"

"No matter. I'm here now. Shep and I actually met last night."

"Yes, we did. But daylight is kind to you."

Tia used her affected southern belle accent. "What a sweet thing to say, nephew." Then, with an amused smile, she resumed her normal dialect and continued. "Come on in, both of you. I have a wonderful day planned." She sounded like the recreation director of The Queen Mary- eager to share the proposed, yet heretofore undisclosed itinerary.

The first day the trio spent together was fun and frivolous. They piled into Tia's Renault convertible, affectionately nicknamed Ren the Renault, after her favorite brother-in-law. Shep drove with Cristin in the front seat and the top down. They headed for the Chartreuse massif, a prominence of the French Alps which lured both native and foreign audiences year round. They dined at Saint Pierre d'Etremont where, prior to selecting their entrees, they politely insisted on a tour of the kitchen, where they witnessed the preparation of food as a living art form.

By late afternoon they drove to Voiron where along the way they stopped to buy a large bag of juicy ripe tomatoes from a vegetable vendor. The farmer's wife who manned the stand had dirt under her fingernails and hair that was wind-whipped and sun-dried. The lines in her face had so deepened that she would not likely have been recognized by her childhood friends. She bagged the tomatoes with the agility of a Las Vegas dealer and the care of a bird incubator. She smiled a toothless smile, only once, in response to Shep's remark that he loved the French countryside. Tia was delighted with the purchase because she had creative designs on the tomatoes. Vinaigrette, tomatoes stuffed with olives and dates, piled with feta cheese, stewed, baked with garlic, etc. Upon discovering that the scoundrels in the front seat had eaten all of the tomatoes in a mere fifteen minutes, the threesome had a communal laugh replete with scolding, guilt and roguishness.

Arriving in Voiron, they drove directly to the Chartreuse Cellars where they partook in a wine tasting session, learning the subtleties of French wine and their companion foods, and enjoying each other's company as if they'd been friends for years. It was the kind of day that one dreams of, that is captured in musicals of The Fifties and written in diaries of famous people. Exhausted and inebriated, the threesome returned to Grenoble. Cristin conjectured that they'd all had a different read on the day. Her best guess was that Tia was probably thrilled with the camaraderie; Shep's pain was lessened, even if only fleetingly; and she had been genuinely surprised by the pleasure of his company.

Shep left early the following morning to settle into his accommodations with the French family he had contacted, leaving both Tia and Cristin dissatisfied with his arrangements.

Cristin sulked. "Why doesn't he just stay with us?"

"I wish he would," agreed Tia. "But my sister Katie says he needs time alone these days. You know, since Peri died."

"I don't understand why a guy who's supposedly so rich would choose to stay with a family with moderate accommodations when he could stay in a fancy hotel with room service and a view of the city."

"I know. I think it's a self-imposed immersion program. He wants to learn the language and experience a life that doesn't remind him of her."

"It sounds like he was really in love, doesn't it?"

"Yea. Pretty romantic story, if you ask me," concluded Tia. "I wonder what it would feel like to be loved by a man like Shep."

~ ~ ~

Days passed with no word from him. Tia started back to school and Cristin returned to the studio she'd rented prior to her travel. The studio was small, but she had chosen it because of its northern light exposure. She was adamant about one rule: no one was to visit her in her studio. No one gained entrance. It was her private world and she would be the one to determine if and when she was ready to share it.

Cristin became increasingly preoccupied with thoughts of Shep and was disturbed by the time lapse since their first encounter. Word came back that he was settled and had met a young woman named Camille who was tutoring him in French.

"That's why we've not seen him," Cristin exclaimed.

"I think it's terrific. I hoped he'd meet a woman to take his mind off Peri. Good for him," said Tia.

"I'm going for a walk." Cristin grabbed her sweater and left the house.

It was a long walk across town. It would have been easier and faster to have taken a taxi, but she needed time to think. She walked past a group of old men playing bocce ball; past children playing tacks and fighting over turns; past lovers on a park bench; past a bicycle accident that had attracted a crowd of bystanders and curiosity seekers. She saw none of it.

When she arrived at the house on Boulevard Lamartine, she was greeted by a young French woman, petite in stature, striking in appearance, and wearing fashionable black-rimmed sunglasses. She stood behind a screen door which impaired their detailed vision of each other.

"Bonjour."

"Bonjour, I have come to speak to Mr. Shepard. Is he here?" Cristin confidently inquired.

"An American, n'est pas? Mr. Shepard is not here, but I am expecting him. Can I tell him who called?"

"My name is Cristin. If you don't mind, I'll wait for him," she replied.

"Actually as soon as he returns, we have an engagement together. It perhaps would be more suitable if I just tell him you stopped by."

"Who are you?" Cristin drilled her, controlling her own fury.

"My name is Camille. Au revoir."

The door closed. Cristin was left standing on the porch with a pigeon cooing at her feet and begging for a handout. She kicked the bird with all of her might and he flew squawking onto the nearest rooftop. He was used to gentler humans.

~ ~ ~

Days later, Shep called Tia's home and Cristin answered.

"Well, you certainly do take your time to respond to a lady caller, Monsieur Shepard," she scolded.

"What caller? Did you come by?" he asked.

"I most certainly did. I spoke to a very unhelpful woman named Camille."

"She must have forgotten to tell me. Sorry."

"I doubt that," said Cristin.

"What do you mean?"

"There's little question that she has her eyes on you, that's all."

"Peculiar choice of words, isn't it?"

"I just meant that she sounded possessive. She implied that you and she had plans that evening."

"We did. Camille is my French tutor and we had an outing planned with some of her friends at her school so that I could practice my conversational skills."

"Isn't she a little old to be still going to school?"

"No, it's a school for the blind. Camille is blind."

Cristin had played the part of a jealous fool well.

"Shep, I'm sorry. I thought... No matter what I thought. Please accept my apologies."

"I do. Now tell me why did you come to visit last week?"

"I missed you. We, Tia and I, had such a wonderful time the day we went to Chartreuse. I just hoped we could see more of you."

"Well, that certainly can be arranged. As a matter of fact, that's why I'm calling. How about a trip to Ardeche to explore the caves on Friday? There are some archeological findings there and it should a beautiful day. Besides which, I hear that the weather will turn for the worse over the weekend. What do you say? The three of us on Friday?"

"It sounds wonderful. Count me in. I'll talk to Tia tonight."

The message was never delivered to Tia who left on Friday for her university classes. Cristin left a note on the kitchen table explaining that she'd be back by midnight. Somewhere in Cristin's youth, she'd adopted the idea that it is easier to ask forgiveness than to ask permission. And using a variation of that theme, a deception by omission was justifiable. After all, what was the worst that could happen? Tia might be peeved, but she had classes. And Cristin needed time with Shep to give him the chance to know her.

The ride to Ardeche was vintage French. Throughout the early afternoon they watched the sky bleed from azure blue to indigo, like India ink moving through a porous celestial fabric.

Shep was a true gentleman, conservative for an American. His conversational style was sensitive and unselfish, his voice was low and deep and his profile was worthy of a Michelangelean bust. She watched him mindfully.

She'd never explored caves before. At one point they broke from the main cave to investigate an ancillary cave with much tighter and darker quarters. Using their lanterns, they created shadows and shapes on the walls which neither one of them had done since grade school. In the heart of the next large cavity, the only sound they could hear was a drip of water from some tiny capillary in the ceiling. They sat down and rested against the wall of the cave to experience the silence.

Shep spoke first, leaning forward, but without making eye contact. "It feels eerie, doesn't it? No one knows we're here."

"It's actually rather creepy. Do you feel safe?"

"Of course," he replied.

"Shep, what's your real name?"

"Franz."

"Like in Schubert?"

"Yes, but I think my Dad had Franz Joseph, the Austrian emperor, in mind when he named me."

"You don't like your name?'

"It sounds too foreign for my taste."

She pried. "Did Peri like it?"

He didn't answer for the longest time.

"I guess you've heard about her. I'm not surprised." He paused momentarily and Cristin had the sense not to interrupt his silence. Silence could be alienating or intimate. Cristin awaited the verdict.

"I miss her. When she died, I frankly didn't know what I would do. I felt lost in a world that I'd known all my life, but suddenly felt no desire to be part of it. Everyone was so good to me. Hell, my family loved her as one of our own. My poor mother felt like she'd lost a daughter."

"Katie?"

"Yes, Katie. She and Peri grew very close. But it's time to move on. Peri will always be a part of my life. She comes to me in my dreams now. It's very real. I wake up heartbroken and angry that our meetings are so fleeting. I swear, on one occasion, I held her and told her that if I had known I could feel her embrace again, I wouldn't have been so despondent. Although I know she's dead, I no longer believe she's gone. It's strange, but comforting."

"Shep, do you believe in life after death?"

"Not in the orthodox sense. I mean I don't believe that there's a place called heaven and a white-bearded benevolent father sitting in judgment. But I think that when one dies, the state of consciousness changes and it's just as real, just like a dream feels real when you're in it. Peri explained it to me one time. She thought that the dream state is nature's way of assuring us that different states of consciousness exist. I buy it. I've actually read metaphysical books since she died. She left me her library, one of her many gifts. She knew I'd read anything that had been important to her and she knew I'd be a better man for it."

Cristin began to shiver. The cold from the floor and walls seeped into her pores.

"We need to warm you up," said Shep, as he put his arm around her shoulder. "We should be thinking of heading home."

"I'd rather not go," whispered Cristin. "I love being here." Cristin used her voice like an instrument, sometimes soft and sometimes strong, retarding or accelerating her delivery to fit the intended melody.

She jumped up and said, "Let's experiment with the light! I want to see how dark darkness can be. Let's turn out the lanterns, just for a minute.

They extinguished the lanterns and there was nothing. They witnessed pure blackness.

"Wow. This is wild. Where are you, Shep? Touch me."

He knew where she was by the direction of her voice and held out his hand. She grabbed hold of it and pulled herself into his arms and hugged him tightly.

"I'll never forget this," she cooed.

A minute passed. "What's that?" she asked as she jumped.

"Bats," he replied. "Turn on your lantern! It's time to leave. Hold my hand and follow me." Cristin did as he asked. His lantern no longer worked so without saying a word, they exchanged them. They silently retraced their steps through the tunnels. The sense of adventure had diminished as the light from the remaining lantern dimmed.

"Shep, are we going to make it out? God, what if the lantern goes out. We'd be in here with bats all night in pitch black."

Shep said nothing, but continued to forge their way on a seemingly endless trail. He tried to give no mental energy to the nagging fear that he'd taken a wrong turn and was headed farther into the interior of the cave. In retrospect, he'd remember thinking that being stuck with Cristin in any other situation would have been pleasurable. But being swallowed by a mouth of cold darkness, at the mercy of unknown nocturnal creatures, would never have been a choice.

Then they heard a distant crash, thunder perhaps. Cristin gasped. They had to be near the mouth of the cave. They were no longer hunched over in low passages. Standing almost erectly their widened eyes frantically searched for light. Gradually, they detected the peripheries of the floors and walls. And finally, in the distance, they saw the opening and realized that not only was rain pelting the outside world but darkness had descended. Cristin broke from Shep's hand and ran into the rain to dance like a wood nymph. Laughing, he sat on the floor inside the entrance of the cave and watched her. She was a mystical blend of child and woman, of Madonna and Siren. Caught up in her exuberance, he acknowledged what Peri would have wanted him to do: care for another.

"Come in out of the rain." He laughed as he watched her frolic. "You're soaking wet! What are you thinking?"

Cristin ran to him, but not wanting to get him wet, stopped short.

"Cristin, you know this is bad news."

"After that adventure, any bad news is relative to a dungeonish sentence of darkness and bats in my hair, so let me have it!" She beamed.

"This's true." He smiled. "But nevertheless, we can't go home tonight. We need to stay here."

"But I'm soaking wet."

"That's also true. But it doesn't erase the fact that we've exited this cave at a different spot than we entered it and with the blinding rain and nonexistent moonlight, I have no idea where we are. We are safer to stay until daybreak."

"Shep, I'm too impetuous. It's one of my worst qualities. I shouldn't have run into the rain. But I was just so happy to be out there."

"You were beautiful. I'll never forget it. But you're going to have to take off your wet clothes. You can wear my shirt. It should cover you."

"But what about you?"

"I'm not wet. Here, take my shirt and change. I won't look." He smiled as he unbuttoned his shirt. Together they crouched in a corner that was encircled by stalagmites. It was somewhat protected from the winds of the storm that now whirled like furious mini-tornadoes at the door of the cave. The interior was as cold as the granite of castle walls and just as hard. They huddled together. Shep held her and they rubbed each other to keep warm. He could feel the outline of her female contour and imagined the softness of her skin through his shirt. He rubbed her legs, smooth and long, painfully cold, lean to her feet. Hours passed. They told stories, revealed fears and secrets they'd never shared with anyone. Cristin quietly wept from time to time. He kissed her fingertips, her forehead, her cheeks, her lips.

The night seemed endless, but came to pass. At the first glimmer of dawn, they rose to find their way. The rain had stopped and the morning had been christened by the sweet smell of green. Cristin, weak from cold, tripped and badly twisted her ankle. Shep carried her through the forest for what seemed like hours, her arms clutching his neck, her legs dangling. He could feel a fever from her forehead pressed against his cool moist neck. And from time to time, he whispered, "I'm sorry."

~ ~ ~

"Cristin! Shep! Where have you been? What happened? I've been so worried," cried Tia, who looked like she'd had as much sleep as they had.

Shep carried a half-conscious Cristin into the house, as Tia ran before him, clearing a path and turning down her bed.

"My God, Shep. What happened?"

"I'll tell you the whole story. Call a doctor, Tia. Find all the blankets you have in the house. Run a hot tub. She'll need some hot tea and some food, something that will go down easily, nothing too rich. Fruit, how about fruit?"

"One thing at a time. I'll call the doctor."

~ ~ ~

The following weeks were devoted to restoring Cristin's health. Tia took time off from her studies to nurse Cristin's "cave "pneumonia.

Shep visited every day, oftentimes bringing bouquets of local wildflowers.

"Please don't feel guilty, Shep. You didn't will this to happen," Tia suggested.

"I should have kept track of the time. The hours just flew. It was as if there was no time. I feel totally responsible."

"She was just as unaware, just as much to blame." Her attempt to comfort him fell on deaf ears.

"No, I'm the man."

"What's that supposed to mean?" An indignation saturated her voice.

"I mean, I'm the man. I should have taken better care of her."

Tia cajoled with her thickest French accent. "Mon ami, chivalry is alive and well in the spirit of Monsieur Shepard!"

The evening folded into night without a crease. Cristin ran a fever that worsened in late afternoon and peaked in late evening.

One night Cristin screamed in a heated pitch. "Fire! Burn, burn! Faster!"

Tia ran into the Cristin's room to find her patient delirious with fever and acting out a nightmare. Sitting up in bed, she maniacally laughed as if she were enjoying the experience. "Yes, yes, burn, burn!"

Tia witnessed the disturbing scene alone and tried to calm her friend.

Inconsolable, Cristin initially fought her off, but became fatigued. Tia applied cold cloths to her forehead and Cristin fell into a deep sleep, not stirring again until the following morning. With the fever broken, Cristin looked refreshed, as if in some mysterious manner her nightmare had been cathartic. Tia told her about the fevered hysteria the night before. Cristin repeatedly asked what she had said, questioning if it was all she had said. She then laughed it off as hallucinatory. Shep agreed. In his words, "What else can you speculate it meant?" But Tia reserved judgment.

When Cristin regained her health, Shep offered to take her away for a short recuperative trip, to get her out in the fresh country air for a change of scenery. Tia reiterated that he needn't feel guilty.

"I'm not going away with her out of a sense of guilt, Tia. I've grown fond of her. As a matter of fact, we shared a great deal that night in the cave. She's had a rough life, you know."

"What do you mean? I know she was adopted and that's about all. She doesn't relish talking about her past. I've broached the subject on a number of occasions and she turns me off."

"She's a private person. I wouldn't know her at all if we'd not been stranded together."

"What's been so tough in her life?" Tia asked.

"Her father abused her and her mother didn't defend her."

"Good God, Shep! I'm sure that Tess doesn't know this. I could have sworn that Tess said Cristin had a happy childhood. I'm positive she did." Tia pursed her lips, frowned and squinted into space, and for a second resembled her older sister.

"Well, I'm sure there's a logical explanation." Shep dismissed Tia's confusion.

Leaning her elbow on the arm of her chair, Tia's finger nervously tapped her right temple.

~ ~ ~

The trip to the Dijon area was splendid. The fields surrounding the city were blanketed with yellow mustard, the plant that had made the town famous. The change in scenery was only an hour away but a curtain pulled down from the sky to set a new stage. Travel injected new exhilaration into the bloodstream of life; it not only made one more aware of life's rich diversity but more appreciative of the familiar.

Cristin had never looked lovelier than their first morning in Dijon. She wore her hair in a thick, silky braid down the middle of her back. Her soft brown almond-shaped eyes were framed by naturally perfect brows. Her lips were full and when she smiled, her straight white teeth brought attention to her sensual mouth.

Dijon, a charming village on the east side of the Alps, was one of the few areas not destroyed during the war. The town of 13th century architecture housed Celtic ruins. The main street was a string of chocolateries, fromageries, charcuteries, and patisseries. While strolling the cobblestone streets, they nibbled on Pain d'especies, a gingerbread delicacy indigenous to the area. They visited Le Mollon de Bois, a charming little wooden mill. They walked the walled medieval city of Baume and drank wine in the caverns of Chateau Mourin in Nuits-St. George.

On their first night in Dijon, they dined at "La Dame D'Aquataine." The restaurant was located in a crypt which was amusingly conducive to morbid comments during the course of the evening. Accompanied by a fine wine, an Appalachian Vougeot from the Clos des Prierres, the feast began with Escargot Bourgogne and finished with tarts and dark chocolate truffles rolled in dark chocolate powder. Shep was much more sophisticated in the art of food and wine; Cristin was an adventurous and eager student.

From an outdoor amphitheater in Lyon to the Romanesque ruins in Cluny, every day presented a new opportunity to explore. One evening outside the Chateauneuf in Auxios, they laid down together in a grassy moat and stared at the sky while playing an imaginative game of connect-the-dot stars. The grass smelled cool and green and they laughed like children on a young summer night. They talked about life as if they were going to share the years ahead. They spoke of visiting the moors of Scotland, the rain forests of Brazil, the fjords of Norway, the waters of Fiji. Their conversation was easy and unguarded. Neither appeared to hold back visions or dreams of their individual futures because they were wrapped by a silver cord that was as long as time and as strong as knowing. They made the evening their own by making love.

~ ~ ~

Tia received no word from Shep and Cristin and tried to mind her own business in her little cottage in Grenoble. But it occurred to her, more than ever, that it wasn't fair that she, Tia Lauren Monson, should live without her Prince Charming. Hope sprang eternal, but no one knocked on her door.

That afternoon a summer storm hit Grenoble. Tia built a fire and went upstairs to investigate a banging sound. A branch outside her bedroom dormer window was loudly tapping on the pane. As she opened it to silence the annoyance, she noticed a familiar figure in the wind and rain, crossing the street and approaching her home.

"Yvette, is that you?" she hollered.

"Oui. May I come in?"

"Of course. I'll be right down." Tia looked across the park where the tops of colorful parasols were in motion like wheels of a locomotive. The view was a three-dimensional Pissarro.

When she reached the downstairs level, there stood Yvette, wet and cold, and ready to be pampered by a caring friend.

"Take your coat off and sit by the fire," said Tia as she helped her friend remove her damp garment. "What a miserable day it's turned out to be."

"Merci. Do you have any hot tea? I must be crazy to stop by unannounced like this, and in the rain no less. My apologies."

"Don't be silly. It's wonderful to see you again. It's been weeks. Tell me about your travels."

A few hours passed as the friends shared their stories. Hearing about Yvette's journeys kindled Tia's wanderlust like a match to paper. Somehow academic life interfered with her ability to take off for other lands.

"Tell me, did your friend Cristin ever come back?" she interjected. "I met up with her in St. Tropez, you know."

"No, I didn't know. She didn't mention it. She's back but not here at the moment and I don't actually know when she'll be returning. She's with my nephew in Dijon."

"Really? They didn't know each other in America, did they?" Yvette inquired.

"No, but they've hit it off. They're inseparable. They've been gone for ten days now and I'm beginning to wonder if perhaps my mourning nephew has found solace in the arms of my beautiful roommate."

"I certainly hope not," Yvette announced.

"Why do you say that?"

"Frankly, I don't trust her. She's strange. More than strange, she's evil."

"For God's sake, Yvette. Why in the world would you say that? What has Cristin ever done to you?"

"Nothing. But I watched her and I listened to her the night we all had dinner together. Tia, you know how strong and accurate my instincts are. This woman is trouble."

"You're scaring me. What are you referring to?"

"Did she tell you about the little boy who was killed?"

"No."

"That doesn't surprise me. The rest of us have been reeling from the incident ever since it happened. But not Cristin. Tia, we all witnessed a child die before our eyes and she made some bizarre remark about a scarf. She is cold, vain, and self-centered. I watched her walking past the stores on the boardwalk without her knowing it. I followed her, if you will. She stared at herself in each shop window, admiring her own reflection, a regular Narcissa. She couldn't keep her eyes off herself. It was nauseating."

"That may be vain, but it's certainly not a crime."

"I then listened to her bark at the shopkeeper's daughter. She was indignant. She made the poor girl cry. Oh, but you should have witnessed her change of persona when she recognized me. It was dramatic and so two-faced. I asked her to dinner to meet my friends. Believe me, I didn't want to share her company that night, but I did want to watch her again, to make sure that I wasn't overreacting to her callous rudeness. I wasn't. I thought you'd better know."

"I can't believe you're saying this about Cristin."

"It's true. She's no good. Where did she come from anyway? How do you know her?"

"My sister Tess and her husband Ren sort of adopted her. She lived with them for a while."

"What's your brother-in-law's name?"

"Ren. Remember, I named my car Ren the Renault? Why do you ask?"

"I think I've said enough. I'm probably mistaken anyway."

"Why would you stop now? What were you going to say?"

Yvette reluctantly spoke. "Well, we'd all been drinking quite a bit that night and Cristin rather casually talked about wanting to have an affair with a married man."

"So? What are you saying?"

"She called him Rennie."

Tia stood out of her chair and starting pacing the room. "That's impossible. I don't believe you. You must have misunderstood!"

Their room crackled with the energy of fire.

"I'm curious, Tia," Yvette asked, "When did Cristin return to Grenoble?"

Tia responded as if in a trance, not taking her eyes from the fire, watching the demon flames dance before her eyes. "I remember exactly when. The day before Shep arrived. I was surprised and so pleased at her timing. She didn't even know he was coming and voila, she was there."

"Oh, but she did know he was coming."

"No, she didn't. I vividly remember. She was as surprised by the news as I was to receive her call."

"No, she wasn't, my friend. I told her the night before that your handsome, unattached, and very rich nephew was due to arrive in two days. Prior to hearing my news, she had no intention of coming back so soon. I wanted to see what she would do. I'm just sorry I didn't tell you sooner. We all ended up going to Greece and didn't return until two days ago. Forgive me?"

Tia mumbled words of pardon, then said good night to Yvette. The islands of floating puzzle pieces that previously hadn't fit together began to lock into place and create a new picture that Tia was forced to look at. She needed to talk to Shep.

Chapter 20

Spring in Minnesota was brief that year. From her porch every day, Serena had watched the snow melt and buds burst forth with nature's sleight of hand. It was humbling that so much beauty in motion had arrived and departed, undetected and unappreciated by so many. Summer was her favorite time. She was more mobile, more apt to leave her home to take short walks. There was no bitter wind to chill her bones and only an occasional rainstorm. But summer too had sprouted wings and flown across her life like a mallard across the marshes, leaving nothing but impressions. Shakespeare was right, she thought, "Summer's lease had all too short a date."

Living alone she was prone to have spells of melancholia; not depressions exactly, but philosophical musings that sometimes took her for walks that ended in dark alleys. She played devil's advocate, taking a position, and challenging it, just to keep her mind vigorous. On this particular day she thought about judgment, starting with the premise that she must make judgments in order to make decisions. But "Judge not according to appearances." How could she place trust if not by judging according to what she saw and heard, according to appearances? Perhaps time was the factor. Perhaps she needed to know a person for a reasonable period of time in order to measure character. Some people were so easy to trust. They were exactly what they appeared to be: no hidden agendas, wearing their hearts on their sleeves, speaking their minds without straining through a sieve of pretense or deception. Tess was one of these. Cristin was not.

Serena watched her neighbor with more than casual interest. Initially Tess had been thrilled to play the part of surrogate mother. Then prior to Cristin's departure, Tess had been anxious and preoccupied. But with Cristin in France, Tess was more tranquil, unperturbed. In June, the household sighed; in July, it relaxed; and in August, it smiled.

It was September. Tess was preparing for a book tour in various cities, as her book was soon to be released. Ren buried himself in work, so their long hours apart were at least mutually satisfying. He cooked more dinners and they took more frequent walks together along the creek. And Serena observed the change.

~ ~ ~

Cristin had only sent one postcard, hinting where she'd been and leaving the rest to their imaginations. But she hadn't left a clue as to when she would return. Sondra had dropped off the radar as Tess had hoped she would. Troy had begun divorce proceedings and had hired an English nanny who was "brilliant" with the children. Day by day, Katie's family was recovering from the loss of Peri. Lissa was visiting them more often and with a more amiable disposition. There was a sense of well-being and serenity in the Parker home

Then one night, not able to locate his leather bound edition of Wordsworth poetry, Ren asked, "Tess, do you know where it is? It's always in our room. If I take it out, I bring it back."

"It has to be there. I'll look as soon as I'm finished."

"Don't bother. I've looked everywhere!"

"When was the last time you read from it?"

"When Cristin was here, last spring."

"Well, maybe it's in her room."

"No, she wouldn't take it."

"If she enjoyed it, she may have borrowed it. I haven't been in her room all summer. She's on the other side of the world, so I doubt she'd mind if we took a look."

"Oh, I think she would mind, but she'll never know," Ren replied.

Tess jumped from the sofa and headed upstairs, two steps at a time with the grace of a tigress. Dressed in jeans and a mid-drift T-shirt, she looked about twenty years old. Within a minute, she called to him.

"Ren, come here."

As he approached her in the hallway, he could see her rigid stance, hands on her hips and fire in her eyes.

"Did you put locks on the upstairs bedroom doors?" she asked.

"No, they don't have locks."

"This one does."

"Well, it didn't."

"She must have installed a lock."

"Why?"

"She had no right to do this."

In a matter of minutes Ren had taken a pipe wrench and twisted the knob until it broke. He then used a screwdriver to trip the lock mechanism and open the door. They entered Cristin's private domain, a normal looking room, practically vacant, and stuffy.

"I don't see any books, Ren. Maybe we should leave."

"Relax. I'll check her desk." He opened the top drawer. "Tessa, look."

Tess peered inside to discover not what one would expect to find in a desk drawer. Not an organized assemblage of pens, paper clips, and supplies. But rather, four distinct contents; Ren's book of Wordsworth ; a pile of artist sketches; a photograph of two young girls with nothing to identify them but the date "August 17, 1994" inscribed on the back; and a key, a lone key, with no tag or identification. As they examined each object, it was difficult to pinpoint which article was the least mysterious.

"We shouldn't have come into her room, Ren," said Tess. "You know how furious she was when I did last year."

"This is our house, Tessa. We have the right to know what goes on under our own roof."

"Yes, but all she asked of us was to respect the privacy of her room."

"Tell me, what is my book doing here? She never asked to borrow my book." Ren picked up the reams of graphics done in elaborate calligraphy. His name inscribed on each page. "What the hell is this about?"

"Well maybe she had a crush on you and we just didn't realize it."

"I don't buy it."

"Who are these girls, Ren? These girls in the picture. Neither one of them is Cristin. I never heard her talk about any girlfriends from her past. Of course that doesn't really mean anything. But the girl on the right, the older one, looks familiar... but that couldn't be."

Ren picked up the key. "I wonder where this goes."

"Rennie, I'm sure there's a simple explanation. Just take your book. Let's go downstairs."

Ren walked to the closet and turned the doorknob. It was locked. He inserted the key. It fit. Before he opened the door, he turned his head, raised his eyebrows, and shot her an expectant, mistrusting glance. In the closet, there were no clothes, no shoes and no boxes; just an empty walk-in closet painted red, orange, yellow, and black. They turned on the light and realized they were surrounded by flames of a fiery inferno. On the walls were three long, gaunt faces, exaggerated in Munchian style and peering from the flames in horror. Their eyes were black and terrified. Their vertically stretched faces, accentuated with long oval mouths, suggested screaming for help, reminiscent of Holocaust figures. In the middle of the closet floor was a single chair.

Ren broke the silence "Good God! What is this? This is sick. It's a goddamn shrine."

Tess stared, remembering the smell of paint that had angered her months before. But never in her wildest dreams had she surmised that something so aberrant had been going on behind Cristin's closed doors.

"What are we going to do?" she asked.

"She's going to find somewhere else to live, that's for damn sure. She's disturbed, Tess. Was she doing drugs?"

"I don't know. You saw her practically as much as I did. Did you suspect that she was capable of behavior this bizarre?"

"I don't know what's more disturbing: thinking she was on drugs or thinking she could come up with this twisted idea in an unaltered state. What kind of a world is she living in? It looks tormented, or worse yet, perverted. What's this chair doing in here? Did she come into this simulation of hell and sit here alone?"

"Let's get out of here. I want to leave." Tess turned and walked out of the room like a zombie with no sense of direction except "away from." Ren found her minutes later sitting cross-legged on the sofa with a slow tear working its way down her cheek.

"Tess, we need to talk."

Her sad, stunned expression didn't break. She said nothing.

"Tessa, talk to me." He sat next to her and folded his wife's hands into his own like a priest about to comfort his parishioner. "I took my book and put it back in our room. I left the picture and the etchings in the drawer. I'm going to repaint the closet white and change the doorknobs of the two doors. When she comes home, we'll talk. But she will find another place to live, don't you agree?"

Tess didn't move a muscle but stared straight ahead. After a few seconds she softly replied, "Yes, I agree."

During the next weeks Ren restored Cristin's closet and doors to their original condition. But a day didn't pass in which they didn't refer to the strange findings in her room. Had the picture of the two young women been one among many, it would not have conjured the curiosity that it did. But one lone picture indicated significance. The calligraphies of Ren's name was disturbing, no matter how one looked at it. The key had symbolically opened a world of demons that they hadn't suspected existed in Cristin's seemingly normal world.

~ ~ ~

Over the years, Tess had learned to appreciate Serena's eccentricities. Tuesday evenings still filled the neighborhood with the smell of goulash and paprika. Strange music rooted in her home still floated on staffs of summer breezes, subconsciously educating young children to sounds of distant cultures. Serena was eclectic and authentic, but not strange. Time with Serena seemed to alchemize what had once appeared laughable into lovable, and bizarre into respected. Serena was a human potion for Tess. She had not only lived longer, but she knew more than Tess. She was Tess's Merlin. Serena had the ability to ask the right questions and tell the right stories to illuminate a problem with clarity. She had the knack of pulling answers out of Tess, as if Tess had known them all along. Serena was her mentor. Serena was her confidante.

"How do you feel about the closet incident now?" she asked Tess one autumn evening as they raked leaves in her back yard.

"I want to hear what she has to say when she calls me, if she calls me."

"You are far too compassionate and not very vigilant. I understand you want to believe the best of this girl. There was a time that I did too."

"What are you saying?" Tess stopped raking.

"I'm saying that I'm not surprised at any part of your story and I think there's more to this than meets the eye."

"What could possibly have been an indication that something was wrong?"

"I may be mistaken, but I think our Cristin weaves lies as easily as spiders weave webs. And her beautiful, beguiling exterior may house within it a scorpion's sting."

"Why didn't you tell me this before, Serena?"

226

"I tried to. Do you recall when I told you that I thought she had lied about her past and I warned you then to be careful? I don't trust her and you shouldn't either. There's something very unusual concerning this girl's appearance in your life...the way she came to you. I don't know the whole story, but more critically, I don't think you do either."

Tess looked at Serena like a guilty child but said nothing. "My legs are getting tired, dear. Let's sit down for a while." Serena plunked herself in a wrought iron patio chair and motioned with her hand that Tess do the same. The afternoon smelled of autumn leaves and firewood. The two friends sat in silence while they surveyed the piles of their labors.

Serena began. "Tess, she has lied to you. She has broken your house rules. She has obsessed about your husband. And she has created some kind of demented shrine in your home. These are not normal behaviors. They are simply not acceptable."

"I know, Serena. I dread confronting her."

Serena took Tess's hand in hers and patted it gently, saying "I think you can leave that up to your husband."

"No, Serena. Rennie may be willing, but I brought her into our lives. I need to be the one to take her out."

~ ~ ~

Preparing for her book signing tour was a welcomed diversion. Ren was supportive and insisted she buy a new wardrobe that was fitting for an author on the rise. Eager to experience her notoriety, she was also anxious. What if she was not what they expected? What if her readers were smarter than she was? Maybe she wasn't ready for prime-time. She knew she wasn't Eudora Welty. She was just Tess Monson. She could scarcely remember what she'd written. But both Ren and Serena assured her that if she were just her unpretentious self, the rest would fall in place. And even if the book was not a colossal success, she hadn't written for an adoring public anyway; she'd written because she had stories to tell. She remembered reading an interview with Isaac Asimov in which he was asked what he would do if he found out that he only had a few months to live. He said, "I would write faster." She understood it. She wrote because she couldn't imagine not writing.

After a shopping spree, she spent hours trying on each ensemble, modeling in front of her full length mirror. Positioning a wide brimmed hat, accessorizing with scarves and jewelry, lipsticks and shoes, she came to the conclusion that she could stand to lose five pounds. She was naturally slim and clothes fit her well, but she was modestly aware not to wear any article of clothing that clung or appeared too tight or revealing. As she modeled her Chanel suit, she looked at her Chanel shoes and followed her thin, yet shapely, legs past the perfect fit to her earrings and her face. She stared at her face and for an instance flashed upon the picture of the two girls in Cristin's desk drawer. Tess stepped out of her shoes and ran down the hall to Cristin's room and opened the drawer. Yes, that was it. One of the girls looked like herself, maybe more of a resemblance to Katie or Tia at that age. But neither girl was Cristin. Very strange. When she returned to her bedroom, she was no longer in the mood to model her new clothes, so she put on her jeans and began dinner before Ren came home.

~ ~ ~

One evening in late September, Ren was star-gazing, trying to locate a minor constellation in the autumn sky, when the phone rang.

"Hi, little sister! It's Katie."

Whether it was Katie's putting her life back together or Tess's instinctive protectiveness of her sister's secret, Tess felt closer to her older sibling than she ever had.

"Well, if it isn't my favorite voice from Bean Town. What's going on? Haven't heard from you in ages."

"Are we going to see you next week?"

"Of course. New York is my third stop. And Katie, you better have everyone you know lined up outside Brenigans. I need at least one confidence builder."

"We'll be there with bells on, honey. We can hardly wait to see you. I'm so proud of you. I think I'll take out an ad in *The Times* announcing your arrival. We're all taking the train into the city. Ingrid will be there with a group of her friends. Heidi has to go to school and she's so disappointed. But we want you to come back to Boston with us and have dinner on Saturday night at the house. Promise me."

"Katie, they've booked me a room at The Plaza. Why don't you come back to the hotel after dinner and we'll have some girl time? I know how much you love those posh hotels."

"You don't have to twist my arm. I'll send the kids back to Boston. We're all so looking forward to seeing you next week, honey."

"You haven't mentioned Shep. Isn't he living in Manhattan?"

"No. He's still in Europe. Remember, he went to France to visit Tia months ago. You're playing games with me. You knew that."

"How would I know that? No one tells me anything anymore."

"Tessa, knock it off. Don't you think it's wonderful?"

"What? What's wonderful?" she asked.

"Now I know you're kidding. Aren't you thrilled? The world is so small. Nothing like keeping it in the family."

Tess paused, a bit irritated, then said, "In the family? I'm afraid I've missed something. What are you talking about?"

"Shep and Cristin."

"Shep and Cristin what?"

"They're in love."

Sometimes news comes in slow motion, as if the universe wants you to listen so carefully that the words sound loud, slow, and deliberate. The rest of the world disappears because all you can hear is your pulse and the surging of adrenaline.

"What did you say?" She heard the echo of her words inside her head.

"Oh, my God. I'm sorry. I should've let Cristin tell you herself. I feel terrible. I just presumed that you knew."

"Knew what? We haven't spoken to Cristin since she left in June."

"Oh. Really? Um. Well, when Shep took his hiatus to France this summer, he met Cristin in Grenoble at Tia's. After Peri's death, he was so miserable. He needed someone else in his life, and voila, I think that someone else is your Cristin. Stefan and I could not be happier for them."

As Tess looked around the room, the images darkened into fuzzy silhouettes, as if she were about to faint. The percussive shushing sound in her head corresponded to a loss of balance. Her knees buckled and she leaned against the nearest chair and fell into it.

"Tess, say something."

"I don't know what to say. I'm stunned."

"I thought you'd be so pleased."

"Katie, I'll call you back, maybe tomorrow. I have to go."

Tess hung up the phone in the kitchen she knew so well and, like a blind woman, she bumped into the furniture as if it had been moved by some sighted prankster to fool her. She called to Ren in the back yard and said that she was tired and going to bed. Alone, she retired to the privacy of their room. In the dark she stared at the ceiling of her mind and imagined the ruins of the bomb that was about to detonate her closest relationships. She could see the faces of the lives she most loved about to be irreparably damaged by one truth. How could someone with such good intentions as she cause pain for so many innocent people? It wasn't fair. Where would she begin? She did know that she couldn't stand by and allow a romantic love between Shep and Cristin. But before they were told, she would have to tell Ren and Katie. She couldn't think of any task more threatening to life as she knew it. But to keep quiet was unthinkable. She would call forth the courage to utter the right words, to right her own wrongdoing. All the months of rationalizing converged into one consolidated point of no return.

And try as she might to justify her actions, she was left with nothing but a lie, told and retold, lived and relived. Now she faced a twist of fate: Shep and Cristin had met and had fallen in love. It was the single scenario she hadn't considered.

~ ~ ~

Dawn cracked like lightning. Never had a day been greeted with more demand and less ardor. After a nerve-racking morning, Tess knocked on Serena's door like a child coming before a Mother Superior. Serena would give her courage and not shun her.

Serena's house smelled of some unidentifiable but familiar scent, reminiscent of the incense that permeated the Catholic church. Tess rarely saw Serena's cat, Emily Dickinson, but on this particular morning she came out from under the easy chair in the living room and greeted her in the hallway, as if she could sense Tess's neediness. The cat, a Scottish Fold, was a strange breed with a flat face, small ears, and yellow eyes that shone like polished marbles from within a tiny black face.

"I see Emily has come out to greet you. That's a first. This is a day that will go down in history." Serena laughed.

"It certainly is."

"My dear, you have dark circles under your eyes. It looks like you haven't slept in days. What's going on?"

They walked through the house and took seats opposite each other in the porch. The storm windows hadn't been installed so the breeze sifted through the screen, filling the room with cool fresh air. Emily jumped up into Tess's lap and purred like a furry motor as Tess stroked her silky back.

"Serena, I need to talk to someone because I must tell the truth about something that I've hidden from everyone. I never meant to hurt anyone. I'm absolutely terrified. But something has happened and I know what I have to do. I just don't know how I can do it."

"Slow down, Tess. Nothing could be as bad as you're making it out to be."

"It's worse," said Tess as she heard her own voice tremble.

"What is it, dear?" Serena looked deeply concerned like a mother who would, in a flat minute, trade places with her child to allay the pain.

Tess began to impart the chronology of how Cristin had come into their lives.

Drawn into the drama, Serena interrupted. "What did Ren think about all this?"

"I didn't tell him. He doesn't know anything except that I helped a young girl in need. Cristin doesn't even know. I denied any connection to her. But Serena, she is my niece. I couldn't turn my back on her."

Tess began to sob. Emily Dickinson leapt to the floor, perhaps not feeling safe in the lap of someone unhappy and potentially unpredictable.

"Everything seemed to be going so well until last winter when Cristin's attitudes and behavior changed. But she never behaved differently in front of Ren so it was difficult to confirm...until more recently, of course."

"So the visits from your friend Sondra this past year are related to Cristin?" asked Serena.

"Yes. I hadn't seen Sondra for twenty three years. But after my inquiry concerning Katie, she paid me a visit. Unfortunately, Cristin appeared and Sondra put two and two together...and was horrified at what I had done. She threatened to go to Katie and tell her everything because she felt so guilty for corroborating my theory. But I convinced her that the ease of her conscience was secondary to the damage that the information could potentially do to Katie and her family. After all, Kate was in a rehabilitation center when this whole thing surfaced. She wasn't strong enough to face her past and serve it up to her family. Sondra's visits have been a nightmare for me, but I couldn't tell anyone."

"So what has triggered your conscience to spill the truth at this stage of the game?"

Tess sensed disappointment in Serena's tone. She didn't hear the blessing of absolution she had counted on. She felt an urge to run away, but she stayed glued to her chair, as if the priestess wouldn't allow her to escape until she had expelled the truth from her tortured soul.

"Oh, Serena, you won't believe what has happened. I heard from Katie last night. She informed me that her son, my nephew Shep, has been in France this summer."

Tess felt a large fist in her throat as she struggled to unclench it so that she could continue.

"Shep has been in France and you know that Cristin has been there as well, staying with my sister Tia. Well, Shep and Cristin have met and they have fallen in love. Serena, Cristin is his half-sister. I have to say something before it goes any further. My whole life is unraveling before my eyes. I have lied to Katie, deceived my husband, and misled Cristin. I have endangered every important relationship I have. I can't bear being the cause of such pain."

Serena moved to the chair next to Tess, swallowed her up in her motherly arms and rocked her. After a few minutes she spoke.

"It's good you have finally told someone, Tessa. We'll sort it out together and you'll do the right thing. Remember, time can be your ally or your enemy. That's why you must think clearly. The longer you hold this inside, the more treacherous it becomes, not only to those you love, but to yourself. Very few things in life are as terrible as we believe them to be. Tessa, take a deep breath. Breathe. Don't hold it. Breathe with me."

For what seemed like a long time, Tess allowed Serena to rock her gently back and forth, and help her breathe. When Tess calmed, Serena released her younger friend and took a chair across the table so she could see Tess's eyes.

"May I ask you a few questions?"

"Of course. Ask anything. I have nothing to hide now. It's ironic that I say that with a sense of relief."

"Why didn't you tell Ren?"

"Because I knew he would say no. He wouldn't have wanted to play a part in withholding the truth from anyone. I just figured that if Cristin could be near us, I could watch out for her. She's my own flesh and blood, Serena. And I've never had a daughter. This seemed like my only chance to be a mother. No one needed to know. No one would get hurt."

"How can you be sure she is who she says she is?" asked Serena. "Maybe she came across the letter and made a move to integrate into a happy, well-to-do family."

"No, she's Katie's daughter. She had my mother's locket, the only possession Katie left with her."

"Well, Tessa, when are you going to tell your husband? He deserves to know the truth."

"I'm terrified."

Serena asked the million dollar question. "What's the worst thing that could happen?"

Tess blurted, "He could leave me."

"On what grounds?"

"That he no longer trusts me."

"Highly unlikely. But even if he did, you'd survive. Love often survives these foibles of human nature, Tess. Start giving some of the people in your life more credit. Or do you really think they are so self-righteous that they could not forgive you? If you justified your decisions, however ill-fated, don't you think they could come to understand your actions?"

Tess hardly heard a word.

"But if Cristin and Shep are truly in love, I'm destroying their chance to be together. After Peri's death, this would be unendurable for Shep. And Cristin? I've not only hidden the identity of her true mother from her but she has fallen in love with her brother. Oh, God, I hope it's not too late."

Tess broke down and began sobbing like she'd never stop, as if on the track of a runaway train, recklessly accelerating, and doomed to crash. The task that lay before her was not only arduous, but imminent, and she was without hope of grace. Somehow she would have to reach into the recesses of her panicked, apprehensive spirit and pull out the courage she would need.

She sat up straight, abruptly inhaled, and stopped crying.

"Tess, you need to find out if this whole romance is true. What if they're just friends and their friendship has been inferred by Katie to be something that it's not?"

"I hadn't thought of that. Maybe it's just an exaggeration of a friendship. Oh, if that would only be true, I wouldn't have to tell anyone what I've done."

Serena shot a sharp glance that ricocheted off Tess's conscience like a rubber bullet.

She corrected herself. "Of course, I will tell Rennie everything. I promise."

"And how do you propose to determine the nature of this relationship?" asked Serena, keeping Tess focused.

"I'll call Tia. Tia will know the whole story....Tia! I probably should have been talking to Tia about Cristin, but if Tia hasn't called me, there's probably nothing going on, nothing wrong. I should have thought of this before. I've probably jumped to the wrong conclusion. Serena, I have to go. Ren isn't home yet and I need to telephone Grenoble."

She ran out the door with guarded optimism, but not before hugging Serena and muttering words of gratitude and affection. She left Serena on her front steps as she ran through an imaginary tunnel; a tunnel that would lead her to safety and possibly leave her unscathed and undiscovered.

Chapter 21

Serena remembered. She remembered the time when she was in love, that sweet summer that carried the scent of lilies on every breeze. Sprays of lilacs and towering Lilies of the Nile tinted her world purple and sprinkled aisles of jacaranda blossoms blanketed the pavement of each side street. Purple became the color of love. At a time when girls held sacred their inviolate reputations, when dishonor and shame were real consequences of passion outside the confines of marriage, she'd fallen in love with the only man she would ever love and threw caution to the wind. She laid beneath him, night after night, as they filled their senses with each other's warm, erotic scents and rode the sound waves of escalating cries of pleasure. They made love every time like it was their first and their last time together. And she knew they would never part. But at the end of the summer, they did part. He left with not so much as a final goodbye and he left her with child. For years after he was gone, she would awaken from a dream at the peak of orgasm, merely remembering his touch.

Serena also remembered having made a decision that would change her life; a choice that would alienate her from those she loved; a decision that would stigmatize her until she became so old that no one knew her anymore; a judgment that had branded her son at unknown cost to both of them. She remembered the people who were righteous and hypocritical, the people who refused to forgive her. Her life had been lonely. She'd often wondered if her decision to keep Jamie had been in his best interests; for try as she might, she'd never been able to be both mother and father to him.

She was only half of the parental equation that guides an innocent child.

But no life was complete in wisdom. Wisdom truly came as pearls, and when gathered, could string a bracelet, or if fortunate, a necklace. People gathered different pearls to create different lengths and value. She wished that she could lend her pearls to Tess, but that's not how the universe worked. Pearls were not transferable. Tess would have to string her own, one at a time.

Serena enjoyed her position on life's timeline because she could look back on her story and claim it as her own. There were not always rights or wrongs, merely choices which had consequences, all of which she had survived. She felt a sense of detachment from everyday life that only age could bring. Her detachment didn't imply apathy but rather, perspective. Her ability to detach from worldly agonies isolated her from others at the deepest level; it was just another facet of her loneliness. But her tears had made her joys deeper, her confusion had paved the way to understanding, and only in the darkest of times came the opportunity to see her inner light shine the brightest. Now it was Tess who was searching for a way out, but sooner or later she'd have to deal with the sorrow of a past decision. It was to be a lonely road.

~ ~ ~

The train station in Grenoble was merely a place where people came and went. But to Tia, it was now so much more. Too many welcomes and goodbyes had been said.

The train screeched as it pulled away. She stood on the platform and watched her world change once more as she waved to Shep and Cristin through the steamy window. They were most certainly a handsome couple; she with her thick, silky dark hair framing her smiling face, and he with the physique of Adonis, towering over her as he leaned into the train window to wave his final farewell. They were off to Paris for a few days before returning to Boston to announce their engagement. Tia thought that Tess and Katie would be pleased.

She was stunned and quite unhappy about the whole affair, but she knew she wouldn't find a sympathetic ear back in the States, so her modus operandi was to say nothing. Time would tell. At Yvette's prompting, Tia had questioned Shep about the discrepancies and non sequiturs of Cristin's behavior. But the search for the truth was met with glib, flip responses, and Shep's defense of Cristin's position only seemed to alienate Tia from her nephew. The man was in love.

The drive home was a flash in time. Absorbed in thought, she neither remembered starting the car nor driving it. Only when she'd crossed the bridge that was two kilometers beyond her cutoff did she realize that she'd been paying no attention. She shook her head, exasperated by her lapse in concentration, but only peripherally realizing the extent of her absent-mindedness. Under her breath, she mumbled the words that one mumbles when no one is there to witness self-annoyance. She turned the car around and headed for home.

As she opened her front door, the phone was ringing. She fumbled in the dark to find the light switch, but the light had burned out and the phone stopped ringing before she could get to it. She found her way into the kitchen and pulled the tassel of her Tiffany lamp. The colors of the shade were gaudily bright and always reminded her of a kaleidoscope and analogously of changes.

She heated the teapot on the cast iron stove, poured herself a cup, and plopped into the cushy chair that swallowed her in one gigantic gulp. The chair was the bearer of her most vivid dreams and the keeper of her innermost thoughts. It had held her during her daydreams and sometimes straight through the night. She knew that when the day came to leave her home in Grenoble, she would have to take the chair. It was like a member of the family, a security blanket- a security chair. She hoped that whoever had called would call back, and it occurred to her that she ought to get an answering machine like the rest of the modern world. But somehow she couldn't bring herself to further mechanize her life. She'd rather just take life as it came to her, naturally, in its own rhythm.

The phone call had probably been Yvette. Despite knowing her for only a little over a year, she knew her as well as she knew anyone. Yvette had introduced scores of her friends to Tia during her first semester at the university. They'd formed the backbone of Tia's support system and social circle. Despite the fact that Yvette had many friends, she had no family. She'd been orphaned at a young age and spent her formative years at Gramercy, an orphanage in the Beaujolais region of France. It was there that she'd also learned German and Italian, not through formal education but from listening to the children who lived there. By her own admission, Yvette had always been attracted to strangers who spoke foreign tongues and brought with them exotic traditions and curious ideas. She called herself "The Xenophile of Gramercy." She told astonishing stories about her years at the orphanage, and although not always happy ones, they were flavorful and fascinating to her listeners. Some people were natural alchemists, creating substance out of nothing, while others evaporated their God-given blessings. Yvette was the former. Yvette was a survivor.

Yvette and Cristin had both been orphaned. In that respect, they had more in common with each other than with Tia. They even shared some similar traits. They were intelligent, shrewd, and acutely perceptive. But that's where the similarities stopped. Yvette was straight-forward and reputably honest. Cristin was evasive and had the instinctive knack of twisting a circumstance or discussion to gratify her self-serving ends. But she did it with such finesse, such ease, one hardly noticed except in retrospect.

Cristin often asked Tia about Yvette's life and was especially fond of Yvette's name. *Yvette Vandall, Yvette Vandall*, she would say to herself. One night Tia had found a sheet of parchment paper, with Yvette's name calligraphied in beautiful script, written over and over and over again, as if the name were a mantra. But that made no sense, so Tia dismissed the thought.

The telephone rang, shooting a shock through Tia's body. She had fallen asleep and her adrenaline fired her off the chair and into the kitchen like a rocket.

She sharply yelled into the receiver, "Hello!"

"Tia, is that you?" inquired the American accent.

"Yes. Who is this?"

"Honey, it doesn't sound like you. It's Tess. Are you all right?"

"Hi! Yes, I'm fine. I'd just drifted off to sleep and the phone startled me out of my wits. Did you call a little earlier, Tess?"

"Yes, about an hour ago."

"I heard the phone ringing when I came in, but couldn't get to it in time. I can't believe I fell asleep for an hour."

"Tia, you have no idea how glad I am you're home. I was scared that you might be out of town."

"What's wrong? You sound frantic."

"I just need some answers and you're the only one who can help me."

"Ask away."

"It concerns Cristin. Tia, I haven't heard from her since she left. But I've heard from Katie that Shep has met Cristin. Is that true?"

"Yes. That's true." Tia's voice didn't disguise her disapproval.

"Why do you say it that way?"

"What do you want to know, Tess?"

"Are Cristin and Shep, friends?"

"Oh, I guess you could say that. They're on their way to Paris as we speak before they head home to Boston to announce their engagement to the family."

"Oh, my God. Oh, my God. You have to stop them."

"Tessa, what are you talking about? I thought you'd be thrilled. What's going on?"

"You have to stop them, Tia."

"I can't stop them. I have no idea where they are. Why would you want me to stop them?"

"Forgive me, Tia. I can't explain it over the phone. Oh honey, maybe they're just friends. Maybe it's not as serious as you think.

It's only been ten months since Peri died. Shep couldn't be serious."

"Well, I know they're heading for Dalian's Jewelers when they hit Paris, and I suspect that Cristin will be donning a titanic diamond on her dainty little ring finger before long. Why are you so upset?"

"I promise I'll explain later. I have to go now. I'm sorry this seems so mysterious, but trust me; I have to speak to Katie before I discuss it with anyone else. Just trust me, pet. I'll talk with you soon. Bye for now."

Tia held the phone in her left hand and stared at it. Never in her life had she heard her big sister so agitated and ambiguous. Tessa, the anchor of the family. Tessa, whose life was Tia's oasis in the desert, her constant. Since their mother's death, Tessa had assumed the matriarchal role of the family as a natural ascension of rank. And suddenly, with one phone call, the security Tia had taken for granted felt threatened. There was nothing to do but exactly what Tess had requested of her…to trust her and wait.

On the other side of the world, Tess's darkest hour had descended. She would speak to Ren that night, as soon as he walked through the door. She would candidly, remorsefully, tell her story, in hopes that he would align himself with her. Without his support and his understanding, she would not have the courage to face Katie. She busied herself packing for her trip to the East Coast, the trip she'd looked forward to for months. She'd planned every detail and now she didn't care. Her excitement had been eclipsed by a closer, more overwhelming danger, in her "soul-ar system. "

Suddenly she heard the doorbell, her favorite chimes. Never before had they sounded foreboding.

"Honey, I'm home."

"I'll be right down." She adjusted her necklace, her belt, her earrings. She nervously changed her blouse to appear fresher and prettier. Her hands shook as she reapplied her lipstick and lengthened her lashes with mascara. She quickly turned to pouf her hair in the mirror and realized how silly she was to be concerned with her looks at a time like this. She gracefully walked down the stairs and hugged her husband.

"Well you must have had a good day," he said as he hugged her tightly. "What's up?"

"No, you go first. Come into the living room and tell me all about your day. I'm already anticipating how much I'm going to miss you."

"Well," he said as he stretched one arm across the back of the sofa and held her with the other, "I had lunch with Lissa today. She said to say hello."

"She did? Well, that's a first, isn't it?" Tess smiled.

"We had the best talk we've had in years. And I owe so much of her progress to you."

"To me? What are you talking about?"

"She's at a very impressionable age. She loves her mother, because, after all, Mel is her mother. She's been fed garbage for years about my leaving ten years ago, but I think she's starting to understand how that all came about. It's the old "actions speak louder than words" scenario. She watches her mother at home, living off alimony payments, getting fatter, bitchier, and more miserable as each month passes. And she looks at you, active, happy and taking a bite out of life every chance you get. And she's come to the conclusion that she likes your style better. She as much as said so."

"That's wonderful, Rennie. I'm so happy for her. Boy, what a difference a year can make!"

"I had no idea how big an impression getting your book published would make on her. She has apparently told everyone, including her teachers at school, that her step-mother is Tess Monson, the author. And she asked that I give this to you tonight."

Ren pulled an envelope from his inside coat pocket and handed it to his wife. Smiling, but not saying a word, he nodded for her to open it.

Dear Ms. Monson,

It has come to our attention that you are Lissa Parker's step-mother. May we be among many to congratulate you on the publication of your book? We understand that you are presently preparing to go on a book signing tour in the East. However, upon your return, if you could find time to contact us, we would like to talk to you about being a keynote speaker at an upcoming program.

Once again, congratulations. We eagerly await your response.

Sincerely,

Janis Forster,

Principal/Jefferson High School

"What a lovely invitation, Ren."

"Get used to it. You're about to be thrust into the hyper-space of media attention, my darling."

"That's not what I want. I just want to be able to tell and sell my stories. I don't want anything else to change. I want the world to stay just like it is, right now, tonight, here alone with you. Oh Rennie, I'd give anything if that were true."

"You sound distressed. This is a wonderful time of our lives. Your writing is acclaimed, you're setting out to meet the world, and even my teenage daughter is looking up to you as a role model. I love you, Tessa."

~ ~ ~

Hours later, Tess, pondered the irony of the evening. She'd been fully prepared to tell him everything, but had been defused by his adoration, and unable to resist his amorous disposition. They'd lain on cool white sheets and felt the chilling autumn breezes drift over their bodies, as if shrouding them with protective auras, making them strong for what was to come.

The next day dragged. Tess set an appointment with Ren to meet at the swings down by the creek at five. It was a beautiful Indian summer day and somehow the big out-of-doors seemed safer to Tess than their own home. She packed a picnic dinner, and grabbed red woolen blankets from the cedar closet so they could clear a patch of fallen leaves and eat under the balding canopy of elm trees. She had visions of curling up in his arms, and together, watching the frigid water head for the Gulf of Mexico. Perhaps the romance of the setting and the closeness they would feel would soften the news she needed to relay.

She arrived at the chosen spot. In the middle of the blanket/tablecloth, she turned a bowl upside down and covered it with a tangerine napkin, on top of which she placed a yellow pottery vase with orange and rust asters. She then placed an eggplant vertically in the middle of a large platter and stuck fringed toothpicks with shrimp and sesame-sprinkled cream cheese squares into its body. Around the eggplant, she lay slices of roast beef, alternated with small bunches of chilled asparagus on lettuce leaves and decorated with bands of pimento. She emptied a glass jar of marinated olives and tomatoes into a crystal dish that Ren's mother had given her and displayed a platter of his favorite sugar cookies. Ren had taught her years ago how important presentation was. She knew he would appreciate her efforts.

She waited and waited. She barely noticed the school children kicking a ball back and forth across the leafy carpet and laughing with warbling glee. She only incidentally noticed lovers, arm in arm, following the serpentine path that traced the creek's winding course. She only peripherally observed a couple of Barrows Goldeneyes that were uncommonly seen and had to be lost, vagrants among the more common Mallards that clung to the reeds at feeding time. Her thoughts were on Ren. Why was he late? What words would she choose? What would he say?

Suddenly her trance was broken. She heard a voice yelling, "Heads up! Heads up!" It was Ren, running toward her with the enthusiasm of a young quarterback, his arm cocked to throw a football. She leapt to her feet and ran backwards with blood surging competitively through her veins. She caught the ball and before she knew it, he'd tackled her and they were rolling in the crunchy leaves that smelled of oak and maple and sycamore.

"Where have you been? I thought you'd forgotten me, big boy,"

"Sorry. I was running late and couldn't very well come here in my suit, so I went home to change, and the phone started ringing. You know how that goes. By the way, Tia left a rather cryptic message on the machine, something about calling her when you were ready to talk. She sounded so serious."

"Oh, I talked to her yesterday. And I realized I have to talk to Katie first. Honey, let's eat. We'll talk about that later. I'm starved."

"Whatever you want, Madame Book-Signer. What have we here? Your presentation is outstanding."

"Thank you. The Cabernet is in the cooler. I even brought our Baccarat crystal, in the box, of course."

Ren uncorked the bottle and poured two glasses of dark ruby wine. As they interlocked arms and toasted their good fortune, Tess began to doubt the execution of her courageous intentions. As the banquet depleted and the sun expired, the air chilled and Tess's mission seemed compromised.

She inhaled with a nervous gust of air. "Let's go for a walk."

"Babe, I'd rather not. Let's put all of this in the car and head home."

"Rennie, wait. There's something I need to tell you, something I need you to hear."

"I'm all yours, sweetheart. But it's getting cold; let's do it at home. Grab the blankets and the football. I'll get the basket and the cooler!"

Anxiety torpedoed her courage, and anger now fueled her ineffectiveness.

~ ~ ~

The confession began awkwardly.

She pleaded, "Rennie, I have done something wrong. I didn't think it was, but it was. And now I have to tell you... and Katie...

and Cristin. But I have to tell you first. Please, tell me you love me one more time before you hear these words. Please."

"Tessa, nothing could be as bad as you're making it out to be. Just tell me," he said with tenderness as he took her hands in his.

"Okay. I'll just say it. Do you remember a year and a half ago when I received that letter from Cristin? Well, the letter wasn't exactly misdelivered. She sent it T. Monson, whom she thought was her mother."

He nodded, puzzled.

"Well, of course, you know that I'm not. But I didn't tell you or Cristin the whole truth. I thought it would never matter. I thought I was doing the right thing. I swear I did, Rennie."

"Continue."

"I am not her mother." She paused, her hands trembling. "But Katie is."

"What? How can that be? Cristin is younger than Ingrid."

"Katie had an affair with another man. Stefan doesn't know about the child, and neither do their children. About twenty years ago, she went away for a few months to 'clear her head.' You know how rocky their marriage has been. Anyway, she never told me, but I put it together and Sondra confirmed it."

"Enter stage right, the mysterious Sondra."

"Rennie, I'm so sorry I didn't tell all of this to you up front. I just thought it would never come out."

"No, Tessa. You knew I would have objected. Go on."

"I just thought that we could include Cristin in our lives and be sure she had a family, our family. Rennie, she's my niece."

"She's our niece. But more to the point, she's Katie's daughter. Why are you telling me now?" Ren's voice assumed a tone of sarcasm that chilled her confidence.

"Oh, Rennie, please don't be angry with me. This is difficult enough as it is." She felt a stabbing in her throat, as if she couldn't speak.

"Just go on."

"The bottom line is this. Cristin and Shep have met in France. They've fallen in love and are en route to Boston this week to announce their engagement."

Ren looked at his wife as if she were a stranger. He stared at her as he silently analyzed the extensive consequences of her cover-ups. He panted in consecutive exhales like a bull. Then he stood up and walked away from her.

"Rennie, please say something."

With the vacant stare one sees in a fighter after he rises from a near knockout, he turned slowly and looked at her.

"Rennie?"

"Be quiet! Don't say a word."

The abyss between them widened and deepened with each leaden second. Focused, he paced the room with powerful strides, then turned to her and said, "Don't say another word, Tessa. Let me talk. I just need to get this straight. You have known that Cristin was Katie's daughter since shortly after you received that letter. You elected not to tell me because you knew I would disapprove of any deceit. You decided not to tell Katie to protect her past. And you determined that Cristin did not have the right to know about her birth mother, but you did have the right to play surrogate mother. Meanwhile, Katie's daughter is romantically involved and about to marry her own brother?" Ren's voice had crescendoed. "Tell me, are you enjoying playing God?"

"No, Rennie, no!"

"I'm not through! I thought I knew you. I thought I could guess your every move, that I understood your integrity, and could trust your judgment. I had no idea that you were capable of such deception. I thought we were partners, that we shared equally in life's decisions that could affect us. You betrayed what we stood for. You compromised our alliance. You violated the sanctity of our trust. What were you thinking, Tessa?"

Hearing the sound of her name gave her an opening to speak. "Rennie, I couldn't let her go. She had no one. She is part of my family, my blood. I know now that I should have let her go. But I thought it was harmless."

"Harmless? So harmless, you couldn't tell me? So harmless, you chose to lie to me?"

"I didn't see it as a lie."

"It was a lie of omission, Tessa, and every bit as venomous as a bold faced lie. Can you see what this is going to do to your family? I presume you will tell Katie as soon as possible. She needs to stop this marriage. And the ripples of this 'harmless' omission go on and on. What do you think this will do to your own sister's marriage? What is Stefan going to say about this twenty-two year old child who has appeared out of nowhere? What will this do to Shep? The loss of Lady Love number two. To hell with Cristin."

The rest of the night was black and empty. Tess didn't hear another word from Ren. He left the house, and wouldn't return until morning. But he left behind words that would torment her for the rest of her life; words of hurt that would never completely heal; words of distrust that could never be retracted. She was alone, perhaps for the first time in her life. It was the first time since her childhood that she wished she were older. This time she wished time away because she was desperate to see how it would all resolve. But this time life demanded that she experience the pain.

As the night lived out its hours, she became more philosophical and less emotional. Her anguish didn't lessen, but her clarity improved. She didn't have the strength to examine the damage to her own marriage, so she moved on to the next task at hand- her talk with Katie. It was as if the dustbowl of her mind had cleared and she distinctly saw what she must do and how. She would plow her way through, cutting a swath through the lives of the people she loved most, but she would do it and accept the consequences. She now considered Serena's insightful suggestion to look at the worst conceivable repercussions and accept them as possibilities. Through some mystical madness, her despair evolved to strength. And with that strength came a dispassionate relief that enabled her to fall asleep, escaping into a valley of calm where no one could touch her.

~ ~ ~

Ren returned to the house in the early morning hours. He'd anticipated a scene of hysteria and agitation, but, instead found his wife sleeping in their bed, on his side of the bed, on her back with one arm extended like a ballerina. She was as graceful sleeping as she was in her waking state, he thought to himself. The room smelled of Tess, that female fragrance that was uniquely hers, mixed with lavender lotion that she always used before retiring. As he stood over her, he traced her form with his eyes, following the curves of the body that so delighted him, the body of the woman he thought he knew. She was dressed in the silk ecru nightgown he had given her for her birthday, and she looked like an angel with wings spread. In her left hand she held a picture of the two of them that Cristin had taken the previous spring, when the poppies had bloomed in the backyard. As he stared at her, he wondered how this exquisite creature could have shut him out of such an important decision in their lives. His anger had quelled, but he felt betrayed, and time would either heal his wounds, or not. The intimacy and devoted trust he had cherished was no longer, and the best he could promise her was to give it time.

Tess stirred and awakened to find her husband standing over her. Startled, she sat up.

"Rennie, you're back."

"I've been back for a while."

"How long have you been standing there?" she asked, acting self-conscious and pulling the sheet to cover herself.

"For a while. When does your plane leave?" he asked.

"At eleven. What time is it?"

"It's eight o'clock."

"I have to finish packing."

"I'll be downstairs," he said as he turned from her, leaving no open doors for discussion.

The morning was staid and formal. They made separate breakfasts, and went to great lengths to avoid one another. Mid-morning, Ren drove her to the airport with few words passing between them.

"Thanks for the ride, sweetheart."

"You're welcome. Have a good trip."

Then she spilled.

"Rennie, I have to say something before I leave. I'm so sorry about what I have done. I was self-serving and wrong. I wish I'd understood the consequences of the decision, but I didn't. I don't blame you at all for feeling the way you do. I would do anything to take it all back. I only hope you can find it in your heart to forgive me, Rennie. I know it will take time. Please, give it time. You must know that I love you. I always will."

Tess exited the car without looking back. Ren watched his wife walk away, strong, determined, and scared. He respected the fact that she wasn't crumbling, but that was the only support he could muster. She had turned their world upside down and he wanted her to feel remorse. He wanted her to suffer for her wrongs. To have forgiven her at that moment would have rendered him ungratified. To have forgiven her would have forged himself a better man.

Chapter 22

The first stop of the tour: Toronto, Ontario. Tess hadn't questioned why they'd schedule her to begin her journey in a foreign country, because she'd always wanted to see the stellar cosmopolitan city of eastern Canada. "Canada" had a magic ring to it. She enjoyed meeting Canadians. They were more wholesome, less affected than Americans. They were better educated and spoke the English language with a fluency that put their southern neighbors to shame. They spoke of stars, rather than movie stars, and ideologies more frequently than fashion. Tess was particularly fascinated by their sophisticated political awareness, on the one hand, and their almost adolescent infatuation with the royal family, on the other.

Her second stop was Montreal which was an enigma, since her book had not been translated into French, and the general populace spoke only French. Nevertheless, as she signed their purchased copies, she felt like a prize in a curiosity shop. Before taking leave of Canada, she took a side trip to the provincial capital of Quebec City, pronounced "Kabek," as she soon learned. She stayed at the beautiful Chateau de Frontenac, which overlooked the St. Lawrence Seaway, the eastern gateway to the Canadian heartland. The Chateau was dressed from head to foot in fleur-de-lis: fleur-de-lis patterns in the carpet, fleur-de-lis ensconced in the ceilings, fleur-de-lis flags, serviettes, silverware, dinnerware, sheets, towels, and bedspreads. She was transported into a foreign world, boldly proud of its rich cultural heritage. For the first time in her life, she yearned to visit Ireland and Scotland to discover her own roots and experience pride of her origins. She hungered to belong to something bigger than she, a family bigger than she had previously known.

Having been a bright child with a vivid imagination and an active dream life, Tess had always looked forward as much to going to bed as she had to waking up, sometimes more. This led her to having trouble distinguishing reality from fantasy. She didn't remember when she became aware of the contrariety, but it was vaguely related to her parents telling her not to lie. And she hadn't understood. But that was then and this was now. She now needed to define and defend the boundaries between the kingdoms of Right and Wrong.

Ren was constantly on her mind. Her emotions were raw but controlled. She made it through the days one hour at a time, and dared not think past the present. At times, she couldn't suppress the pain, but, as Serena had said, it was an inevitable part of her human experience. The facts would not change, no matter how she crafted and manipulated them; no matter how often she played and replayed each detail; no matter how she took apart the puzzle and tried to reassemble it, the picture remained intact. How she handled her feelings, and how she conducted herself, were the variables and the potential key to the door marked "Survival," beyond which she might salvage her relationships and her self-respect. Or not.

She had time to herself to invent scores of scripts she could use when facing Katie, but she realized that she wouldn't know exactly what to say until the moment was upon her. She, the master of words, knew that her explanations and contrivances to soften the truth would probably be ineffective. Surely the Muses would come to her rescue and save her from the monstrous tale that with one big breath of fire could consume her life. Her thoughts see-sawed between clarity and paranoia, until their dizzying effect threw her into a state of panic.

She arrived in New York City and was driven to The Plaza, passing the Vanderbilt Chateau, St. Patrick's Cathedral, and a successive string of townhomes and galleries. Throughout her adult life, she'd read brochures on The Plaza, describing it as "New York at its best," but she was not prepared for the superlative grandeur of the Beaux Arts palace dressed in French Renaissance elegance. The center of the main lobby coughed up the Palm Court, enclosed with large arched windows, towering marble columns and crystal chandeliers. Lush green palms softened the palatial atmosphere, rendering it comfortable, and suggesting a European outdoor café. The antique marble tables were set with fresh floral arrangements, and the corridors leading to the elevators were wide and bordered by walls, dripping with exquisite masterpieces from the paintbrushes of inspired artists.

From her room on the eighteenth floor, she overlooked Central Park. She walked onto her balcony and to either side she saw turrets, gables, and architectural designs she couldn't name, but would never forget. Then she paid the bellboy, laid down on her bed, and cried. She wanted to share The Plaza with Ren and feel his unscarred love. She'd wanted Katie to visit her above Central Park as they had planned, without having to transpose their evening together into the calamity that it was destined to be. She wanted the world to go away.

Tess awakened to a knock at her door. Her publisher had expected her to join him in the Edwardian Room of the hotel at seven 'o' clock and she'd overslept. She arrived forty-five minutes late, assembled like a perfect package with a ribbon in her hair. No one suspected her misery. She unwittingly matched the decor. Her blush floral suit complemented the flower design on the backs of the chairs, and her gold accessories matched the gold utensils on each side of the Plaza china dinnerware. She was picture perfect, right on cue. Yes, she was dining at The Plaza. And Ren should have been there with her.

After dinner, she returned to her room to find a message from Katie confirming that she, Ingrid, and their entourage would leave for the city the following morning and would see Tess at the bookstore at noon. Katie further explained that Ingrid and her friends would take the train back to Boston that night and she would spend the night with Tess. Her words were touching. *"I'm so proud of you. Can hardly wait see you."* If Tess could have postponed the inevitable, she would have, but there was no mercy. Time was marching on, with neither pity nor compassion. The clock ticked away the hours until the dreaded truth was to be spoken and Tess was a prisoner of the universe.

~ ~ ~

Not at all like the old, musty store she'd envisioned in her mind, the bookstore smelled of leather and cherry pipe tobacco from the Scottish Pipe Store next door. The leather smell was intoxicating. All of the furniture was leather, even the mirror frames and lamps. It was cheerful for a New York City shop, bright with fresh flowers and lilting with Baroque music. The cool granite floors were sectioned by subject categories, and the corresponding sitting areas were decorated with mauve carpet and comfortable navy leather chairs that welcomed people to take their time and browse through their selections before finalizing their purchases. There was a coffee bar toward the interior where customers could order a latte or a cranberry juice and, on occasion, listen to a local artist perform on a lute or sitar. On this particular morning, Tess Monson was scheduled to sign copies of her new book. The store manager, Geraldine, greeted her with uncommon cordiality. She was a plump woman in her mid-sixties with slumped shoulders and a silver ponytail that slithered down her back like a snake. Within minutes, Tess concluded that Geraldine had to have been a former librarian. Her ghost would undoubtedly haunt libraries and bookstores for centuries; her spirit, incestuously bound to her beloved volumes.

Geraldine ceremoniously ushered Tess to the table where she would sit and meet her readers. There was a stack of books on the left side of the table, and a beautiful purple fountain pen to be used for the inscriptions.

"Would you like a cup of coffee? Or will the caffeine just rattle your nerves?" She twittered like a young girl with an old woman's voice.

"I'd love a glass of juice," Tess replied. "I noticed they had a tropical blend of papaya, mango, or some other exotic flavor at the bar. That would be perfect. Thank you."

"Your wish is our command, Ms. Monson." The ever-pleasing Geraldine twinkled.

"Please call me Tess." Tess smiled to herself, as she was not accustomed to being addressed by her pen name. In recent years, Tess Monson had been a name she'd only seen in print.

The first two hours flew. The pace was not hectic but constant. She wondered what it would be like to have so much time on her hands that she could leisurely stroll from store to store. She wondered who the casual, unhurried people were. They would be the bloodline of her commercial success. All in all, they were pleasant, a little pushier than in the Midwest, but amiable for "New Yorkers." They asked predictable questions, such as` if she were married, or were any of her characters based on real people she knew; then, the typical inquiries like how long had she known she wanted to be a writer, did she know what her next book would be about, and would she be home from her tour before the holidays? Her favorite inscription of the morning was "To Tillie Louise, The Spiderwoman."

As the clock approached twelve noon, Tess became fidgety and less focused on her duties. The last three customers before her lunch break received autographs on their inside covers minus the well wishes. Never in her life had she been more anxious to see someone she didn't want to see. She repeatedly smoothed her skirt over her knees and her breathing became less and less audible. The only sound that registered was an asthmatic hacking at the rear of the store. Suddenly there was a banging on the window to her right. Ingrid and five of her friends were tapping and waving with irrepressibly excited faces, like children trying to win the attention of a puppy in a pet store window.

Tess waved them in and stood up behind her station.

"Aunt Tess, I can't believe it. Look at you, the author! Everyone, this is my famous Aunt Tess." Ingrid beamed. "This is Marissa and Anne and Shaina and Hiroko and Joni." She squealed as she introduced the delighted audience. "And we all want to buy your book!"

"Sweetheart, why don't you buy one and pass it around?"

"Don't be silly. We've already discussed it. In the spirit of your success and this memorable outing, we'll each buy one! Oh, by the way, Mom is parking the car. She'll be right here. Can we take you out to lunch, Aunt Tess? Mom knows an Irish pub that's walking distance from here."

"Terrific. I don't resume my duties until two o'clock."

The bell over the bookstore door rang and in walked Katie, looking as beautiful as Tess had ever seen her. Sobriety and a few pounds agreed with her sister, and the light in her eyes that for years had been dimmed, now gleamed. She wore a long camel cashmere coat with a deep gold scarf that accentuated her Irish complexion and deepened her hazel eyes. Katie said nothing as she approached Tess with open arms and an exuberant smile.

"Hi!" she said warmly as she hugged her little sister. "I'm so excited to be here with you. Mum and Daddy would be so proud, Tess."

Tess responded as she melted into Katie's heartfelt hug. "I miss them too."

"Mom, we'll walk down to the pub and get a table. You and Aunt Tess take your time, okay?"

"Fine, honey. See you soon." Turning to Tess, she continued. "So tell me, how has it gone this morning? And how was Canada?"

"It's been wonderful, Katie. The accommodations have far exceeded my expectations. You should have seen the Chateau de Frontenac in Quebec City. We must go there together someday. And the food, oh my God, the food has been to die for. Going from French cuisine to The Edwardian Room at The Plaza! I'm going to be a very large woman."

They laughed together like they had when they were little girls with seemingly not a care in the world.

"Tell me, what about the actual book signings? How have they been going?"

"Well, they are a bit more mundane than I'd anticipated. Like one might expect, they aren't as glamorous as they sound."

Katie nodded and smiled as they began walking arm in arm, down a busy street in Manhattan. Two sisters, watching only the sidewalk as they planted their steps side by side, basking in the sunshine of being together again. For Tess, from that afternoon on, the cacophony of honking horns would forever trigger an association of love for her sister Katie.

The day passed swiftly. After lunch, they returned to the store, then later had dinner in an Italian section of town before putting the girls on a train back to Boston. The conversations had focused on stories that Ingrid and her girlfriends shared. It had been years since Tess had been with a group of young women who had yet to forge their lives. It brought back a myriad of forgotten memories and made her feel old.

Tess and Katie returned to The Plaza after nightfall. Katie insisted on a tour of the lobby level before adjourning to their room. Then effervescently, she entered their suite, bounding from room to room on a mission of discovery, while Tess watched her sister enjoy the fruits of her success. They poured virgin daiquiris she'd ordered and had sent up from the bar, and they relaxed into the arms of the evening. Katie shared that she'd never been happier, that her life with Stefan was solid and loving, and for the first time she could remember, all of the stars were aligned. She reiterated time after time how proud she was to have Tess as her sister. She kicked her shoes into the air and dramatically flung herself on the nearest sofa, striking a pose. Then raising her glass, she made a toast.

"To my little sister, a star among planets. Here's to your continued success as an author, as a paragon of virtue to all who love you, as my dearest friend. Skal!"

Tess looked horrified and Katie mistook it for loneliness.

"Honey, it's a shame that Ren couldn't be here with you."

For the first time in the course of the perfect day, a sensitive subject had been broached. All day Ingrid and her retinue had provided a protective buffer between the outer world and inner issues.

"Yes, I miss him terribly."

"How is Ren, anyway? I haven't even asked."

"He's okay."

"That doesn't sound very convincing, Tessa. Just how okay is he?" Katie prodded, sitting out of her relaxed posture.

"He's not," Tess admitted.

"Is he ill? Has he lost his job?"

"No, nothing like that."

"Well, for God's sake, what then?" asked Katie, trying to extract meaning from her sister's disturbing evasiveness.

The moment had come and Tess felt stronger than she had imagined she would.

"Kate, I've done something terrible. I didn't think it was at the time, but I have unwittingly betrayed a lot of people whom I love. Rennie, for one."

The following pause was excruciating, but Katie said nothing. All the frivolity and joy was sucked out of the moment by an invisible pump and she waited in the fearful vacuum for Tess to finish her confession.

"You, for two. Sondra. Your entire family." Tess made no eye contact. Instead she stared straight ahead into an empty fireplace as she spoke. "I only hope and pray that you will forgive me. I didn't mean any harm. But now, with Shep falling in love, I have to tell you."

Katie looked pathetically confused.

"Tess, you're making too much out of whatever it is. It couldn't be that bad."

"It is, believe me, it is."

Frustrated, Katie raised her voice. "What is it? What have you done?"

Tess looked into her sister's eyes and said, "I should never have opened the letter."

"What letter?"

"The letter from your daughter, Katie. The daughter you gave birth to twenty-two years ago and put up for adoption. The one nobody was supposed to know about."

Katie sat still-stunned, frozen, and breathless.

"Go on."

"When I realized who she was and she was alone in the world, I brought her into mine so that I could watch out for her. I didn't tell you because I didn't want to upset you. I contacted Sondra who reluctantly told me that Stefan didn't know about your pregnancy, so I surmised that the kids didn't either. I didn't even tell Rennie who she was."

Suddenly, Katie, obviously deducing the answer, heard herself scream.

"Who is she, Tessa? Who is she?"

"Oh, Katie, it's Cristin. Cristin is your daughter."

Katie's fingers loosened from her glass, sending it crashing to the floor.

"How can you be so sure? How do you know this for sure?"

"Because she had the letter that you gave the adoptive parents, and because Mum's initials were inscribed on the back of her locket, Katie."

Katie started to hiss with catlike sounds issuing from her throat that were primal and clearly inconsolable. Like a wounded panther looking for an escape, she paced the room. Tess watched her sister work herself into a state of hysteria, hyperventilating until she dropped to her knees, then slumped against the table. There was no attempt to communicate, only mutual solitary pain.

Eventually, Tess moved toward Katie in an attempt to comfort her, but was contemptuously waved away with a look of violent rage that defied consolation and bludgeoned Tess's heart.

What seemed like eternity passed before either uttered a word.

Then Katie spoke. "My son. My son." She whispered something indecipherable and began to sob.

Tess's tears felt selfish and unworthy, born of shame. She watched her sister, at the self-professed "happiest time" of her life, face a pain from which she might never recover. Katie's tears were forlorn, her heart devastated.

Anguish hung in the air like pockets of invisible vapor, which expanded to press against every nerve.

Finally Katie stood and delivered her decree.

"Don't say a word. I am going now. Shep and Cristin are coming to town the day after tomorrow, and I need to speak to Stefan before they arrive. This is a nightmare. No, it's worse than my worst nightmare."

"Katie…"

"No. I don't want to talk to you, Tess. Don't call me. Maybe someday we'll speak of this. But until that day comes, I don't want to see your face or hear your voice. Leave me alone."

Katie walked to the door without so much as a glance.

The confrontation, the confession, had been every bit as difficult as she'd expected. Unlike so many things in life that are exaggerated in anticipation, this reality was worse than her distempered imagination had conceived. Katie didn't want to see or hear from her again. There was not even a slightly cracked window of forgiveness. But of course, there wouldn't be. The buck had been passed. It was now Katie's turn to tell her loved ones of her past. It was now Katie's turn to lose everything that mattered to her.

Tess robotically twisted the silver bracelets on her wrist as she watched the night descend over Central Park until the silhouette of the tree line became less and less distinct- until it was erased into nothingness. She thought of calling Ren, but checked her impulse, hoping that he would place the call first. He didn't.

Chapter 23

The road from New York to Boston was longer than it had ever been before. Katie despaired without focus to find a solution. She felt a pounding in her temples as if she had taken a drug to amplify every pulse. For the first while, she hardly breathed, holding her life force and pressing it down hard against her body from the inside until she'd gasp for breath. Her nerves were like jagged teeth of a saw, ripping, grating, and tearing her insides to shreds. The agonizing secret from her past was about to be exposed. She inadvertently bit her lower lip until she tasted blood, then, on purpose, bit it harder to squeeze the blood until there was no more.

As she approached Boston, her logical mode kicked in. Her survival depended upon her ability to strategize. She no longer saw the road on which her stare was fixed; she was on automatic pilot to get herself home. She thought back to twenty-two years ago. Stefan had known that something was wrong but had he suspected an infidelity? Probably not. Not an infidelity, and certainly not a child. As she neared her home, through the autumn fog, she hugged the street like a rodent whose vision is limited and close to the ground. Stefan would not be expecting her as she'd intended to stay in the city. And sure enough, every light had been extinguished and the house was asleep.

She quietly opened the door and wiped the dampness of her shoes on the mat that welcomed her into her own home with braided cloth ribbons, spelling "Home Sweet Home." The house smelled of garlic and popcorn, undoubtedly vestiges of take-out pizza and Stefan's late night snack. Her keys dropped into her coat pocket and hit her pager with a jingle which startled Charley. He met her in the hallway, his big, padded paws sleepily plodding their way to greet her. His eyes were at half mast, indicating that he'd been sleeping, but he'd never miss an opportunity to give her his big slobbery licks. His tail whacked the floor as he rolled over to accept his gratuitous tummy scratch. Man's best friend, loyal and nonjudgmental, never wavering in dutiful affection.

She removed her coat and climbed the stairs to her bedroom. The house was cold because only days ago they had removed the window screens and hadn't yet put on the storm windows for the winter season. In their bedroom, Stefan had forgotten to close the windows, so that the white sheers ballooned outward into the fog like translucent jellyfish of the night. Stefan was snoring, the familiar snore that occurs deep in the back of a man's throat and resonates exponentially loud, even with his mouth closed. One of life's little mysteries. His snores wouldn't bother her. She knew she wouldn't sleep soundly anyway. What she needed was time to think- time to feel close to her husband before he pulled away.

~ ~ ~

His voice broke the silence of the dawn.

"Katie, what are you doing home? I thought you were staying with Tess in New York last night."

Stefan's face loomed over her like a mask suspended from the ceiling.

"I decided to come back."

"Did you two have a quarrel?"

"No. Not exactly. Is Ingrid here?"

"No, but she called last night to say that she'd swing by late this morning because she forgot her coat the other night."

"Good. I want to talk to her about something. I want to talk to both of you, actually, but together."

"What's going on?" Stefan inquired, clearing his throat with a gruff, manly cough.

"I want to spend the morning in bed with my husband, if you don't mind. Everything else can wait."

Katie rolled over on top of him and sat up, straddling and mounting his hips. She knew he loved it when she became aggressive, her mane of auburn hair covering her shoulders and the brown flecks in her hazel eyes, blazing like fiery opals. Minutes later, she melted into his body until she couldn't tell where she ended and where he began. She whispered over and over how much she loved him, asking him to always love her as much as he did that morning. On the cold rainy morning in October, faced with the possibility of losing his love, she convinced herself how much she cared.

As Stefan took his shower, she reevaluated her decision to talk to her husband and daughter together, realizing that he had the right to privacy when being informed of her love affair that had resulted in a daughter, a daughter who was hers, but not his. She took a bath and asked Stefan if he would join her in the family room.

He looked especially handsome in jeans and a denim shirt, his dark hair, peppered slightly with silver flecks at the temples and over his ears. Having just been the object of her sexual attention, he appeared transparently smug. Wrestling with the need to remain calm, Katie met him with a kiss and a cup of coffee.

"What's with the ceremony?" He smiled, actually flirting with his wife of twenty eight years.

"I have something I need to tell you, Stefan." Her mouth felt like it was filled with cotton balls, her lips smacking from the dryness. She put down her coffee cup, her hand trembling, and her eyes nervously twitching.

"Katie, what's going on?"

"Give me a moment to compose myself." Her eyes spontaneously welled with tears, so completely that she could only see the outline of her husband sitting across from her.

"Stefan, I made a terrible mistake, years ago, and circumstances force me to tell you about it now. God knows I don't want to."

She lowered her eyes as she nervously twisted her wedding ring and inhaled a dramatically resonant breath. She glanced at his imposing posture and stare, intent on hearing whatever it was that she had to say.

"Stefan, I'm just going to say this quickly. Do you remember in 1974 when I went out West for a few months?"

He nodded.

"Well, it was a difficult time as you recall. I was very confused. Stefan, what you didn't know was that I'd had an affair, a short-lived affair."

"Who was he?"

"It doesn't matter."

"The hell it doesn't. Who was he?" he demanded.

"Derek Northrup."

"Good God! The senator?"

"Yes."

"Why are you telling me this? That was twenty some years ago. Why now?"

"Because I had a baby, his baby. I gave her up for adoption. I couldn't ask you to be the child's father, Stefan. You would have known anyway. We hadn't slept together for months."

"And you're telling me this now because the child has found you and wants something? Money? Is this an extortion prank?"

"No. I'm telling you this now because until last night I didn't even know who the child was." She paused and gulped. " Last night Tess told me that the child is Cristin. Cristin is my daughter."

Saying the words, Katie began to cry.

"The Cristin who our son plans to marry? Our son and your daughter? We're talking about incest, Katrina."

"We have to stop them. It will break Shep's heart. How will he ever forgive me?"

"You're concerned with whether Shep will forgive you or not? What about me? What about me?"

The tension in the room became stiff and cold enough to slice.

"Do you have any idea what you've done?" screamed Stefan.

"I didn't mean for this to happen!"

"Tess knew this? Who else knew it? Am I the last one to know the sordid truth? Have I been the laughing stock of this family for years? Who else knew, Katie? Who else knew?"

"Only Sondra. I never even told Tess. No one else knew, I swear."

"How did your sister come to find out then?"

"Cristin contacted Tess because she thought Tess was her mother. Tess put two and two together...it's a long story. Tess didn't tell anyone, not even Ren, not even Cristin. Cristin doesn't know anything. She's an innocent party."

"Everyone's an innocent party in this convoluted charade, everyone but you! One truth looms above all others. You might as well have written this one in skywriting – WIFE DOESN'T TELL HUSBAND ABOUT LOVE-CHILD!!! How do you think that makes me look? No, don't answer that one. I'll tell you! Like a fool: Cheated-on, betrayed, a goddamn idiot!"

"How dare you use that holier-than-thou tone of voice on me! You, who slept around all of those years! Maybe deep inside I just wanted to get even. But because I'm a woman, I got caught!"

"No, you don't get off that easily. Because you were stupid, Katie, and adulterous. That's why you got caught. I have a few questions for you. How are you going to tell your girls about the affair you had while you were married to me? How do you think they'll look at you for the rest of their lives? And what about your son? Who, may I remind you has been to hell and back this past year. How are you going to tell him that he's been sleeping with his half-sister?"

"Please, Stefan, don't turn your back on me. I need you to help me through this, please!"

"I'm going for a drive." Fuming, he marched out of the room.

Following him, Katie cried, "Stefan! Please! Look at me! I'm different than I was twenty two years ago. I've grown up. I wouldn't do anything to risk losing you and my family."

He stopped dead short of the doorway, looked her straight in the eye and said, "You already have."

He vanished into a panel of cold drizzling rain. As Katie stared out the window, the yard she loved so well became nothing but an impersonal backdrop to her desperation. Everything was hazy- the trees, the house, the flowers, her past, her present, her future. It was impossible to focus on the details of what had happened. She needed to regroup, to see the specifics of her next moves in manageable steps, one by one, laid out on a cosmic conveyer belt. Heidi was away at school: Thank goodness, one less immediate problem to deal with. Ingrid wasn't home, but would soon be. Ingrid was her next challenge.

Katie threw on her raincoat and walked, crying in the rain, blending her tears with nature's tears. Somewhere in time, she was startled by Ingrid's horn. Her daughter leaned over the passenger seat as the window rolled down.

"Mom, what are you doing out here? I thought you were with Aunt Tess. Get in and I'll drive you to the house."

"No, thank you. I'll meet you at home. Go ahead. Please."

The driveway looked endless in pelting rain. Clumsily stepping on her chrysanthemums, which she'd carefully planted in the spring, and which were now pummeled by rain, their golden crowns leaning onto the sidewalk, Katie walked to the house. Ingrid waited at the front door to meet Agony in the guise of her mother's face. Ingrid's was the first compassionate look Katie had seen in hours and she held her daughter tightly. Together they sat for an hour while Katie shared the story with an honest vulnerability that was tenderly received. Ingrid didn't yell or judge her, but sat next to her mother and held her while she cried.

After Katie had confided everything, Ingrid smiled at her and said, "So I have a little sister. Now I know why I liked her so much."

Shocked and relieved by her response, Katie cried all the harder. The roles between them had reversed. Ingrid supported her mother and assured her that eventually everything would work its way through the tangled and twisted feelings of hurt. Even though Katie didn't believe her, the attempt to assuage her pain was transiently comforting. Ingrid promised to be with her when Shep and Cristin were told, and to stand by her when Stefan returned.

Ingrid left her mother alone on the sofa to steep some hot tea, while Katie watched the rain streaming against the window, chaotic, mesmerizing, and constant. The confession opened a chronic wound that now subjected to the light of day, stung like an angry rope burn on her heart. But the exposure of her grievous error was cathartic. She'd witnessed Ingrid's rite of passage, "unexpected in common hours."

"Mom, do you want a slice of lemon?" Ingrid called from the kitchen.

"No, thank you." Katie's voice was now hoarse and fragile. Her daughter entered the room with the silver tea service and two of her Grandma Constance's English teacups and saucers.

"Remember, Mom," she said, "you always told us that when we're feeling blue, to do extra special things, out of the ordinary things, to brighten the day."

Katie smiled, hearing her own words come back to her like a boomerang, from her once-upon-a-time renegade daughter. Somehow even though she'd believed the advice when she'd doled it out, she didn't believe it now. They were just pretty words.

"Mom, if it would help, I can talk to Dad when he comes back."

"Oh, I don't think so, honey." Katie stuttered. "But perhaps, when Heidi returns, perhaps you could help her understand. She's so young. I hate to think how this will affect her."

"Of course, I'll talk to her." Ingrid audibly swallowed her tea and rubbed her throat in pensive thought. "You know, when I was in the kitchen just now, I was thinking about how you reacted when I told you I'd had an abortion. I had no idea what you went through to avoid that decision. I'm so sorry. I just didn't know."

"Honey, please don't apologize. I was the grown-up. I wasn't honest, and it paralyzed me when you needed me most. If I'd told the truth from the beginning, everyone would have been spared a lot of pain. I'm sorry I let you down. If I'd had the courage to talk to you, if I'd had the courage to talk to your Dad twenty some years ago, even at the risk of losing him, but had I told the truth, then none of this would be happening now."

"What about Aunt Tess? What did you say to her when she told you?"

"I don't remember. I was abrupt. I was in shock. There are no words sufficient to describe what I felt when she told me."

"It had to be hard for her too, Mom."

Katie didn't care how Tess felt.

"Is there any chance that Aunt Tess is mistaken?"

"No, she's not. Cristin is exactly the right age. Nothing about this is coincidental. I don't even need to know the details, although someday I'm sure I'll hear them. Do you remember that locket that Cristin wore last Christmas that Tia mentioned?"

Ingrid nodded.

"I never saw it, but Tess told me it was the locket that Grandma gave me, which I passed on to the baby girl I gave away. Cristin is my daughter."

"When are she and Shep arriving?"

"Tomorrow afternoon. Some homecoming it's going to be. Not at all what I'd planned. I dread the whole ordeal. I wish it were tomorrow night and it was over. I'd do anything to be past the hour when I tell Shep that his fiancée is his sister. Oh God, this can't be happening. I never…"

Katie broke down again and sobbed. Hours passed until the day was spent. She quietly prayed for the time when there would be no more tears, when she couldn't squeeze another tear from her swollen, miserable eyes. Ingrid stayed with her mother until she had to leave. By the time the house was dark, Katie exhausted, had fallen asleep on the sofa. Ingrid covered her with an afghan and tiptoed down the hallway, turning on the porch light before she left. Stefan didn't return.

Chapter 24

Katie awakened with a stiff back, her eyes swollen and stuck together. The imminence of the day's events loomed like a guillotine postured to drop. She took her routine shower and instinctively spent the morning watering and pruning plants. Her hydrangeas and asters were comforting, a reminder of that which was beautiful in the world. Stefan arrived with Ingrid. Katie watched them walk up the walkway together, so she quickly assumed an activity in the kitchen, inattentively busying herself.

"Mom, Dad and I are here."

"I'm in the pantry," Katie replied.

Ingrid appeared in the kitchen, alone.

"Where's your father?"

"He went upstairs." She hesitated. "He's angry, Mom."

Katie nodded and her eyes brimmed with tears.

"I know honey. I don't blame him."

~ ~ ~

An hour before their plane touched down, Shep kissed his bride and whispered a toast in her ear as they took their final sip of French wine. They had celebrated for days in and around Paris, dining in famous restaurants and sleeping in famous hotels. But flying home to Boston to share his good news was the finale of his trip abroad.

"Have you been listening to the man behind us?" Shep remarked.

"No, I've been resting."

"He's been bending the ear of the poor woman next to him, proselytizing for the Lord. What's interesting is that he's a natural. He really believes what he's saying and he's not only ardent but quite charismatic in his presentation. An evangelist."

"I'll have to take a look at him when we deplane," she said.

"You know what's so disturbing about hearing that kind of talk? It's so arbitrary and exclusive. There's no discussion. There's no search for truth because he knows the truth. And it's a truth based on what some men wrote about a man who supposedly rose from the dead. If you ask me, the world must have sorely been in need of a miracle to have bought into that one."

"Shep, you sound like a heretic!"

"Heretic of what? Just because I was born into the Judeo-Christian tradition, doesn't mean that I believe in all the dogma and ritual. Don't get me wrong: I believe Jesus was enlightened. The Golden Rule idea is the best one I've ever heard. But I don't buy the bodily resurrection and 'the only son of God routine'."

"Well, do you call yourself a Christian?" Cristin inquired with a bewildered look.

"No. I think I'm more of a Buddhist."

"Wonderful. I married a Buddhist and I didn't even know it. When did you intend to tell me that you wanted to raise little Buddhists? These are the kinds of discussions we should have had before we tied the knot, don't you think?"

"Don't you love me anymore?" he asked, baiting her with his tease.

"I love you more. I love you for the fact that you figure out what you do believe rather than being swallowed up by doctrine."

"Do you want to hear a great story?"

"Tell, tell." Cristin cooed.

"It's about a farmer whose horse ran away. His neighbor pitied him but the farmer replied, 'Who knows whether it's a curse or a blessing.' The next week the horse returned bringing a herd of wild horses home with him. The neighbor was envious and the farmer said again, 'Who knows whether it's a curse or a blessing.' The following week the farmer's son tried to break one of the wild horses and fell off, breaking his legs. And the neighbor commiserated, but the farmer said, 'Who knows whether it's a curse or a blessing.' A few weeks later some soldiers passed through looking for able bodied young men to join their army, and due to his injury, the farmer's son was not drafted. And again, when the neighbor remarked on his timely fortune, the farmer said, 'Who knows whether it is a blessing or a curse.'"

"I like your story," Cristin whispered. "I'm a blessing, not a curse, you know. And I believe I'm the luckiest woman in the world to have found you. Tonight we're going to shock some people in Boston, my darling!"

"And they're going to love you. I can hardly wait to see their faces."

Within minutes the plane had landed. As Shep gathered their belongings, he was astonished to see that behind him, the man he had pegged as an evangelist was merely a boy, maybe in his late teens. He momentarily reflected on the power and potential influence that the deep-voiced youngster represented to a credulous public.

The airport was always a place of intrigue, a storybook of countless journeys in progress. As they walked through the terminal, they brushed the arms of strangers who were perhaps on a trek to Tibet or a village in Tanzania, or en route to Chile or the Galapagos, or maybe about to visit an elderly grandparent in a prairie town of Saskatchewan. The possibilities were endless.

The weather remained rainy and dismal, not exactly what Shep had hoped for to showcase his corner of the world to his new bride. But despite the poor weather, the landscape was beautiful: Roads that were bordered by century old stone walls, and huge oak trees, whose root systems sprawled for blocks under the earth, erasing property lines and creating a gnarly underground world for burrowing critters and creatures. Just as they approached the house veiled in mist, the sun peeked through the low lying clouds, crowning the earth with a dewy halo

Charley heard their car coming up the driveway, impatiently barking to be released into the world of mud and puddles. Ingrid stood at the front door by her mother's side. They exited the car.

Stefan was not present, and much to Shep's surprise, there was no fanfare. "Mom, Ingrid, you remember Cristin?" Shep cupped his wife's elbow, guiding her up the steps.

"Of course, Cristin. It's lovely to see you again. Please come in." Katie heard her own voice tremble.

"Where's Dad? I thought he'd be here. I've told Cristin all about him."

"Dad will be here a little later."

Shep heard sharpness in her tone, a thinness in her voice, and awkwardness in her demeanor.

"Mom, what's going on? Is something wrong?"

"Actually, Shep, I do need to talk to you right away, privately, if you don't mind."

"Cristin, why don't you come with me?" Ingrid took her gently by the arm.

Cristin looked at Shep as if he should object to excluding her from whatever was going on, but he didn't. He'd been caught off guard and was too stunned by the abrupt request to be gallant.

Suddenly, Katie was face to face with her son and her words failed her.

"You'd better start talking, Mom. This hasn't exactly been a cordial welcome. Are you aware of how important Cristin is to me?"

"I'm beginning to, son. And I have to tell you to do something you're not going to want to hear. I'm so sorry."

"What? Talk!" Shep raised his voice sharply.

"Tia told us that you might be coming home to make an announcement to the family. Is that true?"

"Yes…"

"Shep, you must call off your engagement."

"Engagement?"

"Yes, I saw the ring on Cristin's finger."

"Mother, I've come home to announce that Cristin and I were married in Paris."

Katie cringed in agony, began shaking her head and loudly whimpering like a dying dog. It was an appalling reaction and frightening to witness.

"Mother, my God! What's going on?"

"You can't stay married to Cristin, Shep. You have to annul your marriage. She can't be your wife!"

"Why not?" Shep matched her volume.

"Because she's your sister!" screamed Katie.

Shep entered a zone of confused denial. The blood left his head like mercury falling on a rapidly cooling thermometer. He could only hear the swishing of his heart inside his ears and the dizzying words, "she's your sister, she's your sister, she's your sister."

"What are you talking about? That's not possible."

Initially, Katie's only response was a look of suffering. In the following minutes, Shep listened intently as his mother spilled her story in his lap. His life unraveled at the seams, thread by thread, until the fabric of his world shredded.

When the story was told, Katie whispered, "I'm so sorry. I'm so sorry." She reached out to touch him, but he rigidly waved her away with large, strong waving hands.

"Don't touch me, Mother. Leave me alone. I need to figure out what I'm going to say to her."

"Son, after Cristin is told, someday, please, please find it in your heart to forgive me. I know you can't right now but tell me that …someday…"

"No one else must ever know about this, Mother. No one else."

"I agree. No one but the immediate family will know. You realize that Aunt Tess has told Uncle Ren and, of course, Ingrid and your father were told. Do you want me to talk with Cristin?"

Shep didn't reply.

"Shep, who should tell Cristin?"

"Who should tell me what?" asked Cristin, who appeared at the door, uninvited.

Cristin searched to see strength in her new husband's eyes, but was met with a lifeless, foreign stare.

Katie's voice was the first to be heard. "Cristin, please sit down . There's something I need to tell you".

Cristin obeyed like a trained puppy, never once taking her eyes off Shep until Katie demanded it of her.

"Look at me, Cristin. This will be difficult for all of us, so you must pay attention to what I have to tell you."

"You have my undivided attention, Mrs. Shepard." Cristin stiffened.

"I saw Tess earlier this week, Cristin, and she shared some shocking news. She told me about the letter you sent to her...the letter in which you claimed that she was your mother."

"Yes?" Cristin drew out each sound in the word with interrogative drama and cautious surprise.

"Well, she didn't tell you, or anyone else for that matter, the whole truth."

"Oh my God, does she say that she's my mother?"

"No. Tess is not your mother... I am. I am your mother."

Cristin's mouth slowly dropped, her eyes squinted, then dimmed, as if her sight had been stripped. She bided time. No one said a word.

Then Cristin raised her eyes to Katie and parroted, "You, my mother?" She stared at Shep, and slowly pronounced, "If that were true, that would make you my..."

Shep spoke. "We have to annul the marriage, Cristin. And never speak of this again."

"You are my daughter." Katie repeated it, provisionally hoping to salvage a modicum of affection from the horrific situation.

"No, I'm not," said Cristin with the conviction of someone falsely accused. All of her plans, her scratching out her new life, would not be ruined by an erroneous conclusion. "Tess is wrong. It's not true."

"If it's not true, how did you come into possession of the letter that I wrote to your adoptive parents? How did you come to wear the locket that once belonged to my mother, the locket that I passed on to the child I didn't keep?"

"There is an explanation. I am not your daughter. Shep is not my brother. He is my husband."

Shep's head lifted as he heard her confidence. "You sound so sure of yourself."

"Darling, I need to speak to you privately, please." Cristin pleaded. "I assure you this is all a big mistake. Please, let me first speak to you alone."

Shep took her by the hand and led her out of the room, leaving his mother and sister alone, stupefied. The rain pounded the roof, and the sound of water gushing from the eaves could be heard through a window that hadn't been closed. The aroma of baked apples that Katie had forgotten in the oven sent the message that the apples were over baked. Ingrid mechanically followed her Mother to the kitchen and helped her scrape the apples and caramelized dates off the cookie sheet.

"Mom, what could she be telling Shep? What could be her explanation?"

"I have no idea."

~ ~ ~

Meanwhile, the wheels in Cristin's head spun threads of her story-the story that would defuse Tess's hypothesis and reclaim her marriage.

"Darling, you must believe me. I am not your sister. I promise you this is true."

Shep listened attentively, but silently.

"But I haven't been completely up front. I did something a while ago, something I'm not proud to admit. I was desperate, and

I'm going to beg your forgiveness before I begin. Please try to understand."

"I'm listening."

"As I told you, my parents died in an automobile accident. I was an only child and when they died, I was alone. I had no one, no family, and very few friends. Shep, you have no idea what it's like to feel completely alone in this world. It's terrifying. I had a friend who had a wonderful family: a little sister who followed her everywhere and a mom and dad who thought the sun rose and set upon her. One summer, they paid my way so I could go to camp with her. It was a summer I'll always remember. One night when we were camping under the stars, Trina told me that she was adopted. She told me that she loved her adoptive parents and didn't have any intention of searching for her biological parents. But she did say that, from time to time, she wondered who they were and why they'd given her up. There was a sadness in her voice when she talked about them, as if they'd all been cheated. The next day she showed me a letter and a locket that her adoptive mother had passed on to her. For the first time in my life I felt special. Someone had entrusted me with a secret. After my parents died, I went to her house and asked to see the letter and the locket again, claiming that it was a story that touched me. She showed me, and when she left the room, I took them. I was so frantic to start a new life, I stole them, in search of someone whom I could call family. I wrote to T. Monson in Mississippi and claimed to be her child. When Tess wrote back, she said she wasn't my mother, but she was willing to help me. So, I took a bus to Minneapolis in search of a new family. But Tess never told me that her sister was my mother. And darling, I fell in love with your entire family. This was what I'd dreamed of my whole life. I intended to tell Tess when I returned from Europe, because the guilt was consuming me. I swear, I planned to tell her. But then I met you, the love of my life. I was afraid that if I told anyone, you'd find out and you'd lose faith in me, perhaps not find it in your heart to trust me. I couldn't bear the thought of losing you."

Cristin's beautiful almond shaped eyes welled with tears as she pleaded her case to a jury of one. For it was Shep who would determine her fate.

"Please try to understand. I was so alone. I know now that it was wrong of me. I was young and reckless. I'm wiser now. I will even write to my friend if I can find her and tell her what I've done. I'll make it right, I promise."

"What was your friend's name?"

"Trina."

"Trina? As in Katrina?"

Cristin nodded.

Shep took her hands in his, covering them completely with his own. He gazed into her angelic, penitent face, then kissed her warm tears.

"I believe you," he whispered in the tones of a benevolent god. "I forgive you."

Chapter 25

Three weeks had passed. Cristin stood on the porch of the home she and Shep had rented outside Wellesley. They'd postponed their honeymoon while Shep attended to business matters, but they were packed and ready to leave the following morning. The air was brittle with the crackling cold of dawn; the shriveled flower stalks rimed with frost. Cristin stood wrapped in her robe, and smelled the bittersweet aroma that steamed from her coffee cup. The breeze was scented with autumn forest as she gazed at the quiet that stretched out before her like an unending sheet of gauze. Enormous oak leaves detached from their branches and floated to the ground like paper airplanes. She picked up an abandoned leaf that landed at her feet and crushed it in her hand for the sheer pleasure of smelling it.

Shep had never belonged to her as he did now. She had learned early in life that people believed what they wanted to believe and she'd become a master facilitator to influence their wants and dreams. Knowing this one simple truth made the rest of her life less complicated and more predictable. Nevertheless, one had to be very smart when manipulating the lives of others. One had to remember exactly what was said, when and where, and remain consistent. She rarely felt uncomfortable with people, because generally speaking, she was smarter than they were. Yvette had been a problem. But Yvette was in France. Everyone in Cristin's life served a purpose, even if only as camouflage or diversion. She continued to adeptly juggle stories and position cracked mirrors that distorted and diffused the truth.

The morning fog rolled in and covered the lawn like a blanket as she stared ahead transfixed. Against the screen of gray were projected the faces of her parents and the figure of a faceless girl. She stared at the images suspended in air and she blinked them away. Nothing unwelcome that entered her mind was allowed to stay. She controlled what she thought because she was the gatekeeper of her domain.

As a young girl, she'd despised her family. They were people without dreams: pitiable, pathetic small thinkers. She resented her poor, unambitious beginnings. Because she subscribed to the belief that it was a man's world, she decided early in life that it would be necessary to use a man to escape her life and assume the lifestyle she knew she deserved. Her plan was simple and ruthless-she would win the confidence of people she met along the way who would be stepping stones on her enterprising hike to the top. She deliberately groomed herself to be attractive to men, by studying the habits of wealthy men- the places they ate, the entertainment they sought, the women they pursued. She became an excellent conversationalist and a willing and zealous companion. She understood that admiration was as fundamental to a man's existence as oxygen. Her future was visually clear, as if she were watching a travelogue. Of course, there were times that she would alter her course, but she was never without direction. And she was always in charge.

~ ~ ~

As days passed, Katie's life had become more and more remote, secluded. Despite the relief that Cristin was not her daughter, her family now knew about her past. During Heidi's visit, Ingrid had softened the blow of her mother's extramarital affair. Heidi's only question had been, "where is the real daughter and shouldn't we find her?" Teenagers, by virtue of being teenagers, were self-absorbed in their own worlds to the point of not being particularly concerned with their parents' feelings. Katie actually felt slighted that her life held such little consequence for her youngest child, but she then reflected on how little she had known about her own mother's private life. Her shame usurped her self-pity, and her equilibrium was restored by a sense of acceptance.

Nevertheless, she did ponder Heidi's response on a more direct and personal level. Where was her real daughter? Had she had a happy life? Whom did she resemble- in looks, in manner, in character? Did she inherit Katie's addictive tendencies? Did she resent having been given up for adoption? Was she the only child or the only adopted child in the family? Did her adoptive parents change her name? Did she ever call out for Katie? Had she needed her? Perhaps she wanted brothers and sisters. And if she came forward, would she fit into Katie's family? The things she now wanted to explain to her daughter composed an endless list that tired her heart. She felt different. Her life felt more complete, despite the pain, because of the pain.

And she thought about Cristin. Cristin had not been honest. She had been heedless, conniving, manipulative, and definitely not honest. Everyone seemed to forgive her. But Katie didn't.

Since the confrontation in New York, Katie had only communicated to Tess once, and that was through Ingrid, to dispel the myth of Cristin's heritage. She felt guilty about her distance but whenever she considered calling her sister, her own rage rendered her speechless. After all, had Tess not come forward, Katie's notorious secret would have remained buried in the undisclosed manuscript of time, never to be read by human eyes. And no one would have suffered a loss.

She hadn't spoken to Shep or Cristin since the night of the homecoming. Adult children were not quick to forgive. When parents toppled from their pedestals, their falls were steep and oftentimes fatal. Her first thought was that perhaps they would make a critical error one day and in spite of their own suffering, find compassion for their mother. It had been a convoluted, fleeting thought, and one for which she felt immediate remorse.

Stefan remained unapproachable and childishly humiliated. Had no one else known about the illicit love affair, forgiveness would have come more easily. But his own children knew about it, which mortally wounded his self-perceived machismo. They had attempted to talk on occasion, but tempers had flared and conversations of hurtful accusations inflamed and festered their wounds. Katie's apologies were met with self-righteous silence, which triggered her latent fury against Stefan's past indiscretions. On one occasion, when her defenses were down, she confided her fear about having lost her children's respect, to which Stefan cruelly replied, "You flatter yourself. You're an alcoholic! Respect was lost years ago."

Reconciliation was not an option. Too many incisive irretrievable rounds had been fired. Stefan repeatedly insinuated, "What else haven't you told me?" His insistence of her false character led Katie to believe that he'd been waiting for years for a valid reason to desert her. She eventually concluded that he'd probably wanted to leave her when she was in the rehab center, but it would have reflected poorly on him. But an infidelity involving a child? No problem. The world would condone dissolution of marriage on those grounds. Within weeks, the depth of their years together became shallow and the shores of their lives receded.

Sondra was the one person Katie viewed as an innocent party. She knew Sondra's heart and she believed that Sondra had protected the past and agonized until she was forced to resolve that a betrayal might circumvent an explosive disaster. Sondra, she could forgive.

The house in Boston was a tomb, holding pain like a sealed sepulcher. No matter what she tried, the harmony of her life couldn't be heard, and the continuity was broken. She filled the house with music, playing Bach preludes and fugues so loudly that it was all she could hear. She read Shakespearean sonnets aloud and took long, exhausting runs with Charley. She took up drawing to refocus her attention and recapture a sense of beauty in her life. One afternoon, the sky whitened and lowered like a descending ceiling and snow began to fall. She ran outside, gathering snowflakes on the sleeves of her sweater and studying the pattern of tiny frozen stars. Then, for hours, she practiced drawing snowflakes, trying to capture their perfection. As she compulsively sketched, the phone rang.

"Hello Kate? This is Tia."

Tia had called and left a number of messages which Katie had shamefully ignored, thinking that surely time would ease the suffering of disclosing the truth to yet another loved one.

"Why haven't you called? No one is calling me. I can't get hold of Tess either."

"It's been a difficult time, Tia. I'm sorry."

"What's going on?"

"I'll write you a letter, honey. I promise. I really can't talk about it over the phone."

"You can't just leave me hanging, Kate. Is it Stefan? Is someone sick? No one is leveling with me and it's killing me."

"No. No one's ill. I just have some personal problems that I don't feel up to talking about long distance, kiddo. I'm sorry, Tia. But trust me, I'll write. I promise."

"All right. I'll change the subject. Did Shep and Cristin announce anything?"

Katie gulped. "Haven't you heard?"

"I have to admit. I knew about the engagement before anyone else."

"Engagement? They were married in Paris. They came home to announce their marriage."

"Oh, no."

"Why do you say that?"

"I just thought Shep might change his mind, that's all. They're really married?"

"Married and about to honeymoon...somewhere, of course, undisclosed to the family".

"What does Tess think about it?"

"I haven't talked to her lately."

"I thought you were going to see her in New York."

"I did. Listen, Tia, I'll explain everything in a letter, I promise. But tell me about Cristin. "What do you think of her?"

"Well, I can see how Shep fell in love with her. I just don't think that what you see is what you get, if you know what I mean."

Katie persisted. "What do you mean?"

"She's complex. And I don't want to slander her... but I don't trust her."

"Then she must have given you a reason not to trust her."

"Well, sometimes her stories don't ring true. I have a friend over here named Yvette. She thinks Cristin is a pathological liar. That's a bit harsh but I'd watch her, Katie. Watch her."

"You're scaring me."

"No, I don't mean to. Maybe I'm wrong. Maybe saying anything is unfair. Just watch her, that's all. Listen, say hi to Stefan and the girls. I'll call again soon. I look forward to receiving your letter."

"I promise I'll do it tonight, honey."

Before fulfilling the promise to her younger sister, Katie once again pieced together the mosaic of Cristin's story, holding each fragment up to the light to view its clarity and plausibility. Then she rose, walked to her desk .and composed a letter to Tia that dispassionately defined the chain of events and passionately spilled her feelings.

~ ~ ~

For days Tia watched the mail with unusual expectancy ,but was disappointed with only routine deliveries. One afternoon she received an envelope addressed to Mademoiselle Cristin. It didn't look personal, but more like a bill. Thinking it insignificant and knowing that Cristin was unreachable, Tia opened the envelope.

The lease on Cristin's art studio had expired and the landlord was inquiring if she wanted to extend it. If not, her belongings were to be removed by the end of the week. He was evidently uninformed of his tenant's sudden departure.

The following day, with a key ring that she'd found in the back drawer of Cristin's bureau, Tia drove across town to the studio. The owner was nowhere to be found ,so Tia tried the keys, one by one, until she felt the last one catch. She opened the door. The studio caught light through a window that looked like it hadn't been opened in years, sealed shut with a green patina that was peeling away and coated with dirt. The floor was splattered with color, and the stench of oil and turpentine hung in a rank humidity that smeared the air, but had previously been dissipated by time. The boards of the floor creaked as Tia entered the room where heavy tarpaulins were draped over objects leaning against the walls. Tia pulled off a heavy, musty, paint-speckled tarp and discovered scores of paintings stacked one against the other. She'd never seen any of Cristin's work.

She pushed the paintings apart, one at a time, accelerating the pace with each successive canvas. The gruesome style resembled nothing she'd ever seen before. Dark and fiery, appallingly grotesque, elongated, distorted figures with ghastly wide-eyed mouths and eyes. Each consecutive canvas became more shocking and alarming than the last. Tia felt a nauseous weakening in her legs as she associated the art with the artist. What kind of sick mind felt the need to compulsively paint such horror? This wasn't art. This was psychotic fixation. And this was the woman whom Shep had married? Tia ran out of the building, almost forgetting to lock the door. A blast of fresh air rescued her shortness of breath as she gasped. She fumbled to find the right key and trembled as she secured the unhallowed room.

Retreating from the building, she speculated on whom she must tell. First she would contact the landlord and offer to remove the contents of the studio. But to where? Where would she store the paintings? She had no room at her home. Perhaps she could pay the landlord to dispose of the atrocities, as they certainly held no value. She could not tell Cristin that she had entered the studio without permission. But Shep had the right to know.

Chapter 26

Shep surprised his new wife with a trip to Europe. All he told her prior to leaving was to bring warm clothes. In deference to her wishes to visit a warm climate, he promised her a trip to the Fiji Islands in the spring. But he wished to explore the land of his heritage, Austria, and share it with his new bride. They spent a few weeks driving through Germany, Austria and Switzerland. They took carriage rides through the Black Forest, walked along the Danube, visited the opera house in Vienna, and lodged in Swiss valleys, dwarfed by precipitous mountains.

Early one evening, overlooking Lake Lusanne, they watched the sun slowly drop behind a mountainous horizon.

"It smells like rain, doesn't it?" Shep exclaimed rhetorically. "Look at this view. It's glorious!"

"That's a lazy description," said Cristin. "What exactly do you find glorious about it? Describe it to me in detail. The colors, the lines, the shapes. No, even better, what about the temperature of the air, the breeze that moves over the water, the sounds of the birds, the smell of the pine trees."

"Hey, I thought I married an artist, not a poet."

"An artist is a poet. There is more that goes into painting than copying the lines and colors. One must feel like a poet, hear like a composer, form like a sculptor, and move like a dancer to capture the essence of what you call 'the view.' A painting is to be experienced to be real."

"And I married a philosopher, as well. Let me ask you a question," said Shep. "Articulate. How does an artist go about capturing the essence of beauty such as this? Take me to school as if I know nothing."

"Oh, but you do, my darling. An artist doesn't talk too much about the art she's creating. It would painfully objectify it, distract from the mystery."

"So you're saying that art is mysterious?"

"To a degree, it must be, because everyone who experiences it may have a different reaction. That's an inherent splendor of beauty, the mystery of it."

"Why do you like to paint?" asked Shep.

"I suppose because I like to make form out of chaos, or chaos out of form."

"Fascinating. You know, I've never seen any of your work."

"It's all back in Grenoble. In due time."

"How young were you when you realized you liked to paint?"

"Hmmmm. I scarcely remember." She clicked her thumbnail on her tooth. "Since I was a little girl, I suppose. It was play to me. I was thrilled when I discovered that I could play for the rest of my life. And if I were good at it, I could make a living while I was making a life."

"Funny you put it that way. My Aunt Tess told me once that her writing was play, that art generally speaking, should be play. She said, 'why do you think a work by Shakespeare is called a "play", and people "play" the piano?' She said that play integrates the inner world of impressions with the outer world of expression. Or was it the other way around?"

"Now look who's the philosopher?" Cristin taunted him as she bent forward, deliberately gaping the neckline of her blouse, exposing her breasts. "What else did your Aunt Tess say?"

Titillated by her seductive exhibitionism, he continued.

"Well, she said that art wipes away boundaries. It erases class distinction, language barriers and the boundary of time itself. It outlives us. Now it's your turn. Tell me something I might not know about art."

Cristin thought for a moment, sipped her wine and took up the gauntlet.

"Alright. Art can be symbolic, do you agree?"

"Yes, of course."

"Tell me, what is the antonym of symbolic?" she asked. with a smirk on her face.

"Why don't you just tell me?" He smiled.

"Diabolic. Whereas symbolic means to draw together, diabolic means to tear apart, confuse, throw into discord."

"So what's the point?"

Just then the clouds above them opened and the rain began to fall. They grabbed their belongings and ran for cover. That night as they were falling asleep, Shep thought of the curious remark that nature had so rudely interrupted. But his wife was already heavy with sleep. Too tired to examine her inference, he drifted to sleep thinking that his newly betrothed was brilliant: Absolutely brilliant.

~ ~ ~

Shep's family wasn't aware of the extent of his fortune, and he made it a policy not to discuss his wealth. But one of the detours during their honeymoon was a trip to his bank in Zurich. It was there that Cristin's name was added to his accounts in the event anything happened to him. She claimed that she'd understand any reluctance he might feel to share his assets, but her sincerity only augmented his trust. His unchecked beneficence felt absolute and good and anything less would have flawed his love for her. His refusal to even discuss a "prenuptial" agreement was indeed a sign that he was certain of her faithfulness and love.

One morning, while Shep was on a short business trip to Amsterdam, Cristin found her window of time to take care of unfinished business. She arrived at her studio door in Grenoble.

There, posted to the door, she saw a notice from Tia to the landlord.

"I have tried to contact you to no avail. Mademoiselle Cristin will not be returning. Please release the studio to someone else and do whatever you please with the contents of the room. Apologies for this inconvenience. Tia Monson."

Tia had been there. *What right had she to give the landlord permission to dispose of the contents as he pleased? These were private property, works of art, her mind and heart and soul in form.* But finding the interior undisturbed, she concluded that Tia had not violated her privacy. Cristin worked quickly and without interruption, destroying every canvas, and removing all evidence of her art. Within hours, there was not a trace that she had ever been there. Even the note on the door remained in place.

~ ~ ~

Before she left Grenoble, she paid a surprise visit to Yvette Vandall.

"Do you mind if I come in?" asked Cristin in perfect French.

"What are you doing here? How did you know where I live?" asked the distrusting French woman.

"I'm on my honeymoon. My husband is away on business for a day, so I decided to visit Grenoble just one more time. May I come in?"

"What business have you here?"

"Yvette, I've come to make amends with you. Tia and I are related by marriage now. I know you and I have had misunderstandings. Since the two of you are such good friends, I'd appreciate a chance to clear the air."

"Come in."

With a nonchalant flick of her wrist, she pointed to a kitchen chair. She leaned against the counter, raised her eyebrows, pursed her lips, and with an inquisitive dare on her face, indicated she would not say the first word.

"May I have a cup of tea?" asked Cristin.

"Why of course, Lady Shepard. How rude of me not to offer it," she sarcastically replied "Since when did your ladyship start wearing gloves in the middle of the day?"

"I have a rash on my hands."

Yvette poured her a cup, then resumed her stance against the counter.

"Please, Yvette, you're making this difficult for me. Please, just sit at the table and share a pot of tea with me. Please."

Yvette sat down and poured herself a cup.

"There. That's much better."

"Listen, I don't have time for small talk. We're never going to be friends. I don't like you. I don't trust you. Say whatever it is you have to say and get out."

"Yvette, you have made up your mind without taking time to get to know me. I'm not certain why we got off to such a bad start, but I'm sorry if I've offended you. It would be easier if I knew what it was that I have said or done."

"I see through you. You're a fraud. And you're a dangerous woman to be around because you don't have a conscience. I'm glad you're back in America, away from Tia. Tia is a good person, much too good to be hurt by the likes of you."

Like a cue in a play, the telephone rang and turning her back on her unwelcome company, Yvette left the table. The powder from the capsules dissolved quickly in the heat of Yvette's teacup and moments later, the two women resumed their awkward conversation.

"So what do you want? Does Tia know you're here?"

"Yes. She suggested that I come."

"I doubt that. She's really worried about her nephew, you know. I guess he's one hell of a nice guy. I've warned her about you...."

Cristin jumped in, hoping that Yvette would shut up and drink her tea. "Why are you so hostile? I was........" She could hear her own voice but had no idea what she was saying as she watched Yvette swallow three long sips in a row. Cristin kept talking while the French woman sipped and sipped, and sipped. The poison took affect almost immediately. Cristin watched her clutch her throat, then her chest, then in horror reach out to her murderer, who uninvolved, watched her die as if she were merely watching a movie. When it was all over, Cristin stepped over the body and put the cups and saucers in her purse. She searched Yvette's purse, and then her house, until she found what she needed and never once removed her gloves. She was quiet and thorough and vanished undetected into the evening.

~ ~ ~

Airports were a monstrous annoyance. Too many people, too much waiting. Cristin didn't like people. She put up with them. She especially didn't like having to interact with those she'd never see again. They were just a necessary inconvenience. Standing in lines and being herded into a small space was a particular aggravation. Somewhere she'd heard that such anxieties stemmed from past life experiences, from which she deduced that once upon a time she had been rallied into a gas chamber in Nazi Germany or the like.

Once on the plane, aware of peripheral conversations, she deduced that she'd been wedged between a Swiss midwife and an Austrian undertaker. She kept to herself, determined not to instigate or respond to any exchange. The Swiss woman appeared to be in her late twenties, older than Cristin by a few years. Cristin quickly noticed that the woman was very unhappy, wringing her hands, aggressively biting the inside of her lower lip. Her behavior became increasingly difficult to ignore when quiet whimpering escalated to sobbing. Cristin handed her a tissue, which the woman declined, simpering apologetically through words Cristin couldn't decipher, except to determine that someone had died. But there was nowhere to go. They appeared to be stuck with each other's company for the duration of the trip. When the young woman's crying intensified, Cristin called the flight attendant, who appeared out of the thin germ-filled airplane air and ushered the woman to the galley of the plane.

Finally, alone and tired, Cristin relaxed to a state of semi-consciousness. Her memory randomly visited an event from her childhood. There had been a calamitous fire in an old inner city school building in Chicago with no working fire escapes or escape routes. The newspapers, radio, and television had reported the horror of children's faces appearing in third story windows, with parents below screaming for their children to jump and seeing them pushed away from the window by bigger, stronger children. Smoke billowed and flames engulfed the helpless.

Cristin had relived the hysteria of parents below as they watched their babies disappear into the brick deathtrap that had been a haven. She was scarcely old enough to read, but like a scavenger, she had foraged for news articles and watched and re-watched the news. For months after the tragedy, she dreamed that there was a man in the window well under her bedroom window, ready to light a match and set her home on fire. Then one day she decided that the only way not to be frightened by fire was to enjoy its devastation. Then it couldn't hurt her anymore.

And she saw the faces of her parents and the figure of the faceless girl.

Her next memory was a voyage back to Serena's kitchen while drinking tea with Serena and Tess. They were decent, trusting people. They'd opened their homes and their hearts and offered her an affluent lifestyle. It was interesting how circumstantial life was. She hadn't known when she left Minneapolis that she wouldn't return.

She opened her eyes and watched a sea of marshmallow whip below. In the distance there was what looked like a mountain rising from a blue billowy sea, with a ladder of fleecy steps protruding from its peak and climbing to the great beyond. Her eyes burned from the recirculated air conditioning in the cabin, and she felt congested.

She returned to the wanderings of her mind and recalled how she'd intended to return to "Rennie" and win his heart. And instead, she'd met and married a much younger, and much wealthier, man. Life was safer with Shep, and more promising. He was more trusting, more forgiving, more adoring. It had been a wise choice on her part- less messy.

And Tia. How soon would it be before Tia would discover that her friend Yvette had assumed room temperature? A shame.

As the plane landed, the flight attendant came by to ask Cristin to fasten her safety belt.

"Oh, by the way, the young woman who was sitting next to you has calmed down."

"Who died?"

"Her cat," said the attendant.

Within two hours, Cristin walked the shore of the Danube, where she blended into the ordinary people she so despised. And not a soul knew what she had done.

Chapter 27

Tia was daydreaming in a European architecture class when she heard the news.

"Isn't it shocking? I sat next to her in Medieval Lit last year. Did you ever talk to her?"

"No, but my friend did."

"She was so young," said a girl with the face shaped like a heart, broad around the eyes, angular and small at the chin.

"Who was so young?" asked Tia, only peripherally listening to the common gossip which she ordinarily tuned out.

"That student they found dead," replied a girl with the short uneven haircut and the mouth suggestive of a filly. "You knew her, didn't you? I thought I saw you hanging out with her."

"Who are you talking about?"

"Yvette someone. You knew her. I've seen you talking with her," said a man who resembled a toad as he braced himself against the table.

"Yvette Vandall?"

"Yes, that's right. Vandall, Yvette Vandall."

Tia stared transfixedly at the horse, the heart, and the horny toad. Her blood, sucked from her head, had pooled in her solar plexus, for she felt her heartbeat in her abdomen.

There must have been a mistake. She'd seen Yvette only two days before. But later she'd tried to call her and she hadn't answered.

"Tell me what you know." She stammered, barely pushing the words past the lump in her throat.

"A heart attack, they say. They found her on the floor in her kitchen."

Tia grabbed her books and drove to the police station. The building, having survived decades of wrong-doing and centuries of war, looked like a medieval armory, substantial and covered with ivy. Visiting a police station was the last thing she'd thought she'd be doing that day. She ran up the steps and penetrated the building.

The gendarmes stood in the hallway and joked about their weekend escapades, attending local soccer games. *Why didn't the world stand still and grieve when something terrible could have happened? Everyone was acting normally. Yvette could be dead. Maybe, just maybe, there wasn't a right and wrong in the world after all. Maybe life was just a series of experiences that felt good or bad.*

"Excuse me. My name is Tia Monson. I'm an American student studying at the university. Can anyone help me?"

A tall, thin gendarme stood up from behind his desk and, without smiling, offered his assistance.

"I've just been informed that my friend Yvette Vandall may have been found dead in her house two days ago. I need to verify if this is true. I must speak to the officer who may have found her."

"What was the address?"

"Rue de Cezanne- I don't remember the number."

"I'll be with you in a minute."

The wait was insufferable. The clock on the wall was loud and Tia became increasingly aware of the precious minutes that were hers but perhaps no longer Yvette's. She closed her eyes and prayed: "Please let it not be true, please let it not be true." Perhaps the intensity of her prayer would change the outcome or would alter whatever was already determined. *Doubtful.*

The officer returned to the foyer of the station with another man, both wearing somber expressions.

"I regret to inform you that Ms. Yvette Vandall was indeed found two days ago. Captain Gervais wishes to speak with you if you can afford the time."

Tia nodded. She felt hot tears streaming down her cheeks, tasting the saltiness as they reached her lips. She struggled to maintain her composure, but quietly succumbed to her grief. She followed the captain into a private room where he helped her to a chair. He sat across from her, bending forward with his knees practically touching hers, and one hand clasping the other, like an opera singer.

"I'm so sorry, Mademoiselle. It's terrible when we lose someone so young. I am, however, very grateful you have come forward as we were not able to contact her next of kin. Perhaps you can help us?"

"She has no family. She was raised by the sisters at Gramercy. She was orphaned very young. I can't believe this has happened. How did she die?"

"We presume by natural causes, a heart attack. There is no reason to think otherwise, as there was no evidence of foul play, no evidence of breaking and entering, no indication of a struggle."

"Who found her?"

"The landlady who lives next door noticed that Ms. Vandall's cat was scratching at the door a couple of days in a row and no one was answering. Three newspapers had collected on her porch. Knowing that her tenant hadn't planned to be out of town, she looked in the window and saw Ms. Vandall lying on the floor."

"Oh dear God. I wish I had been there. If only I had been there."

"Mademoiselle, we're grateful you're here now. The landlady told us who she was, which was important because we found no identification in her home, neither in her handbag nor in her desk. Were you close to her?"

"Yes, she was my closest friend in Grenoble."

"Then would you be the person to deal with her personal affects and attend to her funeral?"

"I suppose so. But not now." She sobbed.

"Ms. Monson," Captain Gervais struggled with his English, "would you be so kind as to come back tomorrow and give us a statement regarding your relationship to the deceased , so that the proper procedures are followed?"

"Of course. Of course. Thank you."

Tia walked down the steps of the police station into a world that now looked sadder, yet somehow, more beautiful- a world that Yvette would never lay mortal eyes on again. The grass looked greener, the breeze felt fresher, and the smell of autumn stronger. The changing colors of the leaves that still clung to the plane trees above were a harbinger of their own impending death: even their impermanence, the imminence of their dying, made them more precious.

As she walked through Victor Hugo Square across from her house, she remembered a sobering quotation attributed to him that she'd read once upon a time, but until that moment, had not attached to her life. *"We are all under sentence of death but with a sort of indefinite reprieve."*

The following week distended with funeral preparations. The service was short and sparsely attended by a few students and sisters from the orphanage. Tia was the logical person to deliver the eulogy, and yet she'd only known her friend for less than two years. Privately, she grieved that someone as special as Yvette had been so alone in the world.

After the burial, Tia attended to the task of her friend's belongings. Most of the items were given away to the orphanage, but Tia kept some of the books. Yvette's library was personal and reflective of her thoughts and tastes. The knowing that, for years to come, Tia could read from the same pages that her friend had read was comforting and connective.

The first night that she was not too sleepy to read, Tia opened Yvette's copy of *Peer Gynt*. Ibsen had been her friend's favorite playwright, a kindred spirit of social reform and ethics. Randomly skimming through the pages, Tia stopped at an underlined passage that read,

> *How unspeakably poor a soul can be*
> *When it enters the mist and returns to nothing!*
> *Oh beautiful earth, don't be angry with me*
> *That I trod your sweet grass to no avail.*
> *Beautiful sun you have squandered*
> *Your golden light upon an empty hut,*
> *There was no one within to warm and comfort*
> *The owner. I know now, was never at home.*
> *Then let the snow pile over me*
> *And let them write above: 'Here lives no one'*
> *And afterwards-let the world take its course.*

Mourning the loss of a friend was compounded by youth: youth of the deceased, and the grieving observance of a young friend. The fragile and fleeting aspect of life forced Tia to examine her own mortality. Yvette was gone and Tia was the only one who would intimately remember her. And when Tia died, Yvette's life would slide into the dark, depthless sludge of oblivion, as if she had never existed: her life reduced to nothingness. Tia thought of her own life. Who would remember her when she was gone? Perhaps her children, her grandchildren? And after they died? The answer was no one. Then she, too, would slip into the deep, dark waters of eternal emptiness, as had the billions of nameless souls before her. The ultimate meaninglessness was so depressing that she searched for any argument that could retrieve hope and restore a sense of purpose.

Maybe the ultimate loss of self, which was inescapable, was a clue that ego was a false belief and a trap. Tia forced herself to take a deep breath and experience her spirit; not Tia the human, Tia the body, or Tia the appearance, but the energy and spirit which lived within her body- the prime mover of her thoughts and behavior. Perhaps her mortal existence was an experiment, a playground, an opportunity to feel spirit in spite of physical confinement. The Spirit had to be indestructible and forever. She breathed in rhythm, resonating on a sublime level, a feeling unlike anything she'd ever known. Yvette wasn't lost. Perhaps she was found. Perhaps only when a person exited her transitory physical state could the soul possibly comprehend the Whole.

~ ~ ~

During the following week, Tia received a correspondence from Cristin's landlord. Absorbed with the affairs of her deceased friend, she had completely forgotten about the studio matter. She opened the letter, certain to find a final notice, thinking that the note she had attached to the studio door must have been ripped off by the wind or by a mischievous schoolboy. And she read,

Dear Mme. Monson,

Thank you for your prompt attention to the matter of Ms. Cristin's studio apartment. My wife and I appreciate your taking responsibility for removing the contents so completely. The condition at this time is comparable to the condition when Ms. Cristin took possession, so I am returning her security deposit. Everyone should be so fortunate as to have a friend such as you.

Gratefully yours, Henri Rombeau

Chapter 28

Whenever trust is lost, nothing is ever the same. Love may survive, but its purity is fissured. Like a fractured gem, the flaw, though overlooked, is always a visible reminder of the imperfection. To Ren Parker, his wife's decision to withhold Cristin's identity from him was the fissure and a scarring of the tissue that connected them, which he had believed to be strong, undamaged, and impervious to deception. He no longer looked at her the same way—with reliance and the faith that he knew her heart as well as his own. He no longer trusted that her answers were without omissions or reservations. He subconsciously expected holes, hidden meanings in her explanations, knowing full well that she had suffered abysmal pain as a consequence of her actions, but also knowing that she had been capable of concealing the truth, a significant truth. He knew that had he not loved her, he would have walked away and risked the odds of finding a woman he could trust as he'd once trusted Tess. But he did love her. And despite his reverence to honesty, within the acceptance of his wife's imperfection lay the maturity of his love.

A year had passed since Tess had come to him, a year that had seemed like ten, or more. Days lagged, contrary to the days of past content that had passed so quickly. Although time had narrowed the rift between them, there were moments when he was quiet and Tess looked as if she could read his thoughts. Sometimes when she'd speak to him, he stared through her as if he were turning her inside out, searching for the whole truth that most certainly lurked in the shadows and hid in the corners. In his heart, her innocence was gone- irretrievable, almost as if it had never been. His judgment hurt both of them.

He'd become a more solitary man, spending hours by himself. One night, alone and gazing at the skies, trying to make sense of his life, the stars began to speak. He listened and heard an eternal, immutable truth; the truth was that he needed to rise above his humanness to transcend himself, and to understand that the path to love was to behave lovingly.

Tess was not home. Ren walked into the house and waited for her. He poured a snifter of brandy and sat in his favorite chair, his face serenely softened. He had tapped one of life's secrets and was as grateful as a man could be. He picked up his companion, his leather bound volume of Ralph Waldo Emerson, and opened it to the first page of the essay entitled "Nature" and he read his favorite opening excerpt:

> But if a man would be alone, let him look at the stars.
>
> If the stars should appear one night in a thousand years, how would men believe and adore; and preserve for many generations the remembrance of the city of God which had been shown. The stars awaken a certain reverence because though always present, they are inaccessible; but all natural objects make a kindred impression, when the mind is open to their influence.
>
> Man's intercourse with heaven and earth becomes part of his daily food. In the presence of nature a wild delight runs through him, in spite of real sorrows.
>
> I become a transparent eyeball; I am nothing; I see all; the currents of the Universal Being circulate through me; I am a part and parcel of God.

How many times had he read these words? It didn't matter. It only mattered that the words now helped interpret how he felt. He thought of the responsibility a writer must feel when penning his or her thoughts. Could the philosopher from Concord ever have imagined that his words would inspire a fledgling astronomer from Minneapolis, named Warren Parker, at the turn of the twenty-first century? A man who turned to the stars and was liberated from the bonds of his own selfishness; a man who came to appreciate that the beauty of the outer world could inspire the wisdom of his heart; a man who desperately needed an understanding that would once again bind his spirit with the woman he loved.

When Tess arrived home that evening, she found her partner waiting- her lover, her friend, waiting. No words were spoken that hadn't been shared before, but love had been restored as an answered prayer and a spiritual bequest of two struggling solitary hearts.

~ ~ ~

The following morning, Tess Parker awakened to a world reborn. For months she had bitten and chewed each morsel of her private pain until the pulp had disappeared and she'd been forced to swallow its bitter juice. Her suffering had been an experience of isolation, on a sea of remorse, searching for any passing piece of hope that could help her stay afloat. Her only confidante had been Serena, without whom she believed she would have drowned. But now, by the grace of the heavens, her husband had returned and she felt strong and light. It was a curious phenomenon that having support withheld by a loved one could so dramatically weaken her spirit. She'd carried emotional weight that was so burdensome that at times she hunched over like an old woman. The connection between emotional well-being and physical strength was astonishing. She hadn't realized the fierce correlation until that very morning.

A mild winter snow had covered the back yard with white crystals and called to her to come outside. She bundled up and laid down a path of crunchy footprints. The cold air tickled the inside of her nostrils and in a moment of unbridled spontaneity, she knelt down in the snow like a child and carefully positioned herself to make a snow angel. As her arms and legs waved, up and down, she smiled and stuck out her tongue to catch the gentle flakes that had begun to fall. In her darkest hour, she could never have imagined making a snow angel again. And yet, there she was, in the arms of grace.

Later that afternoon, she walked into her office and stared at piles of writing that had accumulated over the year. Scribbling, at times illegible script, she'd recorded feelings which had no destination or purpose. After all, writers write, even when there is no end. She randomly piled the papers in a box because there was no order. These were not thoughts of a story outline or character development. These were guilty words, born of regret. As she worked, she wondered if she'd ever read them. Had the words already served their purpose? Had the words given life to her feelings when no one would listen? Had the words merely been an exercise to survive?

Ren was home when she returned from the market. She could tell, because the house smelled of pipe tobacco. She panicked, however, when she saw him, standing by the window, his back turned from her, his hand in the pocket of his jacket, as he watched the activity on street below. He had taken this posture so many times before, and, most recently, he spoke to her from this stance, watching the street but not looking at her.

When he heard her enter the room, he turned, removed the pipe from his teeth and smiled. "Hi, sweetheart. Do I get a hug?"

Tess walked to him with open arms and embraced him, relieved that her exoneration had not been short-lived. In the course of the evening, she shared with him her catharsis of stashing away her journals from the previous year.

"I think you might be short-sighted as to their worth, Tessa."

"How could I possibly use them?"

"Have you ever thought of writing your story? Change the names and places. You have to admit, it would make some interesting print. Besides which, there are no other consequences to surface, no more surprises, right?"

"Right." She smiled and with her eyes opening wide to punctuate her affirmative reply, she accentuated her response by one exaggerated nod.

"Well then, I can't think of a subject you are more intimately in touch with than the story of Cristin coming into our lives and the aftermath, of course."

"No, but I can't imagine dredging it all up again, Rennie. I don't think I'm up to it."

"You're the writer." Ren paused as he took a hit from his pipe. "Perhaps it would be better to bury it. The only reason I even bring it up is that the raw material is already written. And perhaps, in the process, you could even help someone out there."

"What do you mean?"

"You know. Writing about what you've learned about yourself and relationships. I could even help you, you know, explaining how I felt."

"You'd be willing to do that?"

"Yes. Yes, I would."

"I love you, Rennie Parker."

"And I love you. I love to see the sparkle in your eyes again."

"Well, you're the one who put it back." She smiled as she squeezed both of his hands in hers. "I'll think about it. The book, that is. I don't think it could harm anyone at this point. Everyone appears to have moved on with their lives."

"Even Katie?"

"So I hear."

"You haven't talked to her yet?"

"No. I hear from Ingrid that she's selling the house. Stefan moved out right away. Apparently their divorce will be final in a month or so."

"That doesn't surprise me. Stefan wasn't ever in your sister's league. From what you've told me, he has a pretty lousy track record. She makes one mistake, twenty some years ago, and he takes off like a bat out of hell. Don't talk to me about Stefan. What about Shep and Cristin?"

"They've been married for about a year now."

"Do we ever hear from them?"

"No. It's as if she's a stranger, a badly mannered stranger, at that. She's removed herself from our lives as if we've never existed. And Shep has apparently followed suit."

How do you explain it?"

"I can't. I suppose she may be ashamed of her deceit. The whole thing stinks. Is she close to Katie?"

"I don't think so. From what Ingrid tells me, they see and talk to Shep from time to time, but very rarely have occasion to see Cristin. The newlyweds travel a lot. It sounds like she's keeping him pretty busy."

"Enjoying her new found wealth?"

"It appears that way, doesn't it?"

"From what I understand, there's a lot of wealth to be enjoyed. Who knows, maybe the whole time she was just playing her cards right and setting herself up for the grand slam. Maybe she just took all of us on *Mister Toad's Wild Ride*, just for the hell of it."

"That's an awful thought. She's our niece now, at least by marriage. We'll see her again someday, and no matter how much time has passed, and how awkward it might be, I expect you to be diplomatic."

"Yes, ma'am. I'll be a good boy."

~ ~ ~

For days, Tess toyed with the idea of writing about their personal saga. Perhaps she could sell her agent on the idea. What had Tia said over a year ago? "All's well that ends well?" Rennie was back. Shep and Cristin were married. Ingrid and Heidi were on with their lives. Stefan was banished from status of in-law to out-law. Sondra had been forgiven. But Katie? As Tess plumbed the depths of the notion of whether or not to write the story, the pain of Katie's life kept surfacing. Her sister's life was shattered and spoiled.

If she wrote the story, could it hurt Katie any further? Could it explain how the whole fiasco came to pass? Could it mend the fences between them? Clarify Tess's motives? Apologize for her actions? That was the key. She could write the story and tell of her own suffering, stemming from the pain she had caused Katie. Katie might not want to see her, but she certainly would read the book. The words would have to be convincing. As Serena had said, the written word could be magic. It could be read over and over, in the solitude of one's own mind, with defenses down, because there was no demand for a response. The reaction could be unprovocative and private. That was why she should write. Her story would serve as an apology to all whom she'd hurt.

That afternoon, with gusto, she ripped the tape off the boxes she'd packed only the day before. When Ren arrived home, a hodgepodge of paper piles, organized according to date, concealed the living room floor.

"What's going on?" he asked.

"I'm going to do it, Ren. I'm going to write the story," she said with a grin.

"Well, that was quick," he remarked with a sense of self-satisfaction. "What made you decide?"

"I want my sister back, Rennie. Maybe this will bring her home."

"Katie's always welcome here, Tess. You know that."

"You know what I mean. I know Katie's welcome. But Katie doesn't come. She doesn't even call."

"And you think the book is the answer?" he asked.

"It could be. You're a genius, honey. It was your idea."

"I'm glad you've figured out your next project, Tessa. There's nothing as impressive as you on the job. By the way, did you pick up the message on the answering machine this morning?"

"No, who was it?"

"Tia. She left for Boston this morning. She's coming home for a vacation. First stop will be to see Katie and the girls in Boston, then here for a visit, then a trip to California to visit Troy and the kids."

"Rennie!! Why didn't you tell me this morning?"

"You were resting, Sleeping Beauty. I didn't want to awaken you. Besides which, you should learn to check the answering machine every once in a while yourself."

"Tia's coming! That's wonderful. Let's throw a dinner party for her."

"I think she's coming to see you, Tessa, not your friends."

"Well, I'll at least bring her to see Serena. And we must go to The Art Center. Maybe Lissa would like to join us, Rennie. What day did she say she'd be arriving?"

"Next Tuesday. I'll be in Chicago that day so I hope she's staying overnight," he said with the poise of a perfect host and love of a brother.

"I'll twist her arm," answered Tess in full voice.

Ren had already disappeared down the hallway en route to the kitchen. *Tia was coming,* Tess smiled to herself. Finally face to face, she would be in a position to hear about Tia's impression of Cristin and possibly shed some light on why Cristin severed contact with them.

~ ~ ~

On Tuesday, Tia blew in like a cool winter breeze. Unlike her former impassioned demeanor, she donned a more mellow costume of manners. Although politely pleasant and genuinely happy to arrive, she was reserved. In fact, she immediately asked for time to settle in and rest before dinner. Tess obliged.

Trying not to make noise in the kitchen, Tess fumbled with pots and pans, clumsily creating a cacophony of kitchen sounds, but unamplified by her sensitivity to be quiet. It had been a long time since her household had housed another person. Of course,

Tia wasn't just anyone. But her arrival had felt awkward. Tess's expectations certainly didn't match Tia's disposition. She'd expected her sister to burst into her home with her usual exuberance. People were entitled to unpredictable temperaments but perhaps Katie had poisoned her with feelings of resentment.

Within an hour, the house smelled of roasted chicken, stuffed with apples and onions, seasoned in lemon pepper and basted with wine. Fortunately, Tess could prepare a three course meal on automatic pilot even when she was preoccupied with other matters. She opened a jar of capers and extracted a dozen with a tablespoon. Anticipating the burst of flavor, she placed a few on her tongue and zealously bit down to taste the tangy spurts. They never disappointed her. The unusual taste of capers was one of those experiences that was impossible to describe, which was a frightening thought for a writer to admit. As she savored the explosion on her tongue, she stared out her kitchen window at the vapory winter sky. The sun would soon disappear, and the rest of the world would take for granted that it would not only set again the following evening, but that they would live to see it. But they'd never see another sunset exactly the same as this one. She instinctively valued the unique beauty of every sunset. She had, since she was a little child. Every once in a while, she snapped the shutter on her stream of consciousness to capture a truth as rich as this one.

"Tess, where are you?" said the soft female voice from the other side of the room.

"Tia, how long have you been standing there?" she said, startled.

"Long enough to watch you lost in space."

Relieved to hear the lilt in her sister's voice, she asked, "Did you sleep well?"

"Did I! I'm sorry I was such a party pooper, but I was up almost all last night with Katie and I know we'll talk late into the night. My body just needed a recharge, that's all"

"I understand. I tell you what. Dinner will be ready in an hour or so. Let's sit down and have a sip. I'm anxious to hear how Katie's doing."

As Tess poured the wine, Tia leafed through a huge unabridged dictionary that rested on an ornamental wrought-iron stand. As she turned the pages, pressed dry leaves fell to the ground.

"Oh, I'm sorry," she said as she bent to pick them up. "Remnants from an autumn once upon a time?"

Surprised, Tess turned.

"I haven't pressed colored leaves in years."

"Look, look, Tess. There are some butterflies too." Tia gently removed a Tiger Swallowtail and a Monarch, their colors somewhat faded by time, still fragile but intact.

"Tess, you always were a collector. I remember eyeing your case of lipsticks and your postcards. Remember your postcards? I was green with envy."

"You couldn't have been over three or four years old, Tia. My God, I wonder what ever happened to them." She laughed, as she handed her sister a long stemmed crystal glass with a frosted dove wrapped around the base of the globe.

"I remember a lot from my childhood. You were my idol. I watched how you tossed your hair, I mimicked your laugh, I even decided that my favorite color would be blue because I overheard you say that it was yours. Actually you said, "Blue, but aquamarine and violet were tied for first place, so you really had three favorites."

"I said that?" Tess said with amazement. "What else do you remember?"

"I remember the day you buried a robin in the back yard under the lilac bush and made us all promise we wouldn't tell Mum and Dad, because they wouldn't approve of having touched a dead animal. I remember the night Donny Anderson came to take you to the Prom and you wore that long purple dress with the low back. I remember how close you and Katie seemed and how left out I felt."

A long, pregnant pause finally birthed.

"Interesting how time changes things."

The next pause lingered until the response took it's breath.

"Not just time, Tess. Time wasn't the only factor."

"No, I suppose not." Tess stopped. The room was tense, but ripe with love. "Tell me, Tia. I need to know how Katie is. She doesn't call me. And she's made it clear that she doesn't want me to call her."

"I know, Tess. But she has lost so much. Her husband, her house, her honor."

"Her secret."

"Yes, but it was her secret. It was her cross to bear."

"Twenty plus years is a long time to carry something unburdened, Tia."

"I know, but it should have been her choice." Silence. "Listen, I don't want to get into the middle of this. You had your reasons, I'm sure. I mean, I'm sure you justified your actions. It's just really too bad that Cristin had to fall in love with Shep. That's where the whole thing fell apart."

"No, Tia. I was wrong to invite Cristin into our lives and think I could keep it a secret from everyone. I wanted her in my life. I felt an emptiness that she could fill. But I was careless. I'm deeply sorry for the consequences of my poor judgment. I just pray that someday Katie will find it in her heart to forgive me." Tess gulped. "Who does she talk to?"

"She and Ingrid have become very close, but Ingrid is carving her own place in life so she can't be a constant companion. Now brace yourself, there is someone else she talks to, but you're not going to believe this one. It's a man who lives down by the Charles River, a homeless guy she calls Uncle Jimmy."

"She mentioned him to me one time; an uncle of someone she knew in rehab."

"That's the one. Apparently she's very fond of him and she always knows where to find him. Life is so strange."

"What about Sondra? Did she mention her old friend Sondra?"

"As a matter of fact, she did. Sondra has been out to see her twice and I think Katie's planning on visiting her when I'm in California next week."

"I see."

As much as Tess had looked forward to the conversation concerning Katie, she felt less hopeful than ever that she would reconcile with her older sister. She shared the idea of writing the story to vent her apology to Katie, and Tia was receptive to the possibility that it might help heal their injured relationship. Evening had fallen into the room, and forgetting that dinner had been prepared, the two sisters sat together, talking in the persistent darkness until they only perceived one another's silhouettes.

Chapter 29

Wednesday dawned to a fresh new blanket of snow.

"Minnesota, land of 10,000 frozen lakes!" Tia marveled at the trees heavy with white.

"Yes, but also 'the land of sky blue waters', the legend of Hiawatha and Minnehaha and..."

"Spare me the details. Did you say we were going to meet the mysterious Serena this morning?"

"Yes. But despite the origin of her name, she's not mysterious. She's uncommonly level-headed and she's a very dear friend of mine."

"Katie has an Uncle Jimmy and you have a Madame Serena. He's not her uncle and she's not a Madame. And both are personal confidantes whom I've never met."

"Today's your lucky day so get ready. We're due there in a half an hour."

~ ~ ~

The walkway to Serena's front door had already been shoveled by the time her visitors arrived. The house smelled of caramel-pecan rolls, freshly brewed coffee, and a faint hint of Emily Dickinson.

"Come in, my dears. Oh, the family resemblance is striking. Please come in." Serena chirped her welcome. She didn't often have company in the winter.

"Serena, this is my little sister, Tia."

"Katia, as I recall."

"Why yes," said Tia with surprise. "How many of the other family secrets has Tess told you?"

"All of them, my dear. Only all of them."

Tia shot a glance at Tess, inquiring if it were true or did this stranger have a peculiar sense of humor.

Tess shrugged her shoulders and winked. "I forgot to tell you that Serena's also a tease."

After a half an hour of small talk, Tess informed Tia that Serena was aware of the events of the past year and had been instrumental in preserving her mental health.

"I don't know what I would have done without you, Serena." Tess squeezed the old woman's fragile blue veined hand.

"That's a bit exaggerated, dear, but I'm grateful you turned to me. Tell me, Tia, how do you like life abroad?"

"I love it. I might even stay. Life has a slower pace in Europe and that feels less complicated."

"In what ways?"

"Europeans on the whole are less concerned with the trappings of life. Instead of obsessing about the size of one's house and the model of one's car, they enjoy fine food, fine clothes, fine wine, and the arts. It's not a matter of right or wrong, it's just more my style."

"I understand. It's a more secular society. But that's another story. Tell me…have you good friends in France?"

"Yes, I do. However I lost my dearest friend about a year ago."

"She moved?"

"No, she died."

"Good heavens, how old was she?"

"Twenty-six, I believe."

"What on earth happened?"

"No one knows for sure. Heart attack, I suppose. It was dreadful. My life will never be quite the same, though. It's a paradox. We all have a false sense of moving forward through life, then when we die, we're swallowed up and move further and further into the past. It's very strange. I miss Yvette."

"Yvette? A beautiful name."

"Yes, Yvette Vandall. I still hear her voice in my dreams. As a matter of fact, I dreamed about her last night. I'm remembering this as we speak. Actually, she was saying something disturbing about Cristin but I don't recall what it was."

"Our Cristin?" asked Serena.

"Yes. But I guess it's not surprising. She hated Cristin, didn't trust anything about her. She told me some things that I initially didn't want to believe. But I eventually..." Tia paused. "Maybe, I shouldn't be talking this way."

"Au contraire, it's important to be honest about what you know. Not what you speculate, mind you, but whatever you know to be true," said Serena.

"That's where Cristin seems to be shrewder than anyone I've ever met. She leaves trails of suspicions, but few traceable facts. There is one thing I personally experienced."

"And what was that?" asked Tess with eyes wide. She gripped the arms of her chair.

"I suppose it doesn't matter if I tell you. I went to her studio, her art studio? I used the key I had found in her bureau. I discovered scores of paintings; grotesque, horrible paintings. They weren't art. They were sick. She calls herself an artist, but from what I saw that day, she's not. She spent hours drawing the same faces over and over again. However, I will give her this: when she talked about art, you believed she was brilliant. She quoted artists, discussed technique. Her patter was convincing and credible. I think she even fancied herself to be a great artist. But artists are sensitive. You should have seen the stuff. She's no artist. She isn't honest enough to be an artist."

Tess sat, expressionless and stunned.

"I've never told that to anyone. I didn't have the heart to say anything to Katie. Cristin is married to Shep now. That's another story. Shep doesn't know whom he's married to, I'm sure of it. She's the Mistress of Disguise. She's so smart."

"I feel sick," said Tess in a whisper. "Serena, remember…"

"Yes, I remember."

"Remember what?" asked Tia.

"After Cristin left, we discovered the closet in her room, painted with the same kind of figures you've described, engulfed in flames."

"Yes, faces engulfed in flames. That's how these canvases were."

"The only other painting I ever saw was one of two sisters, one carrying the other, a limp dead body, and both with the same faces we're describing," said Tess.

"Where are the paintings now? Still in the studio?"

"No. That's the weirdest part. Right around the time Yvette died, I received a correspondence from the landlord of the studio, thanking me for removing all of the paintings and personal property. But I never did. Someone else must have."

"But who?"

"Maybe Cristin," suggested Serena

"No, Cristin was on her honeymoon in Austria at the time. Besides which, if they'd been in Grenoble, they would have contacted me. Suffice it to say, it was strange. I suppose I should have informed the landlord just to set the record straight, but Yvette had just unexpectedly died and very frankly, the art studio was the last thing on my mind. When I finally thought about it, too much time had lapsed to dredge it up."

No one said a word.

Tia added a final thought. "I'll always wonder about it though."

~ ~ ~

That evening, Ren came home in time to visit with his favorite sister-in-law. They spoke for hours about life in France, their mutual love of history, and the opportunities to study abroad.

"I didn't know you had a dream to study on the continent, Ren," Tia remarked.

"Neither did I and I'm his wife." Tess cocked her head, eyebrows lifted.

"Well, actually, Lissa and I were talking about it the other night. You know, Tia, my wife has been a very positive figure in my daughter's life. She's a real student now and I don't mean only in an academic sense. Her curiosity has bloomed like a lotus. She's discovered the joy of learning. I couldn't be more pleased."

"Is Lissa thinking of studying abroad?" Tess asked, trying to make a logical connection with the information shared.

"Yes. And I thought it might be fun for us to live in Europe as well. You could live anywhere while writing, couldn't you, honey?"

"I guess so."

"Well, we can talk about it some other time. It's just a thought. I'm going to let you two talk because I have an early morning. Tia, stand up, woman, and give me a hug."

Tess watched the two people she loved as they joked and hugged each other. As soon as Ren left, Tia shifted, curling up on the sofa next to Tess.

"You didn't tell me that things were going better with Lissa."

"Well, it's true. Thank God, there are a few bright spots in my personal life these days. For a while there my life felt so dismal and hopeless. The only direction seemed to be down. But sometime after my short stories were published, Lissa took an interest in the book and felt some family pride in my success. She started spending more time over here and even brought her girlfriends to the house to meet us. It's made Rennie so happy. I guess if I can't give him a child, I should have the good sense to love his little girl. By the grace of God, I've finally had a chance to be a mother." Seeing Tia's eyes widen, she paused, then continued. "I know. She has a mother. But there's a difference between a biological mother who doesn't know how to be a mother and a woman who wants to guide and guard and inspire a child."

"Wow. Tell me more." Tia urged her on.

"Lissa and I spend a lot of time together. Of course, a lot is a relative term. We each have busy lives, but the quality of the time we do share is mutually satisfying. It's ironic, isn't it? I went through this crisis with Cristin, and the whole time I could have just tried to be a better mother to Lissa. What I wanted was here. I just didn't see it." She paused and shook her head. "I just didn't see it."

The clock in the hallway struck twelve, ushering in a new morning. The two sisters hugged each other good night. The hug said "I love you, I trust you, I'm glad you're with me tonight." The night compressed into the Land of No Time and in a blink it was gone.

~ ~ ~

The next months spun threads of facts and fiction, shaping a story that was designed to touch hearts. Tess discovered the joy of being on the path of a story she really understood. She knew the people, the facts and, most critically, she knew the feelings. She discovered detours and side roads, parallel paths and dead ends that she'd never explored. She realized that the more she understood about human nature, the more creative possibilities opened up to her. Her personal maturity spawned her maturity as a writer.

She spent fewer hours with Ren and Lissa. Instead, she chose a love affair with time. Time could not be replaced, retrieved, borrowed, or stolen. Wasting time was the same as wasting herself. She embraced her writing with full attention. If not writing or thinking about her story, she felt lost, off the path and disoriented. It was a manic state, not balanced or even healthy, but driven by the necessity to re-create in words what had happened in her life. She compulsively wrote and obsessively contemplated. But in her search for closure, there wasn't a tight, neatly wrapped ending. Life wasn't two dimensional.

As weeks passed, she became more reclusive, having long given up discretionary activities. She embellished and exaggerated her story to better hold the reader's attention. Despite the aberrations, the integrity of the characters remained true. Like a sculptor finding the figure inside a pillar of marble, Tess conscientiously chiseled to find the truth.

She tried to understand Cristin in a more compassionate light. What she discovered was how little she'd truly known about the girl. Initially, she needed to make Cristin likable in the eyes of the reader and in doing so, Tess, for a time, became sympathetic to the person who had brutally disrupted their lives through conscienceless premeditation. But in her heart, her forced sympathy for Cristin couldn't endure.

Every day the energy she felt in the morning was countered by the exhaustion she felt in the evening. In the process of having relived her story, Tess's attitude as a writer had changed. Her only competition was with herself, becoming a better writer than she'd been the day before. The world of other authors no longer existed. Her focus wasn't tainted by a fear of failure but enhanced by desire- desire to be her best self.

Chapter 30

Two years later, the book was well into publication when the unexpected occurred. The day began as any other. Ren left for work, and Tess was left to browse through magazines, collecting images of raw material for future descriptions. The smell of Serena's home baked pumpernickel rode the breeze through the screens in the verandah and wafted down the hallway like aromatic feathers. The morning sun filtered through the slats of the vertical blinds that gently twittered in the breeze, clicking against the window sill and imprinting patterns of dancing bars on the polished hardwood floors.

The birdfeeder at the east window swung with the weight of finches and black-capped chickadees. Tess was partial to the little birds. They seemed more fragile and agile than larger ones. Her mind plugged into the nursery rhyme, "and along came a blackbird and snapped off her nose," and she amusingly identified it as the reason she wasn't as fond of the larger birds-except for hawks, and owls, herons and pelicans, egrets and sand cranes, swans and… As she watched the male finches, she was reminded of how the famous ornithologist Roger Peterson had described them as sparrows dipped in raspberry juice and she thought how curious it was that creatures unaware of her existence could bring her so much joy.

The phone rang. One ring, jolting her out of her avian reverie.

"Hello, Aunt Tess. It's Ingrid." The voice was weak and dark.

"Sweetheart, what's the matter?"

"Aunt Tess, something terrible has happened. I don't know how to tell you this."

"Just tell me, honey." Tess felt her knees buckle, and she groped for the sofa behind her.

"There's been an accident."

"Oh God, Ingrid, your mother?"

"No, it's Shep."

"What happened, Ingrid? Talk to me. Just say the words."

Ingrid exhaled repeatedly, with a labored huffing sound, then started to cry. Knowing that she was about to hear terrible news, needing to hear it but not wanting to, Tess felt a nausea grip her stomach.

"Shep is dead."

"Oh my God."

"His plane went down somewhere in the mountains."

"And Cristin?"

"She was with him. They're both gone."

"I can't believe you're telling me this. There must be some mistake. It couldn't be true."

"It's true. They chartered the plane in Malaga, headed for Brussels and lost contact somewhere over the Pyrenees. The plane disappeared five days ago and they found the wreckage this morning. There were no survivors, Tess. They found pieces of my brother in the debris. They found some of Cristin's personal belongings, thrown from the impact. I mean, she must have been burned beyond recognition. Aunt Tess, they must have been so scared. I can't bear to think of their terror when they knew what was happening."

"Honey, they didn't know. They probably hit the side of a mountain without any warning. There's nothing gained by conjecturing about something they didn't experience."

"But what if they knew? I can't stand to think of it."

"Ingrid, listen to me. I've heard that if people know they're about to crash, they go into shock and lose consciousness before impact."

"But Aunt Tess, how can you know that?"

"Ingrid, sweetheart, slow down, take a deep breath. They didn't suffer. Hold on to that thought. Where is your mother?"

"She's right here. She's numb. I think she's in shock. She won't talk."

"May I try to speak with her?"

"Let me ask." Ingrid cuffed the phone and Tess could hear only a muffled tone on the other end of the receiver. Obviously Katie was sitting right there.

Hundreds of miles away, with a scolding grimace because she'd been asked, Katie furiously shook her head.

"Aunt Tess, Mom isn't up to talking right now. We'll keep you informed about the memorial service. I'll talk to you soon."

"I understand. Goodbye."

Her faint voice faded like the last hint of an echo. Why had she said she understood? She didn't understand why her own sister wouldn't talk with her. Punishing Tess for years was enough. She looked out the window. The finches and chickadees weren't aware that Shep and Cristin had died. They just continued swinging from the birdfeeder, oblivious of the human world, and serene because of it.

~ ~ ~

The memorial service was held on the following Saturday in a small chapel in Sudbury. Like dutiful relatives, the Parkers flew to Boston and drove to the gathering that promised to be morosely sad. The air smelled of coming rain and the tender green buds began to open in anticipation of the menacing shower.

"This is an awful feeling," Tess muttered as they approached the church.

Ren grimly agreed. "I can't argue with that."

"What am I going to say to her, Rennie? It's been three years."

"You'll find the right words, sweetheart. You always do."

She hated when people said that. She had to work at finding words, just like anyone else.

"Maybe you don't need to say anything. Maybe it would be better to follow her lead."

"We'll find out soon enough, won't we?"

They turned the corner and saw Katie and the girls entering the church. Tess filled her lungs with fresh air and audibly exhaled. She bided time by allowing Ren to open the car door for her, something he hadn't actually done in ages.

"Allow me." Ren smiled as he offered his hand and pampered his wife out of the car. The door slammed hard behind her and she jumped, startled and visibly irritated.

"God, help me walk through this day. Make it end soon," she murmured under her breath, squinting her eyes and lowering her head. She straightened up as Ren took her arm in his and steered her towards the chapel.

The narthex smelled of old wood, a scent that expanded and deepened with each step. The structure appeared to be two hundred years old. She thought to herself that someday she would like to spend the night alone in a sanctuary and listen to the stories it could tell. She'd often dreamed of spending a night within the inner chambers of the Great Pyramid at Giza, to commune with the spirits of antiquity. But she was willing to settle for the spirits of Sudbury, Massachusetts, if she had to. It was certainly a more reasonable objective.

As they entered the sanctuary, she was momentarily surprised at the absence of coffins. But, of course, there would be no coffins. The bodies were not recovered, at least not intact. The chapel was small. Katie was in the first pew, flanked by Ingrid and Heidi. Stefan sat alone, directly behind them. Tess searched for other familiar faces, but saw no one she even vaguely recognized.

White lilies banked the steps leading to the altar-white lilies and white roses lifting out of prolific sprays of white baby's breath.

Spring flowers, symbolizing birth and new beginnings. How strange, thought Tess, as they were gathered to acknowledge endings, not beginnings. Then again, what flowers depicted death? She answered her own question. Dead flowers. But one couldn't very well display dead flowers. Tess quietly shuddered at the absurdity of her thoughts at a time like this.

They took their seats as the organ began to play a melody faintly familiar, appropriately reverent, and unmistakably Presbyterian. Tess fidgeted with her program until Ren took one of her hands in his to calm her. Fretfully pursing her lips, the truth abruptly hit her like a wrecking ball. Shep and Cristin were dead. Shep, her bright, precocious nephew who climbed into her lap when he was only three years old and informed her that the sky couldn't really fall in *The Little Red Hen* because the sky was only air; Shep, who won a blue ribbon at his junior high school science fair and insisted on giving it to the second place winner, who was hospitalized with hepatitis; Shep, who offered to escort his sister to the senior prom when her date became ill; Shep, the self-made multi-millionaire before the age of thirty, who had remained a generous, kind human being. The world had been robbed. The family had been robbed. Shep had been robbed. Life wasn't fair and Tess powerlessly resented the injustice.

Then there was Cristin: the young woman who came out of nowhere, who assumed another identity in order to ingratiate herself into a new family; Cristin, who lied, manipulated, charmed, and connived until she married the crown prince and almost lived happily ever after. But despite her unambiguously angry feelings about Cristin, she hadn't deserved to die so young.

The music stopped and the minister appeared behind the podium. He was a man in his mid-fifties with piercing green eyes, a coarse complexion, and a nose like an eagle's beak. He was very tall, and when he spoke, the arms of his ministerial gown flapped, and his enormous hands flexed and appeared to grow even larger. It was difficult to hear what he said as his presence was so commanding. It didn't matter what he said because Shep and Cristin were dead.

Somewhere in the middle of the service, a woman in a smart black suit, with hair tucked underneath a stunning black hat, walked to the front of the church. Only when she turned around did Tess and Ren recognize her. It was Sondra. She spoke briefly on behalf of the family, as they were "stricken with grief." The words didn't seem at all melodramatic to Tess's ear. The knife in Tess's stomach turned deeper and sharper, with the realization that Katie had turned to Sondra, someone outside of the family, to represent the family.

The service was brief. The chapel had gradually darkened as the rain began to fall, and by the time the recessional was played, the pounding precipitation provided an eerie percussive accompaniment within the house of mourning. Katie walked down the aisle on the arms of her girls, who both looked up to acknowledge their aunt and uncle. Katie made no eye contact with anyone. But as Sondra walked by, she reached out her hand to Tess and smiled with a compassion that let Tess know that she was approachable. Tess's teary eyes darted to Ren's to confirm the subtle interchange, and the lump in her throat painfully released as she began to audibly sob. Her knees gave in and she sank to the pew, her hands covering her face, and her head despairingly pressing into Ren's shoulder in an attempt to disappear. The pain of rejection, the hope for reconciliation, the grief of loss and the gratitude of love were emotions so intense, so conflicting, yet so real, that she couldn't identify one as predominant. They were all wrapped up in a strangulated knot of pulsing emotion that reinforced the truth that living involved suffering.

The church emptied and Ren held his wife in the cell of the damp chapel that had lost the warmth of breathing bodies, a complement to the temperature outside. At that moment, Tess was overwhelmed with love for her husband. "Ren thank you for loving me. I don't know what I'd do without you."

"And I, without you."

"I love it when you talk that way," she whispered, smiling through tears.

"What way?"

"So proper, so British."

Ren rocked her from side to side. He had his Tess back again.

"I will never withhold my troubles or worries from you again. We're in this big, bad, beautiful world together." Tess looked into his eyes with a childlike need of approval and a promise of good intentions.

"I believe you, sweetheart. Now it's time that we show the world our alliance. It's time to meet the family. Come." He stood and led her to the car.

Rain had fallen on the church, on the trees, on the floor of the earth, saturating the dirt, perfuming the air, collecting in puddles, and flowing into streams that reflected the street lamps above. Like a relative that shared the same traits, but with a different personality, mist caressed the air and awakened the wild smell of dark moist bark and dying chrysanthemums.

Tess pressed her temple against the car window as they drove away in silence. Detached from the world, she watched frames of passing impressions as in a Fellini film. With hands clenched and shoulders slouched, she felt like a small frightened animal. The margins of her mind were annotated with frantic scratchings of a life in process, without confidence, without form. In an attempt to connect, she heard herself say, "It's going to feel strange not going back to the house in Wellesley. I hate change. It's uncomfortable." She paused. "And cruel."

"That's a mega leap. All the way from uncomfortable to cruel? It won't be long until Katie's new place will feel normal, and the house in Wellesley will dim to a vague memory."

"No way. Wellesley was magic. That old colonial with its hardwood floors and scatter rugs, the brick fireplace hearth- it was sheer magic."

Ren stopped and exited the car, closing his door as his wife's voice continued to reminisce. When he opened her car door, he could hear her continue "...those towering conifers that dropped pine needles in crunchy, woven ground covers..."

"Tessa, hold my hand." He urged his maudlin wife whose nerves were frayed like exposed wires. "We're going to pay our respects to Katie and her family now. Come with me."

At the front door, Heidi appeared with a warm embrace, a welcoming angel at the gate of the Purgatory. Behind her appeared Ingrid. "Aunt Tess, Uncle Ren. We're so glad you're here. Come in out of the rain. The weather fits the mood, doesn't it? Mom says the heavens are weeping today. I think it makes her feel better."

Tess hugged the girls, who regrettably no longer smelled like shampoo and bubble gum, but scented with Poison and Calvin Klein. The townhouse was dark but warm, crammed with over-sized furniture from the four thousand square foot home in Wellesley, and decorated in true East Coast fashion. Navy and burgundy sofas and rugs, smells of candles and wood, family photos in silver frames. On the entryway table was a raft of pictures of Shep from babyhood to manhood, with only one diminutive picture of him and his wife.

As soon as they'd shed their coats, Tess asked to be taken to Katie. People whom they'd never seen filled the living room and spilled into the narrow hallway. *What were all of these strangers doing in Katie's home at such a private time?* Tess resented the intrusion but realized how separate their lives had been. If the roles had been reversed, Katie would not have known Tess's friends either.

"How did you know her son?" asked a stranger as they passed.

Tess shot him a scolding look as if he'd not only been insensitive, but it was none of his business. "He was our nephew," she said.

As they passed him, Tess heard him say to his wife, who had elbowed him with disapproval, "I only asked her how she knew him."

"Mom is in here," said Heidi as she opened the door to the den. Katie sat in a large swivel chair with her back turned to them and she said, "Heidi, I don't want to talk to anyone right now."

"But, Mom, it's Aunt Tess and Uncle Ren. They've come all the way from Minneapolis."

Ren broke the awkward silence. "Tess, I'll let you be with your sister. Katie, words cannot express our sadness and loss. Our hearts are with you."

Without turning around, Katie said, "Thank you, Ren. You've always been kind to me."

The large pine door closed with the abrupt sound of solid steel.

After an awkward silence, not moving, and with her back to her sister, Katie said, "Thank you for coming. I know you loved Shep."

"Yes, I did." Tess tightened her jaw, and her heart feverishly raced. "I love you too, Katie. I want us to be close again, like we were before Cristin came into our lives."

Katie swiveled around in her chair to face Tess, and with a voice in high volume and intimidation she said, "Don't you ever say that girl's name in my house again! Do you understand me?"

Tess gasped and held her breath in traction. "I'm sorry, Katie. I didn't mean to upset you. I..."

"I want you to leave. Leave me in peace. I don't want to talk to you."

"But, Katie..."

"Go! Now!"

Tess ran out of the door, past all of the strange faces, and tearfully asked Ingrid to find their coats. Ren, who'd been speaking to Sondra, swept through the room to her aid.

"Rennie, I need to go. We need to go."

"Of course."

Sondra interrupted as she clasped Tess's hand. "Tess, please let me say something. Give Katie time. She's in so much pain and she associates her pain with you, with your part in bringing Cristin into their lives. Try to understand. It's not you. It's the association. It's going to take time."

"Thank you."

Sondra reached forward. And whispered in her ear. "I'll visit you if you'd like. If you want to talk, let me know."

"Thank you." Tess attempted to smile. Through a veil of tears, she hugged her nieces.

A blast of cold air slapped their faces as they opened the door to the outside world, adding insult to injury, as they headed silently toward their car. The trip had been necessary, but more excruciating than she'd imagined.

Chapter 31

One could only plan one's life in the short term and sometimes not even then. Unforeseen events make it impossible to calculate the future. And so it was one afternoon in February. The doorbell rang. Expecting to see the mailman, Tess was surprised to see a young woman, perhaps in her late twenties, standing at her door.

"Is this the home of Tess Monson?"

Surprised to hear her pseudonym at her personal residence, she replied, "This is the Parker home, but yes, I am Tessa Monson."

"Ms. Monson, may I speak with you? I have read your recent novel..."

"Do I know you? You look familiar," asked Tess.

"No, we've never met, but I believe we do have a connection."

"And what might that be?"

"I believe you are my aunt."

Tess stared at the woman who stood before her, this woman with auburn hair, Irish eyes and thin lips; this woman who appeared familiar because of her uncanny resemblance to Katie. Tess's heart began to thump until her manners eclipsed her alarm.

"Please, come in."

As the stranger passed into the front hallway, she spoke. "I know this has to be a shock and believe me I have no intention of upsetting your life. But after reading your last book..."

"Excuse me, before you go on...."

"I believe I'm your sister's daughter."

"Why would you say that?"

"Because that's what happened in your book. A young girl came to you and claimed to be your daughter. But she was really your sister's daughter."

"But that was a story. I'm a writer."

"I beg your pardon, Ms. Monson, but I have reason to believe that it was a true story. But more importantly, I need to know about the girl who came into your life."

"Who are you? What's your name?" asked Tess.

"My name is Trina Shanihan McClaren."

Tess stared at Katie's daughter. No words came. Only a long penetrating stare.

"Please, sit down," Tess finally said. "I'll get us some tea. Do you drink tea?"

"Yes, thank you. I'll wait here," replied Trina as she took a seat near the bay window.

Outside, the snow swirled off the rain gutters and pirouetted across the yard like pixies at a winter dance. Trina unwrapped the scarf from her neck and eased out of her long navy blue coat. She then noticed the pictures in the room and stood to examine closely each photograph, looking for the girl she knew.

In the kitchen, Tess heated water and prepared the tea service. Outside her window, the snow looked like someone had picked up her world like a glass dome, and brutally shaken it for the sheer pleasure of watching it settle.

When Tess returned to the living room, she found Trina holding a picture of Katie when Katie was in her early thirties.

"This is my Mother, isn't it?"

"I'm not answering any questions until I understand how you found me and what you want."

"Fair enough. Where shall I begin?"

After a sip of hot chamomile, Trina spoke.

"I was raised in a small town in Iowa, one of two adopted daughters of Sean and Kathryn Shanihan. We lived a good life. I was first told that I was adopted when I was thirteen, a rite of passage, I guess. I felt so loved by my parents and sister that although I was surprised, I wasn't disappointed. As they put it, I was one of the chosen children, which made me feel special. I'll never forget the day that they told me because my father was so nervous. I suppose he was afraid that the news would traumatize me, but it didn't in the least. They gave me a letter that my biological mother had given them, along with a locket with the initials CLM on the back. I cherished these treasures and shared them with very few people. You can see how, when I read your story of the letter and the locket, that I knew there was more than coincidence involved. Besides which, I knew you were a writer published by *The Mississippi Press*. Thinking that you were my mother, I read everything you published. It was through your publishing house that I was able to finally track you down."

"Trina, why are you here now? What do you want from me?"

"I don't want anything, Ms. Monson."

"Please, call me Tess."

"All right, Tess. I'm not here to cause you trouble. I can tell by your story that you've already suffered."

"You speak as if you know more than you could possibly know. Please get to the point."

"Can you show me a picture of the girl?"

Tess walked to the escritoire and took out a picture of Cristin, Ren, and herself, taken on a summer day shortly after Cristin had arrived in Minneapolis. She handed it to Trina and watched her face.

"What's the matter? Did you know Cristin?"

"This isn't Cristin. Her name is Hunter Cross."

"To me, her name was Cristin. How did you know her? Who was she?"

"Hunter Cross was a friend of mine in school. I shared a letter from my birth mother with her. I showed her my locket, and she stole both the letter and locket from me. She used my story to get what she wanted."

"What are you talking about? I don't understand. This so-called Hunter arrived on my doorstep with identification stating that she was a Cristin Shanihan. She even had a Social Security card because she needed it for employment. I saw it with my very own eyes."

"It was a valid social security number. It belonged to my sister."

"Who is your sister?"

"Her name was Cristin Shanihan."

"I don't understand. Where is she?"

"My sister is dead."

"Dead? How? How did she die?"

"Until I read your book, we thought she was the victim of being in the wrong place at the wrong time. But not anymore."

"What are you saying?"

"I'm saying that Hunter Cross killed her. It was an act of premeditated murder."

"Trina, these are horrific allegations."

"My sister died in the same fire that killed Hunter's parents."

"But Cristin said that her parents were killed in a car accident."

"Well, they weren't. A number of years ago, there was a terrible fire at the Cross farmhouse, outside Muscatine, Iowa, where we lived at the time."

"But she said she was from California."

"She lied to you. She was from Iowa. Anyway, Mr. and Mrs. Cross and my sister perished in that fire. My sister hung out with Hunter, so it wasn't unusual for her to be at the farm, but Hunter was supposedly in town at the time of the fire.

"And you're saying that you think Hunter deliberately set the fire to kill her parents and your sister?"

"I know she did. She always talked of wanting to be in another family, a family with money. She even told me one night that she'd go to any lengths to make it happen. I never took her seriously. But now that I know what's she's done, I need to find her and hold her accountable for the pain and loss my family has suffered. Where is she?"

"She's dead."

"Don't protect her. She's a cold- blooded murderer."

"I'm not protecting anyone, Trina. She died last year in a small plane accident over the Pyrenees. She was married to my nephew. Yes, just like in the book. He died as well."

Tess excused herself and reappeared with the picture of the two mystery girls.

"This is you, isn't it, Trina?"

Trina examined the picture, and her eyes welled with tears.

"Yes, with my sister Cristin.".

"I'm so sorry."

"Well, it's over then. Done. Justice, that is," she said.

"I did lose a nephew in that plane crash. I'd hardly say that justice was served."

"I'm sorry. I just meant that Hunter can no longer hurt anyone. She was evil."

"You sound so sure that she committed these crimes."

"I know she did. I was young, but I should have been more wary. The red flags were there. Did you ever see her paintings?"

"Just a few."

"I saw enough to know that she dwelled in a dark and hideous place that I hope I never see. But it's all in the past now. I won't be bothering you or your family. I just had to know for myself if my hunches were right. And they were. You can only imagine how shocked I was to be reading your book and read about the locket with your mother's initials...and the same horrible paintings, and to realize she had assumed my dead sister's identity? Your story isn't coincidental to mine. It's a slice of my life."

Silence. Tess trembled. "But hearing that she, this impostor, may have orchestrated the deaths of three people..."

Trina abruptly interjected. "Not may have-she did. It's important to me that you know this, that you know the truth."

"Well, on a more positive note, I have met you, Trina. And you are Katie's real daughter."

"Katie? Is that my mother's name?" Trina asked as her face softened with a smile.

"Yes, her real name is Katrina and she goes by Katie. You look so much like her."

"What is she like?"

"She's special. Giving you up was the hardest thing she ever did. She kept the secret her whole life."

"Just like in the book. Is she angry with you for exposing the truth?"

"Yes, I'm afraid she is, but I hope we'll find our way back to each other...eventually."

"Just so you know, I don't intend to contact her, so please keep my identity to yourself. I have a mother who raised and loved me and I love her. But I do have one question. Is the story in the book close to the truth?"

"To the letter."

"Do I really have three half siblings?"

"Only two now. Shep died in the plane crash last year but Ingrid and Heidi are quite well. What about you, Trina? Tell me about your family."

"I'm married with two daughters; Cristin, who is four, and Elizabeth, who is a year and a half. Tess, I need to be going. I flew in this morning from Lincoln, Nebraska, and I'm leaving in a couple hours. I won't be in touch with you again, but I hope you understand why I had to meet and talk with you."

"I do. And I will honor your decision not to contact Katie."

"I'll leave my address with you. The matter is between you and me. It must remain our secret, right?

Tess nodded.

"It's been a pleasure meeting you, Tess. Thank you for your hospitality."

"No, thank you. Thank you for making the trip. I'm terribly sorry that you lost your sister at such a young age, Trina. And regarding Hunter...."

"I'm glad she's dead. Her greed did lead to her downfall. Perhaps her karma ran over her dogma, so to speak." She smiled. "Goodbye, Tess."

"Goodbye, Trina."

Tess closed the door on another chapter of her story, an epilogue of sorts, an after-the-fact discovery that was disturbing, but done, finished, over, sealed in the Universe's vault of secrets.

She watched Trina gingerly walk down the icy latticed walkway, placing each foot with caution, the same caution and prudence she probably exercised with every move she'd ever made. Tess liked her. Katie's daughter was smart, forthright, and courageous. Katie would be proud.

Tess curled into the curve of her sofa, pulled the fleecy afghan over her knees and, in her mind, ran her memory recording of the visit. Trina resembled her mother. She had a straight-forward and kind manner that Tess trusted. There was no reason to discount her. She had come on a mission to find not her mother, but someone whom she believed to be the killer of her sister. Tess flashed upon first meeting Cristin in the Chinese restaurant downtown, finding her work as a nanny for the Taylor children, inviting her to live in their home, sharing her family, encouraging her to visit Tia in France, hearing of her marriage to Shep. All of this had occurred without the knowledge that she may have been a murderer in their midst. Tess stared through space with wide-eyed astonishment and punctuated the thought with a cold shiver that sent a shock down her spine in a mere second. How could she have been so trusting? She thought for a moment. Cristin had been that convincing.

Trina had used the phrase "red flags." There must have been red flags. The closet shrine, the dictatorial insistence of privacy, and Tia's stories of her lies and manipulations. And what about "Cristin's" lie that she thought she was Tess's daughter? After all, Trina claimed that "Cristin" not only wasn't Cristin Shanihan, but that she'd killed Cristin Shanihan in order to take on a new identity. It was so twisted. It played in her mind like someone else's nightmare. For the first time since the plane crash, Tess felt relief that Cristin was not alive. If she'd lived, Trina would have found her, and the family's wounds would have been reopened and publicly infected. A public bleed would have been unbearable. Tess's guilt for having led this stranger into their homes would have been insufferable. She quietly gave thanks that "Cristin" was no longer.

Ren would be home shortly. There was no benefit in telling him about the visit. As Trina had said, "It will remain our secret." It was history, like the Peloponnesian Wars, over and done with, unalterable and with no consequences whatsoever. It may take years, she thought, but maybe she could even erase the memory from her own mind. Perhaps someday the whole incident would seem like a vague and distant dream.

The doorbell rang and Ren entered with his briefcase and an armful of flowers, which he'd bought from the kid who stood at the off ramp of the freeway.

"How many did you buy this time?"

"All of them. I felt so sorry for him, I bought the lot, as they say in jolly old England. It was freezing out there. I told him to go home and have a bowl of his mother's beef stew."

"You have such a good heart, Rennie. One of the many reasons I love you so."

"How was your day, Mrs. Parker? Did anything exciting happen?"

Tess heard herself answer. "Oh, not really. Just an ordinary day."

Epilogue

Three years passed and Katie had visited Tess twice. The book about Cristin's intrusion had accomplished what Tess had hoped it would. Words were powerful. As Tess had so often heard, it was not always what you said but how you said it. The fact remained that the story of Cristin, incomplete as it was, had not changed. But the point of view had made the difference.

Serena died the year before. The cancer that was diagnosed in April quietly took her in September. Tess missed Serena. There were times when she'd hear something and her first instinct was to run next door and tell her friend. But her friend Elizabeth "Betty" Chapman, a.k.a. Madame Serena, wasn't there anymore. During one of their last visits, Serena talked about dying. "It's interesting," she'd said, "people who are dying want to talk about it. They want to talk about their childhood and review their lives out loud, to make sure their memories are known to someone. I've always thought it amusing that everybody wants to go to heaven, but nobody wants to die to get there."

Tess could hear Serena's laugh more easily than she could conjure her mother's or father's. She wondered if Serena and her parents had met. Probably so. The common denominator of her love for them would be a tie that bound. In a queer way, she was envious of those who had passed on because of what they now knew. They were definitely her guardian angels, and she listened for their direction in her moments of reflection. She wondered what the opposite of a guardian angel would be. If a spirit could help her from the spiritual realm, could one harm her, as well? In a dark moment, she prayed that Hunter Cross could not harm her loved ones.

One morning in late May, Tess awakened after a fitful sleep. She'd been chased all night, narrowly escaping her pursuer, but not knowing from whom or what she was running.

"Rennie, did I keep you awake last night?" she asked, as she watched him lather his face with shaving cream.

"Good morning. You were dead to the world this morning, that's for sure. Probably because you were exhausted from running all night long. Your feet were very active."

"So I did keep you awake."

"Only a little. I was pretty tired. What were you dreaming?"

"I don't remember much except that I was being chased."

"What kind of animal were you?" Ren chuckled.

"Animal?"

"Yeh, I figured you were probably an animal because you kept saying 'hunter', 'hunter'."

Suddenly the dream surfaced. She'd been running from Hunter Cross, the person she kept buried in a chamber of her emotional caves, the name she could never share with anyone, the name that now haunted her in her dreams. But Hunter Cross was dead. She had no power.

"So what kind of animal were you, Tessa? Let me guess, a coyote?"

"No, I was a lynx," she replied, making it up as she went.

"Is that a hint? You're not the type to wear a fur coat. You're an animal rights activist, for God's sake."

"All right, Carnak, game's over. It's definitely time to get up."

After Ren left the house, Tess poured a steamy cup of green tea and headed for the verandah. The air was still nippy in the early hours as winter was lingering. The backyard teased her with baby buds and promises of bursting blossoms. One season was about to be born, and another to die. Year after year, cycle after cycle. Birth and death, birth and death, as normal as breathing in and out.

Grateful that she was warm inside her long fleece robe, she sat down on her chaise lounge and heard the padding beneath her crack from the cold. She sipped her tea and, as she looked up, she saw him. The hawk had returned. Sitting in the same sycamore tree and staring at her through those intense yellow eyes, once again as if he knew her every thought. The hawk, the observer, guardian of vision and perspective. She remembered what Mum had said about a hawk appearing in your life. He was the sign to circle over and above one's life and examine it from a higher perspective. Tess smiled. She loved the remembrance of playing the medicine cards with her mother and sister.

She jumped up from her seat and walked to the library, where she searched for her old copy of *Native American Animal Medicine*. She remembered it was a faded blue volume with frayed corners, about the size of *The Prophet*. And there it was, wedged between *Crime and Punishment* and her high school Palmer/Colton European history book. She dusted it off and clutched it like a new found treasure.

Resuming her spot on the verandah, she turned to "Coyote."

The coyote is the master trickster who fools himself. No one is more astonished than Coyote at the outcome of his own tricks. He falls into his own trap. He blindly does himself in with grace and ease. He cannot see the obvious.

She thought to herself. *What does this mean?* Deep down, did Ren think she was a trickster? Deceptive? Why did he say that she was a coyote in the dream?

She leafed through the pages to "Lynx." Maybe what she thought was more nearly correct. Granted, she'd manufactured the idea out of thin air but she hadn't said she was a bear or a wolf. She'd said she was a lynx. So she read,

> *The lynx is a keeper of secrets, a knower of secrets. A lynx gets mental pictures of others and what they have hidden, either from themselves or from others. The lynx sees their deceptions and lies, but tells no one.*

Tess shut the book and stared at the hawk that hadn't moved an inch, but continued to stare at her as if his only focus in the world was her heart.

Later, that afternoon, she opened their front door to discover a package on the doorstep. It was postmarked Lincoln, Nebraska, with no return address. Inside was a magazine called *The New and the Obscure*, with no letter. Upon first glance, it appeared to be an arty publication that examined and spotlighted eclectic artists around the world. On the cover was a note that merely said, "Page 44." Tess opened the magazine to the designated page to discover a picture of a young girl carrying a dead girl, both with the hideous, elongated faces that Tess had seen before. Next to the picture was a brief article about the artist "whose sense of the grotesque is startlingly unique; a wealthy young French woman presently living in Switzerland, who prefers to remain anonymous."

Tess stared at the reproduction of the painting. In the corner was a signature, small and scribbled. She strained to read the inscription until she clearly deciphered each letter. The name was Yvette.